Also by Norman G. Gautreau

Sea Room
Island of First Light
The Sea Around Them
Iniquity

THE LIGHT FROM THE DARK SIDE OF THE MOON

A NOVEL

THE LIGHT FROM THE DARK SIDE OF THE MOON

A NOVEL

NORMAN G. GAUTREAU

bsp

Blank Slate Press | Saint Louis, MO

bsp

Blank Slate Press | Saint Louis, MO 63110
Copyright © 2019 Norman G. Gautreau

www.amphoraepublishing.com

Cover and Interior Design by Kristina Blank Makansi
Cover Photography: Wikimedia Commons and Shutterstock

Set in Adobe Caslon Pro, Neuzit Grotesk, and Escrow Banner
Manufactured in the United States of America

Library of Congress Control Number: 2019935300
ISBN: 9781943075614

To my granddaughters
Francesca Grace Gautreau
&
Calliope Rose (Callie) Gautreau
whose names I have borrowed for two of my nicer characters

and
to my father
Norman J. Gautreau
who did his part in WW II

and
to refugee children of every age,
everywhere,
and in every time

CONTENTS

AUTHOR'S NOTES

Élodie is pronounced AY-low-DEE in French and
AY-low-dee in English

The French Jewish organization that helped save many
Jewish children, the *Œuvre de Secours aux Enfants*,
or OSE is pronounced "Ozay."

PART 1
MOONRISE

When to the sessions of sweet silent thought
I summon up remembrance of things past,
I sigh the lack of many a thing I sought
And with old woes new wail my dear time's waste.

—William Shakespeare

Chapter 1
An Ancient Moonlight

L etting a hurt chafe for years without doing something to soothe it, letting grief linger for decades without confronting it will bring a person to the brink, and that's where I am after seventy years. At the brink. It's been that long since I lost Élodie and only now, after a life lived, am I ready to do what I should have done a long time ago: face the grief squarely, ennoble it, dignify it. Embrace it. That is the purpose of this journal, this memoir-in-progress. I hope the process of writing about what happened will help me recover more complete, more electric memories of the woman I loved, memories I've denied myself all these years.

And to do this, I will return to France before it's time to make my final bow.

From my balcony overlooking Boston Harbor, I listen to the thrum of ferries and ships, the slap of halyards against metal masts, the distant clang of a bell buoy, faint as a memory. The soft euphony of wind chimes from a floor below, reminds me of Élodie's laughter and I almost hear her voice again.

Across the harbor, the sinking sun flares in the windows of the office buildings in the city's financial district and butters the clock at the top of the Custom House Tower. The moon, full and fat, rises low over Logan Airport. I watch an airliner lift into the sky across the face of the moon like a great Pyrenean eagle, its red beacon flashing, its white, wingtip strobe lights slashing the dark, and a thrill runs through me at the thought I will soon fly to France again. Only, this time I will step from the plane trailing carry-on luggage, and smiling at the flight attendant, rather than leaping from an open bay door into a barrage of flak.

In less than two months, I will attend the 70th observance of D-Day, then retrace my long-ago journey with Élodie to see if being in the fields and the barns and the caves and the houses where we had been, inhaling the lavender air of the South of France we shared, hearing the rush of meltwater in the Ariège River where we bathed each other's bodies, and seeing the snow-capped Pyrénées in whose shadows we lived and whose breezes raised goosebumps on our flesh—to see if all these things will help me recover more charged memories of her.

I've already made the reservations.

And I will lay a red rose on her grave—if I can find her grave. And if I'm not too crippled to make the journey. Or too weak to face the grief.

When I speak Élodie's name, it flows melodious from my tongue, whether pronounced the English way, a dactylic AY-low-dee, or the French way, a cretic AY-low-DEE. A three-note song. A melody.

Élodie.

Sometimes when I lie awake and say her name, my little dog stirs in his sleep and gives a soft huff and crawls under the blankets and I feel the wet of his nose on my hip and I am stirred to remember Élodie's lips. But the memory quickly fades. For, no matter how hard I concentrate, I can never tease out memories of her beyond a half-lidded blur, scumbled images, murky as if seen through a film of cracked varnish. I have nothing like Proust's madeleines to fire my memories with scent and flavor.

If I'm not too crippled to make the journey.

Sometimes, I swear I can feel the synovial fluid seeping from my 92-year-old joints. My engine losing oil as elbows, knees, neck, hip, knuckles choke with thirst. My right knee cracks. For years, I've promised myself I would do anything to avoid arthritis. I swallow chondroitin sulfate and glucosamine pills, I consult a dietitian about anti-inflammatory foods, and I have adopted a Mediterranean diet of fish, vegetables, olive oil, soybeans, cherries and other foods thought to prevent arthritis. I even started choking down broccoli! I go to the gym to lift weights while younger people stare at me with incipient smiles and some pretty woman in spandex tights compliments me on being "over ninety years young" and I feel like clobbering her with my cane because I hate that goddamned, condescending euphemism.

I am determined to avoid a wheelchair because I dread living with my eldest daughter and her husband. Natalie would insist she clean for me and make me coffee in the morning and button my shirts or buckle my belt or tie my shoelaces. The first time that nightmare occurred to me, I bought walking loafers, two sizes too large, so I could avoid bending over to tie shoelaces and, instead, could wiggle my feet into them while bracing against a doorframe. As it is, I catch myself at the supermarket welcoming the support of a grocery cart even if I have only one or two items on my list. I also hired a maid service, so my condo is always neat when Natalie visits. I won't allow her even the tiniest opening to become my caretaker. If that ever happens, I know it wouldn't be long before she admitted it was too much for her (she never stays with things) and I'd have a fight on my hands to avoid a nursing home. I'd rather die than stand unsteadily in a walk-in tub while some grouchy, punctilious aide washes my butt and my balls and asks, for the umpteenth time, about the old, red disfigurement of my war wound, which I would say is a cicatrix just to baffle her nosy self.

Arlequin appears at my feet, clenching his leash between his teeth. I close my notebook and rise. As I pass through my study, I stop at my desk and lift the aging black-and-white photo taken at a barn near the Normandy beaches during the height of the invasion. I remember the red sheen of the apple Élodie held in her hand, the wavering reflection of a candle flame on its skin, the crunch of her teeth as she bit into it. I can even see the remaining flecks of bright red polish on her fingernails. With a shiver, I recall the weep of juice at the corners of her lips. And I remember how Jean-Baptiste came along and snatched Élodie's apple from her hand and took a bite of it, leaving a moist cream-white crater, and how Élodie and Jean-Baptiste exchanged those hate-filled glances that were my first inkling of the trouble that was to come.

The photo shakes in my hand as I stare at it, trying to remember her face as it was when alive, animated, impassioned, not calcified by the microsecond trip of a lens shutter. But it seems fruitless. The juice at the corners of her mouth is as fossilized as amber. All I can summon of those days, beyond the dry reportorial minutia of where, what, when and why, is a sense of the moonlight that dominated our time together. It weighed heavily on us. It seemed everything we did, we did in a wash of moonlight. On that first night, I saw my buddy's face, drained of blood, bleached white by moonlight. Moonlight reflected in the terror-stricken eyes of the children and in bombed out cities and burnt out villages and in savaged fields until it seemed the entire miserable world was inundated by a density of moonlight.

And then there were the nights we made love in the moonlight.

I place the photograph on the desk next to the brochure titled "Normandy Celebrates Liberty, 1944 – 2014" detailing the events in France for the 70th observance.

When I finally emerge onto the sidewalk holding Arlequin's leash in one hand and a cane in the other, I am greeted by a neighbor, a young woman who jogs frequently along the roads and wharfs of the Navy Yard, her alluring ponytail swaying side to side in cadence with the swing of her hips.

"Good evening, Mister Budge," she says.

I switch Arlequin's leash to my cane hand, doff my herringbone newsboy cap, and give a shallow bow, stopping at the first twinge of pain. "Good evening to you Maddie. Have you had a good run?"

"Enough to work up an appetite. Ted and I are gonna order pizza later. Would you like to join us?" She bends down to pat Arlequin.

"I've already eaten, thank you. And Maddie, you forgot your promise."

"What promise?"

"To call me Henry."

"Oh, of course. I'm sorry. It's hard to get used to."

I smile. "Because it's hard to think of me as a contemporary?"

"No, that's not it. I just—"

"That *is* it, but I forgive you. It must be hard to think of a ninety-two-year-old man as one of the gang. But I plan to be sharing this earth with folks your age for some time to come, so you might as well get used to it and call me Henry."

Maddie laughs. "Henry, it is, then. And let's make a date for pizza tomorrow night. You can tell us about your book."

"You'll eat pizza two nights in a row?"

"We could eat pizza every night of the week."

This makes me laugh, and I silently curse the broccoli I force-feed myself. "I guess it's a good thing you two run all the time."

"So, you'll come?"

Again, I try a slight bow. "How can I refuse a date with a beautiful lady, even if her husband will be present?"

"Great! Come by at seven. And, of course, you must bring Arlequin." She bends and scratches Arlequin behind his huge ears, and he wags his tail as she stands and disappears through the revolving doors into the condo building.

I take a deep breath. "Oh, to be young again!"

Arlequin gives a little bark, and we begin our stroll along the boardwalk that edges Dry Dock 2. Soon three women pass us from the direction of the Pier 6 Restaurant and one pauses and exclaims, "Oh look! How cute! Can I pet your dog?"

"How can I refuse?" I say with a smile.

She squats to give Arlequin a pat. "What's her name?" She looks up at me.

"*His* name is Arlequin."

"How lovely. What does it mean?"

I explain the name comes from a zany stock character in *commedia dell'arte*. When she raises an inquisitive eyebrow, I say, "Think of it as Italian vaudeville from three hundred years ago."

"So, is Arlequin zany?"

"All the time. A regular comedian."

"What breed is he?"

"Papillon. Means butterfly in French."

"He's adorable. How old is he?"

But before I can flash my most endearing smile and say, "Not as old as I am," the woman's companions, who have continued along, call out to her. "Sorry. Gotta go." She gives Arlequin a final pat, stands, and hurries to catch up with her friends.

She walks away gracefully, blue jacket, matching pencil skirt, sunglasses propped on her head. I look down at Arlequin. "Everyone thinks I got you because I was lonely after Anna died. But you and I know it's because you're so good at attracting the ladies." I laugh and draw a glance from a man waking in the opposite direction. "Did you notice her perfume, Arlequin?" He looks up at me. "*Vol de Nuit*[1]. It's what Anna wore. The two women I've loved each wore distinctive scents associated with moonlit nights. *Vol de Nuit* for Anna and *Nuit de Longchamp*[2] for Élodie. I'll bet you experience something similar. Do you detect the scent of a lady friend at that fire hydrant over there, and another one at that light pole? We are a pair of sniffers, you and I. Like Al Pacino in *Scent of a Woman*."

We come to the end of Dry Dock 2 at First Avenue and turn left. Moments later, the woman who'd stopped to pet Arlequin dashes past us in the opposite direction. "Forgot my phone at the restaurant," she says, breathlessly, and is past us before I can think of a clever reply. I shrug, and we continue walking along Constitution Road until we come to the Marriott Hotel where we turn and head back in the lessening light. By the time we arrive back at *Old Ironsides*, the sky is drained of daylight, and the street lamps create a path of alternating light puddles and dark patches. I stop to admire the full moon through the rigging of the frigate, an old sight a sailor strolling the docks might have seen two centuries ago. The ancient smell of tar on the rigging, like the smell of Latakia pipe tobacco, ferries me back in time. Scent has the power to do that. That's why, a few years ago, I bought a vial of *Nuit de Longchamp* to remind me of Élodie. Foolishly, I kept it on the corner of my writing desk, which gets a lot of sunlight, and the heat oxidized the fragrance, and it lost its potency. I'll replace it soon and put it some place safer.

In the dimming light, I nearly trip and plant my cane hard to arrest a stumble. Arlequin scuttles out of the way and looks up at me with concern.

"My boy," I tell him, "I should go about in a red shirt with a big

---

1   Night flight

2   Night at Longchamp (a Parisian horse race track in the Bois de Boulogne)

yellow cross on it and have a sweater made for you out of the signal flag for the letter 'U'. You would look quite handsome sporting the four alternating red and white squares, and together, we would signal 'R-U, Romeo-Uniform.' That's what ships in trouble hoist to say, 'Keep clear of me. I am maneuvering with difficulty!'"

I chuckle at my own joke and then stop abruptly as a cry of alarm cuts through the cool evening air. A woman's voice. I turn to see two figures disappear into the darkness behind a dumpster near the locked entrance gate to *Old Ironsides*.

Another cry. "No!" More like a shriek. Then another, slightly muffled. "Stop! Get off me!"

"Christ!" I mutter. I hobble as fast as I can toward the dumpster, planting my cane hard on the pavement with each step. Arlequin follows at my heels. As soon as I round the dumpster, I see a man prone over the blue-jacketed woman. The waist of the man's pants sits just under his buttocks, which shine in the moonlight as the woman struggles beneath him.

I saw this brutal violation play out seventy years earlier in France, and the anger I felt then rushes back, cascading onto and reinforcing the anger I feel now. I raise my cane over my head and, with all the might I can summon from my ancient body, bring it crashing down on the would-be rapist's head. The man cries out and looks over his shoulder, his penetrating eyes shining up at me, and I bring the cane down again with a sharp crack, and then again, and again, and my senses are so aroused, I can hear the cane whistling in the air and feel the spittle flying from my lips. The man raises an arm to shield his head and some of my spit lands on his face, and I hit him a again so hard, the damned cane breaks in two and the lower end pinwheels through the moonlight before clattering along the pavement and the man staggers to his feet and tugs at his pants, and I, gasping for breath and wiping the slobber from my mouth, turn to the woman who has raised herself to a sitting position, and ask, "Are you—?"

"Watch out!" she screams.

I turn and see a flash as something slams into my chest and it's like being hit with a baseball bat in the sternum and I crumble to the ground and bash my head against the corner of the dumpster as I fall.

And there is only blackness.

When I regain consciousness, the piercing whine of police and ambulance sirens fill the air and white, red and blue flashing lights strobe wildly in the moonlit night, anachronistically streaking across the 18th century rigging of the frigate and across my face, blinding me every few seconds. Suddenly, I am aware of being on a gurney without remembering being lifted. I am being loaded into the back of an ambulance when I catch the eyes of the woman and they are wide with fear and I hear her ask, "Will he be alright?"

"They have great docs at MGH," someone answers. "They'll take good care of him."

I recognize the voice. It's Teddy Eagan, a Charlestown cop with whom I often chat.

Someone else says, "We gotta get a dressing over that wound."

"Teddy," I whisper. "Where's Anna? Someone should tell her what happened."

"What did he say?" a man asks.

I hear Teddy answer, "He asked about his wife. But she died two years ago."

It's like the voices are drifting to me from an echo chamber. Then a thought comes to me. "Where's Arlequin?" Panic rises inside me. I can't catch my breath. I try to raise myself to a sitting position, but instantly feel dizzy and slump back. "Where's Arlequin?" I mumble again before the doors of the ambulance close.

Chapter 2
Night of Nights

The light is wrong. Too white. Too soft.

And where is the noise?

And the pain.

Where is the pain? *Where is the pain?*

Because on this night of nights, under the fullest of moons, the flashes of light are not soft-white, but hard, angry-white and fire-red. And then the pain is real, *excruciatingly* real, as I jump into the inferno and my breath is snatched by the double shocks of propeller wash and the snap and jerk of my parachute opening and I look up through the floating silk canopy to see the bloated moon with its shivering edges and I breathe and exhale at its fearsome beauty.

But the moon is too bright and too soft, and I sway and float in 3/4 time, exposed among the silent explosions, descending with dozens of my buddies like a bloom of moon jellies sinking into the abyss and I watch, helpless and heartbroken, as many of my brothers die, blown to pieces in the fireworks of flak that makes no sound, blasted into shards like irreplaceable pottery as they jump from disintegrating planes or are shredded by hot shrapnel or plunge to earth with flaming parachutes trailing impotently behind, and still others, like suspended targets at a midway arcade game, are torn apart by machine gun fire spewing from silent muzzle flashes rising up from the shadowed ground. All soundless images. Then my right thigh explodes in a painless spray of blood and I let out a voiceless cry and see the murky, moonlit earth rise up to meet me and see how the earth glints back at me because I am descending into water and I remember how, in the previous night's briefing, we had been warned the Germans might flood the fields (but how deeply?) and what if it's not a field, but a pond, or a lake? Will I drown if I can't free myself from my equipment? Will I sink like a dead moon jelly into the depths? And where is Jimmy Carson, my best buddy? Jimmy was immediately in front of me in the stick, number three on the anchor line cable to my number four, close enough that I could smell he had shit himself. Like many others. Was the bar of grace so low that I swelled with pride because my pants remained unsoiled, if a little wet? I look left and right and search the ground below and see no collapsed parachutes, no sign of Jimmy.

The moonlit water rushes up to meet me. It is an unnatural moon-light, as if there is a giant mirror out beyond the moon's orbit reflecting the dark side's light back to the lacerated earth. Yet when I land, I don't sink. Instead, I feel the snap of bone and the expectation of pain coursing through my body from my feet to my shoulders and realize I've come down at the edge of a field flooded in ankle-deep water. *But where is the pain?* And the chute drifts down on me like a shroud, blocking the moon. As I free myself from the collapsed parachute, my blood spreads and dilutes in the water and I see the little finger of my right hand bent inward at an impossible angle and I groan and reach down to my thigh and then throw my head back and grimace. It's then I see a buddy hanging lifeless in a tree, his blood staining delicate white blossoms red under the parachute draped over him like a deflated halo.

But it's not Jimmy. The legs are too short.

I am aware of soundless explosions and machine gun fire all around me before my mind shuts it all out and I see only the sheen of moon-light in the slick mud next to my face. It smells vaguely like whiskey. I see my mother bending over to brush my forehead with a comforting kiss and it frightens me because I'd heard soldiers often call for their mothers when they're about to die, and now here she is as if silently summoned, kissing me goodnight on the forehead as she did every night of my childhood. And she asks, "Is the pain bad?"

I'm confused because there is no pain and it's not my mother's voice.

"Is the pain bad?" The unfamiliar voice asks again.

I open my eyes to a bright light. *Why is the light so wrong?* I reach down to feel my thigh. What happened to the pain? "Um, no," I manage. My own voice sounds like it's coming from somewhere else, someone else.

"It's the anesthesia," the voice says. "Don't worry, we'll give you more pain medication before it wears off."

I look up and see her face, but I don't recognize her. Anesthesia? What is she saying? I feel discomfort in my nose. I raise my hand and find a plastic tube wrapped around each side of my head and ending in my nostrils.

"From the surgery," the woman says. "Those are nasal cannulae to keep you oxygenated."

There's a dull ache in my side. I shift my body slightly to the right.

"Uncomfortable?" the woman asks.

I nod.

"That's the chest tube. They inserted it between your ribs to drain air and blood from your pleural cavity."

I must still look confused, because she says, "Don't you remember being shot? Coming to the hospital? Being prepped for surgery? They said you were still conscious for a moment on the operating table because you were blinking at the operating lamp. They had to put a cloth over your eyes until the anesthesia kicked in."

Suddenly, a series of images appear. A man with penetrating eyes. The flash of a muzzle. The ground rushing up to meet me. A young woman, blue jacket, sunglasses. An ambulance with flashing red lights, and the full moon through the ship's rigging, and police cruisers sweeping the night with stabs of blue, and sirens like the screams of incoming 88s, angry, flashing lights strobing the night like exploding shells, like the hot slash of tracer bullets, the moon above, lights sweeping the rigging of *Old Ironsides* back and forth, back and forth.

And where is Arlequin?

"It's okay," the woman says. "People are often confused when they come out of surgery. It's the anesthesia. You're in post-op at Mass General Hospital. My name is Amy. I'm your nurse. You've just had a bullet removed from your right lung."

"Lung?" I can't seem to shake the damned confusion.

"Yes," she replies.

I try desperately to think, to make some sense of everything. And then it hits me again. "My dog?" I whisper. "Where is my dog?"

"What dog?"

"My dog, Arlequin! He was with me when it happened!" I hear the whine in my voice.

"I'm sorry. I don't know anything about your dog."

"Does my family know I'm here? They need to find him." I struggle to sit up. "They need to *find* him!"

The nurse puts a hand on my shoulder. "You must relax. You've had a stressful experience."

"I don't need to relax! I can't lose—"

"I'm sure your family is being notified. We found your healthcare proxy in our files."

"I can't lose him!" I say again. I feel a tear slide down my cheek.

The nurse tightens her grip on my shoulder. "You mustn't worry about that right now. Somebody will find your dog. Meanwhile, you're a lucky man. The bullet just missed your heart."

More confusion! "I thought it just missed the femoral artery."

The nurse shoots me an incredulous look, shakes her head. "It was nowhere near your femoral artery. That's in your thigh. You were shot in the chest."

"Femoral artery." Those were the words she'd spoken that first time. *"It missed your femoral artery."* A sweet voice. Élodie.

The nurse smiles at me and looks at the band on my wrist. "Can you tell me your name, please?"

"Henry Budge."

"And your date of birth?"

"Uhmm, five … one … nineteen twenty-one."

"You're in fabulous shape for a ninety-two-year-old man."

I feel a heat in my cheeks. "I'm not in fabulous shape, goddamn it, I've just been shot!"

"But you came through the surgery wonderfully. By the way, the surgeon said, when they did a complete check for other wounds, they noticed you'd been wounded before, but in the thigh. Was that what you meant when you mentioned the femoral artery?"

"A long time ago," I manage to whisper. *Normandy. 1944. The night of nights. The Germans will probably flood the fields. A bloom of moon jellies.*

"World War Two?"

I nod.

"Was it D-Day? I just saw something about that on TV. There will be a commemoration and President Obama will be there."

Again, I nod. My mind is beginning to clear. "Seventy years ago," I say.

"You were a young man."

"We all were. Please. Call my family. We must find Arlequin."

"I'll make sure your family is contacted. Meanwhile, I'll give you a sedative to help you relax."

"I don't want to relax!" My eyes prickle with tears of frustration. "I want to find Arlequin!"

But she fiddles with something at the IV pole, that I notice for the first time, and within moments I feel myself yielding to a pleasant, floating sensation.

The first thing I notice when I regain consciousness is the cold, wet mud pressed against my right cheek. I lift my head to see I'm on the edge of a flooded field. I reach down and feel the wound in my thigh and I examine my hand in the spill of moonlight and my knuckles glisten with blood. The dull thumps of 88 mm flak guns and the sporadic sharp mutter of machine-guns, like the earth coughing up phlegm, all seem to come from a great distance. It's as though when I jumped from the C-47, across the face of the full moon, I somehow jumped clear out of the war. Instead of gunfire, I hear the croak of a frog, the rasping caws of crows, a dog barking in the distance, the moos of cows.

And ... and splashing footsteps rushing toward me!

I scan the ground around me. Moonlight glints off the barrel of my rifle ten yards to my right and half buried by my collapsed parachute.

I try to drag myself toward it through the ankle-deep water, but I can only move slowly and with excruciating pain. When, at last, I am near enough, I reach out to grasp the barrel of the rifle, but in that instant a boot comes down on the barrel pinning it to the earth with a little splash of mud, and a man's voice says, *"Non, nous sommes amis!"*[3] It is instantly followed by a woman's voice. "Claude, speak English. He's an American." The woman leans over me and says, "We are friends. Are you badly hurt?"

"My right thigh," I answer, gazing at her beautiful face.

"Is the pain bad?"

"Uhmm."

She uses a knife to cut away the leg of my pants and leans close to examine the wound. She says, "I can't see very well in this light, but it appears to have missed the femoral artery. You're lucky. You'll probably live. It was a bullet or shrapnel. It's hard to tell." Gently, she takes my right hand into hers. "Your little finger is broken." I can't take my eyes away from her face. Then she says, "We found another paratrooper. Dead. American. He had morphine with him. Do you have morphine?"

"We were each issued a syrette. It's in my first aid packet. Did you see a name?"

"A name?"

"The dead American."

She nods. "Carson."

"Oh, fuck!"

"You know him?"

"Fuck! Fuck! Fuck!" I spit the words.

"I see," she says, wiping my mouth. "I'm sorry about your friend. But, your first aid packet. Where is it?"

---

3   "No, we are friends." There is both French and German in my narrative. It's important to note that I didn't know these languages then; I learned them later via the G.I. Bill. I leave the phrases in their native language to show how confusing it could be for me and my buddies, quintessential strangers in a strange land.

"I think it's under me."

She searches under me and finds the packet. She tears it open and pulls out the contents: sulfadiazine, sulfanilamide, dressings, a tourniquet, and the morphine. "First, I will sprinkle sulfanilamide on your wound." I close my eyes while she does that, and then she says, "There's a tourniquet in your packet. I don't know if I should use it."

"You don't know?" I search her face.

"I'm not a nurse."

What the hell? "Well, I certainly don't know."

"We should use it, just in case," she says. "When we have more light, we can see if the bleeding is stopped. If so, we can remove it." She places the tourniquet around my thigh.

"Uhmm …."

"Don't speak. I must tighten it now. Ready?"

I nod, suck in my breath.

She cinches the tourniquet. The pain isn't nearly as bad as I expected.

She rips open the morphine box, pulls out the syrette, and says, "It will absorb faster if I use a large muscle with good vascularity. Is it permissible to use your buttocks?"

"Vascularity? I thought you said you weren't a nurse."

"I read the medic's manual. Also, my father was a doctor, and he taught me a lot."

I force a smile. "Lead on, Macduff."

"That's a British expression. Can you roll onto your side and loosen your belt?"

"I was in England before the invasion."

"I received my resistance training in England. Help me lower your pants, if it's not too painful." She tugs at the waistband of my pants. I feel the cool air on my ass cheeks.

"You have a handsome butt," she says, and I can almost hear the smile in her voice. "Here comes the injection." I flinch at the jab. "Sorry. It will absorb quicker if I massage around the injection site. Do you object?"

"Do you hear me complaining?"

Her hands are cool on my right butt cheek. As she kneads the muscle, she looks up to her companions and says, "Jean-Baptiste, you and Claude go back to the barn and bring a litter. And bring Marcel. We'll need help carrying him. I'll stay with him in the meanwhile."

The man she addressed as Jean-Baptiste hesitates a moment, glares at me, then the two men start back in the direction from which they came.

"We are staying in a barn, our hideout for the invasion." Her voice is warm, silken. "We are resistance fighters. My name is Élodie."

"Henry."

"Uhnree." I love the way she says it. My nostrils twitch. Through it all, a scent has come to me, heady and repulsive. "What is that awful smell?" I ask. "Is that me? My pants? My thigh?"

She gestures toward a short, round tree bursting with white blossoms. It cradles a body. "Your comrade came down in a hawthorn tree. They stink."[4]

"It smells like death."

"It will take some minutes before the morphine fully takes effect."

"Your English is good," I say, tearing my gaze from the hawthorn tree.

"Just moments ago, I told you I trained in England. You don't remember? You must be knackered." She takes a handkerchief from her pocket and wipes my forehead and then under my eyes. "You have mud on your face."

I figure it's a lie; she's really wiping away tears. I study her face to shut everything else out because it hurts too much—my thigh, my finger, Carson. I stare at her like she's a guardian angel. The moonlight is soft on her features. She has a serene oval face, an upper lip like a Cupid's bow, a graceful, long neck, and opalescent eyes that appear to change from jade to gunmetal blue and back with every movement of her head. "You're beautiful," I say.

---

4   You may wonder how I can remember such details and specific conversations. Three answers: One, I kept a diary. Two: where my diary is sketchy or incomplete, I feel confident I remember enough to re-create impressions and dialogues while still being faithful to my story. Three: if I forgot something or my diary was incomplete, I researched it. That's how I know, today, it was a hawthorn tree, genus Crataegus, family Rosaceae, with an odor like decomposing flesh.

"Don't speak," she replies. "Here, put your head in my lap. The water is cold, and your resistance is weakened with the loss of blood." She lifts my head and levers her thighs under it. "If you get sick in addition to everything else, it will be bad."

This is the first time I catch a whiff of her perfume. I begin to feel drowsy. The morphine? Exhaustion catching up to me? I haven't slept since long before we left RAF Folkingham. It seems a lifetime ago. I feel Élodie stroking my temple and it has a tranquilizing effect and the next thing I know I'm being jostled through the woods on a litter. Above me, moonlight filters through the green canopy and I notice a pre-dawn brightening of the sky and hear the thump and roar of big guns followed by the crump of exploding shells. Probably the navy softening up the invasion beaches. German 88s answering, their sound mimicking their German name *Acht-Achter*, like hacking, like the earth clearing its throat.

I must have dozed again, because the next thing I know, I'm inside a barn. Above me is a hay loft, and the odor of cow dung permeates the air. I hear the *vit vit* of two swallows tracing filaments of flight around each other and look up to see the birds flitting along the walls of the barn, which are transected by morning sunlight. I'm startled to hear violin music. Played softly. I listen for a few moments, then laugh. "I always thought there would be harps in Heaven, not violins."

The music stops, and Élodie's smiling face appears above me. She holds a violin and a bow in her right hand. She wears a gray dress under a white frock. On the starched collars of the dress are red crosses and between them, at the hollow of her throat, a Red Cross medallion.

"Does this smell like Heaven to you?" Her laugh is light and delicate, like wind chimes. "I never imagined cow dung in Paradise, and how do you presume you would end up in Heaven, anyway? But, seriously, are you in pain?"

"A little."

"It's been several hours."

I reach down to touch my leg, but she stops me with a light touch.

"Your injuries are not so bad after all, and the tourniquet was not needed. I took it off. We can give you another syrette if you want. We collected some from your dead companions."

My dead companions!

She leans close to examine my forehead and frowns. "You scrapped yourself badly! Bugger all! I didn't see it before in the poor light. I'm sorry. Let me put some salve on it." I feel the warmth of her breath. On her fingernails, there are tiny flecks of red where polish once was. She pulls out a round container that reads:

BRANDWUNDEN SALBE

My eyes widen. "What's that?"

"It says 'burn ointment.' Don't worry. We're not Jerry."

"Then why…?"

Gently, she applies the salve to my forehead. "We'll be moving out soon. If you only have a little pain, perhaps we should wait and give you another syrette later."

I nod. "The pain's not that bad." I gesture toward her violin. "What were you playing? I've heard it before."

"Charlie Chaplin. From the movie, *Modern Times*."

"Of course! They played that movie in camp only about a week ago. Five days running. I saw them all. What do you mean, moving out?"

"We have a mission to complete. Do you remember me telling you we are a small group of resistance fighters?"

"Uh huh."

"Well, our work isn't finished. We'll be going south toward Toulouse to blow up railroad tracks. We need to block the Boche from sending reinforcements to the beaches."

"And what about me?"

"You must come with us."

"No sirree! Nix on that! I need to get back to my comrades."

"How do you plan to do that?"

"I'll walk!"

"On that leg?"

"Then help me get back."

"No. It will be a few days before you can travel on your own, and we can't escort you back to the Americans."

"Why not?"

"No time. The Wehrmacht is probably already starting to move reinforcements toward the beaches, so we must move now. The other option is we could leave you here, and when you're ready you could drag yourself back to your companions. But it seems clear you are nowhere near your intended drop zone, meaning you have no idea where your American friends are. Who's to say you can find your way back before the Boche find you?"

"But I need to get back. They're my buddies. I have their backs and they have mine."

"You're in no shape to try to get through the lines on your own. And there's another reason we can't escort you back to the Americans," Élodie says. "Here, I'll show you." She turns and calls out, "Claude, Jean-Baptiste, Marcel, come say 'Hello' to our guest. He's awake."

Three men appear, all wearing German uniforms. I bolt to a sitting position. "What the fuck?"

"It's our cover," Élodie says. "How do you think we operate behind German lines? We pose as a German medical team." She turns sideways to show me the white armband on her left arm which has a red cross surrounded by the words, "*Deutsches Rotes Kreux*.[5]"

"But you speak English."

"We're fluent in German, also. That's why we were seconded here; we're language specialists. The invasion troops are all American, British, Canadian, and Free French, and the defenders are German. Except, of course, for the Poles, Mongols and other conscripts."

"How did you get the uniforms?"

The man called Claude turns to Élodie. "How does one say, '*nous les avons embusqués*'?"

"One says, 'We ambushed them'," she replies, and turns back to me. "It was easy to surprise them and take their uniforms and equipment.

---

5   German Red Cross.

Now, we are free to travel anywhere behind German lines without raising suspicion. And it's natural for us to be heading in the opposite direction of the Wehrmacht. They'll only assume we're going to a field hospital behind the lines. But Claude is wrong. 'Ambush' is not the right word; it makes it sound like we jumped them with guns firing. But what good would uniforms with holes in them do us?"

"So, what did you do?"

"We came on them in the night and garroted them. We couldn't afford for there to be blood if we were going to take their uniforms."

I guess I made a face, because she says, "Yes, it was ugly. But it had to be done. As you Americans might say, 'It's the fucking war, Sweetheart!'" She gives a little laugh that sounds forced. Her cursing in a second language surprises me, but it makes me feel less like a lost boy and more like I'm in a barn with my buddies. She continues, "Fortunately, there was a nurse among them." She pauses, frowns, and says again, "It had to be done. But in order to complete the disguise, we had to give up our Sten guns for standard-issue Karabiner 98s and Walther P38s which is all the medical unit people had. And, see over there? That lorry is part of our equipment."

Sitting on the opposite side of the barn, under a hay loft, is a German army truck marked out as an ambulance with a red cross on the side, and the black-and-white cross of the Wehrmacht on the door. Next to it is a similarly marked motorcycle with a sidecar.

"But what about me?" I ask. "Do you have a German uniform and identification for me?"

Élodie shakes her head. "No uniform. No *ausweis*.[6] And, speaking of that, we need to get rid of your dog tags if we're going through German lines."

"German lines?"

"What better way to hit the enemy than to go where he is?" She smiles. "Your dog tag says, 'Budge, George H.' But you call yourself Henry. Why?"

"The army won't let you choose your own name. George is my

---

6   Identification card.

father's name. I didn't want to be 'Junior.' Besides, try saying George Budge many times in a row. It's an ugly sound."

"Well, I will call you Henry."

"Thank you. So, if you can't return me to an American unit, and you can't pass me off as German, what the hell are you planning to do with me?"

"We discussed that whilst you were sleeping. I don't think you will like the answer."

"Tell me."

"We have the trousers from a Wehrmacht medic's uniform. You'll wear those. We'll say you are a burn victim. We'll bandage you from the waist up, including your head. You'll be a mummy. Unfortunately, it might be horribly uncomfortable. You won't be able to scratch an itch. Then there's the pain from your real injuries, survivable as they may be."

It sounds awful. "The waist up?"

"Yes. I think it's best we keep you heavily sedated with morphine. Best for your comfort, plus it will guard against anyone questioning you. We're certain to encounter German troops. Do you agree with this plan?"

"What choice do I have?"

"None, really."

"Well, then. I guess I agree."

After jabbing me with a morphine syrette, Élodie leans over, wipes my forehead, and says, "We'll be leaving in a couple of hours. Meanwhile, there are some railroad tracks nearby we have to take out. Relax. We'll be back shortly."

And they are gone. The morphine must already be working, for there is little pain in my leg. I can hear the Navy guns and the answering 88s and know they are marking my way back toward my buddies. *Just follow the sound!* I rise from the cot and instantly realize I can't put much weight on my leg. I scan the barn for something I can use as a cane and see a two-tine pitchfork with a long shaft leaning against a wall. Probably used to bale hay.

I hop on my left leg, dragging my right behind be, and grab the pitchfork. I test it. If I hold it in my right hand and plant the tines on the barn floor, it seems to hold my weight. It's slow going, but I manage to hop and drag myself out of the barn and turn toward the sound of artillery. I know, from reconnaissance maps, Utah Beach should be east of my position and I'm relieved to see the low morning sun is throwing shadows to my left. I estimate I should be close to the village of Sainte-Mère-Église, one of our first objectives, which is about six miles inland from the beach. If all has gone to plan, I should find some American units there, maybe even the 82nd. My own moving shadow, with its lurching gait and the pitchfork jabbing ahead every step of the way, is like a bad Bugs Bunny cartoon. The ground is getting soggy; the pitchfork tines are digging deeper into mud. Ahead of me is the thump of Navy guns and German 88s.

I quicken my pace. I'm feeling weak and a bit dizzy. The morphine? Suddenly, there is a tremendous boom close by that leaves a ringing in my ears. Instinctively, I jam the pitchfork into the mud and it sticks when I go to pull it out and it catapults me forward and onto my face. There is a second concussion. The earth under me convulses and spits mud into my face. I try to pull myself up, hand over hand, on the shaft of the pitchfork, but all my strength is gone and I sink down into the mud again.

I must have passed out, because the next thing I know, I'm back on the cot in the barn with Élodie leaning over me. Maybe it's her perfume that awakened me.

"So you decided to go back to your comrades?"

I look up at her. It takes a few moments for her words to register. Finally, I say, "Yes. We are brothers in arms. That's just the way it is."

"No, *this* is the way it is: There are German patrols between you and your comrades. You would never make it, especially on that leg."

"Then I'll find another way."

"Brilliant, Idiot! You can walk back, then. But it will have to be through the South of France, over the mountains into Spain, then Portugal and back to England! Which, by the way, is what will happen anyway because that's what I do. I escort downed English and American airmen out of France."

"I thought you were a resistance fighter."

"That's only temporary for the invasion. Now, it's too soon to give you more morphine, but I'll slather you with *Mückensalbe* in the places that might chafe before we bundle you up."

"What's that?"

"It's a wound ointment[7] used by the Wehrmacht. But we only have a few tubes of it."

"You got it from the medical team you attacked?"

"Yes." She frowns.

"You're troubled by what you had to do."

"It had to be done."

"Of course. You're a soldier."

"I'm a musician."

I study her face a long time. Finally, I ask, "What is the perfume you're wearing?"

"My perfume? It's *Nuit de Longchamp*. It means 'Night at Longchamp' which is a hippodrome in Paris, a horse race course. It covers the stink that comes from not being able to bathe very often in this bloody business." She smiles and tilts her head toward her companions. "I wish they would also wear it."

"I don't think it would sit as well on them as on you."

All the while she's talking, she's unbuckling my belt. Finally, she whips my pants off so violently my butt bounces off the cot. "Ow! What the fuck? What's got your dander up?"

She leans close and whispers, "You're making it hard on me. When we first found you, Jean-Baptiste wanted to leave you here. I insisted we take you with us."

"What about the others?"

"They mostly follow Jean-Baptiste. We'll dry these pants as best we can but they'll still be wet. If you are uncomfortable, or you get a fever and die, it will be your own fault!"

Less than an hour later, my upper body is entirely swaddled in bandages and my legs are itchy in a damp pair of pants. My head is also

---

7   It's really mosquito ointment, I learned after the war. I suppose it was the best they had.

wrapped except for two small openings, one for my nose and mouth, and one for my eyes.

"Does this mean I'm your prisoner?" I mumble through pinched lips.

"If you must see it that way, Idiot!" Once more, Élodie leans close enough for me to catch the scent of her. "Here. Take my hand," she says, placing her hand in mine. "You have a choice of riding inside the ambulance where it will be hot, and you won't be able to see anything, or on the sidecar of the motorcycle which is designed to take a stretcher. If we put you there, you'll have fresh air, at least, but the ride will be rougher. Squeeze my hand once for the motorcycle, or twice for the ambulance."

I squeeze her hand once, then let my hand linger in hers for several seconds before she smiles and moves away from me. I see Jean-Baptiste frown as he grasps the poles at the foot of my stretcher. Marcel leans down to lift the poles at my head. I smell his breath. They jostle me as they carry me to the sidecar and strap the stretcher down. Jean-Baptiste mounts the motorcycle with a last, hostile glance at me, and the others climb into the ambulance. Moments later, both engines roar to life and we are off.

The stretcher jerks and bounces and I wonder if Jean-Baptiste is deliberately trying to hit every rut we pass. Now, for sure, my guard is up. I know I'll have to be careful around him.

Chapter 3
Soon You Too Will be at Peace

I am awakened by a disturbance in the hospital corridor outside my room. I hear an all-too-familiar woman's voice saying, "I am Natalie Frowd. I'm his daughter. This is my husband, Marshall. How is my father doing?"

Natalie is using her pissy, hectoring voice, and I am trapped in a hospital bed, unable to escape. I hear somebody reply but can't make out what is said. Anna and I never understood where Natalie got a varnish-blistering voice that could strip a tree of its bark or cause a snake to shed its skin. We never spoke loudly, but from the time she uttered her first sound, Natalie's voice was ear piercingly loud. So much so, we even took her to an otolaryngologist to have her hearing checked, thinking she just didn't realize how loud her voice was because her hearing was poor. But it checked out fine and we were forced to accept Natalie's voice was a form of aggression. She attacked people with it. This was confirmed when she started school and began behaving like a bully. It never got better, and Anna and I were frequently called to teacher-parent consultations.

Her voice booms out again.

"Well, please keep me informed. Since my mother passed away, I'm his healthcare proxy." Her voice grows louder with every word, a Doppler effect that warns me she is approaching my room, and all at once she bursts into the room.

"What the hell is this all about, Dad?"

I force my most sugary smile. "Hello, Sweetness. Hi Marshall. I need someone to find Arlequin. I don't know what happened to him."

"He'll probably show up at your place," Marshall says. "Someone will find him."

Natalie peers down at me. "How're you feeling, Dad?"

"I'm fine."

"Bullshit! You've gotten yourself shot."

"Would you like to step outside and try your entrance again? Perhaps with a more civil, sympathetic attitude?"

"How the hell did it happen?"

I wink at Marshall. "I guess she's not interested in trying this again."

"Don't try to be funny, Dad," Natalie says. "You could have been killed. How many times have I said you shouldn't walk alone at night in the Navy Yard?"

"Lots. But I wasn't alone. I had Arlequin with me."

"Please stop with the jokes! Why do you insist on walking alone?"

"Because I enjoy it." I grimace as a wave of pain runs through my body.

Her voice softens. Just a tad. "You're in pain. Shall I call the nurse?"

"It's not that bad. They pumped me with morphine just before you arrived. It'll kick in soon."

"They said on the news you attacked a guy with your cane. What happened?"

I try that saccharine smile again. "If you saw the news, you know more than I. What can I say? The man was behaving badly so I crowned him. By the way, I need a new cane. Could you ask the nurse if they have loaners?"

Natalie shoots Marshall a look of exasperation, turns back to me and says, "You're impossible!"

"Would you have been proud of me if I had done nothing while a woman was raped?"

"But, Dad, you're over ninety!"

"Look, Sweetness, age may be an excuse for not shoveling the fucking snow, or even not shaving every day, but it doesn't give anyone a pass on humanity."

"But you take such risks. And watch your language. You're in a hospital."

"What's a hospital got to do with it? Look, I have less to lose. A twenty-year-old guy? Now, he stands to lose maybe seventy, even eighty years of life. Countless lovely women he'll never get to know. Me? Not so much. Have you heard from Johnny and Judy?"

"Johnny called from O'Hare. He was off on some business trip. I haven't called Judy yet. You're crazy. You have lots to lose."

"What time is it now? They put my watch somewhere."

"Nine. Maybe they put your watch away because there's a big clock on the wall facing you."

"Oh," I say, lamely. "Well it's only six on the west coast. Give her time. What about Callie?"

"She'll be here when she can. We stopped at her floor on our way up. She's on the overnight shift but will see if she can get another doctor to cover for her. I can't get over it. Are you crazy? Attacking a man like that? What do you think Ma would have said?"

"About the same as you. You *are* your mother's daughter." My lids suddenly feel heavy. The morphine. A pleasant sinking sensation. Or am I just trying to escape?

The last thing I remember before drifting off to sleep is Natalie saying to Marshall, "One good thing will come out of all this. It will end his silly talk about going to those D-Day ceremonies. There's no way he'll be able to go now, thank God!" Then there was some talk of getting me a mobility scooter, and I'm not sure if I told Natalie I didn't want one, or if I only thought it.

After Natalie and Marshall leave, I open my eyes. I'm awake enough to fumble for the button to call the nurse. A tear tickles my cheek. *Arlequin!* I try to sit up higher, but the morphine drags me back to the pillow.

Late in the afternoon, they move me from post-op to a private room. After my new nurse, an older woman named Martha, asks me to confirm my name and date of birth, she says, "I'll turn the TV on. You're a celebrity. You made the news."

"Uhmm." My arm aches like a horrible toothache. I squeeze my eyes shut.

"Pain?" Martha asks.

I nod.

"Look at your right arm."

I pull the sleeve up and look. What the hell? It's black and blue from the biceps to the wrist. I rotate my arm carefully. It's black and blue on the inside, too. All the way around!

"In addition to the bullet you took to the chest, you suffered what's called a distal biceps tendon tear. You must have really clobbered that guy with your cane to rip your muscle that badly!"

"It hurts," I say.

"Not as much as it hurt that guy. I'm told he was still staggering when the police caught him. It's hard to believe he could shoot straight. I guess you're just unlucky." She hands me a plastic device with a button. "It's connected to that machine beside your bed. It's a PCA pump, patient-controlled analgesia. Press the button and you'll get a shot of morphine. And don't worry, it's set so you can't overdose."

That nagging sense of panic returns. "What about Arlequin?" I ask.

"What's Arlequin?"

"*Who's* Arlequin. My dog. He disappeared when it happened. Poor fellow must have been frightened out of his mind!"

"I'm sorry. I don't know anything about your dog. Maybe when your family returns."

I turn away from her and look out the window. I press the PCA button and squirt morphine into my body. And I try not to cry.

Later, on TV, there is commentary about a Red Sox walk-off win the previous night, followed by a weather forecast, then footage of *Old Ironsides* comes on that shows a ribbon of yellow police tape fluttering in the breeze. I listen to the syrupy voice of the anchorwoman:

"And now for one of those stories that restores your faith in humanity. Last night Henry Budge, a historian with several best-selling books to his credit, and all of ninety-two-years-young, saved a woman from being molested and possibly raped. It happened in a lonely area of the Charlestown Navy Yard, not far from *Old Ironsides*. Mister Budge, a veteran of World War Two, who courageously parachuted into France on D-Day seventy years ago, displayed his extraordinary courage once again when, while taking his nightly constitutional with his dog near *Old Ironsides*, he came across a woman struggling with a man in the shadows. Listen to the woman describe what happened. We've disguised her voice and image to protect her privacy."

"I was with friends at the Pier 6 Restaurant. After an early dinner, we were walking to North Station when I realized I'd left my phone at the restaurant, so I went back to get it and as I was heading back, and came near *Old Ironsides*, I was suddenly grabbed from behind. I screamed and fought, but the man was strong, and dragged me behind a dumpster, and threw me to the ground. He started to tear at my clothes. But, suddenly, I saw somebody standing over us. This man—who turned out to be an elderly man, with a cute dog that I had met earlier—started to beat the attacker with his cane, over, and over, and over again. I couldn't believe the energy and strength he had. I've never seen a person so angry. It startled me. My attacker jumped up and started to run away. But then he turned around. He was staggering and tripping over his pants. But even so, he shot at the old man. I thought I heard the bullet ricochet off the ground before it hit my rescuer. He fell immediately and hit his head on the dumpster. I called nine-one-one. And, well, you know the rest. That angel of a man is a hero, and I hope he'll be all right."

"A hero, indeed!" says the news anchor. "They don't make them like that anymore. The latest information we have is that Mister Budge was undergoing surgery at MGH. We are following the story and will keep you informed. In the meantime, we have news about the D-Day commemoration. The White House, which had previously announced President Obama will join world leaders in Normandy to pay tribute to American and Allied forces who fought and died in the D-Day landings seventy years ago, further announced the president will meet with Vladimir Putin who will also be at the observances, marking the first opportunity the two men will have had to meet personally since the Ukraine crisis that was precipitated by the Russian takeover of Crimea. More on the situation in Ukraine after the break."

"Ninety-two-years-young!" I mutter.

"What?" Martha asks, reappearing in the doorway.

"Why do they say that? Ninety-two-years-*young*? Ninety-two is decidedly not young."

"I suppose to compliment you on your youthful vigor."

"It's not a compliment. Who wants to be associated with foolish youth? I'm old, damn it. I've earned it. It took a lot of years to get here."

She shrugs. "Whatever."

"Whatever," I grunt, part pain, part annoyance. Usually I'm a cheerful man, not always so tetchy. But then on most days I haven't just been shot and haven't lost my dog. Thinking of Arlequin makes another wave of panic roll through me. I squeeze my eyes closed.

"Is the pain increasing?" Martha asks. "Don't you want to press the button for more morphine?"

"I'm fine! I'll press the damn button in my own good time. I was only out for my damned walk. Nothing heroic about it." I lean back against the pillow. Also, it was not a goddamned "constitutional" near the *U.S.S. Constitution*. Christ! This new generation of newscasters think puns make them clever! Where are you, dear, old Walter Cronkite? I'm not a hero. A helpless person cries for help and either you help, or you walk off the pier and separate yourself from humanity. And the news lady with the cloying, talking-down-to-children voice doesn't even know what the word "ironically" means. "Coincidently" would have been the right choice. I punch the "off" button on the TV remote.

"Well you must admit," Martha says, "it's not every day someone goes out for their walk and something like that happens. The right man in the right place, I'd say."

"What do you mean 'their'?"

"What do you mean, what do I mean, 'their'?"

"You said, 'someone.' That's one. Singular. One person. Then you said, 'their.' That's more than one. Plural. Are you confused about how many of me there are? Perhaps I had a clone walking alongside?"

She furrows her brow and shakes her head. "I don't follow."

I feel sorry for being rude to her. But the pain and the worry are overwhelming. What will I do if I lose Arlequin? I raise my head, but it instantly falls back onto the pillow and, within seconds, I'm out.

I wake some time later to sunlight streaming into the room. A slant of light lays across the bed. The morphine has worn off. The pain has returned. I punch the PCA button with my thumb several times. A nurse I haven't seen before draws the blinds and turns to me. "Ah, you're awake. I came in to say you have a visitor. Shall I let her in?"

"Who? Is it my daughter?"

"She said she's a neighbor. Her name is Maddie Callahan."

"Oh yes, Maddie. Please tell her to come in."

Moments later, Maddie appears by my bed. "How are you feeling, Mister Budge?"

"Henry."

"Yes, of course. *Henry.*"

"I've had better days."

"Well I hope I can make the day a little better for you." She pulls out a tablet computer, touches the screen a few times with a long, neatly manicured finger, and holds it before my eyes. I see a video in which Maddie's husband, Ted, holds Arlequin in his arms and says, "Say hello to your Papa, Arlequin."

Arlequin gives a yip.

I can't hold it back. It's a dam bursting. My eyes well with tears. "You found him!"

Maddie says, "He showed up at the outside door. We were really worried for you. We were about to call the cops, and go out and search for you, but just then the news came on."

"Thank you," I manage to choke out. "Thank you!"

"No, Henry. Thank *you* for restoring our faith in people. It was a brave thing you did. They're calling you a hero."

I give a dismissive wave. "Pouff!"

"Pouff yourself! Ted and I can't wait till you're well enough to share that pizza we planned. In the meantime, we'll be happy to take care of Arlequin for you."

"That's wonderfully kind of you."

"It's the least we can do."

"You'll need to take him outside to poop."

"No problem."

"And I haven't trained him to run."

"Again, no problem. We'll walk. I'll run later. And now I'm gonna let you get some sleep. The nurse said it was important that you rest." She places a hand on my shoulder.

I lay my hand over hers, and say, "Thank you, thank you. I don't know what I would have done if I lost him."

"Our pleasure," she says, and turns to leave.

"Oh, Maddie, one more thing. Arlequin really likes Milk-Bone biscuits and Cesar brand wet food. I'll pay you back when I'm out of here."

"You rest. Don't worry about Arlequin."

෯

Mummified as I am in the bandages, I have no idea where we are, only that we have been heading in a southerly direction for a long time. I know this because we started out from our last stop in the early afternoon and in the moments when I woke from a morphine-induced sleep, the sun has always been to my right. My throat tightens. I realize now there's no way I can get back to my outfit near Utah Beach. I don't even know where I am! I squeeze my eyes shut and think, but I can't come up with any alternatives. It looks like my only option is to let Élodie escort me over the mountains and out of France. My chest feels hollowed out at the thought. Every instinct, every moment of training, screams at me: *You're abandoning your buddies!*

The warmth of the sun and the effect of the opiate combine to make me drowsy, and I fall in and out of wakefulness. By now it's clear I don't need the morphine for my wounds and I'm using it only to numb myself to the discomfort of the full body bandages they've used to disguise me.

I am barely awake when the motorcycle's engine sputters to a stop, and Jean-Baptiste hops off the bike and joins the other men as they go off into the bushes, presumably to pee. Moments later, Jean-Baptiste returns and grabs Élodie by the arm and drags her away from the rest of us into a small copse of trees. I can't see them, but I hear them arguing vehemently in French, each saying the word "American" several times. When Élodie finally returns to my side, she says, "Marcel will help you walk to the bushes, so you can relieve yourself. It will be a long time before we stop again." As I stagger unsteadily toward the bushes with an arm around Marcel's shoulder, I pass Jean-Baptiste who glares at me but says nothing.

Some hours later—I gauge it must be mid-afternoon—I hear a man's voice call out *"Achtung!"*[8] The word is snapped off as if it had splintered in his throat. *"Halt!"*

Élodie appears at my side. I smell her perfume. She whispers, "We've come upon a German platoon. *Herr Leutnant* will undoubtedly question us. Remain silent. I'll stay here beside you."

Moments pass. I hear voices some distance off. Soon I hear approaching footfalls, the clatter of hobnailed boots. I sense the man standing beside me and speaking to Élodie in German with the rising inflection of a question.

"Wer bist du?"[9]

"Ich bin eine Krankenschwester und meine Kollegen sind Kampfmediziner.[10]*"*

There's a pause, then the man says, *"Bitte beenden Sie dieses Gedicht: Über allen Gipfeln ist ruh, in allen Wipfeln spürest du kaum einen Hauch.*[11]*"*

I hear Élodie's quick reply. *"Die Vögelein schweigen im Walde, warte nur, balde ruhest du auch.*[12]*"*

---

8   "Attention!"

9   "Who are you?" This, and all future translations I either got from Élodie after the fact or reconstructed them after I studied German and French in the post-war years.

10   "I am a nurse and my colleagues are combat medics."

11   "Please finish this poem: 'Above all the mountain tops it is calm, in all the treetops you can hardly feel a breath.'"

12   "The birds in the forest are silent. Wait, only, soon you, too will be at peace."

My head immobilized by the bandages, I jink my eyes from mouth to mouth like a spectator following a tennis ball.

"*Gut,*" says the man. "*Sie übergeben können.*[13]"

Moments later, the engines roar to life and I feel a jolt as the motorcycle lurches forward. We ride for what seems like another ten minutes before again stopping. Élodie comes to my side. "Water?"

"Please," I say.

She places a ladle to my lips. The water is cool and some of it drips onto my neck where it isn't covered by the bandages. Élodie wipes it dry with a handkerchief.

"What was that all about back there?" I ask.

"He just wanted to know who we were. I told him I am a nurse and the others are combat medics. Then he gave me a test to make sure we were truly who we said we were. He asked me to finish a poem by Goethe. It's one every school kid in Germany learns. It's like an American asking someone about Babe Ruth."

"You know about Babe Ruth?"

"We prepare carefully," she replies with a smile. "We could pass for American, German, British, even Canadian. Do you know the nickname of Maurice Richard of the Montreal Canadiens hockey team?"

"No," I say.

"It's 'Rocket.' Do you know what number he wears?"

I give a short laugh. "I haven't the faintest idea."

"Fifteen. You wouldn't pass for Canadian, but I would … *eh?*" She smiles.

"Do you ever mix languages up?"

"Only British English and American English. It's very frus*tra*ting. Or, since you are American, I should say, *frus*trating. And, while we are on the subject, you said I had 'my dander up' when I treated you harshly—and appropriately, I might add!—after you tried to pitchfork your way back to your American friends and we found you nose-down in the mud. Is that an American expression?"

"Yes. It means being pissed off."

---

13   "Good. You can pass."

"Got one's dander up. Is that how you say it? Always with a possessive pronoun?"

"If you mean 'my' 'your' 'his' 'her.' Yes."

"Hmm. Then, we must be careful about getting Jean-Baptiste's dander up. I am increasingly amazed by this woman as, later, Jean-Baptiste kicks the starter, the engine roars to life, and we are off.

⁂

I sit up in bed to watch the Red Sox game—more to drown out the sounds of beeping machines, doctor pages, and ringing telephones than a real interest in the game—when my granddaughter Callie appears in the doorway. Callie! She always brightens my life!

"Hello, Papa. May I come in?"

"Of course, Callie. Come give Papa a kiss."

She approaches the bed and leans over and plants a kiss on my forehead and says, "I arranged for a colleague to cover the rest of my shift."

"I'm delighted." I still have happy memories of traveling to California with Anna to watch Callie graduate from Stanford Medical School, and even today I tell people my granddaughter is a doctor every chance I get. Of course, I do. I'm a grandfather!

"They said you might be sleeping."

"I've been dozing on and off, but I'm glad to be awake now."

"How are you doing?" Her eyes expertly sweep the medical readouts beside my bed: heart rate, heart rhythm, oxygen saturation.

"So foul and fair a day I have not seen."

"Shakespeare?" She checks the IV drip and the PCA Infusion Pump. *"Macbeth."*

"What do you mean by it?"

"Foul or fair depending on when I last juiced up with morphine."

"And how is the pain now? Fair or foul?"

"Fair since they let me shoot myself up."

Callie laughs. "That's this machine," she says, touching the PCA pump. "It tells me you gave yourself a dose just a little while ago. Sounds like it helped."

"Like a charm."

"You're lucky the guy was a small-time hoodlum with a small-time pistol and not some gun lover with a Magnum. I've seen what those monsters can do."

"I don't want to think about it."

"I talked with your doctors. They're confident about your recovery, thank God. I don't think I could handle losing you."

I place a hand on her forearm. "Well, I'm not goin' yet," I say. "But when the time comes, you'll be able to handle it quite fine."

She smiles, brushes the backs of her fingers across my cheek. My whiskers stand up with the sensation. It's like when she massages the bottoms of my feet after trimming my toenails. It's a secret Callie and I keep from her mother. If Natalie knew her doctor-daughter was giving me pedicures, we'd never hear the end of it. She assumes I go to a pedicurist, but it's treasured time I get to spend with Callie.

"What makes you so sure?" Callie asks.

"You were trained to cope with loss the right way."

She chuckles. "What's the right way? Is this gonna be one of your lectures?"

"I've often thought circumstance should introduce children to loss—to the inevitability of loss—little by little, starting with small losses, then gradually escalating them, as their ability to handle things grows. It's far better than having a piano dropped on you from the word 'Go!' Believe me, I know." I remember the children in France. I remember Élodie.

"What's a little loss?"

"The best example I can think of is a balloon."

Callie gives a short laugh. Her voice inflects high. "A balloon?"

"You may not remember, but when you were about five, Nana and I took you to the Topsfield Fair."

"I think I vaguely remember."

"Do you remember begging us to buy you one of those animal balloons, and we did, and the balloon man made you a puppy with balloons of assorted colors forming the body, the tail, the snout, the legs and the ears, and you loved it so much that you gave it a name? Do you remember that?"

"Yes, vaguely. It was mostly red and blue. But I don't remember the name I gave it."

"Waffles."

"Waffles? Why would I name a balloon puppy Waffles?"

"You don't remember? On the way to the fair we stopped at IHOP for breakfast and you had waffles."

"Really? Was I that unimaginative?"

"Nana and I loved it. Waffles! But within the hour, first one balloon burst, then another, and another, until you were left holding an empty stick. You cried your eyes out. To tell you the truth, I almost cried, too. It always got to me when children were sad. Still does." I look out the window for a long moment, thinking of those children in the Pyrénées. I turn back to Callie. "But then I realized there was a kindness there."

"A kindness?"

"Yes. It was a loss, but it was a little loss. One you could deal with. Far better than if the first loss you experienced was a pet." A shudder passes through me at the thought ... thank God Arlequin showed up! "Or, God forbid, a parent, or a sibling. Or a grandparent. That's why it's a kindness when we experience the loss of pets before grandparents, grandparents before parents, oneself before one's children. It's the natural order of things. It allows you to build reserves of strength and the wisdom to deal with the terrible pain of great loss."

Callie leans over and hugs me around the neck. "I love you so much, Papa!" It's amazing how the heart can feel so full when she says those words.

"And I love you."

"I suppose according to your philosophy, doctors like me build up extra reserves because we also experience the loss of patients."

"I suppose."

She shakes her head emphatically. "No! Not nearly enough for me! If I lost you, it would be like losing the balloon, the pet, and the parents all at once. Nothing will ever have prepared me for that. So, I insist you stick around! Doctor's orders!"

I laugh. "I guess if you put it that way, I'll have to keep hangin' on."

"Good. Now, speaking of which, I talked with your surgeon and with your hospitalist. They agree on transferring you to Spalding Rehab in a few days. The people there will help you get back on your feet."

"And do you agree with them?"

"I'm an emergency doctor, so it's not my field. But, yes. Hedrick is one of the best trauma surgeons we have. I've worked with him before. And Osborn is a great hospitalist." Callie pauses, hesitates, and I sense this is one of those good news, bad news things. "Papa, there's something else," she says. "They don't think you should fly any time soon. And I agree with them. I know you were planning on that D-Day ceremony, but …."

Damn! "Why not?"

"See that tube between your ribs? It's to remove excess air from the pleural space, that's the space between your lung and your chest wall. Otherwise, you could end up with a pneumothorax."

"Pneumothorax?"

"Collapsed lung."

"And that stops me from flying?"

"When I was working a field hospital in Iraq, we wouldn't let kids fly to Germany for more complete medical treatment if they had sustained sucking chest wounds. We waited until they had recovered enough. That was generally at least a week or two. The problem is air pressure at altitude."

"But it's a good four or five weeks before my flight to France."

"And you're over ninety, Papa. Frankly, we don't get many nonagenarians who have been shot in the lungs. Those guys in Iraq were young and fit. With you, there's too great a risk of a recurrence."

I turn my face away from her and stare out the window. I'm trying not to show how much this galls me. *Goddamn luck!*

Callie grasps my hand. "That was really something you did, Papa. Saving that woman. I'm so very, very proud of you. Everybody down in the ED has been talking about it."

"Your mother isn't happy. She thinks I'm too old to be doing things like that."

Callie frowns. "How do you even put up with Mom?"

"Oh, she just wants to be needed. She was always that way. But

I swear, she talks more and more like Nana every day." Callie's face tenses, and she looks away for a moment. "You look like you want to say something."

"No, I—"

"Go ahead. Say it."

"Nana was never as much of a bitch as Mom is."

I chuckle. "Well, perhaps you never saw her the way I did. She had her moments. But, so do we all. I loved her anyway."

Callie smiles. "Yes, I know you did."

"And as to your mother, I love her, too. She's a rose. A thorny one, perhaps, but …."

"She always wants to take charge of everything."

I sigh because I know it's true. "She means well. You need to cut her some slack. She was great in Nana's last years."

"I appreciate that. But I had to grow up with her always hovering over me."

"Maybe she was wise. Look how wonderfully you turned out."

Callie laughs. It's a tension releasing laugh. She walks to the window and looks out for a moment, and returns to my bedside, and pauses, then asks, "Papa, who is Élodie?"

As Élodie, herself, would have said, I'm gobsmacked! "What?"

"The nurse in post op, Amy, is a friend of mine. I saw her a little while ago and she said when you were coming out of anesthesia you mumbled that name several times. She said she never knew my grandmother had such a beautiful name."

"And what did you say?"

"I just smiled and said I always called her Nana." Callie narrows her eyes playfully at me. "So, *who is* Élodie?"

"*Was.*"

"Was?"

"She died a long time ago."

"Oh, God! Obviously, she was important to you. But who was she?"

"A French resistance fighter I met during the war. That's all."

"That's all?" She gives me a skeptical look.

"And she played the violin."

Callie smiles. A knowing smile. "Seventy years later, you come out of surgery and call her name—*her* name, not Nana's—and all she was to you was a resistance fighter who played the violin?"

"It was before I met your grandmother."

"So, you were in love with her, and you kept it a secret all this time." Callie touches my hand. She's having fun. She loves to tease me. She sits on the bed and hugs me.

"Your grandmother knew about her," I offer, weakly.

"You told Nana?"

"We were always honest and open with each other."

"Were you with her when she died? Élodie I mean."

"No. I was in Austria. I only learned about it after the war when I went to find her. It was Jean-Baptiste who told me."

"Jean-Baptiste?"

"Another one of the resistance fighters. I was with them for a time while I recovered from my wounds. My parents were told I was missing in action."

"I never knew that!"

"I never talked about it much. I asked Jean-Baptiste to show me where she was buried, but he said he had no idea where her grave was."

"So, you weren't even able to say goodbye to her?"

"No." I pause for a long while thinking of that foothill in the Pyrénées, all those years ago, then say, "That's probably why I called her name in the recovery room and not your grandmother's."

"I don't understand."

"Your grandmother and I, our story was complete when she died. It had a beginning, a middle, and an end. It had come full circle and it was good. As much as it broke my heart when she died, there was a sense of completion, I guess. Perhaps even a satisfaction for a life well-lived. I think she felt that way, too."

"But with Élodie there was no closure?"

"Closure. That's the word people like to use these days, but, no, no closure. There is never closure. You only learn to survive better. Instead, I always thought of Élodie and me as a story without a true ending, with the final chapter unwritten."

Callie's eyes shine and she hugs me again. "Oh, Papa!"

"Please, Callie, don't tell your mother any of this. I'll never hear the end of it."

"Don't worry. It's our secret."

"She'd pester me about it as if it happened yesterday, or as if I was carrying on an affair while married to your grandmother."

"I promise not to tell, Papa. Now I'll let you get some sleep. It's obvious the pain meds are making you drowsy."

"Better living through chemistry," I say. "It's like floating."

"Can I get you anything before I leave? More water?"

"No. Wait, yes. Please get my phone. It's over there on the window sill. And the earphones, too."

"Of course." She retrieves the phone and hands it to me.

"Thanks. Now one last favor. I can hardly move my right arm, and I'm useless as a southpaw with these small buttons on the phone. In my music files you'll find a piece called 'Song of the Birds.' Would you pull it up for me, please, and put my earphones on my ears? I want to drown out the noise from the nursing station."

"Was this a piece she played on her violin? Élodie?"

I nod. You could never get anything past Callie.

She smiles. "Drown out the noise from the nursing station, my ass! You want to dream." Callie pauses a minute, then says, "Wait a minute! So, your Élodie played the violin?"

"She was a musician," I say, "and she played beautifully."

"Those door plates in your condo Mom was all over you for buying. What did you call them?"

"You mean the escutcheons?" Following my move to the condo in the Charlestown Navy Yard, I'd hired a smithy to fashion custom escutcheon plates for the light switches and door hardware. Callie's mother, the ever-practical Natalie, protested that it was a silly waste of money.

"Yes, those. The one leading to your balcony is an embossed violin, split right down the middle so it's only whole when the doors are closed. And some of the light switches have moon jellies and I remember you telling me you thought of yourself and the other men who parachuted into France as moon jellies because they look like parachutes. And the cross with two cross bars, I'll bet it has some special meaning for you, too."

"It's the Cross of Lorraine, a symbol of the French Resistance."

Callie gives a falsetto laugh. "You rascal! You created a secret code with all those symbols on your doors and light switches! You made a *museum* of your memory of her! A memory palace of Élodie!"

I'm stunned. "What do you know about memory palaces?"

"Papa, do you think I don't read your books?"

A thrill passes through me. "You read *The Architecture of Memory*?"

There is a gleam in her eyes, a knowing grin on her lips. "You mean *The Architecture of Memory in Prehistory, Antiquity and the Middle Ages* by G. H. Budge with chapters on Cave Art, Cicero, Simonides of Ceos, Matteo Ricci, Giulio Camillo, and Giordano Bruno, among others, for which you won the Otto Gründler Book Prize in Medieval Studies? Is that the book you mean?" She throws her shoulders back and places her hands on her hips. She looks just like she did as a little girl when she thought she outsmarted everyone.

"I'm flabbergasted! I didn't think anyone in the family read my arcane books."

"I would have been a dull doctor if I spent my entire med school years buried in books like Netter's *Atlas of Human Anatomy and Human Histology*."

"Indeed," I say with a laugh.

"I've noticed, Papa, most of your books deal with memory, especially of things lost. I've always wanted to ask you about that. Now, I think those escutcheons are part of the same thing."

I smile. Damn, she's sharp! "Vainly had I sought to borrow from my books surcease of sorrow."

"Shakespeare again?"

I shake my head. "Poe. *The Raven*."

"So, am I right? Those escutcheons make up a kind of memory palace?"

"Don't tell the others."

Callie throws her arms around my neck. A tear slides down her cheek. I feel the wetness on my own skin. "I love you so much, Papa!"

She hugs me tighter. "Though I ache for your loss of Élodie. Even if it's seventy years on."

I don't want to let her go, even though her embrace is hurting my right arm like crazy. "I love you, too, Callie. You've made an old man feel at least some of his writing has a purpose. Now please give me my music and let me get some sleep."

"*Song of the Birds?*" she asks, searching my files.

"That's it."

She pulls up the music and places the earphones over my ears and presses play and kisses me on the forehead. "Pleasant dreams, Papa," she whispers.

I watch her leave then lean back into the pillow and allow myself another little squirt of morphine as I sink into the music.

Chapter 4
Nine Day's Fall from Heaven

I remember how, not long before Anna died, she reached out from her hospital bed, held my hand, and said, "We are bound together, you know. Always." It was something she'd said often, but it was only after she died, and I first experienced life without her, that I finally came to fully appreciate what she'd meant. I now see how so much of our lives was intertwined—our passions, physical and spiritual, our love of life, our wonder at rearing children together, our shared delight in grandchildren and the bewitching but sobering appearance of great-grandchildren, the pleasures we shared of music, books, movies, Shakespeare, poetry, our delight in food and wine at fine restaurants, and our discreet comments about couples at adjoining tables. And, also, the sadness we sometimes endured together including the deaths of our parents and other relatives; the deaths of children anywhere in the world through war, famine, natural disaster or unnatural savagery; the death of a friend; the death of a pet; public tragedies like the assassinations of the Kennedy brothers and Martin Luther King and John Lennon. Anna and I would talk about these things, share our thoughts, share our grief. It was during one of these conversations (this one about the assassination of Bobby Kennedy) that I conceived the idea of a giant, wrathful mirror, suspended somewhere out beyond the moon's orbit, that reflects the unnatural light of the back side of the moon on us all—the hellish light the Janus-faced moon keeps turned away from us.

And now that Anna is gone, I miss her every time I see a news event on TV and can't ask her what she thinks, or every time I go to a movie and can't ask if she enjoyed it, too, or each time I go to a restaurant and I can't give her a bite of my prime rib in exchange for a taste of her salmon, or a sip of my martini in exchange for a sip of her daiquiri. Come to think of it, I hardly ever do those things anymore. Movies and restaurants are just no fun without her.

I mention all this because these things were promises—*potentials*—of the love Élodie and I shared, that never came to be, that were still-born. Those thousands and thousands of daily affinities, this accumulation of both grand and trivial things, are exactly what made my life with Anna complete, and what leave me wanting more of Élodie. Christ, we never even had a chance to quarrel and make up! I suppose in all ages war is like that. It so swamps your spirit with the need to stay alive, you have little time for anything else except war's antithesis, the overwhelming need for love. This is why I invent conversations with Élodie about trivial things as if she were still alive. *What would you like for breakfast, Élodie? Where would you like to dine after your concert? Should we have red or white wine? What are you going to wear to the theater? What should I wear?* I'm not being unfaithful to Anna, you understand. After all, Élodie and I loved long before I met Anna, and anyway, Anna and I are a finished book, complete and whole. Rather, it is a deep sense of the opposite of what I'd had with Anna—that stinging incompleteness—that drives me to try to reconstruct the memory of Élodie. To resurrect her.

❦

After running into the German patrol and passing the Goethe test, we continue south. Avoiding main roads, we arrive at a small commune called Saint-Christophe where we spend the night in a barn, owned by a friend of the Resistance, who feeds us and leaves us with several bottles of wine.[14]

---

14 Yes, I know morphine and wine is a dangerous combination. However, we didn't know that much then and, besides, we were young and thought we were

The following day, we meander southeastward on little-used roads, past irregularly shaped farm fields, and soon arrive at a lonely cross-roads east of a small village called Javerdat. We pull the ambulance and motorcycle into a copse of chestnut trees at the edge of a meadow to hide them from the road and stop for a rest. Immediately, we notice a faint smell of smoke coming from the southeast—acrid, sulfurous. It stings my nostrils. "It smells like someone is cooking bad meat," I say.

"There's no such thing as good meat these days," Élodie says. "Only in Paris and only at the Hotel Meurice, I suppose."

"The Hotel Meurice?"

"Where the Germans have their headquarters," she replies, spitting on the ground.

While her colleagues share one of the remaining German cigarettes they had taken from their victims in Normandy, Élodie unwraps the bandages from my head and helps me off the stretcher. She guides me unsteadily to a boulder. The wind veers to the northeast and stirs the vegetation in a meadow surrounding the copse. I sit and stretch my back and neck and I inhale the perfumed air coming from the sun-saturated field of purple, fragrant orchids and blue periwinkle. The scent momentarily masks the odor from my own sweaty body, my blood-soaked bandages, and the mysterious, acrid smell of smoke from the southeast. There is a buzz of insects. Butterflies flit over the open meadow. The twittered songs of warblers fill the air.[15]

In the distance squats a small stone house surrounded by a low stone wall. The shadow of a hawk ripples across the rolling landscape. A bulge suddenly appears under the moist carpet of dead leaves and moves off like a wave—a critter scurrying for safety from the sharp-eyed hawk whose shadow suddenly slows and circles.

Élodie sits beside me with her violin case. "Comfortable?"

"Yes. I'm beginning to like this morphine stuff."

---

indestructible.

15   While lifting these colors, these sounds, and mostly these scents from my diary, I got a momentary impression of Élodie. It was so vivid, yet so fleeting, my hands shook, and I had to take a break.

"We must start to wean you from it. You shouldn't keep taking it."

"This journey over the mountains to Spain and Portugal, how long will it take?"

"Still eager to get back to your American friends?"

"I signed up to fight the Krauts alongside my buddies. I went through jump school side-by-side with them, and I shipped out with them. I belong with them. So, how long?"

"It depends."

"Depends on what?"

"Things."

"Goddamn it! What things?"

"Germans, for one. Have you given them your schedule? Do they know you're in a hurry?"

"Fuck!"

"And then there is the weather. Those mountains are high. There are many storms."

"Great. Anything else?"

"You."

"Me?"

"How much you can tolerate. Your strength. Your endurance."

"Don't worry about me."

"Okey-Dokey." She flashes a cherubic smile.

I chuckle. "Where did you learn a phrase like that?"

"I watched *The Little Rascals* to help learn colloquial American English. Porky says it."

"Jesus!"

She removes the violin and a tuning fork which she hands to me. "Now, you can help me tune."

"Swell. Action at last! It's what I joined up for."

Élodie gives me an acid smile and says, "When I give you the sign, hit the fork on your knee."

"It will be my pleasure. I've always regretted not taking music lessons when I was a kid."

"Well we can start now with a single note, an A." She stands the base of the instrument on her thigh, presses her left hand hard against the scroll, and nods to me. I knock the tuning fork against my knee, like an uncle playing the spoons, and it rings out an A note. Élodie turns a peg and plucks the A string several times. Finally, she says, "These pegs are forever slipping. I need to get new ones fitted when the war is over." She continues tuning the other strings by referencing the A string and when she is done, she starts to play scales up and down.

"And here I thought I was gonna get a recital," I say.

Élodie shakes her head. "I need to practice."

"She's always doing this," says Marcel. "Always practice, never a concert for her companions."

"I need to practice," Élodie says, "so I'll be ready to give concerts again when the war is over."

"The war seems very far from here," I say. "Play something for us."

Élodie gazes at me for a long moment and I'm afraid I upset her. Finally, she nods. "I'll play a piece Pablo Casals taught me. He said it's a prayer for peace. It's called 'Song of the Birds.' In it, you'll hear the urge for freedom. He wrote it because his homeland, Catalonia, was not, and is not, free." She begins playing at a very slow tempo and as she plays, she gazes into the distance. It's an empty stare, and when she finishes the piece, she continues to stare at the sky for long moments before putting the violin back in its case. "I think it's going to rain," she says, nodding to the west.

I shield my eyes from the dazzling sunlight and gaze toward the west where I see a line of pewter clouds with darker underbellies hanging like overfull udders.

"That's not just ordinary rain," says Marcel. "It's a storm. We should keep going. Perhaps we can find shelter."

We travel on for a short distance until we come to a stone house with blue shutters. The door is ajar and swings on a tight arc with a sudden gust of wind, its hinges creaking. The storm is quick-moving and passes to the east of us. There are blooms of lightening, distant thunder claps, but no rain where we are. And there is no sign of life, either in the house or in the adjoining barn.

"I don't think it's abandoned," Élodie says. "I saw laundry hanging on a clothesline out back."

"Let's see if anyone is inside," says Marcel, leveling his rifle toward the house. The other men also ready their weapons.

"Not wearing these uniforms, idiot!" says Élodie. "If somebody is there, we'll either scare them to death, or they'll see a chance to kill some Germans before we can explain who we are."

"We need to get rid of these uniforms," says Jean-Baptiste.

"Not until we're past the main body of the Wehrmacht," replies Élodie.

"But this far south we're more likely to get shot at by our own comrades than by the Boche."

Élodie shakes her head. "Not until we're certain most of the Germans have left for Normandy."

Suddenly, there is the simultaneous crack of a gunshot and a zing as something hits the stone wall and a chip of granite leaps into the air. I whirl. A bearded man is aiming a rifle at us. The gun seems to draw all the light of day to it. The barrel flashes sunlight. More men have weapons pointed at us. One of the men shouts something in German.

"He's warning us not to move," Élodie says to me.

The same man shouts again, *"Lassen Sie Ihre Waffen auf der Boden.*[16]*"*

Marcel and the others lay their weapons on the ground.

Élodie says, *"Nous sommes des combattants de la résistance comme vous, et cet homme est un Américain."*[17] She turns to me. "Confirm to them you are American."

What can I say? I shout, "It's true. I'm an American paratrooper. I know who Babe Ruth is! Viva de Gaulle! Viva Roosevelt!"

"What are you doing here?" the man asks in heavily accented English. "Why are you not with your comrades in Normandy?"

"I was wounded. These people helped me," I reply.

Élodie turns to the man. "You speak better English than German. It's *auf DEN Boden,* not *auf DER Boden."*

The man shrugs. "Why is the American with you?"

---

16   "Leave your weapons on the ground."

17   "We are resistance fighters like you, and this man is an American."

Élodie says, "We couldn't return him to his unit because we had to come south quickly to help prevent German reinforcements going to the beaches."

"Why those uniforms?"

"We took them from some Boche we killed. A medical unit. They allow us to pass as German to get through the lines."

"What do you call yourself?"

"My *nom-de-guerre* is Azalais."

"Your real name?"

"Élodie Bedier."

"The violinist?" the man asks, glancing at the violin case that hangs from a strap looped over her shoulder like a rifle.

"Yes. You are very observant." I can hear the sarcasm dripping from her voice. *I can almost hear it today.*

"I've heard of you."

"I'm flattered."

"But how do we know it is really you?"

One of the man's companions says, "It's her. I saw her perform in Paris before the war." This man looks at Élodie. "Mozart's Third Violin Concerto. You were wonderful."

Élodie smiles. "Thank you. It's one of my favorites."

The first man says, "I am Auguste Pauly. Your admirer is Isaac Benjamin. He's a doctor. And these are my men," he says waving his arm. "We are Maquis d'Aquilac."

"I know of you," says Élodie. "One of your leaders is the pianist Aliénor Breasiac with whom I have performed chamber music."

"Yes. But now tell me where you are headed."

"South to join the Resistance around Toulouse."

"What about the American?"

"Perhaps the doctor can examine his wound and predict when he'll be recovered enough to travel on his own two feet. And, when we can, we'll take him through the Ariège and over the Pyrénées, and out of France, so he can get back to his American unit."

"But first you will kill Boche?"

"First we will kill Boche."

I stare at her. Had her voice faltered a little?

"In that case, we must find other clothes for you. Also, we must give you different weapons. After yesterday, it would go very badly for you if people thought you, yourself, were Boche."

"What do you mean? What happened yesterday?"

"We'll tell you, but first we will find clothes for you there," says August Pauly nodding toward the house.

"Shouldn't we ask the people who live there?" asks Élodie. "We can't just walk in and take what we want."

August frowns. "I'm afraid Monsieur and Madame Argoud and their two sons won't be back."

"Why won't they be back?"

"Between them, there should be clothes that will fit all of you."

"Why won't they be back?"

August frowns, says nothing.

In an irked voice, Élodie says, "I ask you one more time, August: Why won't they be back?"

August's shoulders slump. He gestures for a young boy, who is standing with the others, to come to him. The boy walks shyly toward August and Élodie. "This is Gabriel Bazin," says August. "He will tell you what happened yesterday in Oradour-sur-Glane, which is only a kilometer from here, then you will understand. Unfortunately, Gabriel does not speak English, so you must translate for your American friend." He turns to the boy and says, "*Dites-leur ce que tu a vu.*"[18]

The boy begins in a small, shy voice to tell us what he had seen. He talks haltingly. Élodie interrupts a few times to ask questions. Finally, she turns to me. "He says the Germans came at two in the afternoon. The day was sunny, and he remembers hearing birds singing." She turns back to the boy, asks another question. When the boy answers, she says to me, "It was the second SS Panzer Division. That's the one they call '*Das Reich.*' It's an elite division of the Wehrmacht."

---

18   "Tell them what you saw." Footnotes are not needed for what follows because Élodie made certain I understood by translating simultaneously. She could have worked for the U.N. after the war!

The boy continues to talk, and Élodie translates. "They came into the town marching people from outlying farms before them."

"Including Monsieur and Madame Argoud and their two sons," says August.

The boy starts to tremble. *"Le bruit de leurs bottes … Le bruit de leurs bottes …."* Tears slide down his cheeks.

Élodie puts a hand on his shoulder. Turning to me, she says, "The sound of their boots. He's talking about the sound of their hobnailed boots. It must have been terrifying." She takes young Gabriel into her arms and speaks soothingly to him, encouraging him to go on.

He continues in a quavering voice, and Élodie translates. "They forced everybody to stand in the fairground."

Gabriel seems to be steeling himself to tell the story. He starts to speak rapidly and Élodie translates as quickly as he speaks.

"The men, including Gabriel's father, were taken to the garages and barns and the women and children were marched into the church. His mother was among them. They took more children from the school, including his two older sisters—even children from the school for toddlers where Gabriel's youngest sister was—and forced them into the church."

"Ils ont crié, 'Raus! Raus!'"

"They screamed in German, 'Out! Out!'"

Gabriel speaks. Élodie translates. "That's when Gabriel escaped. He slipped out the back door and hid behind some trees."

"Puis j'ai entendu les coups de feu …."

"Then he heard the gunshots …"

"Et je savais … je savais dans mon cœur que papa … était mort."

"And he knew … Dear God! … He knew in his heart his father was dead." Again, she takes the boy into her arms and holds him. His entire body trembles. Élodie's shoulders shake.

Through sobs, Gabriel mumbles something.

In a trembling voice, Élodie says, "Then there was a great explosion. Much black smoke."

"Ma mère … et mes sœurs …."

"His mother and his sisters …."

August rushes forward. "Stop! This is too painful for him. I will tell you the rest. I am an idiot for asking him to tell you about it!" He stares at Élodie and me. His nostrils flare. He draws in a sharp breath, and says, through clenched teeth, "The fuckers blew up the church with everybody inside! It was a mistake to ask the boy to tell you what happened. The poor boy has suffered enough." He puts an arm around the boy's shoulders and hugs him close.

He turns back to Élodie and me. His eyes glisten. "There was one survivor from the church. This is what she told me. As the children were marched to the church, there was a great clatter of the people's sabots,[19] and the German boots. The church was filled with mothers, many with babies in their arms, some with babies in prams. There were several hundred people in the church. Then came the explosion Gabriel mentioned. Thick, black smoke. Women and children screaming. One door gave way under the pressure of ... *les gens paniqués.*" He looks to Élodie for help.

"Panicked people," she says.

He nods. "Some people escaped the church only to be mowed down by machine guns. Women and their babies. And then the Boche threw straw, firewood, chairs, anything that would burn, on top of the bodies. Then they lit the whole place on fire. The fuckers!"

"Mon dieu!" Élodie murmurs.

"I arrived in Oradour the following day. That was yesterday. The stench of burnt flesh was unbelievable. Dogs roamed the place with tails between their legs and whining and yipping as they sniffed around looking for their owners. The fuckers returned yesterday morning and tried to cover up what they'd done, but it was impossible. They couldn't bury the evidence, so they simply gave up. I saw a man who had been incompletely buried, his hand was sticking out of the ground like he was reaching for something. There were between six and seven hundred bodies! *Six to seven hundred!* How, by all that is holy, do you hide something like that?"

"Jesus Christ!" I mutter.

---

19   Wooden shoes.

Élodie shakes her head and puts her arms around Gabriel. Tears fall freely from her eyes wetting the boy's cheeks. She looks up at me, bitterness in her eyes. "Do you want to know what the word 'oradour' means?"

"What?" I ask.

"It comes from an Occitan word, *oradores*—a place of prayer."

⁂

That is one image of Élodie I can coax from my memory with some precision: the way sunlight glistened in the tears under her eyes. The wet, sunlit trails of her tears on Gabriel's cheek. The lines of her face twisted in grief and anger. It's all burned into my memory.

My face must have been clouded with the same hatred and outrage. And I saw it in the faces of Jean-Baptiste. And Marcel. And Claude.

I once read, on the internet, how a new village had been built after the war, but only on a nearby site. The original site was established as a permanent memorial and museum on the orders of Charles de Gaulle. I promise myself I will visit the site when I go to France. I know in my heart it will hold a memory of Élodie. I believe there are only a few places in the world that could arouse living memories of her, and Oradour-sur-Glane is, sadly, one of them. The cave at Lascaux is another. The home of Pablo Casals in Prades in the Pyrénées-Orientales, where she was as happy as I had ever seen her—that is another. And, of course, there are the Pyrénées themselves where we risked our lives together. These are the places I will revisit when I return to France.

⁂

With the help of August Pauly, we exchange the ambulance and motorcycle for a less conspicuous Citroën confiscated from a farmer. It is fitted with a cylindrical wood gasifier that hangs over the rear bumper which will allow us to run the car without relying on hard-to-find gasoline.

"This will be safer than the truck and motorcycle," August says. "The further south you go, the more likely you are to run into resistance fighters rather than Boche."

"You also said something about exchanging our weapons," Élodie says.

"Yes. We'll give you all Sten guns[20] we've taken from dead comrades."

"You've been an immense help, August," says Élodie. "And we all thank you for the new clothes and weapons."

August gives a sad smile. "Madame Argoud's dress does not flatter you, but I suppose it will do."

Isaac Benjamin steps forward. "I have examined the American's wound. The shrapnel hit nothing vital. Only muscle. You have done a very good job. He should recover very quickly."

"When will he be able to walk?"

"With a limp? Now. Freely? Quite soon. There'll be some pain, but he should be able to manage," says Benjamin. "And there is no need keep him wrapped in bandages."

Élodie looks at me. "They are a disguise only."

"He should wear regular clothes," says Benjamin. "The open air will help the wound to heal."

I could have kissed the man right then and there!

"Is it true you are heading for the Ariège?" Benjamin asks.

"Yes."

"Then you will pass close by Aquilac. Perhaps you will deliver a message to my wife and daughter. Please say I am alive and well. Their names are Ruth and Elsie and they are in hiding there."

"Hiding?"

"We are Jews."

"Benjamin! Of course," Élodie says. "I know many of the people in Aquilac. Who are they with?"

---

20   The Sten gun was a British-produced submachine gun, that could fire fully- or semi-automatic and that cost only $10 to manufacture (in 1941 dollars). It was capable of emptying a 30-round magazine in a single 5-second burst. It was a devastating, lightweight weapon favored by resistance fighters.

"Gaston and Odette Dupont."

"I know them well. I'll be pleased to deliver your message."

After I change into ordinary clothes, we exchange a round of kisses, one on each cheek, and leave. We drive slowly through the drifting smoke coming from the direction of Oradour-sur-Glane, a thick smoke that slides shadows along the ground, hunches over boulders, stumbles into ruts, brushes the trunks of trees, marking them with the stench of something hideous smoldering around the next bend, or on the next stretch of road, or in the next few kilometers.[21]

Toward evening, under a gibbous moon, we arrive at the outskirts of the village. I feel we have entered Dante's 7th circle of Hell. Or, to put it like Milton, we have somehow fallen nine days from Heaven. Stone houses stand gutted on both sides of the road. Broken. Roofless. Jutting from the earth like giant swollen knuckles in the unnatural moonlight. Piles of wooden furniture with red-glowing embers hunkering deep inside. Coils of smoke like noxious incense snaking up from unclean thuribles worm into my nostrils. Over there, a burnt-out Citroën. And there, a charred sewing machine, a destroyed fuel pump. Melted eyeglasses! Some poor soul's fucking, melted eyeglasses! An indecent tomb-like stillness hovers about the village, softened only by the sighing of wind through the broken walls, and the cavities, of buildings. And bodies. Human forms. Blackened. Unrecognizable. The silence curls around us like tentacles.

Someone mumbles, *"Merde!"* The deeper we go into the village, the more the smoke assaults our eyes and nostrils. I am forced to squeeze my eyes shut repeatedly and wrinkle my nose against the acrid bite of smoke.

Élodie stares at the destruction. "We cannot stay here. We must leave."

---

21 Now, seventy years later, I can see I wrote these details, and those that follow, in my diary with considerable anger about the things that followed. The ragged-edged puncture where I broke the pencil tip is still plainly visible and the writing becomes shaky because I was forced to squeeze the stub of my freshly sharpened, and shortened, pencil between the tips of my thumb and my forefinger.

I know she's right, and I wonder who gave the fucking moon a spin and turned that dark Janus face toward us.

No one objects. We accelerate down the road, chased by miniature, swirling dust devils. Soon, we are clear of the village and, after a few kilometers, we pull over to the side of the road. No one speaks. Élodie pulls her violin case from the car and climbs a small hillock. At the top, she sits on a boulder under a spreading chestnut tree and takes out her violin. She begins to play a sorrowful, slow tune. It is that Catalan tune, "Song of the Birds," she'd played before. We remain silent, listening, lost in our own thoughts.

And a rain begins.

It is a soft, feminine rain, a nurturing mizzle, the kind that nourishes fields and shivers leaves. It comes with the clean, ozone smell of fresh rain. I turn my face to the sky and open my eyes, blinking to allow the drizzle to rinse my burning eyes, to sooth my nostrils. The rain releases the steamy perfume of the earth, the bouquet of plants, the faint ozone of the rocks—the petrichor that accompanies rain. And there is the essential oil of lavender in the air.

Several hours later, under a fat, hunchbacked moon, we round a bend in the narrow road and abruptly come face to face with the lights of a Wehrmacht staff car escorted by three motorcycles with attached sidecars.

Claude stomps on the brakes and the Citroën skids to a sudden stop, catapulting all of us forward. I jam my broken pinkie painfully against the dashboard. Obscured by a moonlit dust cloud kicked up by the tires, we scramble out of the car and fling ourselves to the ground behind the Citroën, even as the Germans open fire. Above me, a Sten gun barks angrily. I look up. Élodie stands, scarcely shielded by the car, sweeping the stuttering Sten gun right and left. Her teeth are barred. She wears a crazed expression. The night is filled with frenzied muzzle flashes. I tear my gaze from her and take aim with my gun and crack off several shots and I am aware of the others firing their weapons and bullets rip the ground around me and ping off the Citroën and there are shouts of pain and, already, three Germans are sprawled on the ground but one of them is still alive, his legs jerking, and I aim, carefully, and fire and the man's legs go still. Fuck! This is the first man I've ever killed! I make a quick count. There are at least six more Germans. I aim. Fire. A hole erupts in the forehead of an officer and the man crumbles to the ground. One German hops aboard a motorcycle. Another man vaults into the sidecar. Élodie springs out from behind our car. She slaps the Sten gun against her shoulder, grabs the magazine that juts at right angles from the barrel, and rips off a stream of bullets, mowing the Germans down with several short bursts of fire. The motorcycle with its sidecar runs off into the trees and flips, spilling the two Germans to the ground. *"Merde!"* Élodie cries when she pulls the trigger again and nothing happens. She snaps the empty magazine from the gun and flings open the door of the Citroën and dives into the rear seat where she snatches another magazine and slams it into place. I'm vaguely aware of shots coming from my left. I swing my gun in that direction but stop when I realize the shots are coming from Jean-Baptiste and Claude who have somehow scrambled into the trees and now have the Germans in withering enfiladed fire. Suddenly, there is no return fire. There comes a cry of *"Nicht schießen! Nicht schießen! Wir kapitulieren!"*[22] Slowly, two Germans appear from behind the staff car, hands raised. *"Bitte, nicht schießen!"* one repeats. He is trembling. He is young. He is a boy. *Ein Junge.* So is his companion.

Élodie approaches the first boy. She asks him what unit he belongs to, even though, as she tells me later, she already knows the answer, for she sees the *Wolfsangel,* or wolf's hook, shoulder patch of the *Das Reich* Division. But she wants to hear the boy say it.

"Der zweite SS-Panzerdivision,[23]*"* he replies.

She asks him if he was in Oradour. *"Waren Sie in Oradour?"*

The boy glances nervously at his companion but remains silent behind his smooth, cherubic face.

Élodie's face reddens. Her nostrils flare. She leans forward and stares flinty-eyed at the boy. *"Waren Sie in Oradour?"* she shouts. She insists he answer yes or no: *"Ja oder Nein?"*

---

22   "Don't shoot! Don't shoot! We surrender!"
23   "The 2nd SS Panzer Division.

Still, the boy remains silent. His lips quiver. Tears slip from the corners of his eyes and leave rills through the dust on his cheeks.

"Ja oder Nein?" Élodie repeats. Her eyes are wide. Her voice is a screech. Her cheek muscles twitch. I shiver at the sight.

"Ja," the boy answers weakly.

She asks if it was two days ago. *"Vor zwei Tagen?"*

The boy's forehead is creased. His raised hands are shaking. His eyes are pleading. Finally, he says, *"Wir wurde uns befohlen, es zu tun."*[24]

Élodie turns to me. In an acid voice she mutters, "Following orders!"

I reply, "Fuck!"

Jean-Baptiste approaches Élodie. "What will you do with your young prisoner?" he asks with a little smirk.

Élodie takes several steps backward. She levels the Sten gun at the boy. She mumbles, "Fuckers!"

"Don't," I say, reaching out for Élodie. But she takes another step back.

"Nein!" the boy cries. *"Nicht schießen! Nicht schießen!"* He turns to run.

Élodie cuts him down with a long burst of fire. She empties the magazine into him. She empties the whole, fucking magazine into him.

The other boy starts to run.

I glance at Élodie who is reaching for a new magazine and, before she can snap it into place, I take careful aim and shoot the boy in the back of the head. I hear Jean-Baptiste give a soft whistle of amazement.

Birds in the trees that had fallen silent, begin to twitter again.

There is a rustling in the underbrush, an unseen critter scrambling for cover.

The wind soughs softly through the treetops and I can scarcely hear a breath.

No one speaks for several long moments.

Jean-Baptiste and Marcel and Claude busy themselves rummaging through the dead German bodies, collecting weapons, ammunition, other items. Élodie approaches one of the dead Germans from the overturned sidecar and kneels beside him.

---

24   "We were ordered to do it."

I crouch alongside her. "What are you doing?"

"I want to see his *Erkennungsmarke*."

"His what?"

"Dog tag. I want to know who he was." She reads the tag aloud. "Fritz Dürbach."

A camera lies on the ground beside the man, a Voigtländer. Élodie picks it up. "Maybe there are photos I can send to his family after the war." She lays her Sten gun on the ground, gently, like putting a child to bed. With the camera slung over her shoulder, she walks slowly toward the trees by the side of the road. She leans against the trunk of a chestnut tree. She vomits. I come up to her and put my arm around her shoulders. I squeeze. I say nothing. Her shoulders convulse as she heaves over and over again, the camera tapping lightly against the tree trunk.

Jean-Baptiste comes up to us. Smiling, he says, "You see, American, it is good policy never to anger a woman."

I want to kill him. "Fuck you! Get away from her!" I scream. Jean-Baptiste's face reddens. I struggle to hold back tears. I level my gun at him. "Get away from her, now! Clear out, or I'll fucking kill you where you fucking stand!"

Jean-Baptiste backs away, a look of deep hatred in his eyes.

"Who the hell gave the moon a fucking spin," I mutter.

Élodie shoots me a quizzical look, but I don't explain, and she doesn't ask.

Chapter 5
Moon Jelly

I have never been able to erase the image of that damnable giant mirror. I can picture it up there, beyond the moon's orbit, wrathful in its precise reflection of the dark side, and I am filled with dread. This sense has never left me. Almost anything can bring it on: a news bulletin about children being harmed in some way, the view of a swollen moon in a sullen sky, a neo-Nazi parade anywhere in the world, a dead moon jelly on the beach. It happens, and tears come to my eyes. They don't tell you the nightmares never go away. Never. There's no such thing as closure. And now I wonder if my plan to return to France isn't, at least partially, an attempt to exorcise the Lucifers of my dream world—to see, first hand, a France where life has returned to normal, to see that Élodie's sacrifice was worth something, and to somehow ennoble the grief.

꙰

As much as a year before my encounter with the would-be rapist in the Navy Yard, I had formed the idea of returning to France for the 70th observance of D-Day, and as soon as that idea took hold, I realized Natalie would organize family resistance to it. So, I decided I needed, not only to announce my plan, but to demonstrate I knew what I was doing. I told my other children what Natalie already knew, that I was awaiting results from the tests my primary care doctor had ordered. Then, a week later, I called again to say I wanted them to gather for the weekend to celebrate my 91st birthday at the family home in Gloucester because I had something important to tell them. And when I asked them, collectively, to bring along the entire family, all thirty-two of them—spouses, children, grandchildren, great-grandchildren—they, of course, assumed something was wrong and wanted to know what it was. But I only insisted I wanted everybody to hear it directly from me, and all at the same time. Sure, it was a cunning ruse, a bit of dissembling for which I felt only a tiny shiver of shame because it was well worth it if I could get them all together, something I'd longed for since the time everybody gathered for Anna's funeral reception two years before. And besides, the ruse was nothing like the one I'd pulled off almost seventy years earlier to avoid a firing squad!

How could they refuse? Natalie planned to drive up from the South Shore with Marshal. My son, Richard, booked a flight from Seattle with his wife, Sandra, and my daughter, Judy, said she would fly in from San Francisco with her husband, Denis. And, acceding to my wish, every one of them planned to bring their full complement of children and grandchildren. Richard's son, Fred, planned to travel with his family from their home in Hermosa Beach, near Los Angeles, thus completing the West Coast contingent. Even better, a few days before the gathering, Callie called and said she would arrive early with her two children, Danny and Ashley, to help me prepare.

"What do you say to having lobster, Papa?" she'd asked.

"Perfect! We can get corn, too."

"A regular New England clam bake."

"Except we won't be on the beach, and we won't have clams and potatoes. Unless you think—"

"No. The lobster and corn will be enough. Too many in our family don't like clams the way you and I do."

"Primitives!" I said with a chuckle.

Callie laughed with me and volunteered to take care of cooking the lobsters if I'd pick them up that morning.

Except for Callie and her children, everybody was scheduled to arrive in the late afternoon on the first Friday in June. That morning, I climbed into my old '71 fire-red Ford Mustang and drove the few miles to the dock across from the State Fish Pier in Gloucester. I'd bought the car, new, forty-two years earlier, but when Anna and I leased a more practical Toyota about ten years ago, I garaged the Mustang. Then, after Anna died, I had it restored and got rid of the Toyota.

As I drove, I listened to the 8-track tape player which played Pablo Casals' "Song of the Birds" and thought of Élodie and the way moonlight would glint off the body of her violin and how the light would play along the bow as it moved across the strings and how it reflected in her cheeks and how she made the strings shiver with grief for Oradour, the place of prayer. It's like that often with scents or sounds. A memory comes into sharp focus, then disappears in an instant. In the time we were together, she played that piece often, almost obsessively, as if to lift herself from some dark place, as if grasping for a form of redemption for the things she had to do to fight the Nazis. Often, she'd said, "The worst thing about the Nazis is they drag you down to their level. You don't want to go to that place in your soul, but it's the only way to survive, the only way to fight them." And then she'd play the music she learned from Casals during his exile in the South of France and she'd play it over, and over, and over again. I often think of that music as the soundtrack of our love affair and I listened through to its conclusion after parking the Mustang and sitting with the window open.

The weather was clear, and I could see beyond Gloucester Harbor out to the Atlantic Ocean. There was the briny tang of sea breeze and, for the briefest of instants, I experienced another fragment of memory: Élodie's hair floating on the wind and the salt-sea breeze rising up from the Mediterranean to where we stood high above Argelès-sur-Mer at the eastern end of the Pyrénées, peering through binoculars at a German column snaking along the moonlit shore toward Saint-Cyprien.

I let the memory linger until it faded, then went into Captain Carl & Sons where I always bought my lobsters. Several large tanks lined the walls to my left and right, and directly in front of me was a polished oak counter, leopard-spotted with burn marks where long-ashed cigarettes had fallen from ashtrays. Behind the counter stood Carl, a burly man wearing a soiled apron that extended to his knees. "Henry!" he said, "I *thought* that was you pullin' up in that ancient buggy o' yours. What the hell were you sittin' in the parkin' lot for, anyways?"

"That car's a lot younger than me," I replied. "Just listening to a piece of music."

"Come for your two one-pounders as usual, have you?"

"Not this time, Carl. I'm needing three dozen for tomorrow night."

"Three dozen? You havin' a gang over?"

"The whole family," I said. "First time since Anna died."

Carl gave a slow shake of his head. "Still miss her, I do. Loved it when you two came in together and she picked the lobstahs. How many people we talkin'?"

"Thirty-two."

Carl frowned. "You sure three dozen'll be enough?"

"A bunch of them are kids. They'll prefer hot dogs."

"Kids! Gotta love 'em. You want all chix like you usually buy?"

"Not necessarily. Whatever you have, but nothing over two pounds. Too old and tough. Like me."

"Aggh! You ain't that old! You're still drivin', ain't yuh?"

"You may be the first person in the world to say ninety-one isn't old."

"Ain't the years, Henry. It's the fitness. You're fitter'n most people half your age."

I had to laugh at that. "Maybe I'll send my daughter, Natalie, over to see you. She's always harping on me to quit driving. Wants to pack me away in some goddamned nursing home."

"You in a nursin' home? Bullshit! Ain't where you belong."

"Tell that to her."

"Sure, send her over. I'll set her straight."

"No, I wouldn't subject you to that, Carl. I'll drop by around noon tomorrow to pick up the lobsters."

"They'll be waitin' for ya."

After leaving Captain Carl & Sons, I stopped at the shopping center and bought two new 20-quart stockpots—the 5-quart ones I already had were too small—and several nut crackers to augment my supply. I was thrilled Callie planned to arrive early to help me set everything up on the deck. I loved nothing better than spending time with her and Danny and Ashley. The previous evening, when we'd talked on the phone to make final arrangements, I'd told her, "Low tide is a little after three tomorrow. Come early and the four of us can go for a walk along the beach before everybody else gets here."

"Perfect," she'd replied. "The kids can't wait to see you."

"Tell them I'm eager to see them, too," I said. "And, of course, you."

After we said goodbye, I mixed myself a martini and sat on the deck overlooking Salt Island. Several neighboring flagpoles, newly stripped of their flags as sunset approached, cast long thin, undulating shadows over the sand. I stared at the shadows while metal hooks on the halyards clanked raggedly against the poles.

I stared at the shadows and remembered.

❧

Later that day, when we pull off the road and stop for a rest, Élodie goes off by herself into a stand of walnut trees. She unpacks her violin and plays "Song of the Birds" so slowly and so sadly, we can only listen without speaking. A listless cloud shadow undulates over the rolling hills like a long, slow, oboe accompaniment. In the distance, there is thunder. Not long after she finishes playing, the rain begins. Élodie places the violin in its case and hovers over it, like a mother over a child, to keep it dry. "He was some mother's little boy," she whispers.

I don't have to ask. I know she means the German boy. I embrace her. Rain streaks our faces. I feel her body tense with a sadness so deep, tears won't come. "Fuck following orders!" I whisper.

Early the next morning, we arrive at a small commune in the Corrèze department about 180 kilometers north of Toulouse. Sensing something amiss, we stop abruptly at the outskirts of the village and hide the car behind some trees.

In the cemetery, some 200 yards away, the rising sun projects long, thin shadows that stretch along the ground and ripple over tombstones in the hillside cemetery like drifting smoke. In the rising light, these are revealed to be the elongated shadows of black-robed women who stand motionless atop tombs.

At first, I see three women near the top of the hill. But as the sun rises, it's light travels down the hill until, one after the other, a dozen motionless women are revealed to me, all with long, black diaphanous robes fluttering in the wind, floating behind them in waves as elongated as the women are tall. The robes appear to be transparent gossamer ending at the knees, and the low sun seems to penetrate the material, revealing the nakedness of the women under the fabric—black transparent gossamer drifting behind them like angry, soot-filled smoke. Transparent, except for the veil over the faces of the women, faces which remain hidden.

"What the hell is happening?" I whisper.

"Look to the left, at the base of the hill," replies Élodie in a quiet monotone, fragile and dry and trembling like the last leaf to fall from a tree in autumn. "There are four or five new graves."

I look. I see the freshly turned earth. And I see a small procession of carts and people on foot following their lengthy shadows to the new graves. They are guarded by German soldiers with drawn machine pistols.

Élodie says. "When the Boche kill resistance fighters, they insist they be buried quickly at dawn so as not to arouse the people. No doubt, that is what's happening."

"But why are the women standing on tombs?" I ask.

"The Corréziens have a custom. Whenever someone is buried, the women stand on their own family tombs. It's a show of respect for the newly dead. It's a way for the ancestors, going back through the years, to participate."

"But why are their robes transparent? Why are they naked underneath?"

"What are you talking about?" Élodie asks. "The robes are not transparent at all. We must wean you off the morphine. You don't need it, and it's been known to cause hallucinations."

⚜

The elongated shadows of the flagpoles on the sands of Good Harbor Beach morph into twelve black-robed women, which, in turn, by some trick of my mind, become a lone woman standing with her back to the sea. Somehow, over the years, the near-naked women (whose robes were solid black, not diaphanous as my addled mind had insisted), are like an over-painting that has faded and summoned Élodie to appear half-formed at the surface, a pentimento rising from the ocean. Now it is her legs I see below the hem of the diaphanous robe, it's her body both hidden and revealed by the transparent fabric, backlit by the moon-streaked waves. It's her face veiled by layers of gossamer. And I know, with certainty, what will happen next. The face behind the black, smoky veils will slowly resolve into Anna's face as if my wife were appearing to reassert some sort of *jura possessionis,* a kind of right-of-possession, to my thoughts and affections.

I raise my martini glass to my lips with an unsteady hand. The mingled gin and vermouth rock in the glass and emit low refracted moonlight, an acoustic map of sine waves that I feel dance across my face. "Don't have more than two," I hear Anna say from somewhere among the deep synapses of my brain. "Remember what the doctor said."

I nod and hold my glass at arm's length toward the moon. It is my third martini. "I loved her," I mutter.

"Of course, you loved her," says Anna. "I would have loved her, too. She was so committed, so loving, so compassionate. And killing was so entirely against her nature."

"But she had to do it," I say with a shudder. The martini has me on the edge of tears.

"Of course, she did. It was war."

"She felt things deeply."

"Haven't you told me many times how passions become more intense during wartime?"

"Yes, they do," I say. I hold the glass toward the moonlight and examine the prism of light I've created.

"So, you see," Anna says. "You can't blame yourself for loving her."

"No."

"It was long before we met."

"Yes. But there were other things she felt. *We* felt. Not just the passion. I was never able to tell you the whole story about those other things. Mainly because I didn't fully understand it. There was Oradour. Other things that happened. The German boy-soldiers. She would play beautiful music. Later, there were the children."

"Of course. From what you say, she was a beautiful person."

"It was impossible not to fall in love with her."

"You were young and impressionable."

"We were all young. Some younger than others. But that explains nothing."

"It explains everything," Anna says. "And it was before you knew me."

"Of course, it was."

"I think you were just in love with the idea of being in love."

"No."

"Yes."

"No," I insist. "I truly loved her."

"Did you love her more than me?"

I jerk forward in my chair. "No! No!" Quickly, I shake my head. What am I thinking? Anna would never have asked that! Never! I sip from my martini. I watch my ancient hand shake. The ice clinks against the side of the glass. For the briefest of instants, Élodie appears before me, and I suck in a breath. But just as quickly, she's gone, impossible to grasp, no more animated than the olives that wink back at me. Anna's voice comes again, from deep in my mind. "Is she the reason we always traveled to Italy and Switzerland and Greece, but never to France? Is she the reason you never took me to France?"

"I don't know."

"Don't you remember how I always wanted to rent a river boat or a barge and go along that ... what was it called?"

"The Canal du Midi?"

"Yes, that. Why did we never do that?"

"I don't know."

"Were you afraid she would appear, and it would cause trouble between us?"

"Of course not. She was dead."

"Was she?"

"Yes."

"Really?"

"Yes, of course she was."

"Well, what does that matter? I'm also dead, but I have a hold on you, still."

I have no answer. I wait and watch the moon slip behind a cloud and the beach fade into darkness and the shadows of the flagpoles dissolve into the sand and disappear and I wait, but Anna's voice has gone silent.

The cloud passes and a bright streak of moonlight lays heavily on the undulant waves.

Anna! I remember her almost child-like excitement when we first saw the house on Salt Island Road in Gloucester. It was a small Dutch colonial with brown, weathered shingles, a deck overlooking Good Harbor Beach and Salt Island, and a spacious, insulated sunroom abutting the deck for when the weather was less welcoming. The house was as old as I, and just as battered by hostile storms and scoured by salt-laden Atlantic winds. A flight of steps descended from the deck to a small lawn where a flagpole vibrated with the thrashing of a wind-whipped flag. The metal snaphooks of the halyard beat an erratic rhythm against the pole. From the lawn, a path of flagstones led to a concrete staircase that wound its way downward through boulders before emerging onto the beach. The rocks were sun-bleached white and brown above the high-tide line, and dark and barnacle-encrusted where they were submerged twice a day with the diurnal tide cycle.

Next to the door opening out to the deck hung a polished brass tide clock that Anna and I would consult frequently because we liked to time our daily walks to the hour or two on either side of low tide when the beach was flat and exposed below the high-water mark and the sand was compressed smooth as a clay tennis court. Sometimes we walked at sunrise, sometimes at sunset, sometimes in the middle of the day. We allowed ourselves to fall into the rhythm of the tides, varying the time of our walks by almost an hour as each day passed. When the water, which often snaked down from the Labrador Current, wasn't too cold, we walked ankle-deep at the razor-thin edge of the ocean. Even in the winter, we seldom missed a day. We stepped into boots, and the salt-encrusted rime crunched under our feet as we watched the play of horses with their riders, and dogs chasing tennis balls launched by their owners. These were the people, and animals, who reclaimed the beach each year after the tourist season. Anna and I especially liked walking hand in hand, when the night draped itself over the sand and waves spilled dense diamonds of moonlight onto the shore.

❧

But on this day of the family gathering, it was mid-afternoon when Callie arrived with my great grandchildren, Danny and Ashley. Like a child with a new puppy, I introduced them to the little eight-pound rescue dog I'd recently adopted. The children *oohed* and *aahed* and patted the dog whose tail wagged excitedly.

"What's her name?" Ashley asked.

"His name is Arlequin."

Both Danny and Ashley repeated the name softly.

I looked at Callie and said, "It's the French form of Harlequin, one of the stock characters in *commedia dell'arte*. Kind of a zany character."

"That's unusual. Whatever possessed you to choose that name?" Callie asked.

I shrugged.

"When did you get him?"

"A few weeks ago, from the Northeast Animal Shelter in Salem. It was getting a little lonely around here."

Callie placed a hand on my shoulder and squeezed. "We all miss Nana, but I can't imagine how it must be for you."

Something caught in my throat.

"What breed is he?" asked Callie, to my relief

"Papillon," I answered. "It's French for 'butterfly.' Because of the ears."

"The Northeast Animal Shelter?"

"Yes."

"Papa, that's a pure breed dog. It's highly unlikely you'd find him at Northeast. Where did you really get him?"

"Can't get anything by you, can I?"

"No."

"Londonderry, New Hampshire."

"You drove all the way to New Hampshire to get a dog?"

"It's only up ninety-three. Exit four after the border. An hour and a half, tops."

"Why was it necessary to get a papillon? Why not a lab or a hound or a mix? They have lots of those at the shelter and it's nearby."

All I could do was shrug and say, "I like papillons, I guess. And he won't get much bigger, and he'll likely outlive me. I made sure to check with them."

"You asked them how long he might live?" she asked with a rising inflection.

I nodded.

"Why?"

I shrugged. "Didn't want to go through losing him, I suppose."

Callie gazed at me and her eyes began to shine. "It breaks my heart to know how very, very deeply you feel Nana's absence."

I thought of Anna. And Élodie. And I gave Callie a weak smile. "He loves to walk on the beach. Come on, I'll show you."

"How terribly lonely you must feel!"

I force my lips not to tremble. "Come, let's walk Arlequin. I grow old. I grow old. I shall wear the bottoms of my trousers rolled. I shall wear white trousers and walk upon the beach."

Callie said, "Eliot wrote 'white *flannel* trousers.'"

"Close enough. Just can't get anything by you! I'm impressed you know it so well."

"Did you think I was just some uncultured doctor? I have a grandfather to live up to."

She always knew the right things to say! I stopped and kissed her on the forehead. We walked down to the beach, the children before us, and removed our shoes. It was a nacreous sky, iridescent blue-white like the polished inside of an oyster shell. The sand, still wet from the ebbing tide, was cool on the soles of our feet. A gibbous moon, demure in the soft brightness of the afternoon sky—not looking so hunchbacked as it sometimes can—tugged at the seawater. We walked the gull-loud beach out to Salt Island along the sandbar that was exposed only at low tide as waves rippled toward us from both sides and sluiced around our feet with waters that still carried a cold rumor of the far-off Labrador Current.

In the filtered light, Callie, Ashley and Danny had sunglasses propped on the tops of their heads. My sunglasses were firmly fixed before my eyes. Since my cataract surgery, I am especially sensitive to sunlight. Also, advancing age—and martinis—often leave me lachrymose and the sunglasses hide the tears.

Some distance before us, a hermit crab scuttled toward the water. Arlequin bolted after it, barking. Ashley took off after the dog. The crab stopped momentarily at a gelatinous mass, then disappeared into the water seconds before Arlequin arrived, tail curled over his back like a comma.

"Eew!" Ashley cried, jumping back. What's that?" she asked, as Arlequin nosed a small viscid object.

I raised my sunglasses and looked. It was a dead moon jelly that bobbed slowly on the rippling water. My whole body shivered, and I sucked in my breath.

"What's wrong, Papa?" asked Callie.

My eyes filled. I couldn't hide it.

Callie put a hand on my shoulder. She frowned. She looked to see the children were still gazing at the jellyfish, turned to look me in the eyes, and silently mouthed, "You're crying!" I lowered the sunglasses back over my eyes. "Papa, what's wrong?" Callie mouthed, her forehead creased.

I shook my head.

"Papa," asked Danny, "How can the waves be going in opposite directions at the same time?"

"What?" I asked.

"The waves," Danny said. "See how they go toward each other? What causes that?"

I forced a chuckle. "They didn't always. Three hundred years ago they went in the same direction, but then a Swiss mathematician named

Bernoulli came along and said fluids around an object can go in different directions."

Callie shot me a skeptical glance.

I gave her a weak smile. "It's true! Well, *almost*. The waves always behaved that way from the beginning of time. Bernoulli only explained why."

"So, why is it?" asked Ashley who was a year younger than her brother.

"It's called, if you can believe it, the Bernoulli Effect. See out past Salt Island? The waves are coming at us in a northwesterly direction. But when they run into the island, they must go around it. So, the wave splits and some of the water goes around the northern end of the island and some of it goes around the southern end. But, then, the two sides of the wave arc like a brother and a sister who have been separated and want desperately to come back together again. So, after they pass the island, they rejoin from opposite directions, and the wave is happy once more. See how the water leaps for joy when they meet again?"

Danny and Ashley giggled.

"In fact," I continued, "that's why this sandbar exists. As the wave comes back together it scours up sand from the bottom at the two ends of the island and deposits it where the two parts of the wave meet."

A cacophony of cries drew our attention to a flock of seagulls circling over a dark patch in the water fifty yards ahead of us.

Arlequin dashed toward the commotion.

"What's got the seagulls so excited?" Danny asked.

"Probably a dead fish," I replied.

"Why don't you and Ashley run up ahead and see?" Callie said to Danny.

The children took off at a run, splashing water around their ankles.

Callie turned to me. "Now, Papa, tell me what's wrong. Please. And stop deflecting with arcane facts about wave formation."

For a long time, I said nothing. There, in the wrathful moonlight, I saw the dead man hanging amidst the white blossoms of the hawthorne tree. We had leapt from the plane and descended like a bloom of moon jellies, sinking into the slaughter. I survived, but he, like some many others, did not.

"Papa?" Callie asked in an uneasy voice.

I saw the kids out of the corner of my eyes. "Here come Danny and Ashley back," I said.

Callie snatched a glance over her shoulder, turned quickly back to me, and said, "Will you please, please, tell me what is wrong? I'm begging you!"

I shook my head. "It's nothing."

Danny and Ashley came up to us. "It was a fish," Danny said.

"I thought so," I said. I pointed to several seagulls perched on the rocks of Salt Island. "See how some of the seagulls are standing on one leg? Do you know why they do that?"

"They have sore feet?" Ashley replied with a giggle.

I laughed. I tousled Ashley's hair and said, "It's to help them stay warm. They have veins in their legs and when they tuck one leg against their bellies, they warm the blood."

"Really?" asked Callie, still frowning.

Danny said, "Really?"

"Yes, really," I said. We turned and started back along the sandbar. "Now tell me this: how do you tell the male seagulls from the females?" I asked the kids.

"The males are white, and the females are sort of grey-brown," said Danny.

"Who told you that?"

"Mom."

"Well, your mother is smart in many, many ways, as a doctor should be. But she happens to be wrong on this one. The difference in plumage only tells you their age. The white gulls are adults; the grey ones are juveniles. I don't know how you would tell their sex except maybe to hold them upside down."

"Oh, Papa!" Danny said. He took off running and Ashley chased after him, laughing.

Élodie laughed like that. When she laughed. Pure, child-like, bell-clear.

"You just went all sad again," said Callie. "Is it something to do with why you called this weekend's gathering?"

"It's nothing, I tell you. I just flashed on a war memory."

"You're evading," said Callie.

"No. It's nothing. Just a war memory, like I said."

"After seventy years?"

"It never leaves you." A tiny shudder passed through me.

We walked for several moments in silence, then Callie said, "You know, if it's something else … well, whatever it is, the family will stand behind you. You know that, don't you? We'll have your back. All of us."

I nodded, flashed a quick smile, and said, "See those two gulls? See how they fly low over the water, even rising and dipping with the contour of the waves? It's called ground effect. The air between them and the water is more compressed and therefore provides more support. If the sandpipers were out today, you'd see them skimming the waves, too."

"You're deflecting again," she said. "I mean it. We will always have your back."

I put an arm around her shoulders and drew her to me. "I know, Callie. I know. And to put your mind at rest, I'll only say it has nothing to do with my dying, as I'm beginning to suspect is what you think. In fact, quite the opposite."

She let out a breath. "That's good to hear."

"Now I only hope you all don't hate me for not dying," I said with a mawkish laugh.

"Papa! Don't be silly. What an awful thing to say."

"I only mean you might be annoyed by my little subterfuge. Well, maybe not you. But your mother? I'm not so sure about her. Or the others, for that matter."

Callie gave me a quizzical look but said nothing.

Chapter 6
The Pleasure of Love

It is dark. The moon is a thin cradle in the eastern sky. We arrive at an abandoned barn several kilometers west of Corrèze, and near the rail line between Montauban and Limoges. We hide the car in a copse of trees behind the barn. Now, as midnight approaches, Jean-Baptiste, Marcel and Claude pack explosives into their rucksacks and leave on a mission to find a spot to blow up the railroad tracks. Before Jean-Baptiste leaves, he argues that Élodie and "the American"—what he's taken to calling me—should accompany them. "That way, we can just continue south instead of coming back here," he says.

"No, idiot!" Élodie replies. "You can't take the car because of the lights, so you'll have to come back here anyway. Henry needs to rest."

"Then he can stay here while you come with us."

Élodie shakes her head. "His wound needs to be cleaned and re-bandaged. You three go. You don't need a woman to blow up some tracks. It doesn't take brains."

I see the sullen look Jean-Baptiste gives her.

Claude says, "But we may not be back until dawn."

"Then, you are not back until dawn. Just leave the lantern. And don't worry, we won't drink all the wine," she adds, referring to the wine we confiscated from the adjoining house.

Jean-Baptiste mutters, *"Merde!"* and stomps out of the barn. The others follow.

Élodie and I sit on two old milking stools we find in a dusty corner of the barn and open one of the bottles of *Château de Tiregand* from the nearby Begerac region. Somehow it has survived the Nazi occupation when much of France's wine was shipped east. It is rumored the best wines ended up at Berchtesgaden and in the bellies of Goering and Goebbels.

I put my arm around her shoulders. "Aren't you afraid of pissing Jean-Baptiste off?"

"You mean getting his dander up?"

I laugh. "Wow! You learn fast!"

She lifts the bottle to her lips. "That's what makes me good at what I do." Light from the lone lantern, sitting on the floor between us, flashes along the bottle's length. She takes a long draught and hands the bottle to me. "We have no glasses. Sorry."

"I'm not complaining," I say. I drink and hand the bottle back to her.

"And no. I'm not afraid of Jean-Baptiste getting his knickers in a twist. That's how the British would say it."

A pair of barn swallows flitter high among the rafters, crying, "*Vit, vit.*"

A half hour later, the bottle is empty and Élodie sets about cleaning and re-wrapping my wound.

"While you're doing that," I say, "tell me how you came to be a resistance fighter."

"It's a long story." Light from the lantern dances in her face, her eyes.

"We have till dawn."

"But it's mostly a sad story."

"It's wartime. Most stories are sad. Tell me. I want to know."

"Don't speak. Let me finish wrapping your wound."

At last, she is finished with my bandage. "Now will you tell me your story?" I ask.

"I told you it's a very sad story."

"Then open another bottle of wine."

She stares into my eyes for a long time and finally nods. Without speaking, she drives the corkscrew deep into the cork and twists it from the bottle with a pop and spins the cork from the corkscrew and flicks it with a snap of her thumb to a dark corner of the barn and takes a long swig, then another, and hands the bottle to me. "It began in Paris," she says.

❧

Paris. June 11, 1940.

Élodie is temporarily staying with her parents in their spacious apartments across from the Musée Guimet in the 16th arrondissement because she is scheduled to perform Rodolphe Kreutzer's 17th Violin Concerto at the Salle Pleyel on the 14th. However, the concert is cancelled because more than half the orchestra's musicians have already fled Paris in advance of the Germans who are already bombing factories in the suburbs.

Doctor Yves Bedier, Élodie's father, says, in his impeccable English, "We must do that, too. Soon, maybe, they'll be bombing in the city itself. The animals!"

"Even if they don't bomb in the city," Élodie says, "we must leave. Whilst I was out, I learnt that people are waiting in line five hours for a loaf of bread. There's no pork, no cauliflower."

"And I know, for a fact, there's hardly any petrol," says her father. "I curse myself for waiting too long. It's just that I couldn't believe France would collapse so easily."

"Somebody told me people are smashing pigeons with bricks to make soup," Élodie adds. "Even, *mon dieu*, people are eating their pets," She shudders, pats her papillon, Arlequin, on the head.

Louise Bedier, Élodie's mother, makes a hasty sign-of-the-cross. *"Au nom du Pere et de Fils et du Saint-Espirit. Ainsi soit-il."*[25]

"Yes, of course, we must leave," Dr. Bedier says.

Madame Bedier's forehead wrinkles with worry. "But where will we go?"

"I saw a large blackboard around the corner on the Rue de

---

25   "In the name of the Father and of the Sons and of the holy spirit. So be it." The French sign-of-the-cross.

Longchamp. It was a list of where people should evacuate to, depending on where they live. For us, in the sixteenth arrondissement, it is the department of Eure."

"Then that will be Gare Saint-Lazare," says Madame Bedier. Like her husband, she's always practicing her English. They pride themselves in being multilingual, a trait they passed on to their daughter.

Élodie shakes her head. "I was there yesterday. It was like a can of sardines. There were so many people, you could scarcely move. Everyone is trying to escape by train and there's not nearly enough space."

"Then what will we do?"

"We take the car," says Élodie's father. "As I said, I curse myself I didn't fill it with petrol when I had the chance!"

"How far will it get us?"

Monsieur Bedier frowns and shrugs.

"We should take only what we absolutely need," says Élodie's mother. "There are bound to be people walking who will need a ride. We should save room for them."

Élodie says, "I only need what I'm wearing, my violin, and Arlequin."

"Of course, Élodie," says her mother. "We couldn't bear to leave Arlequin behind."

"We must leave now," says Monsieur Bedier. "I heard down at the café the government has already escaped to Tours. It must mean German tanks will be rolling into the city any time now."

It is unseasonably hot when they emerge onto the street and climb into Doctor Bedier's 1938 Delage D8, a commodious luxury car which he justifies because it enhances his standing among his medical colleagues. Élodie helps her father remove the convertible top so they can carry more items. They are soon off. Élodie sits in the back seat with Arlequin in her lap and her violin, in its case, beside her.

As soon as they are outside Paris, they are forced into a huge evacuation column. Thousands upon thousands of refugees extending to the eye's horizon, a cacophony of sound rising up from them—horns, shouting, crying. The road is choked with cars, vans, trucks, bicycles—even hearses and wheelbarrows—all scarcely moving. Men and women push prams, some with babies in them, and others occupied by elderly people, their legs dangling over the sides in a kind of sad, macabre second childhood. It is so slow, people walking can keep up with the motorized traffic. More shouts, children crying. Curses, as people fight over water. Some of the cars have mattresses on top. Élodie and her parents soon come upon an elderly man and woman who are obviously having difficulties. They are leading an old, broken-down horse who is pulling a two-wheeled cart with milk buckets hanging from its rails. The old couple stagger arm-in-arm like a wounded creature with six legs, their own gimpy legs, plus a cane each. Doctor Bedier stops the car, steps out, and offers them a ride. In French, he says, "We won't be going much faster than you can walk, but at least you can rest for as long as we have petrol."

"Mais nous ne pouvons pas laisser notre cheval et notre charrette."[26]

Élodie says she and Arlequin will lead the horse for a time.

The old man's eyes fill with tears and he hugs Élodie, then Doctor Bedier, and kisses them each on the cheeks. *"Merci, merci!"*

His wife does the same. She, too, is crying in gratitude.

"We have been walking for more than a day," the man says. "It's very difficult. I worry for my wife, here."

The woman puts her hand on the man's cheek. "But I worry for you, *mon chou.*"[27]

Élodie learns their names are Monsieur and Madame Prideaux and they are trying to get to Caen where their son and daughter-in-law live. She notices they smell like they haven't bathed in a while, but that doesn't bother her. She offers them one of the baguettes she and her parents threw into the car before they left. Monsieur Prideaux grabs the bread eagerly, breaks off a piece, and hands it to his wife. She takes it and says, "You eat, too. It's been too long."

For the next several minutes they tear at the bread. Crumbs fall to the seat and Arlequin eagerly licks them up.

Once she is satisfied Monsieur and Madame Prideaux are comfortable, Élodie leads Arlequin to the horse, takes up the reins, and

---

26   "But we cannot leave our horse and our wagon."
27   Literally, "My cabbage." A French form of affection roughly equivalent to "Sweetie."

sets out. She is startled by a small explosion and sees a flash low and to her left. It's a photographer who has just snapped a picture of her.

Several hours later, they come to a fork in the road. Élodie sees a sign for Giverny pointing to the right, and a sign for Evreux indicating the road to the left.

"Everybody is taking the road to the left," says Doctor Bedier. "Perhaps we should go towards Giverny, so we can move faster."

"No, Papa," says Élodie. "The German armies are in that direction. Just a week or so ago they drove the British across the English Channel at Dunkerque. That's why everybody is staying to the south."

"Of course," he replies. "You are right as always. We'll stay toward Evreux. Perhaps the traveling will become easier after all."

⁂

In the barn, as Élodie tells me her story, her eyes are sad. Light from the flickering lantern glints in a tear that slides down her cheek. Something startles the swallows. They flitter under the roof and among the rafters, panicked. Have they sensed a predator? A peregrine falcon? An owl? Élodie looks at me and says, "I wish with all my heart I had never said that to Papa. How things might have been different if we had taken the road toward Giverny. The first indication of what was ahead for us were the posters I saw when we passed through Fauville, a tiny commune east of Evreux." She pauses, takes a deep breath.

I offer the bottle of wine to her.

She reaches for it. Our hands brush. She lifts the bottle to her lips and takes a long draught.

"What about the posters?" I ask.

⁂

On the wall of the mairie in Fauville are dozens of hand-scribbled notes and posters looking for missing children, missing parents, relatives. Families trying to re-unite. A breeze flutters the corners of dozens of notes and there is a quiet slapping sound like flies being swatted. In the town square, the boulangerie is shuttered with a sign saying, *"Pas de pain."*[28]

Also closed is the épicerie whose shelves are nearly empty of groceries and canned goods. And, not surprisingly, the boucherie is also closed since meat has been hard to come by recently. At the prefecture, a line of people, seeking petrol coupons, snakes out the door and up the street. People converse with one another in subdued voices.

It is getting increasingly difficult to find something to eat, and tempers are beginning to flare. Élodie is surprised by the sensation of hunger; the pangs are something she's never experienced in the comfortable life provided by her parents. Even Arlequin whimpers from hunger, and it breaks Élodie's heart. But she refuses even to consider mercifully killing him the way other pet owners have done. She resolves to give him her own food, if it comes to that. So far, there's been enough, at least, to keep them alive.

A few kilometers west of Fauville, the vast column comes to a stop. There is the bleating of car horns. Vehicles of every kind are backed up as far as Élodie can see, both before them and behind them. Already, they have passed many cars—some piled high with household items and furniture—that have been abandoned on the side of the road because they have run out of fuel. But now, even the non-motorized vehicles are stopped: the mule carts with cows and horses tethered to them; the wheelbarrows carrying elderly people; the baby carriages filled with prized china; and birdcages with songbirds. Some even with the babies for which they were intended.

"What has caused this stop?" Élodie's father asks.

"A child has been run over by a truck," someone near them says.

"Mon dieu!" cries Élodie's father. "I must see if I can help."

"I'll go with you," says Élodie. She drops the reins to the wagon horse. It's not going anywhere in this jam, she reasons.

They push their way through the throngs of people, her father shouting repeatedly, "I'm a doctor. Let us pass. I'm a doctor."

---

28   "No bread."

It's more than a half mile to the front of the column. By the time they arrive, they are panting heavily and sweating profusely. Several people are crouching by a little girl of about five who is sprawled motionless on the ground, a trickle of blood issuing from her mouth. Her eyes are closed. Dr. Bedier kneels beside her. "I'm a doctor," he says, as he reaches to feel for a pulse in the girl's carotid artery. Nothing. He tries the wrist. Nothing. He lowers his ear to her mouth to see if he can detect any breathing at all. He looks up. "I'm afraid she's gone," he manages to say in a strained voice.

"*Non!*" screams a young woman. She drops to her knees, takes the lifeless body in her arms, and falls back on her haunches, resting the girl's head in her lap. "*Ma fifille! Mon bébé!*"[29] She rocks the child in her arms, tears streaking her cheeks, humming what sounds to Élodie like a cradle song.

Élodie's father shakes his head sadly and motions they should return to their car. Élodie nods and they turn to go. But at that moment, the mother glares at Doctor Bedier and says, in French, "I thought you said you were a doctor. You are useless! Useless!"

"There was nothing I could do," he replies. "I am so sorry for your loss."

"It's the Jews," she shouts. "They have sold us out! They have betrayed us!"

"Yes, the Jews," a man says.

Doctor Bedier stares at the man, speechless.

Élodie takes her father's hand and urges him to follow her. They head back to their place in the column.

After a while, the column starts to move again, but long shadows now stretch out behind them. Élodie's father pulls to the side of the road, west of the little commune of Glissoles. He says, "Soon it will be too dark to go on, and we can't use our lights because of the possibility of German planes. We'll rest here for the night."

The sun is low in the west. The blanched moon is low in the east. He has chosen a spot opposite an open field, at the back of which is

---

29   "My little girl! My baby!"

a barn. Near the barn, stands a large beech tree, loud with the warbles and whistles of starlings. Élodie hears a faint rumble coming from the north. Thunder? In Paris, they had removed the convertible top from the car. What can they use to cover themselves if it rains? She looks to the north. There is scarcely a cloud in the sky. Then out of the corner of her eye she sees Madame Prideaux walking across the field toward the barn. "Where is your wife going?" she asks Monsieur Prideaux.

He gives a shrug and a shy smile. *"La toilette."*

More rumbling.

Louder, still.

Again, Élodie looks to the sky. Now she sees several flashes of light. It takes her a few seconds to realize the light is the low sun reflecting from airplane canopies. And now comes a low screaming, growing in intensity, like a siren, and she guesses these must be the infamous Stukas that, she'd heard, made a terrifying shriek and she turns to warn the others, but Monsieur Prideaux is already lumbering across the field as fast as his ancient legs and one cane can carry him and the shrieking of the Stukas is louder and people in the column scream and scatter in every direction and there is a crackling of guns and across the field, clods of earth are thrown in the air as the Stukas strafe the field in a ragged line that in seconds will reach the throngs of people in the column and Élodie hears Monsieur Prideaux cry out, "Lucette! Lucette!" and Madame Prideaux turns toward him, and, in that instant, her body erupts in blood, and bits of bone, and flesh, and is thrown several meters through the air before it crashes to the earth. "Lucette! Lucette!" Monsieur Prideaux is almost to his wife when his cane explodes a split second before his body slumps to the earth and his left arm reaches out, hangs in the air for a second or two, then falls to the ground, and now he lies motionless, and Élodie starts into the field after him.

"No, Élodie! No!" cries her father, grabbing her wrist and pulling her down beside him and Madame Bedier as bullets tear into the ground around them, spewing dirt and blood and flesh into the air. It lasts for several long, shuddering breaths, then the bullets stop and there comes a chorus of moaning from the people.

Élodie's father says, "I must do what I can."

"Where's Arlequin?" Élodie cries.

"He must have run off. He's probably frightened."

Élodie looks to the woods on the other side of the road, hesitates, then says, "I'll help you, Papa." And she is thankful her father has imparted a great deal of medical knowledge to her despite his disappointment that she chose music over medicine.

They start through the crowd. There are at least two dozen dead and wounded. Men. Women. Children. Two babies lie lifeless in their prams. Doctor Bedier comes to a woman who is moaning. "She needs a tourniquet immediately," he says. "I'll treat her. You go ahead and triage for me. See if you can decide which ones are too far gone and which ones I should treat."

"Yes, Papa."

As she maneuvers her way through the scattered bodies of people and horses and donkeys, the sky has fallen silent. Perhaps the planes have gone away. Up ahead, she hears cries for help. She rushes to the sound and comes to a mother holding her little boy whose severed right arm lies on the ground. The woman looks at her and says, "You! Your father is the doctor. Please bring him here. We need help."

There is a new shrieking. Rising in intensity.

A screeching from the sky. A stridency.

And from the people, a ululation of horror.

Élodie stares at the woman for a moment, mouth slack. She turns to see if she can locate her father. She sees him about fifty meters away.

The scream of the planes is louder. This time, she sees bombs fall from their shining bodies, fired by the low sunlight.

"Papa!" She starts to run back.

There comes a deafening crump. She is knocked to the ground. More bomb blasts. She sees the large beech tree near the house and barn explode into flames. Moments later there comes a strange pattering, like soft hail on a metal roof. She wrinkles her brow. *What can it be?* And at once she is horrified to see roasted starlings falling out of the sky all around her. She leaps to her feet. "Papa! Mama!"

As she runs back toward their car, she sees a young woman emerge from the house carrying a bird cage with a songbird inside. But the house and its barn are raging infernos and their appetite for oxygen is so great the bird cage is snatched from the woman's hand and sucked into the flames the way the tongue of a frog sucks in insects. The young woman can only stand and stare, dumbstruck as the air is tortured with the terrified bellowing of cows and the screaming of horses. And then the inferno sucks her, too, in to its maw.

"Papa! Mama!" Élodie continues to run toward the car. Then she stops abruptly. The car is no longer there. She scans the road and finds it upended on the other side of the road. Beside it, she sees the lifeless bodies of her parents.

⚜

Flickering light from the lantern glistens in Élodie tears. "Papa," she murmurs. "Mama."

"This is too painful for you," I say. "Perhaps you should leave the story there."

"I can't. I want to leave it at a better place."

"Of course, but it doesn't have to be now."

Élodie is silent for a few moments. Finally, she swigs from the bottle, wipes her lips with the back of the hand holding the bottle, and says, "What could I do? I couldn't give them a proper burial on my own, so I begged a local farmer to help me. He was very kind. He got some others to help, and we had a very quick service the next day. Every time I think about his kindness, it makes me cry. Amid all that hatred and fear, amid all that broken humanity, there was this one man who managed to find compassion in his soul. His name was Aristide Charnay. When this fucking, goddamned war is over, I will try to find him. I swear it! And I will kiss him on the cheeks, over and over, until he can stand it no longer!"

I am afraid to ask, but I must. "Your dog? Arlequin?"

Élodie squeezes her eyes shut, shakes her head slowly. "I searched for hours. I was in a daze. I even cried out to God and asked Him, if he was going to take my parents, at least leave me Arlequin because he's only a dog and he's innocent and he's so very vulnerable and he can't be blamed for all this the way we humans can. But I could never find Arlequin. The poor little guy must have been so frightened. Maybe he just didn't trust humans anymore. Even me. Or maybe he was dead under some rubble."

I put an arm around her shoulders and pull her toward me. She sinks back into my chest. She looks back and up at me. "Sometime in the days after that—I can't say exactly where or when; it's all a blur—I heard a radio broadcast by General de Gaulle. He appealed to French people to join him in London to continue the fight. That became my single-minded focus. Eventually, I walked all the way to Granville. Perhaps four hundred kilometers. It took almost two weeks. I thought the blisters on my feet would never heal."

"Granville?" I ask.

"It's a small coastal commune north of Saint-Malo. I went there because I was afraid the Germans might already be in Saint-Malo. I'd once given a concert there and I knew it had good port facilities they would want. But I had to get to the coast."

"To escape by water?"

She nods. "I found a fisherman from Chausey who agreed to take me there. It's a little island about twelve kilometers off the coast. We had to go at night, without lights, except for the moon, for fear the Germans were in the area. From Chausey, another fisherman took me to Jersey. From there, I managed to get to Guernsey. Of course, those two islands are British, but that didn't mean I was safe. They were expecting the Germans to invade at any moment. In fact, they had already evacuated almost half the population."

"So, you joined the evacuation?"

Élodie shakes her head. "No. By the time I got there, they had a priority system for who got on the boats and, of course, French refugees were not one of the categories."

"So how did you get to England?"

She gives a guilty smile. "I became a *passagère clandestine*." She pauses, wrinkles her brow. "What is it in English? Oh, yes, 'stowaway.' I hid in a lifeboat. The crossing was very rough, and I became seasick. But I was afraid to crawl out of the lifeboat which had a canvas cover.

Eventually, we arrived at a port I later discovered was Weymouth. From there, I took a train to London."

"How did you afford a ticket?"

"I had taken all the money my father had on him, which was quite a lot. Both French and British, because he used to travel to London often to give talks. Of course, much of it went to bribing fishermen, but I still had a lot left and, if I was unable to find people willing to take French francs, I could always use the pound sterling."

"So, you got to London."

"Yes. And I went straight to General de Gaulle's headquarters near Saint James Park and got a job."

"Just like that?" I ask.

"They needed secretarial help. I was willing to do anything. I even entertained with my violin when the general had guests for dinner."

"They made a musician as talented as you do clerical work and entertain?"

"It was the war effort. Besides, it wasn't as bad as all that. I ate with them at the main table. Even sat next to Churchill once."

"What was he like?"

"He kept bumping my knee with his. And his cigars stank. And he drank. He surely did drink."

"So far you haven't told me how you became a resistance fighter." With my thumb, I carefully wipe the tears from under her eyes.

She touches my wrist and caresses it with a single finger. The moon slides out from behind some clouds and slants heavily through large cracks in the barn's siding. Moonlight sizzles on the tines of a pitchfork. "That started almost exactly two years later. May of nineteen-forty-two. They encouraged me to join the SOE."

"SOE?"

"The Special Operations Executive. It is part of the British MI9 which is their military intelligence people."

"So, you became a spy?"

"In a way. The primary mission of the SOE is to help British prisoners of war and downed airmen escape out of France. But they also have a small French unit, F Section, which I joined. Its purpose, as they said in the briefing, is to help start up, train, and arm local resistance groups to perform acts of sabotage and be at the ready to support an eventual invasion. They sent us to a tiny village called Arisaig on the Inverness coast of northern Scotland. We stayed in a small country house for several weeks and were taught how to survive behind enemy lines. We studied and practiced everything: rock climbing, finding our way in unknown territory, making it through an obstacle course, hunting, canoeing, judo."

"From what I've seen, you learned well."

"But that was only the beginning," says Élodie. "After Arisaig, we were sent to R.A.F. Ringway, near Manchester, for jump training because we would be parachuting into France."

"You became a parachutist?" I ask, astonished.

She smiles. "Did you think you were the only one in this barn who's crazy enough to jump out of an airplane?"

"Were you nervous?"

"A little. But then I realized I had nothing to lose, so it became easier."

"When did you jump into France?"

"Autumn of forty-two."

"Tell me about it," I say, handing her the third bottle of wine.

☙❧

Tempsford, England. September 24, 1942.

Carrying a parachute on her back, Élodie walks past the squat, heavy blockhouse of a control tower, and across the grass field of RAF Tempsford, a secret airfield about seventy kilometers north of London. A slight breeze cools her cheek. Dense moonlight reflects off the canopies and propellers of idle aircraft: Vickers Wellingtons, big Handley Page Halifax bombers and several Lysanders. Smoke filters back to her from the cigarette of one of the other women. There are four of them. They are among the first women to be dropped into France by the SOE.

Élodie tries to control her shaky legs as she climbs awkwardly aboard a Whitley bomber, a two-engine, twin-rudder plane known not so affectionately as the "flying coffin." With a crew of five plus the four women, they are soon juddering across the field and then with a roar of engines they lift over the bordering trees. The plane banks and a slash of moonlight streaks across the bulkhead. Élodie sits on the floor of the fuselage, her back supported by the packed parachute which she has jammed against the fuselage wall. Her feet almost stretch to the opposite bulkhead. She reaches behind her to touch the parachute. She can feel the vibrations of the plane's metal skin deep in her bones. None of the other women, all similarly positioned, speak. Once more, she reaches behind her to touch the parachute. And, for a third time, she reviews in her mind that morning's task of packing the parachute: check the rigging lines, lay out the yards of canopy silk on the long table, precisely arrange the folds of cloth, feed the rigging lines into their holding straps, pack the pilot chute, adjust the harnesses. It must be perfect if she is to live through the drop and, after running over the steps one more time in her mind, she satisfies herself she's done everything properly.

It is almost two hours later when a man emerges from the cockpit and announces they will soon be over her target. Élodie reaches behind her to touch the parachute pack yet again. The man opens the trap door in the floor of the fuselage and Élodie hears the wind screeching by. And she hears the roar of the engines. She cannot see the ground. Everything is black for several moments. Then the moon appears from behind clouds and she can see vaguely outlined forms of trees and fields below. She reminds herself to push forward enough for the folded parachute to clear the back edge of the hole. She remembers a woman who failed to do this in training, got tilted forward, and broke her nose on the opposite rim of the jump hole.

The man yells, "Go!"

Élodie pushes forward and drops through the hole. A breathless shiver runs through her loins and stomach. The parachute opens, and she is violently jerked upwards. And suddenly, the rumble of the plane's engines grows distant and she floats earthward with the only sound a barely discernible silken whisper of air across the parachute, like the sound of a bridal train sweeping a dance floor. Below her, the serpentine bends and loops of the river Lot glitter like a silver necklace carelessly dropped on the bedroom floor. She looks up and sees moonlight illuminating the giant mushroom of her parachute. Who can see her from the ground? Only the people secretly slated to receive her? Or others? Germans? A dog barks some distance away. Now, in the moonlight, she sees she's coming down into a large, fallow field. She knows it is west of Cahors in the South of France. The field is bordered by stately van Gogh cypresses the halves of whose thin, conical shapes are moonsilvered bright. A pinpoint of light wavers at the edge of the field, then starts to bounce toward the spot where she'll be meeting the earth, as though someone is running with it. She hits the ground with a thud and stumbles forward several steps before falling to her knees and wrestling the parachute under control. She closes her eyes briefly and whispers, *"Merci, mon ange dans ciel."*[30]

Two people appear at her side. "Come quickly," says a man of about sixty in French. "And bring the parachute."

A woman of about the same age says, "We must bury it."

They turn and rush toward the edge of the field. Élodie struggles close behind, her legs still stiff from being crammed in the airplane.

❦

Élodie hands the nearly empty bottle of wine back to me, draws the back of her hand across her lips, and says, "They were wonderful and courageous, Monsieur and Madame Lemieux. They hid me for two days until two British pilots were delivered to us through the underground railway. This was why I was dropped into France in the first place. I was to be one of several who escort downed Brits and Americans into Spain from where they are guided to Portugal and eventually back to England."

"Sounds like a tall order. How will you manage it?"

"I grew up in the Ariège. I know the area. And, by the way, that's where we're headed."

---

30   "Thank you, my angel in heaven."

"You're escorting me to Spain?"

"That's the way it has to be."

I stare at her. It feels like there's a tiny hummingbird caught in my throat. I say nothing. We are startled by a sudden movement. A mouse scampers through a shaft of moonlight, followed instantly by the pounce of a cat. For a few seconds, there are tiny animal cries. Then silence.

Élodie takes a deep breath. Lowers her head. Wipes a tear from under her eye.

"You're crying," I say. I draw her to me. "What is it? Is it the mouse?"

"No, of course not."

"Then, what?"

She touches my cheek with the back of her hand. "Wine makes me weepy."

"It's more than the wine. A sadness came over you."

"A short time ago, I learned that Monsieur and Madame Lemieux were discovered by the Milice and summarily executed. They were such a sweet, old couple. *Mon dieu,* I hate this fucking, goddamned war!"

"The Milice?"

"French militia. They work with the Boche."

I hold her closer. We fall silent for several long moments before finally Élodie asks, "Is there more wine in that bottle?"

The bottle standing by my hip is still half full. I hand it to her. As she lifts the bottle to take a long draught, it catches a shaft of light. The refracted redness of the wine brushes her cheek, giving her a flushed look. She takes a second mouthful, coughs once, and says, "The others won't be back for hours."

There's that hummingbird fluttering in my throat again!

She presses closer to me and touches my hand. Our breathing becomes heavy. Moments later, she touches my knee. Then my thigh. "Yes?" I ask.

She nods. "Yes."

I embrace her.

"Wait," she says.

"What?"

Élodie's right thumb and forefinger tremble as she unbuttons her shirt. Then, pausing, with a demure glance at me, she reaches into her rucksack and pulls out a vial of perfume. She opens it, shakes a few drops into her hand and rubs it between her breasts. "To cover the stench," she whispers as she leans back into my arms.

A release of *Nuit de Longchamp* wafts from her now exposed breasts and I take in an aroused breath, and a whisper of wings stirs the air in the rafters, and the swallows flit and unspool ribbons of flight around each other among the roof beams, under the roof, and Élodie and I lie back onto a bed of straw, and I feel the softness of her in the sparse peach fuzz on her arms and breasts that glistens in the moonlight, and in the delicacy there is roundness by the soft light of the lantern, and a coyness and yearning and tenderness and breathlessness, and there is fragrance, and we make love with yesses and *ouis, ouis* and yesses, and there is wetness and dewiness, and there is a blessedness and a deepness and a devoutness, and there is giving and receiving, and receiving and giving, and soon there is a stillness and a calmness and a sacredness and a sereneness in the wash of moonlight, and we lie together, arms wrapped around each other, and I breathe in her fragrance and she lays her head on my chest and we stay like that until we drift off to sleep. And when we wake, she wraps her arms around me and tucks her nose in the hollow of my neck, and says, "I love snogging with you after we make love."

"Snogging?"

"It's what you Americans might call necking."

I'm enchanted. I stroke her hair. "I've never experienced such pleasure," I say.

She sighs and burrows deeper into my neck and kisses me. "I was afraid you might think I was one of those khaki-wackies sent by Hitler and Hirohito to give you syphilis, or gonorrhea, so you wouldn't be able to fight."

I'm stunned. "How in God's name do you know that expression?"

"I told you before that we do our research. The Americans also call such women good-time Charlottes and bags of trouble and—I love this one—Patriotutes."

"Incredible!"

"Oui, incroyable!"

From above comes the *vit vit* of the swallows as they whirl and dip and dive around each other. Beneath the fork-tailed swallows, Élodie and I lie naked in the night, in the hay, a cooling breeze drying the wetness from our bodies, silken moonlight blanching our flesh.

An hour later, we are dressed when the others return.

"How did it go?" Élodie asks.

"We blew up a bridge," answers Jean-Baptiste. He narrows his eyes at Élodie. His nostrils twitch. "They won't be able to use that railway for a while. But now we must go to a place called Montignac." Another twitch of his nostrils.

"Where is it?" asks Élodie. "And why go there?"

I know Jean-Baptiste is smelling her perfume. It lingers around my nostrils; surely, he can smell it, too.

"About fifty kilometers east of Périgueux," says Marcel. "We used up almost all the explosives. Just enough for one more operation. I have a cousin who lives in Montignac. He's in the Resistance. He might know where we can get more."

Jean-Baptiste looks to where the hay is disturbed on the barn floor, then back at Élodie. "You have straw in your hair," he says.

Élodie reaches behind her head and pulls out a strand of straw. She averts her eyes from him and says, "I took a nap on the floor."

Jean-Baptiste continues to stare at her. He glances at me.

There is silence in the barn.

There is silence above, in the rafters.

Chapter 7
The Grief of Love

The seagulls over Good Harbor Beach dip, dive, and swirl, carving out slices of flight, then hover and squawk "*kyie, kyie*" so close to the deck that they reflect distortedly on the surface of my martini as it rocks in my glass, and suddenly I'm reminded of the barn swallows and the wine we drank the night Élodie and I first made love, when she told me about her parents and how she ended up in the Resistance. And I remember the look on Jean-Baptiste's face when he saw the hay sticking out of the back of Élodie's hair.

For the briefest of instants, she is with me now, but then she dissipates with far less permanence than the dissolving ice shavings floating among my olives.

Callie and I had decided to set up the feast on the deck. With the help of Ashley and Danny, we butted two long tables together, end-to-end, and surrounded them with the wicker chairs that always sat outside, dragged out chairs from the house, and added several folding chairs I'd had stowed away in the garage. Callie draped the tables with a pair of floral Jacquard tablecloths that had been Anna's favorites. Finally, Ashley and Danny placed a vase with flowers at the center of each table. Red roses, pink carnations, white lilies. My cheeks ached from so much smiling! I had long dreamed of such a family gathering.

Before everybody arrived, I'd set my music system to play on the deck and created a play list that included Bach's *Goldberg Variations* and *The Well-Tempered Clavier*—both played by Glenn Gould—several of

Beethoven's late quartets, his Archduke Trio, lots of Mozart and pieces of Chopin played by Arthur Rubinstein. I also sprinkled, throughout the play list, so they would play several times, pieces I associated with Élodie: "The Song of the Birds," the "Adagio Expressivo" from Amy Beach's Piano Quintet, and, finally, a recording of *"Plaisir d'Amour"* a traditional French love song Élodie had played for me. I'd fallen in love with a recording by Nana Mouskouri, but then, about a decade later I'd been riveted by the television mini-series *Band of Brothers* about men like me and my comrades. One episode was dedicated to the Battle of the Bulge in which I participated, except it was focused on the 101st Airborne, not my unit, the 82nd. Nonetheless, I was moved to tears when I heard *"Plaisir d'Amour"* on the sound track sung by a children's chorus—their innocent, vulnerable voices. When I saw that episode, called "Bastogne," something cracked inside me, and I wept. Anna sat beside me on the sofa and put her arms around me and comforted me and said, again, as she had often, that I should see a doctor. "They now have people who specialize in this kind of thing," she'd say. "They call it PTSD."

But I never saw a doctor.

And Anna died.

It was that children's performance of the song that I now put on the play list.

Plaisir d'amour ne dure qu'un moment chagrin d'amour dure toute la vie.[31]

Everyone arrived within half an hour of one another and gathered on the deck where a soft sea breeze wafted in from Salt Island. Arlequin became overexcited at such a large crowd. The breeders warned he would be very active and would probably bark a lot, but I got him anyway. Now, he repeatedly jumped up to paw at people's thighs. When he did this to Natalie, she stepped back and shooed at him with her hand. "Whose damned dog is this, Dad? One of your neighbors?"

"No, he's mine."

---

31   The pleasure of love lasts only a moment, the grief of love lasts a lifetime.

"Yours?"

"Got him a week ago. He's a rescue. Keeps me company."

"And what will you do with him when you have to go into a nursing home? *We're* certainly not taking him!"

I felt the muscles in my cheeks twitch. "You won't need to." I said. "I'm not going into any goddamned nursing home."

"Dad, you're in your nineties, for God's sake!"

"Believe me, I know full well how old I am. I'm just not going into a nursing home and that's that. Now, can't we have a nice evening without you and me fighting?"

"But, Dad—"

"I don't want to hear another word about it! If you're gonna harp on me about that, you can leave now."

Several people gasped, and others glanced at each other. Natalie stared at me with a look of incredulity painted on her features.

"Well I guess that's that," Callie said. "Papa, how about we go into the kitchen and make drinks for everybody?"

"Good idea." I gave her a smile and followed her into the kitchen. Callie closed the door and turned to me.

"You're upset about more than the nursing home business, Papa. It's not like you to fly off the handle like that."

"I know. It's just that your mother angers me. Her reaction to Arlequin."

"She can be a real harpy, sometimes. Believe me, I know. I grew up with her. But, at this moment, I'm worried about you. How you behaved this afternoon on the beach, and now this."

"Nothing is wrong. Like I told you, I've been having flashbacks to the war years lately and some of them are, well, a little upsetting."

Callie gave me a wavering smile. "Okay. Look, I have some colleagues at the hospital who specialize in this sort of thing."

"Now you sound like your grandmother."

"How?"

"She was always telling me I should see a doctor about the ... the memories."

"She was right."

"I don't want to lie down on some shrink's couch and talk about the freaking war."

Callie shrugged. "If you say so."

"I say so."

"Okay, for now. But don't think I give up that easily. If you thought Nana was a pain in the ass about it, buckle up! You haven't seen anything yet!"

"Message received," I said, and kissed her on the forehead. "Now let's make those drinks."

After we delivered drinks and appetizers to everyone on the deck, we made small talk and watched the waves roll in and folks stroll along the half-mile stretch of sand in the low-slanting, late afternoon light. Several boys rode boogie boards and skimmed on the shallow water toward two attractive young women who laughed and jumped out of their way.

Natalie, whose sour expression from our earlier confrontation hadn't changed, plucked at the eyeglasses suspended by a gold chain on her bosom, raised them to her eyes, and asked, "Isn't this part of the beach supposed to be private?"

"Theoretically," I replied.

"Which means those people are trespassing. Shouldn't you complain to the city?"

"Why would I complain? I can sit on my deck and be feasted with—what do the young people call it? Eye candy?"

"Dad!" Judy gave an exaggerated sigh. The comment even garnered a reluctant chuckle from Natalie, and Callie flashed me a smile and announced she was going to get the water ready for the lobsters.

"Where did you get the lobsters?" Judy asked.

Callie tipped her glass toward me. "Papa got them. Captain Carl and Sons, right?"

"I didn't know they delivered," Judy said.

"They don't. I picked them up this morning."

Natalie's face darkened. "You drove?"

"No. I hopped in a little red wagon and Arlequin towed me." Arlequin gave a yip at the mention of his name. Callie snorted. "I gave up driving at night. Partly because of the glare of headlights and partly because it's near my bed time."

"Maybe your cataracts grew back."

I could feel myself tense. I knew exactly where the conversation was headed. "Cataracts don't grow back. But that doesn't mean you can't end up with blurred vision again."

Natalie frowned. "Don't you think you should give up driving entirely?"

"No. And the Registry of Motor Vehicles doesn't think so either. They just renewed my license."

Natalie blew out a long breath and rolled her eyes. I excused myself and joined Callie in the kitchen. "Do you mind if I join you? The gathering is barely underway, and I already need a break from your pain-in-the-ass mother."

"Hey, she may be my pain-in-the-ass mother, but she's your pain-in-the-ass daughter. You owe me for my childhood trauma."

The banter could have gone on as it often did, but soon everyone had migrated from the deck to the kitchen making the room as crowded with bodies as the stove top was with stock pots. "Everybody out! Into the living room, now!" Callie said as she waved at the columns of steam floating around her face and mushrooming toward the ceiling. "I can't work with you people hovering over my shoulder!"

"Callie's right," I said, shooing everyone out of the kitchen. "Go into the living room or back out to the deck. Don't let the gulls eat the appetizers! Go on, everyone. I'll bring another batch of gin-and-tonics."

"Hold up, Dad," Callie's father said, "I'll make them. You go relax in your recliner."

"I'll make them. I don't need help."

"But, Dad—"

"Don't 'but Dad' me! Get your ass out of here. I'll bring you your drink when it's ready." For emphasis, I gave a hard twist of the cap on a bottle of tonic water which hissed when I screwed it off. Maybe I was being a bit theatrical, but sometimes Natalie and Marshall annoyed the hell out of me! How Callie turned out so lovable was a mystery.

Marshall shrugged at Callie and left the kitchen.

Callie and I exchanged smiles. "You tell him, Papa."

"I'm not infirm yet. Despite what they all may think. And I don't intend ever to be infirm. I swear I won't let it happen."

Callie whipped her head around and stared at me, her brow furrowed. Christ! What had I said to make her react like that? "Papa, you're not saying …."

"What? What am I not saying?"

"You know …. You said you have an announcement …."

I gazed at her for a few seconds before realizing what she was implying. "No, no, no, sweetheart! I'm not suggesting I'll …. That's not what this evening is all about, not even close."

"Oh, thank God!"

"Besides, give me some credit. Do you think for one moment I would make that kind of announcement with the little ones present?"

She hugged me close and lay her head on my chest. "Of course not. It was silly of me."

"Never, ever, would I do that." I watched a bead of steam condensation slide down her forehead and brushed it away with my thumb.

"I know." Her voice was muffled as she pressed her face into my chest. We stayed locked in an embrace for a few moments before she pulled back, touched my cheek, and turned back to the stove. I busied myself with a large bottle of gin, several bottles of tonic water, and a bucket of ice cubes. After a few moments, I turned back to her.

"It never occurred to me that's what people might think," I said.

"Well, you've hinted at it before."

"I have not!"

"You have, too."

"When?"

"Almost every time Mom brings up the idea of a nursing home."

"Well that's just to shut her up. But if that's what people think, I'll make the drinks stronger than usual."

Callie laughed, the kind of exaggerated laugh that comes from relief. "Make mine first and leave it here," she said.

"You got it." I pulled a bowl of sliced limes from the refrigerator.

"The water's ready, but I won't put the lobsters in until the drinks are finished and you've made your announcement. I'm sure some of us are going to need a third round by that time."

"I fear you're going to be disappointed. I'm not joining a commune or moving to Outer Mongolia or anything like that."

"That's a relief."

I finished pouring the last drink. "Help me carry them out. I might as well get the announcement about my real travel plans over with."

"Real travel plans?"

"You'll see."

We made two trips between the kitchen and the living room with trays full of clinking crystal highball glasses. Finally, when all the adults had drinks and the children had their sodas, I turned to face my family. "I told you all I had something important to say, so here it is." The room went silent. The screech of seagulls came through the open French doors leading to the deck. A voile inner drape fluttered inward on the breeze. "I love you all," I said.

No one spoke.

"That's really all I had to say."

Natalie shook her head in bewilderment. "You mean you let us think you had some terrible news to tell us and all you wanted to say was that you loved us?"

"Is that so bad? It got you all here, didn't it? And besides, who said I had terrible news? You just made assumptions."

Callie gave an un-ladylike guffaw, covered her mouth, raised her glass with a tinkle of ice, spilled a little, and said, "Way to go, Papa! You're the best!"

I smiled at her and said, "Well, actually, there is one other thing."

"Okay, here it comes," muttered Natalie.

I looked around the room. "Yesterday was the sixty-ninth anniversary of D-Day. Meaning, of course, next year will be the seventieth. There will be big ceremonies, as there are for every decade observance. I plan to attend. Maybe some of you would like to accompany me."

"Are you crazy?" Natalie said.

Callie's hand shot into the air. "I'll go."

"No, Callie," Natalie said. "Don't encourage him. We need to be discussing Dad's ... Papa's ... need to move out of this house, not some silly trip he's too old to make."

"What the hell are you talking about?" I asked. At the open window, the linen curtains wafted inward on the sea breeze, brushing my elbow. I side-stepped from the window and the ice in my gin-and-tonic clinked against the side of the glass. "Who says I'm too old to travel? And this is not some silly trip. Goddammit," I almost shouted.

Natalie looked around the room as if to ask for help. "It's just that we worry about you. Even here at home. This house has three floors, all of which you use. You should be on a single level and have help. There are nursing homes that—"

My youngest daughter Judy piped up, "You should at least get one of those stair-lifts like in that brochure I showed you. The stairs can be dangerous."

"I agree with Judy," her husband, Denis, said. "If you fell and broke your hip at your age, it could be very serious."

"Denis is a nurse," said Natalie. "He knows about these things."

I glared at her. "And Callie is a doctor," I shouted, perhaps too loudly. "You don't hear her complaining about every step I take. And, besides, have you forgotten I've written several books on healthcare? Well-received books, I might add. Don't you think I also know a thing or two about aging?"

"But when it comes to your own aging, you've turned a blind eye."

"The hell, I have. I'm intimately aware of my limitations. I curse them every day! Every time I bend a damned knee, I curse them."

With her glass in her hand, Callie made a time-out sign. "Time out everybody. I slaved in the kitchen to make us a nice dinner. Let's table this discussion for later."

"No, Callie," I said, shooting her what I hoped was an impish smile. "We might as well have this out now." I took a sip of my drink, looked each of them in the eye, and said, "Which means, it's time to make the announcement I really called you here for."

"You mean it's not about this D-Day trip, Dad?" Richard asked.

"Well, that still stands, but it's not the primary reason."

"And saying you love us all wasn't the real reason either?" asked Natalie, the snark evident in her tone.

"That, too, stands," I said. "And, in a way, that's my most important message. But there's something else. And it's the reason I refused to install one of those damned stair-lifts." I paused and looked at each of my children in turn. "I've sold the house."

My announcement had the effect I hoped it would. For a few seconds, a stunned silence settled on the room. The only sounds were the cries of seagulls, that damned lawn mower in the distance that always seemed to be going, and the chink-rattle of ice in crystal glasses. Finally, Natalie asked, "Are you serious?"

"Would I joke about something like that?"

"But, why?"

"You all seem shocked. I thought you'd be happy."

"I am," said Natalie. "*We* are," she added, looking around the room and getting nods of assent. "I think we're all happy about it, but why did you suddenly decide to sell?"

"It wasn't sudden," I said. "I'd been thinking about it even before your mother died. All of you are right about the stairs. I started to think I'd be better off living on one level. I'm not as bull-headed as you all seem to think I am. But the clincher came when Luana retired and went back to the Philippines. I realized how much your mother and I depended on her and I'm not about to go through the hassle of finding another housemaid who would have to learn my habits."

"Did you and Mom talk about it before she passed?"

"Once or twice. But I only made the decision after she died."

"And then you just decided to sell without telling any of us?" Natalie asked.

"I'm telling you now."

"But, Dad, Marshall's a real estate agent. He could have helped."

"What? From the South Shore? It would have been an imposition."

"But he would have been—"

"Besides, he doesn't know the Gloucester market. No offense, Marshall," I added, offering a toast with my highball glass. "You need a local for this sort of thing, and I found a good one."

"No offense taken," said Marshall who turned to Natalie and said, "He's right, you know."

"So, Dad, where will you live?" Judy asked.

"Would you consider assisted living?" Natalie asked. "It's the perfect time, and you can afford it."

"No."

"But it would be so good for you."

"What? Eating when everyone else eats? Pick any one of three items on the menu? Let's see, it's Tuesday, must be meatloaf or spaghetti-and-meatballs or beans-and-franks. Playing Bingo or some such crap game with a bunch of old coots? And on Friday nights—Jesus Christ, save me!—on Friday nights dance to the music of Lawrence Welk with some doddering old lady? Sorry, that's not for me. And your mother hated the idea of it, too."

"No, she didn't," said Natalie. "She thought it was fine. Sensible."

"Well, then I hated it for her."

"But who will take care of you?" Judy piped up again.

"*I* will take care of me!"

"Sure, but for how long?" Natalie continued to look around the room for support, but they seemed to be happy to leave it to her as the oldest child.

"Until I'm freaking dead!" I shouted. "That's how long!"

"Dad, the children!" said Judy.

"That's why I said 'freaking' instead of what I wanted to say. Besides, they probably drop the F-bomb more than all of us put together."

That elicited snickers from a few of the older children, making me think I should have a private word about language with them.

"But you can't predict when you'll need help," Natalie said. "Before he died, Marshall's father had to have an aide wipe his butt and help him shower. And he wasn't even ninety."

"Well, I'm not Marshall's father. And my butt resents you talking about it in its presence," I said with an exaggerated wiggle of my hips.

More snickers from the children. One of them shouted, "Look! Grampa is twerking!"

At least I was getting through to *them*.

"It's only because we love you, Dad," Natalie said.

"Yes," several others added.

Richard leaned against the door jamb and swirled his drink. "So, if you won't accept assisted living, where will you live?"

"I'm working on that. I don't close for a few months. That was part of the deal. And, I need to oversee some minor repairs. Also, part of the deal."

"Marshall and I would be happy to build an addition to our house."

My biggest goddamned nightmare! I shook my head emphatically. "First off, that would be imposing and I—"

"It wouldn't be an—"

"And I don't intend to impose. On anyone. So, don't any of the rest of you offer to take me in like some orphan. Besides, none of you live near the ocean and I may be giving up this house, but I sure as hell won't give up walking out the door to breathe in the sea air. I've been researching the condos where Callie lives."

"The Navy Yard?" exclaimed Callie, her eyes round.

I smiled at her, my greatest ally among the whole crowd. "There are several nice buildings there. I could have walks along the water and I would be able to see Danny and Ashley more often. And, of course, you."

"That's brilliant!" Callie said. "I'll help you look."

Danny and Ashley waved their hands in the air like eager teacher's pets waiting to be called on. "We want to help, too! We'll pick the best place in the neighborhood!"

Everyone seemed satisfied that the eldest grandchild would be helping feeble old granddad, and that put an end to the discussion. Conversation drifted to fond memories and good times had in our house by the sea. It had been a great place to raise the family, and I would be sad to turn over the keys to someone else. But it was time to move on.

A half hour later, the sun was just setting when we sat down to dinner. Soothing moonlight lay on the family gathering. Callie, Danny, and Ashley wore a path between the kitchen and the deck bringing out mini salt-and-pepper shakers, a dozen custard cups of clarified butter, nutcrackers, small plates of lemon wedges and several bottles of Chardonnay which held reflections of moons in their golden glasses. It wasn't exactly Gatsby, but it was bountiful nonetheless. And I never aspired to be a Gatsby anyway.

"The lobsters are almost ready," Callie said. "Who wants a bib?"

Midway through dinner, Casals' "Song of the Birds" came through the speakers. I closed my eyes and listened.

How I would love to have introduced Élodie to these people! How I would have loved to see her reaction to me twerking.

❧

Emboldened by their success in destroying the railroad bridge, Jean-Baptiste and the others decide to make a second foray. "There's another trestle bridge a few kilometers further south over a gorge," Claude says. "They're bound to send a train loaded with troops to repair the bridge we blew up last night. It won't take much to bring the bridge down when they're going over it."

Lighting the short stub of a carefully saved cigarette butt, Marcel looks up. "No one would survive such a drop."

"Then do it," says Élodie. "We'll wait here."

Jean-Baptiste narrows his eyes at her. "You won't come with us?"

"Why? You just said it wouldn't take much to destroy it. What do you need me for?"

"I thought that's what you trained for. To fight."

Élodie narrows her eyes. "I also trained to rescue people. You *know* that. Sabotage was only part of my job and only briefly to support the invasion. You know very well my main job is to help British and American fliers escape over the Pyrénées. It just happens I received my first client earlier than expected."

Jean-Baptiste glares at me, turns and stomps out of the barn. Marcel and Claude quickly follow.

"It's settled, then?" I ask when they're gone. "That's what we're doing? You're escorting me out of France?"

"When you're fit enough. It's an arduous trek. What else can we do?"

"I don't know." I stare into her eyes. She's right, of course, but I don't want to admit it. She returns the look with an unyielding gaze of her own. Finally, I say, "Well, we still have time. No need to decide now. Shall I open a bottle of wine?"

"Yes," she whispers.

We make love again that night and afterwards we lie back in the hay and we hear the patter of raindrops on the barn roof, and the sound lulls us to sleep.

When I wake, Élodie is not beside me. I hear the soft sound of a violin. I rise and walk out of the barn. The rain has stopped and light from a half moon presses down from behind clouds. I inhale deeply. There is that fresh, ozone after-the-rain smell.

Élodie sits on the stump of a tree, playing a sweet melody. She doesn't smile when she sees me. She continues to play. A wine bottle is perched on a boulder next to her. Miniatures of the moon reflect from the bottle, and from the belly of the violin, and crickets form an undertone to the music. When she finishes, I ask, "What was that piece? It's beautiful."

"A traditional French song from the eighteenth century. It's called *Plaisir d'Amour*, the pleasure of love. I told you about it before."

I kiss her on the forehead. "They got that right!"

Élodie looks into the distance and now there are two more miniature moons, one reflecting from each of her moist eyes. "The song has words," she says in a barely audible voice.

"The ones you told me the other night?"

She nods, takes a deep breath. "The pleasure of love lasts only a moment; the grief of love lasts a lifetime."

There is a heaviness in my chest. "But that—"

"The writer goes on to tell how his love is leaving him for another lover."

"Are you leaving me for another?"

She shakes her head slowly. "It's *you* who will be leaving *me* for another lover." She lays her violin it it's case.

"What are you talking about? Not a snowball's chance in hell! Nix on that!"

"The American army is your lover. Your comrades are your lovers, your brothers-in-arms."

"I owe them, yes. But I love you."

"War makes it too easy to fall in love and too hard to stay in love."

The thought of losing her is like a kick in the stomach. "I don't give a shit about what happens to me. I love you. Only you."

"I thought American men didn't like to say, 'I love you.'"

"*This* American man is not shy about it. Damn it, I love you!"

"Then I guess you have a problem. *We* have a problem." Élodie gazes at me a long moment. Finally, she says, "You've ruined things."

"What? What have I ruined?"

"You've made it impossible."

"Made what impossible, damn it?" I can feel the heat in my face.

"Everything."

"What do you mean, *everything*?"

"All the possibilities … everything."

"For Christ's sake, you're not making sense. I don't know what you mean."

"Until there was you, I was willing to take risks. I would jump out of planes. I would fight the Germans. I was free to die. Now I'm too afraid of losing you. I can't even go with my comrades to blow up a fucking, goddamned railroad bridge."

"That's silly. You jumped into France, you attacked that German medical unit. You are not yellow!"

"Besides, it's too dangerous for you to stay with me," she says.

"How is it too dangerous for me? I'm not afraid of my commanding officers."

"It's not that."

"What is it, then?"

"It's that I would rather die with you, than live without you."

A thrill passes through me, and I reach out and pull her to me. "I feel the same way. I don't care what happens to me as long as I can be with you."

"You see," she says, backing away. "That's exactly the point. As long as we're together, we'll allow ourselves to take risks. We'll be like two people holding hands at the edge of a cliff. A lover's leap. As long as we're together, we don't stand to lose each other."

"You're wrong," I say. "We'll do anything to keep each other safe."

She shakes her head. "We'll take foolish risks. It's the way it is."

"I don't believe that." I'm struggling to find the right thing to say.

"Already, you're willing to risk the firing squad."

"That's not true!"

"But, it is true," she replies. "It means the thing that's impossible, is us. You must return to your unit and I must do what I must do in the Pyrénées. I must disappear into the mountains. This is impossible."

"I won't let you go."

She shakes her head. "No. I must disappear into the mountains."

"We'll meet after the war."

"You assume the war will end."

"Of course, it will end."

"But will we still be alive when the war ends?"

I give a heavy sigh. It feels like she's already slipping away from me. "Listen, Élodie. I think it's what happened at Oradour catching up with you. It's best we drop it for now, have some wine, and enjoy what we have while we have it. Yesterday's done, and we'll worry about tomorrow, tomorrow. Okay?"

She remains silent.

"Okay?" I ask again.

She shrugs and picks up her violin. "Don't speak," she says. She starts to play the violin. As she plays, the light of the moon sizzles in the canopies of leaves and in the body of the violin. The bow flashes with a sliver of moonlight.

"By the way," I say. "It's funny when you curse like that."

"Like what?"

"Saying 'fucking, goddamned thing.' Most Americans would say it's either a fucking thing or a goddamned thing. Using both seems overkill."

She turns her back to me. She mumbles something under her breath, but I hear it anyway. "Idiot!" she says.

Chapter 8
Chamber of the Bulls

After several days, my lung has sufficiently healed for the thoracostomy tube to be removed, and, after another few more days of recovery, I am ready to be transferred to rehab. I lie comfortably on the gurney as they wheel me out of Mass General and into an ambulance for the short ride to the Spaulding Rehabilitation Hospital which, conveniently, is in the same Charlestown Navy Yard as my condominium. Indeed, I've often walked Arlequin on the grounds of the rehab hospital and along the wooden walk bordering one side of Dry Dock # 5 which noses into Boston Harbor not far from the hospital's main entrance.

When we arrive, we are greeted by one of those morning fogs that draws everything into itself. I smell the ocean, I taste the salt air, I can hear the softest sound and it fills me with joy. I am home. Well at least I am only a few blocks from home. But when they roll me into my room, I find the window blocks all sound and scent; I can only stare across Boston Harbor, and see planes taking off from Logan Airport, lifting into a sky patchy with finger-painted clouds, a scumbled sky like the one above the airfield in England on the eve of that night-of-nights seventy years ago, and my mood instantly darkens.

Every plane taking off is full of people going somewhere, and here I lie in bed, an old man going nowhere. I grind my teeth even though my dentist has repeatedly told me not to. Has my membership in the human race expired with that bullet? Has my body passed its use-by date? I look at the date on my watch. The ceremonies of the 70th anniversary of D-Day are four weeks away. June 6, 2014. I press the nurse call button twice in rapid succession. Moments later, a nurse enters the room. "You need something?"

"Yes. Do you happen to know where they put my phone?"

"It's in the drawer beside your bed. I'll get it for you." She slides the drawer out, removes the phone, and hands it to me.

"Thank you."

After the nurse leaves, I call Callie. She answers on the second ring. "Papa! Are you in Spaulding already?"

"Yes, and I need your help. When you get a chance, would you please go to my condo and fetch my notebook computer? It's on my writing desk." Silently, I congratulate myself for having given a key to my condo to Callie when I moved in—and for not giving one to Natalie.

"Of course," she says. "I was planning to drop by after my shift anyway. I'll be over this evening."

After we end the call, I lie back against the pillow and close my eyes. *Four weeks to June 6th.* I reach into the pocket of my robe and take out the creased photograph of Élodie I had Callie bring me when I was at Mass General, the one where Élodie sits on a boulder outside a shepherd's barn cradling a Sten gun in her lap. I gaze at the photo and remember that moment.

There's another June 6th I remember. June 6, 1968, the day Robert Kennedy died. He'd been shot the previous night at the Ambassador Hotel in Los Angeles, shortly after winning the California primary and delivering a victory speech. Anna and I had stayed up to watch the returns and Kennedy's speech. It was the wee hours of the morning, and I was in the kitchen pouring us each a last celebratory drink when I heard Anna cry out from the living room. "Oh, God! Oh, God! No!"

I rushed into the living room. "What's wrong?"

"They shot him! They shot him!"

I remember sinking to the couch beside her and pulling her hands into mine. And then we wept. It was one of the rare times, after the war years, when I wept openly, and it was hours before we could fall asleep from exhaustion.

And the following Saturday, we watched on TV as Kennedy's funeral train slowly journeyed southward from New York to Washington, passing enormous crowds. Mothers and children saluted the train as it passed. Boys in baseball uniforms held their caps over their hearts. Twenty thousand people sang the "Battle Hymn of the Republic" as the train passed through Philadelphia Station. Women fell to their knees and wailed, black and white—it didn't matter—crammed together on station platforms, holding each other, crying together. Overpasses were lined with people carrying American flags, people crowded together in building windows and on street corners, police and military men stood at attention and saluted, bridesmaids delayed their receptions to toss flowers at the train, people stood on water towers, climbed signal trees, brandished signs saying *God Bless Bobby*. Nuns huddled in prayer as families stood together—father, mother, children—in order, tallest to shortest, hands over their hearts, and then, finally, the train arrived in Washington and the nation mourned again as one Kennedy was laid to rest next his brother. We watched it all, transfixed. I still remember Ted Kennedy's words when he said his brother should be remembered as a man who "saw wrong and tried to right it, saw suffering and tried to heal it, saw war and tried to stop it."

And now I remember another southward journey filled with tears, the tears of Oradour where more than 600 people were murdered by the Germans, the tears of Tulle where 99 resistance fighters were executed, the tears of Élodie outside the cave at Lascaux. So many dead. So many tears.

And I remember the deep well of compassion inside Élodie, and back in 1968, I wished, more than anything, that I could have talked with Élodie about Bobby Kennedy's life and his death.

There is a discreet knock on the door of my room at Spaulding, followed by a woman's voice. "Good afternoon, Mister Budge."

I turn from the window to see an attractive young woman with a shy smile. "You startled me." I return the photo of Élodie to my pocket.

"I'm sorry. I just wanted to introduce myself. My name is Amélie. I'll be your physical therapist while you're here at Spalding Rehab."

"Call me Henry," I say. "You have a French name and accent."

Her face brightens. "I was born and raised in Caen, France."

I smile back. "Normandy."

"Yes," she replies as she examines my bracelet I.D. "Most Americans confuse it with Cannes on the Côte d'Azur. Do you know Normandy?"

I broaden my smile. "Intimately," I say. "You remind me of horses."

She gives me a bemused look. "*Horses?*"

"The perfume you're wearing ... it's *Nuit de Longchamp*."

"Why, yes, it is, Mister Budge! But how in the world do you know that?"

"Call me Henry. The olfactories have very long memories." Élodie is almost there, almost at the threshold of the room, wanting to come in. Can't I be granted just one moment? Just one?

"I'm sorry. I—" Amélie says.

"The nose remembers," I say.

"But why horses, Mister Budge?"

"Henry."

"I'm sorry. *Henry*. Why horses?"

"That's better. Longchamp is a race track in the Bois de Boulogne in Paris."

"Yes, of course. You have been there?"

If I was the age of my great grandkids, I might have said, "Duh!" Instead, I say, "I made a tour of France seventy years ago."

She stares at me for a moment, then her eyes grow bright. "Oh. I'm sorry. I should have known, Mister Budge."

"Henry, damn it! We're on this earth together, you and I, and everybody else who's alive. Let's try to get by on a first-name basis. Who knows? Maybe world peace will break out."

"I'm sorry," she says. There's that gorgeous smile again. "From now on I'll call you Henry. I promise."

"I may be just a tired historian, but I'm not retired from the world. I'm alive and want to be called by the name I prefer. And, besides, I'm still working, still writing. Don't cremate me yet."

"I understand."

"They always want to separate us: the baby boomer generation, gen X, the millennials ...."

"The greatest generation ... *Henry?*" A teasing smile.

"Yes, that too." I return the smile. *It's the same way Élodie had pronounced it ... Uhnree*

"We'll begin PT tomorrow. How does eleven o'clock sound?"

"The sooner, the better," I say. "I'm hoping to get to Normandy for the D-Day commemoration."

She knits her brow. "I'm afraid that will be impossible. There's not nearly enough time. Your doctors would never approve."

Damn! Why can't I keep things to myself? "I'll make it happen," I say. Weakly.

"But you won't be fully recovered. There'll be pain."

"Do you plan to strap me to the bed?"

She laughs. "Of course not."

"Well then Amélie, my sweet, let's do what we need to do, and I'll take it from there. Deal?"

"I don't know. I—"

"Deal?"

She stares at me, bites her lower lip. Finally, she nods. "Deal."

"Deal, what?"

"Deal, *Henry.*"

"Thank you. And don't breathe a word of this to anyone else. Especially my family."

"Don't worry. I'm not allowed to. HIPAA. Patient privacy rights."

"Good for HIPAA! Score one for bureaucracy."

"And by the way, Henry, if what they tell me is correct, you are more than 'just a retired historian.' I understand several of your books have been quite popular."

I shrug, assume what I hope is a look of modesty. "Yes ... but you must still call me Henry. And there's something else you can do for me."

"What's that?"

"Remove this goddamned Foley catheter. It's uncomfortable as hell."

"Are you sure?"

"I'm damned sure! I don't need it. Why did they put it in anyway?"

"Well, you needed it for the surgery. And then I guess they—"

"They what? Assumed since I'm over ninety I must be incontinent? Well, I'm not, and I want the damn thing out."

"Okay, I'll ask the doctor."

"Don't ask. Tell!"

Good. I've elicited that beautiful smile again!

"I'll do what I can," she says. "If you'd like to be nearer the window, I can bring a wheelchair in."

"No! I don't need …. Sure. Why not?"

After Amélie leaves, I roll the chair nearer the window and place the *Boston Globe* on the wall unit housing the heat and air conditioning, and pull the section containing the crossword puzzle from the rest of the newspaper and start solving it. In ink. I like the challenge of ink because it forces me to hold several intersecting words in mind at the same time to confirm the correctness of the interlocking entries before committing myself to writing the answer in. It is my private test for signs of Alzheimer's and, so far, I've passed easily. I am half finished with the puzzle when I put it down on the wall unit. The pages of the newspaper flutter in the updraft. I place my hand in my pocket to touch the photo of Élodie and lean back to watch planes leaving Logan Airport.

When I saw Élodie's tears that time, when I saw her tears after we had the film developed in the village of Prades in the Pyrénées, I fell even more deeply in love with her. Because, in addition to the photo I took of her—the one sitting in my pocket—there were other exposures on the Agfa film roll in the camera we took from one of the Germans we killed after Oradour. I remember Élodie insisted on knowing the man's name. It was Fritz Dürbach.

In several of the pictures was a smiling young woman with her arms around two children, a boy and a girl. The boy, in turn, held a dog in his lap. On a table behind them was a framed picture of Dürbach. Then, in another picture, Dürbach himself, posed with his family in front of a Christmas tree. That was when tears formed in Élodie's eyes. And it was when she muttered, "To hell with Hitler and his filthy, fucking, goddamned war!" I can almost hear her voice now. *Almost.*

Why, seventy years later, is Élodie's memory calling me back to France? Beyond what I wrote in the beginning about ennobling the grief (which has intensified since Anna died, or since I'm approaching my own end) and to recover more perfect memories of my first love, what do I hope to accomplish? Do I also hope to exonerate myself for what I did at that time—or, more precisely, what I *didn't* do—because of my love for Élodie? Come to a final reckoning? Close the ledger on a long life? It would be easy to avoid going to France. Getting shot is certainly a damn good excuse. Plus there's my age, my family, the doctors, including Callie, who say I shouldn't fly. I never thought going to France that first time was very heroic because I had no choice. The generals made me go. But to go a second time, to bring our story—a story that ended on the rise with no falling action, no denouement—to bring that story to a better conclusion requires a different kind of courage. Now all I need is to figure out how to escape from this place in time to catch my flight and make it to the ceremonies. And I need the courage to write the final chapter.

I roll the wheelchair back to the window and see people moving briskly through chiaroscuro plays of light on the sidewalk. Several physical therapists work with patients in the Therapy Garden, a small park opposite the main entrance.

Why is trying to retrieve memories of Élodie like trying to remember the taste of a fine meal, the vaguest hint of flavor? Or like trying to hang onto a sound when the receding, reverberating, tenth echo had lost its life force? All I can recover are afterimages, like the vague, fast-fading, green-gray mackle you see when you close your eyes after gazing at a backlit window, or after staring at a cell phone in the dark.

Here I am, an expert in memory. I wrote the goddamned book, for Christ's sake! *The Architecture of Memory in Prehistory, Antiquity and the Middle Ages.* I studied the key thinkers on memory—Simonides of Ceos, Cicero, Quintilian, Matteo Ricci, Giulio Camillo, Giordano Bruno—all of whom constructed what they called "memory palaces" whereby an item to be later remembered is stored in one or another imaginary room in an imaginary palace, and when that bit of knowledge is needed, all one has to do is visit the imaginary room in the mind, and there it would be. That may work for facts. But feelings? They are different. I can't use that trick to recover the feeling of making love with

Élodie, her touch, her smell, her warmth, her yearning voice, the taste of her, or even the very look of her impassioned face. So, why do I think it will be better if I go to France?

"Well, aren't you the picture of self-pity, sitting there looking out the window with a hangdog expression?"

I spin the wheelchair. "Callie!"

"Hello, Papa."

"You can't even see my expression from the door."

"You were reflected in the window. And what are you doing sitting in a stuffy room like this? Don't you know you can open a window?"

"What?" I say. "No, I didn't know that. I thought they were fixed so people wouldn't jump out."

"Uh unh," she says. "I guess when they designed the building they figured fresh air was worth a few bodies on First Avenue." She opens the window. A breeze comes in and wafts through my hair. There is the sea-salt smell of the ocean. I hear the flutings of birdsong coming from the trees. I laugh. "Oh Christ, thank you Callie! Thank you! You have liberated me!"

"I brought your computer."

"More liberation!"

"I talked to your physical therapist."

"Amélie?"

"Yes. She said it would be okay to wheel you outside tonight. Want to go?"

"In this chair?"

"Of course. You haven't recovered enough to be walking for more than a few minutes."

"Do you know if your mother is coming tonight?"

"No. She said she was going to bed early. She'll visit tomorrow."

"Okay, then. I'd like to go outside."

Callie tilts her head and gives me an inquisitive smile. "But only if Mom is not coming?"

"She would only have to see me in a wheelchair once and she'd start nagging me all over again about a nursing home. Next thing you know, she'll be suggesting I wear diapers, for Christ's sake!"

"Don't worry, Papa, I won't tell her." Callie takes the brake off the wheelchair and pushes it into the hallway.

When we arrive outdoors by the Therapy Park, the sound of the wind is thready as it rustles through the trees. I see, in a slick of moonlight, a soft breeze dragging cat's paws across the water. I ask, "Are you up to pushing me all the way out to the end of the dry dock?"

"Of course."

A few minutes later, we arrive at the end where it juts into the harbor. Waves suck and wheeze against the pilings. We stop, and I gaze across the harbor at planes taking off and landing at Logan Airport. And though I can't see the lighthouses at Graves and at Boston Light because of buildings in my line of sight, I look in their direction and know that, out there, ships are passing in and out of Boston Harbor.

Ships! Passing in and out of Boston Harbor!

I look to the south and see a Coast Guard cutter at its pier and I know, beyond that, is the Black Falcon Cruise ship terminal.

And I begin to form a new idea. Why risk that pneumothorax thing by flying, when I can travel by sea?

෨ඏ

Some eighty kilometers southwest of Corrèze, we come to the outskirts of Montignac, a small commune in the Dordogne where Marcel's cousin lives. It is a heavily forested area in the valley of the Vézère River where limestone cliffs, honeycombed with caves, rise almost directly from the river. The village itself is medieval with narrow streets and half-timbered buildings dating from the 13th and 14th centuries, including a stone, arched bridge over the river and a turreted château on the outskirts of the village.

Marcel signals for us to pull over. "We must hide the car here and you must wait while I visit my cousin and make sure the place is safe."

"Yes, go," says Élodie. "But hurry. And don't take any chances."

We wait less than half an hour, mostly in silence. There is an obvious rancor among Élodie, me, and Jean-Baptiste which discourages conversation. Élodie and I stand together, resting our backs against the car. Jean-Baptiste leans against a tree trunk, some distance away, smoking several cigarettes in a row. Claude seems to want no part of the palpable tension, so he, too, stands off by himself. Finally, when we see Jean-Baptiste drop the stub of his cigarette to the ground, stomp on it, and start toward us, we turn to see Marcel approaching.

"Well?" Élodie asks.

"Georges thinks the Boche are all over in the nearest prefecture," Marcel reports. "They haven't seen any for several days. My cousin welcomes us and says his wife will kill a few ducks and make her famous *Magret de Canard* with a *Sauce Perigueux*."

"A feast in the middle of a war!" Élodie's voice is like a song. She turns to me. "*Sauce Perigueux* is a truffle sauce. I have no idea how she will manage to do this with the shortages."

We climb into the car and drive into the commune and on to a stone house with an adjoining barn, also stone, behind which we park the car to hide it from the main road.

Georges and Isabeau Bosquet are a middle-aged couple who live alone except for a pig they call Adolphe they plan to eat when food becomes even scarcer—or to celebrate liberation if it comes first. I learn later that, for several years, they have been a stop along an underground railroad, sheltering Jews trying to escape the Nazis and passing them on to the next safe house, from where they are escorted along the chain until they are guided out of France, over the Pyrénées, and into Spain. We sit around the kitchen table and discuss the war while Isabeau vigorously works the lever of a red water pump that emits sighs and asthmatic gasps as it gushes water into a tin bucket. Fortunately for me, Georges and Isabeau speak English, though not nearly as well as Élodie and her companions.

"There has been much sabotage," Georges says. "But the Boche are quick to repair the rail lines. More must be done."

Claude leans forward. "That's why we came to see you. Do you have dynamite you can give us?"

"No. But I can get some tomorrow."

"Then do it." Jean-Baptiste says it like it is a command. "We'll stay the night here."

Isabeau looks at Élodie. "We only have one extra room. You are welcome to it, mademoiselle."

"That won't be necessary," Élodie says quickly. "I'll sleep in the barn."

"We'll all sleep in the barn," says Jean-Baptiste.

Élodie and I exchange glances.

Later, after the meal, Georges opens a third bottle of wine and holds it up as if for a toast. "Enough about war. Let us talk of more pleasant things. Have you heard of the important discovery some local boys made here four years ago?"

"No," says Élodie. "What discovery?"

"An ancient cave with many, many paintings. *Préhistorique.*"

Élodie's eyes widen. "That's sounds fascinating. Will we have time to visit it? How long will it take for you to return with the explosives?"

"I have to go to Begerac for them, but the ordinary route is too close to Périgueux, so I must go indirectly. It will be four or five hours before I return."

"Why too close to Périgueux?" asks Jean-Baptiste.

Georges shrugs, *"Les Boche."*

"Périgueux is the next closest prefecture," Marcel explains. "So you think they're still there?"

"Mai, oui." Georges turns to me. "My apologies. I forgot to speak in English."

"It's okay, Georges," I say. "That much I understood. The Krauts are in Périgueux."

"Will you tell us how to get to this cave?" asks Élodie.

"Mais certainement. I have written it out. We get many requests." He steps into the adjoining room and returns moments later with a piece of paper. He hands it to Élodie. I look over her shoulder. It reads, in French and German:

Environ un kilomètre, sud par le sud-est. 162 degrés

Etwa einen Kilometer südlich von Südosten. 162 Grad[32]

"You will see a path," Georges says, "but, in any case, you may borrow my compass if you don't have one. The opening is bigger than when the

---

32   About one kilometer, south by south-east. 162 degrees.

cave was discovered. You won't miss it. Jacques Marsal, one of the boys who discovered it, pitched a tent so he could guard the opening and charge a fee, but he won't be there until late in the morning."

Élodie looks up at Georges. "Have many Germans visited the cave?"

"In past times. But not so many these days, and none for a fortnight." Georges laughs and pours himself another glass of wine. "I think you and the Americans keep them busy, *n'est-ce pas?*"

That night, when Élodie and I retire to the barn, Jean-Baptiste follows us. I secretly roll my eyes at Élodie who whispers back, "Don't let him bother you."

I sleep with the other men in the open main part of the barn while Élodie beds down in a stall. The following morning, Élodie and I slip out of the barn to eat some of Isabeau's homemade baguette and share with our hosts steaming cups of ersatz coffee, made from roasted acorns. With a laugh, Georges points out at the trees. "This war is hard on the squirrels. We pass our shortage of coffee on to them, and now they have no acorns to eat."

Élodie stares into her cup for a moment and then glances up at me. "War is hell, as you Americans say in the movies."

When we finish our breakfast, Georges goes into the next room and returns with a brass marching compass in a leather pouch and two old, dented, copper lanterns with verdigris patinas. "These will help you find the cave and view the paintings," he says. "Now I am off to acquire some German dynamite."

I loop the compass strap around my neck, and Élodie and I set out for the cave before Jean-Baptiste and the others appear for breakfast. The path Georges mentioned is barely discernible, but the compass guides us past thickets of undergrowth and brambles and through a forest of dense pine, rough-barked chestnuts, and ancient oaks. At last, we find the opening. It is oblong, about six feet high and twelve feet across in the lumpy, irregular shape of a giant potato.

We turn on our lanterns and peer into the mouth of the cave and see a long, almost-vertical shaft with a wooden ladder propped against it. Élodie slings her Sten gun over her shoulder and begins to climb down into the darkness. I follow quickly and at the bottom, we find ourselves in a huge chamber about sixty feet long and maybe twenty or thirty feet across at its widest.

"My God!" Élodie cries. The light from her lantern falls on the cave wall and illuminates a horse's head and neck. It has a woolly mane.

"Look at this," I say. My light beam aims at a strange creature which seems to have two long, straight horns protruding from its head. Moving through the large chamber, we see black horses and some animals that look like oversized oxen.

"I think they are aurochs," says Élodie. "They are *éteint*. How does one say? Ah, yes, extinct."

As we sweep the walls with our lanterns, a line of aurochs and horses, stags, bulls, and a bear appears out of the darkness, painted onto the stone with such confidence and elegance the animals appear to be alive, moving even. At the end of the large chamber, there are two passageways, one leading left and the other right. We choose the left. It is longer than the first chamber, but much narrower, and we find a dizzying array of figures—a huge black bull, a cow, more horses, more aurochs, more bulls, bison, ibexes, and a magnificent black bull that I estimate is about thirty feet long.

"I am gobsmacked," Élodie whispers, her voice full of reverence. "This is the deepest memory of my people, my ancestors. It's as if we are walking through their brains, or their souls!"[33]

Soon, we come to a dead end and we retrace our steps, finally emerging into the first space, from where we enter the passage on the right. This corridor is decorated with hundreds of figures—more aurochs, bison, deer, horses, ibex. At the end of the passage we come to an intersection and we enter the long, wide cavern on the right which has a ceiling that varies in height from a foot or so above my head to three times my height. Here, there are many more paintings, among them a group of seven ibexes, a large, black cow, crossed bison which show skillful perspective, four stags drawn as if swimming in an imaginary stream.

---

33   On book tours, people often ask where I get my ideas for books. It's easy to identify the spark that led to *The Architecture of Memory in Prehistory, Antiquity and the Middle Ages*. It is this brief comment by Élodie.

Élodie lowers herself to the floor and stares, mouth agape, at the procession of animals surrounding us. I sit beside her and put an arm around her shoulders. "I'm stunned," I say, voice low as if in a church. "What's that word you used just now?"

"Gobsmacked?"

"Yes. I've been inside cathedrals that don't leave me as awestruck."

"That's it, my love. Well said, you! *Magnifique!* It's a cathedral of the earth. When I was in England, I saw Stonehenge. Do you know of it?"

"Yes," I reply. "I was based at Littlecote House near Hungerford. That's only about thirty miles away. I saw it several times on weekend passes."

"They say it's a sacred place," says Élodie. "And I can understand it. That's how I felt when I was there. Did you feel it?"

"Very much so."

"I think this cave is a sacred place. I feel I am inside the mind of the human race and these paintings are ideas and memories."

I lean closer to her, my lips brush her hair. "I'll bet you've never made love inside a cathedral."

She turns and looks into my eyes. "Is that a proposal?"

I lean forward and kiss her. Soon, our clothes are scattered on the stone floor, and our bodies are moving together, the only other sound a trickle of moisture dripping from a crevice in the wall.

And then we hear it. A creak. Someone coming down the wooden ladder at the entrance. Élodie pushes me away and whispers, "Someone is coming."

"Jean-Baptiste?"

"Probably."

I grab the pile of clothes and hand Élodie's blouse to her. "I would not put it past the idiot."

We are rushing to put our clothes back on when we hear a second creak. Then a man's voice. *"Un seul baiser."*

Élodie whispers to me. "Only one kiss. French with a German accent."

"Non!" It's the frightened voice of a girl.

"Nein! Ein Kuss. Un baiser!"

"Non!" The sound of shoes running.

"Halt!"

Now come the sounds of a struggle. Scuffling feet. A loud slap of flesh on flesh. A cry of pain. Grunts. The thud of a body slammed to the ground. *"Non!"* The girl lets out a long scream.

I whisper to Élodie, "No time to finish dressing. Let's go."

She nods.

We scramble into the next chamber where we see a man in a Wehrmacht uniform on his knees, straddling and punching a struggling, crying girl. I notice a holster on the man's right hip. Still barefoot, I approach him quietly from behind and wrap my left arm around his throat, squeezing and pulling back hard. With my other hand, I snap open the holster, pull out his Luger, and force the man to his feet. I press the muzzle of the gun to the back of the man's head and over my shoulder, I say to Élodie, "Tell him if he resists, he will die."

Élodie says, *"Wenn Sie sich widersetzen, wird er Sie töten."*

"Now tell him to stand against the wall."

"Stellen Sie sich gegen die Wand."

"I'll watch him while you see if she's all right," I say. I keep the luger trained on the man who, although wearing the markings of a 1st lieutenant or *Oberleutnant,* has a boyish face and unusually long blond hair.

Élodie helps the sobbing girl to her feet, and murmurs something reassuring in French, and the girl's sobs gradually decrease. I catch the word, *"Résistance."*

The German tips his head toward the girl. *"Sie ist nur eine Jüdin."*

Without taking my eyes off him, I ask Élodie to translate.

"He said, she is only a Jewess."

"Do you have your gun trained on him?" I ask.

"Yes."

I spin the man around, pistol whip him across the face, and spit out the only German word I know. *"Schwein!"*

The man gives a cry of pain and drops to his knees.

I risk a glance up at Élodie. "I'll keep him here while you finish dressing and help the girl out of the cave. Then I'll send him up as soon as you're ready to cover him. I'll put my boots on and follow. Tell him that's what we are doing. Tell him you will shoot him in the face if he tries anything."

Élodie speaks to the man, then urges the girl up the ladder. Moments later, she herself climbs the ladder and calls down. "Ready!"

I motion with the pistol for the man to start climbing. Peering up the shaft, I see Élodie with her Sten gun trained on the man. When the German reaches the top, she motions him to stand to the side and calls down, "Okay."

I slip on and lace my boots as fast as I can, then climb to the surface, ignoring the pain in my wounded thigh. With the Sten gun and the Lugar still trained on him, we march the German ahead of us back to the home of Georges and Isabeau Bosquet.

When we arrive, Isabeau is at the front door to greet us, and Élodie explains what happened to the girl—whose name, she has learned, is Hannah Katz. Isabeau puts her arm around the girl's shoulder and ushers her into the house. Over her shoulder, she says, "Hannah lives nearby. I guess the swine wouldn't report her as long as he got what he wanted. I will see she gets home."

I push the German toward the stone barn where Jean-Baptiste, Marcel and Claude now stand at the door of the barn watching. They make way as I shove the German inside so forcefully he stumbles against the rotting hulk of an ancient automobile with flattened tires. He hits the car hard. Dust rises in the air and flakes of red rust fall to the floor.

Élodie follows us inside.

Marcel looks the man up and down and then turns to Jean-Baptiste. "What will we do with him?"

"Execute him." Jean-Baptiste's tone is flat, matter-of-fact.

"No." Élodie says. "That's what the Nazis would do. We are not Nazis."

Jean-Baptiste looks from Élodie to Claude and Marcel and then steps toward the German. "He should be executed."

"No!"

"Tu es une poule mouillée!"

Élodie smiles, turns to me. "Jean-Baptiste said I am a wet hen. It's a French expression which means he thinks I am a wimp or a sissy, as you say in English." She turns back to Jean-Baptiste. "If you are going to insult me, do it in English so everyone can understand!"

"To hell with the American! I don't care if he understands what we say."

"You are an idiot!" she practically flings the words into the air.

"I insist!" Jean-Baptiste growls. "Execute the man!"

"Your problem is that you are a brute with no imagination," Élodie says. "He is my prisoner. I will decide."

Marcel and Claude, like usual, watch their comrades bait each other without saying a word.

"If you won't execute him, what *will* you do?"

"Better to punish the real offender: *Le zob.* His beard-splitter. Please pass me the medical kit." She turns to me. "I'm referring to his penis, in case you want to know."

"I see." I suppress a shudder. "So, what is your plan?"

Instead of answering, Élodie gestures toward a wooden bench sitting near the rusting car. "Marcel and Claude, please place him down on that bench." The two men sweep old auto parts off the bench, which fall to the floor with a clatter. A small cloud of dust rises as they take the German by his arms and legs, drop him on the bench and hold him there.

"Claude, pass me the forceps and sulfa powder

Jean-Baptiste snorts. "You object to executing him because it's what a Nazi would do, yet you would do this to a man? You would castrate him?"

"No, idiot! Again, that's something the Nazis would do. But, circumcise a man? I think that is something a Nazi would have little reason to do." Élodie unbuckles the man's belt and slides his pants down. The German's eyes are wide and he tries to squirm free, but it is no use. He is held in place by Marcel and Claude.

Élodie lifts the scalpel from the medical kit.

"*Wofür ist das? Nein! Nein!*"[34] the man cries.

Élodie is about to sprinkle sulfa powder over the man's penis, when she pauses.

---

34   "What is that for? No! No!"

"Nein! Nein!" the man cries.

Élodie gazes into the man's eyes. Finally, she says, "No. I have a better idea. He has long hair. It seems discipline in the Wehrmacht must be slipping of late. We'll give him a peyot."

"What's a peyot?" Marcel asks.

I have the same question.

"It's the sidelocks an Orthodox Jew wears. I've seen it many times. Remember, I used to work with O.S.E.[35] We had many older children who were Orthodox Jews pass through our care."

Jean-Baptiste gives a sardonic smile and says, "So, you back away from punishing his *zob?*"

"I'm a musician, not a butcher. I'll give him a haircut instead. When he rejoins his friends, he'll know what it feels like to be a Jew among Germans. Maybe he'll have more compassion." She takes a pair of scissors from the medical kit. "Hold him."

Marcel and Claude hold the man tightly from both sides. Élodie goes to work on his hair, cutting most of it short, but leaving tufts in front of each ear. She hums as she works, turning his head this way and that. "Your hair isn't long enough to do a proper job, but your friends will get the idea," she tells him in German.

I frown at her.

Jean-Baptiste draws in a deep breath. "So, you've had your fun. Now what do we do with him?"

"Nothing," Élodie says as she steps back to appraise her handiwork. Marcel and Claude step back, too, and the man turns on his side and curls into a fetal position.

"You mean, just let him go?"

"Why not. He'll be too embarrassed to tell anybody what happened to him and, I promise you, he won't be back."

"I see," says Jean-Baptiste. He walks to the bench as if inspecting Élodie's haircutting skills, then smoothly pulls out his pistol and shoots the man once in the back of the head.

---

35 The *Œuvre de Secours aux Enfants*, or Work for Child Rescue. OSE, pronounced OZAY.

It happens so quickly, so unexpectedly, I jump.

The echo of the gun shot reverberates in the barn.

Élodie turns on him and yells, *"Es-tu un idiot? Pourquoi fais-tu ça ?"*[36]

"Killing those young soldiers after Oradour has made you insane, woman!" Jean-Baptiste yells back at her. "It's crazy to put an enemy combatant back in the field. How would you feel if he was sent to Normandy and killed some of our people? Also, if that girl is a Jewess, it means she is staying in a safe house. And it means, he knew where to find her. He could expose the whole underground railroad. It would have been stupid to let him go."

There is a brief silence, then I say to Élodie, "Jean-Baptiste is right, you know."

Jean-Baptiste gives me a slight smile and a reluctant nod of appreciation.

"I'm going to check on Hannah." Élodie turns and storms out of the barn.

I follow her out and as we pass the chicken coop, I put my hand on her arm. "Sorry for siding with Jean-Baptiste like that."

"I don't hold it against you."

We walk on for several moments. Forcing a smile, I ask, "Beard-splitter? Where did you find a word like that?"

"You want to ask me that, *now*?"

"Yes."

Élodie doesn't answer. Instead she marches on toward the Bosquet farmhouse. Finally, I say, "You should stop thinking about that German. Where did you find a word like beard-splitter?"

"Why do you want to know?"

"I just want to know. Where did you find it?"

Élodie gives an exasperated sigh. "*The Autobiography of a Flea,* I think."

"What's that? I never heard of it."

"It's a racy Victorian novel. I've read lots of them."

I shake my head. "You continually amaze me."

---

36   "Are you an idiot? Why did you do that?"

"What do you find amazing? That I read novels in what is to me a foreign language, or that the novels are naughty?"

"Both, I suppose."

"There's no mystery. When I was in England, a dozen British women and I had a book club. They wanted to read bawdy Victorian novels. More than half of the women were apart from their husbands for the first time." She pauses, then narrows her eyes at me. "You are very clever."

"Why do you say that?"

"That business about beard-splitter. You wanted to switch my mind from what Jean-Baptiste did."

"It's done. You shouldn't let it torment you."

"Like the boy soldier after Oradour?"

"You shouldn't let it torment you."

"This man, today, was some mother's little boy."

"He was a rapist."

"But, was it really necessary for Jean-Baptiste to do that?"

I say nothing.

"I can't stand him," she says with a visible shudder. "Before you dropped out of the sky, he was always trying to seduce me. But I would have none of it. I find him repulsive. Then you came along and now he hates both of us. I should have made my revulsion to him unambiguous in the beginning. I wish I would have done. Then we would not be playing these stupid games."

Later that morning, after we bury the German behind the barn, Georges returns with two wooden crates stenciled in black with the Nazi eagle and swastika and the words, *"Dynamit," "gefährlicher explo-sivstoff,"* and *"gewicht 8.125 Kg."*[37]

Jean-Baptiste and Marcel pry the lids off the crates. They are filled with similarly marked sticks of dynamite packed in layers like sardines.

---

37   "Dangerous explosives," and "weight 8.125 kg."

I estimate between fifteen and twenty sticks in the top layer, and I guess there are, perhaps, ten layers.

"We need to leave straight away for Montauban," says Jean-Baptiste. "Claude, Marcel, help me get this stuff in the car."

Élodie says, "There won't be enough room for everybody."

"Not a problem," says Jean-Baptiste. "You and the American aren't coming with us."

"What do you mean?"

"It's obvious you don't want to fight. You've lost your taste for killing. You're of no use to us."

"What are you talking about? When we found that Boche medical team—"

"When we found that medical team, yes, you did your job," Jean-Baptiste says. "But you shook and threw up for two days afterward. Same thing after Oradour. We can't rely on you. You are, at heart, a pacifist. You should be back at Chabannes with the OSE. You know I speak the truth. You've known it all along. And now, you've let your pacifism blind you."

Élodie glares at Jean-Baptiste. He glares back. There is silence until finally, Georges says, "If that zob knew where that poor girl was, others may know. She needs to be escorted away from here."

"There," Jean-Baptiste says. "You can save lives instead. Escort your American out of France."

"But you have the car."

Georges speaks up. "That is no problem. Old Gaspard Fabry died a month ago, and Madame Fabry doesn't drive. I'll talk to her. It has a wood gasifier just like your car."

Élodie hesitates a few moments, then nods. "We'll take her to Aquilac. I know of some good people. They'll know how to continue her along the escape route."

Later, as Jean-Baptiste and the others are preparing to leave, I ask Élodie, "He mentioned something called OSE and Chabannes. What was that all about?"

"OSE stands for the *Œuvre de Secours aux Enfants* or the Society for Rescuing Children. There were more than a dozen establishments in the south. Sort of orphanages for Jewish children. But Jean-Baptiste is an idiot. They were all closed in the last year after the roundups and deportations started."

"So, what happens to the children now?"

"There's a network of safe houses like the one Hannah Katz lives in."

"And we're taking her to another one?"

"I don't think so. I'll discuss it with Madame Bosquet. I think the girl is too fragile at the moment. Besides, we haven't decided what you and I are doing. It's best to let Madame Bosquet arrange for her to be escorted to the next safe house closer to the Pyrénées."

"Where you intend to escort me?"

"Yes."

"And if I refuse?"

"Then you will be risking the firing squad, and it will kill any chance we have of meeting again after the war."

I stare at her. I have a dark feeling the moon has rotated a little, but by how many degrees?

Chapter 9
A Second Escape

After Callie returns me to my room at Spaulding and says goodnight, I turn the computer on. After a moment's thought, I enter the search term, "New York to France by ship" and am immediately presented with a list of hits. The seventh one down catches my eye. It reads, "*Queen Mary 2* Transatlantic Schedule." I had guessed there would be many more ships from New York than from Boston, and I am quickly proven right. I find there is a sailing on the *Queen Mary 2* that will get me to Southampton, England several days before the ceremonies of June 6th. I enter "England to France, train" and learn I can take the Eurostar from London, through the Channel Tunnel, to Calais. And yes, of course there is a train from Calais to Caen from where, I am confident, I can take a taxi to Omaha Beach and the American Cemetery. Finally, working backwards, I search, "train Southampton to London." No problem.

I stare out the window for several minutes and finally say to myself, "What have I got to lose?" and begin making the necessary bookings on line. It's a sudden change in direction, but one I'm determined to follow. When I finish, I call Maddie Callahan, and she tells me Arlequin is doing fine and eating all his food. And I pull the covers over me and sleep soundly through the night.

"I volunteered with the OSE before the war," Élodie says. "Gave concerts to raise money."

"But you're not Jewish."

"You don't have to be Jewish to want to help Jews." Her voice is caustic.

"Of course not. Forgive me. I was clumsy, and I'm sorry."

"You Americans—"

"What about us Americans?"

"Your countrymen made it clear, early on, they opposed Jewish immigration, even children trying to escape the Nazis. Even your president refused to help."

"I'm not FDR. Don't lay that on me."

"You're not his wife, either. She, at least, did try to help." I stare at her but have no words.[38] After a pause, she takes my hand. "I'm sorry. Of course, there was nothing you, personally, could do. Especially since your government was saying the murder of the Jews was just a war rumor."

"Unlike you," I say with genuine admiration. "You could do something, and you did."

She takes a deep breath and looks off into the distance. "OSE provided homes for children whose parents were either in concentration camps or had been killed. I was scheduled to return to them after my concert in Paris, but then the Germans marched into Paris and you know the rest. I ended up in England. Some of the children made it to America."

"Some?"

"In forty-two, the Vichy police began roundups. They deported children from the orphanages to Nazi concentration camps."

"Jesus!"

"So, the OSE organized underground networks to smuggle children out of France."

---

38   Years later, this brief conversation, and Élodie's passionate defense of the Jews of Europe, became the basis for my book *Reluctant Salvation: WWII Refugee Children and the Roosevelt Administration.*

"And this Aquilac, where we are going, is part of that network?"

"Yes. Gaston and Odette Dupont live there. I know them well. I've guided many children to them."

"Then what happens with the children?"

"When it's the right time, others try to get them to the port at Marseilles or over the mountains to ships in Lisbon."

"The right time?"

"When we're confident there are ships and countries that will take them."

Georges and Isabeau Bosquet return in an old Citroën with a gasifier where the rear luggage compartment ordinarily would be. Georges gestures toward the car with a bow. "Madame Fabry was delighted to help. She said she is too old and timid to fire a weapon, so this is the least she can do."

"It's fine," Élodie says with a determined smile. "It will get us to Aquilac."

❦

When Amélie appears the next day for my physical therapy session, I am ready to do whatever she demands. I promised myself I would be a model patient if it meant the difference between getting to France, and not. I listen closely as Amélie explains the plan of action. "We'll start by doing a pulmonary function test this morning to see what our base line is. That will help us decide how rapidly we can progress. Then we'll go from there. The objective is to get you to the point where you can get from your bed to the bathroom relatively easily and you can do normal chores around your condo, especially in the kitchen. Any questions?"

I'm not about to tell her the real objective is to get me to the point where I can get from my bed to France. Screw the bathroom! Instead, I ask, "Can we do some of this rehabilitation outside in the fresh air?" I reason it will provide me better escape opportunities when the time comes. If they become accustomed to seeing me outside, they might not notice when I gradually extend my wanderings and, eventually, make my escape.

"Not only *can* we," she says. "We've designed the rehabilitation programs so that we *must* do some of our work outside. The grounds are designed with different surfaces to help patients cope with the real world as they recover their mobility."

I force my best saccharin smile. "Good. I'll enjoy the fresh air."

"Are you ready?" she asks.

I give a salute. "Eager and ready. Lead on, Macduff."

"What?"

"It's a British expression. Lead the way. I'm putty in your hands."

"Have you spent time in England?"

"You might say that, but that's not where my British expressions come from. There was a person I knew who spoke better English than the British people themselves."

"I see," she says with an amused smile. "Well, Mister Putty, before we head outside, I'm going to take you to an exam room and we'll do the pulmonary function test." She wheels me out of my room, down a corridor, and into an elevator. In the exam room, Amélie hands me a nose clip to pinch my nostrils together and demonstrates how to use the spirometer. When I'm ready, I inhale as deeply through the mouthpiece as I can, then exhale forcefully. Amélie reads the result, wrinkles her brow, and makes me repeat the procedure several more times.

After the last test, I look up at her. "Is something wrong?"

"On the contrary. Your results are so good, I wasn't sure if they were accurate. Were you an athlete?"

"I ran track. The middle distances. Fifteen hundred, mile, five thousand."

"And you never smoked?"

"Tried it once during the war. Didn't like it."

"When did you run? Was it in college?"

"Yes. And until I was in my mid '80s."

"Seriously?"

"Lots of us old folks run these days," I say. "There are even masters' meets. When I was sixty-seven I won the mile in the sixty-five to seventy age group with a time of five-twenty-one in the national masters' championships in Eugene, Oregon. In the same meet, I won the five thousand in nineteen-oh-seven."

"Most people in their twenties can't run those times!"

"I trained for it. So, what's my score?"

"Your FEV1/FVC ratio is seventy-four percent."

"What the hell is that?"

"Sorry for the technical terms. It's a measure of your lung capacity and how much you can exhale in one second. Normal for a *healthy* man, your age, is sixty-five percent. Over seventy percent is crazy, especially for a man your age who has also suffered a lung injury."

"So, what am I doing hanging around here?"

She laughs. "Not so fast. You still have some healing to do. But what these results suggest is it won't take long at all. And, this much I can say, you won't be needing that wheelchair. Are you ready to walk back to your room?"

"You bet!"

She offers her hand and helps me rise from the wheelchair. As we walk toward the elevator, I must be sporting a huge shit-eating grin because everyone we pass seems compelled to smile back at me.

The next day, my rehabilitation begins in earnest.

After warm-up exercises in the Therapy Garden, Amélie teaches me to place my hands at the lower part of my rib cage and to breathe deeply and exhale through pursed lips. And in the days that follow, we work both indoors and outdoors on abdominal exercises; stretching exercises, walking up and down stairs, lifting weights, and walking—first on the treadmill, then outside along the paths in the Therapy Garden. After a week and a half of this, I know I'm fit enough to initiate my escape plan. So, late in the second week, after Amélie and I walk in the garden, I ask, "Isn't eating one of the things I should be able to do on my own?"

"Yes, of course."

"Then let's go to the cafeteria. I'm hungry and I don't want to eat in my room."

Amélie shakes her head. "I can't. I have another patient."

The thing is, I already know that, and I'm ready with an answer.

"Then leave me in the cafeteria. I want to try some different food for a change."

"But I'm required to escort you back to your room."

"I'll just sit here and enjoy the sea air. You can come get me when you're finished with your next patient."

After some hesitation, she agrees. And on that day, I behave. I stay at the al fresco table exactly where she left me. But on the following day, I saunter about fifty yards to the foot of the old dry dock, then return to my table before Amélie comes to fetch me. A nurse sees me and asks if I need help. "No, no," I say. "Just faithfully practicing my walking."

The nurse gives me a nod of approval. "Well, keep up the good work."

The following day, I repeat my little walk, this time adding another twenty yards to the out-and-back excursion. By the fourth day, hospital staff, including the nurse who had offered to help me on the first day, seem not to notice me anymore. Gradually, day-by-day, I increase my range by small increments until, finally, I make it to the point where, if I were to continue, I would disappear behind some buildings. Poof! Just in time. The *Queen Mary* sails in two days. It's time to move. Tomorrow is the day!

Back in my room, I pull up Amtrak's Acela Express web page on my notebook computer and confirm my ticket for the 1:00 pm train the next day. That will get me to New York around dinnertime on the day before sailing. I also confirm my room at the Waldorf Astoria.

I no sooner close the cover to my notebook when I hear, behind me, "It's good to see you using your computer, Papa."

"Oh, hello, Callie," I say, trying not to act guilty. "I wasn't expecting you."

"You act like a little boy caught peeking through a girly magazine! Aren't you happy to see me?"

"Yes, of course. You just startled me."

"Now that I'm free, I thought I'd drop by."

"Free?"

"Don't you remember me telling you the other day I take my vacation around this time every year to gather my strength to deal with the flood of July interns?"

"Oh, right. That's why I'm supposed to not get sick in July because I'd have some pimple-faced kid tending to me."

"Exactly. And for us doctors, it doubles our workload what with the briefings, answering questions, taking at least twice the time with every patient on rounds, doing intern evaluations. We can get damned cranky. Anyway, since David has the kids, I'm totally free. How about I come over for lunch tomorrow?"

"Tomorrow?"

"Yes."

"But I have a session with Amélie."

"I thought she leaves you to have lunch at one of the outside tables while she works with her next patient. I'll just join you then."

"But I'll be tired. I won't be much company."

"What's with you, Papa?" Callie asks with a bemused smile.

"It's just these rehab sessions tire me out."

"That's not what Amélie says. She says you go through them like a champ."

"Well, I'm not about to give her the pleasure of knowing how much she tires me out, am I? How about the day after tomorrow? I'll go light with the exercises, and then we can have a walk in the garden"

Still with a bemused expression, Callie says, "Well, I suppose. I hope you're feeling better about things then."

She's suspicious. But I think I'm okay. "Oh, I'm sure I will be. I'm regaining strength more and more as each day passes."

She gives me a skeptical look but drops the issue and entertains me with stories from the previous week of Ashley's dance recital and the two goals Danny scored for his junior soccer team.

The following day, after the rehab work, Amélie leaves me at a table on the cafeteria patio. I watch her disappear inside, push my chair back, and try my damndest to look casual as I start toward the path on the right side of the dry dock. When I reach the row of small trees that will hide me from the people on the patio, I give a quick, "Ha!" and continue to the short flight of steps that take me to the Harbor Walk which meanders behind the buildings that front First Avenue. My nerves are on edge. I'm startled when a powerboat pilot guns his engine. A flock of seagulls squawk and scatter into the air as I pass. I hurry as fast as I can. My shoes scrape against the cinder path and I am breathing too hard and I pass the Shipyard Quarters Marina where halyards slap against masts as the wake from that powerboat passes under them. They mimic my jangled nerves. More seagulls circle above me with their cries, *Kyieeee, Kyieeee.* When the path turns from cinder to a boardwalk, my back can't take it anymore. I must rest for a few moments. To my right is a length of heavy chain suspended along a row of posts in sags and peaks like telephone wires. I lean my butt against one of the posts, but it is too high and hard-edged. I should have stopped at the bench I passed half a football field back! I try to sit on the catenary of the chain, but it swings precariously. There is a flap of wings and a seagull lands on a heavy, black bollard opposite me which offers a rounded, smooth top. I struggle to my feet, cross the boardwalk, and shoo the damned seagull away. It flies off with an angry squawk. A squirrel scampers along the boardwalk and dashes into some bushes. The bollard is comfortable, and at last I can rest. Out in the harbor, I see cat's paws raised by the thready wind. After several minutes and some deep breathing exercises, I rise and resume walking toward my condo. My cane taps rhythmically on the boards. I pass Constellation Wharf, and then Pier 6, before finally arriving at the Flagship Wharf condominiums. As I walk into the lobby, the doorman greets me with, "Mister Budge! We didn't expect you back so soon. Welcome home. How are you feelin'?"

"Thank you, Jim," I say. "It's good to see you. Would you mind calling me a taxi and seeing that he waits?"

"Certainly. Where shall I say you're going?"

"Just downtown. I'll give him specifics when I'm in the cab."

Up in my condo, I make a quick phone call to Cunard to learn where exactly I must go to board the *Queen Mary 2*. I throw some clothes into a suitcase and rush out the door. I can buy more clothes aboard if need be. I am tempted to stop in Maddie and Ted's condo to see Arlequin, but last night I told Maddie I would be another week or two at Spaulding Rehab. Besides, it has already been nearly a half hour since I left the hospital and, soon, somebody is bound to realize I am missing. They know where I live. I must be in the cab, and on my way, before they track me down. I drag my suitcase out of my condo and, by the time I reach the lobby, Jim has a taxi waiting. I climb into the cab and wait until we pull away from Jim before I say, "South Station, please."

An hour later, I am downing an Angus steak burger and a half bottle of wine at my seat on the Acela Express and, a little more than three hours later, the train is pulling into Penn Station where I catch a taxi to the Waldorf-Astoria.

⁂

Even in the slow, wood-fueled Citroën, the journey from Montignac to Aquilac should have taken no more than four hours by main roads. But Élodie chooses to travel further east and use secondary roads, hoping to avoid encounters with those Germans who have not yet gone north to Normandy. We circle north of Rodez, then turn south between Rodez and Millau. We travel in silence for the first hour or so, and I marvel at how distant the war seems as we negotiate the lonely, narrow roads between farm fields where neatly rolled bales of hay dot the land. In several fields, we see tan-colored cattle with long, lyre-shaped horns, that Élodie says are called Aubrac.

"They're used mainly for beef," she says. "But farmers also use their milk to make Laguiole cheese. It's wonderful. Rich and creamy. Maybe we can find some for you to try."

"In the middle of the war?"

"We can't let the war dominate everything."

I say nothing, but this gives me hope she won't insist on escorting me out of France. I don't care what happens. I only want to be with her. Occasionally, we slow to pass a horse-drawn cart, or stop to wait for a flock of sheep to cross the road.

Eventually, she says, "Do you remember the Roquefort cheese we had with Monsieur and Madame Bosquet?"

I nod. "Kind of crumbly with a bite to it."

"It comes from those sheep. The breed is called Lacaune."

I smile. "Suddenly you're a tour guide."

She shrugs "I suppose I just want you to know the real France. France without the fucking, goddamned war."

For some insane reason, it makes me happy to hear her cuss in English. I look out the window to see the France she loves. "It's certainly peaceful."

"Look at those fields," She says. "No bomb craters, no burnt-out buildings. You would never know there was a war on."

We drive on for another hour before stopping where the road borders a deep gorge. Away from the edge is a copse of trees that hide us, and the car, from sight. Here, we break out the bread and wine Georges Bosquet has given us. Élodie rips off a chunk from the loaf and tears a piece off with her teeth. Crumbs fall from her lips as she asks, with what seems studied nonchalance, "Have you ever been in love, Henry?"

I'm thrilled every time she pronounces my name. *Uhnree.* "I've already told you I'm in love. With you."

"Yes. But, haven't you ever thought about it at all? It seems to me you could make some girl wonderfully happy."

"I think …. Wait! Where have I heard those exact words before?"

"*It Happened One Night* with Clark Gable and Claudette Colbert, perhaps?" she asks with a coy smile.

"Yes, of course. They played that movie constantly when I was in England. I must have seen it at least seven times."

"I know. You don't remember telling me that?"

"No. When did I tell that?"

"You were probably drunk on wine, or morphine, and have forgotten. And I told you I also have seen it many times. I told you Claudette Colbert was born in Saint-Mandé, near where I lived in Paris."

"Yes. Now I remember. I was—"

"I lived there with Mama and Papa." All at once, her countenance darkens and her voice is almost a whisper.

"You've suffered such a great loss," I say, putting my arm around her shoulders.

She leans her head against my chest. "Bugger all," she says, her voice muffled. "I hate this bloody, awful war! I wish those farmers could just make their cheese, and tend their cows, without worrying about being shot by Germans."

I squeeze her shoulders. We stay like this for several moments until Élodie reaches for the bread and pulls off a piece and hands it to me. "So, *have* you been in love? Have you ever thought about it at all? It seems to me you could make some girl wonderfully happy."

She's testing me. "Sure, I've thought about it. If I would ever meet the right girl, somebody that's real, alive. Sure, I've thought about it. I've even been fool enough to make plans. You know, I saw an island in the Pacific once. I've never been able to forget it. That's where I'd like to take this girl."

She wags a finger at me. "You missed some lines. Also, Clark Gable said, 'I've even been *sucker* enough,' not *fool* enough, to make plans."

"Your memory is that good?" I ask.

She nods and tears off another piece of bread. "I have *mémoire photographique.*"

"Photographic memory?"

"Aha! You see. Already you are learning French! So, Monsieur Henry, what sort of girl would this be?"

"Let's see. The kind of girl who would jump in the water with me."

"Surf," she says. "Clark Gable said, 'surf.'"

"Yes, right. Surf. And love it as much as I did."

"And the nights, Monsieur Henry?" Her eyes sparkle.

"I can't remember," I say. "Give me a hint."

"Nights when you and the moon and the water all become one and the stars—"

"And the stars are so close you feel you could reach up and touch them. Boy if I ever found a girl who was hungry for those things, I'd … I'd …."

Élodie leans closer and says, "You'd swim in the surf with her, you'd reach up and grab stars for her, you'd laugh with her, you'd cry with her, you'd kiss her wet lips." She offers her lips and we kiss.

"Yes, that's exactly what I'd do," I say.

She breaks into a laugh. "Monsieur Henry, you are such a romantic!" Laughter like wind chimes. "Will you take me with you to this little island? I want to do all those things with you. I want to celebrate the end of this war with you. I want to grow old with you. I want you to take me to Hollywood, so I can see what Claudette Colbert saw. Then we can go to our little island in the Pacific."

"I know just the island," I say. "My grandfather gave me an old book of his. It was about the three voyagers of Captain Cook, and there was a long section about Tahiti. *That's* where I want to take you."

"Perfect!" she says. "I fell in love with Tahiti by studying the paintings of Paul Gauguin. The 'Women of Tahiti,' 'Joyousness,' 'The Repas,' '*Eau Mystérieuse*,'[39] '*Et l'or de leurs corps.*'[40] We'll drink mysterious water and live forever, and our bodies will become golden."

"Our bodies will become golden and we'll play in the surf," I say.

"Yes, we'll play in the surf."

"And there will be no more killing."

"No more killing."

"And the moon and water will become one with us."

"Then it's settled. When the war is over we'll move to Tahiti and grow old together and however old we become, our bodies will forever remain golden!"

It should be a happy thought, but our eyes are moist. Both of us. And she reaches out and her fingers feel like shy caresses on my skin and I see a tear spill onto her cheek. I wipe it away as I choke back my own tears. And then it's time to get back on the road.

We're quiet as we resume our journey south, skirting population centers like Millau, Saint-Georges-de-Luzençon, Saint-Affrique and, certainly, Castelnaudary where there are doubtless Germans. Élodie says Aquilac is too close to Toulouse—where there is also a major German presence—for us to take chances, so we give Toulouse a wide berth and approach Aquilac from the south. At nightfall, a few kilo-meters from the village, we hide the car in an abandoned barn and wait for the morning. There is not enough moonlight to drive into Aquilac, and it is too dangerous to use headlights.

---

39   Mysterious Water
40   And the Gold of Their Bodies

The stone walls of the barn are mostly in good repair, but the wooden roof has large gaps through which we can see an extravagance of stars. In the northeast sky is the "W" of Cassiopeia, and not far from it, the Northern Cross. Polaris is plainly visible, as is the broad ribbon of the Milky Way.

"You seem to know the area," I say.

She nods. "I grew up just west of here and know many of the people in Aquilac. Also, I've given some duo concerts with Aliénor Breasiac. She's a pianist from Aquilac. Quite famous."

"What kind of concerts?"

"Standard classical repertoire. Bach, Bartók, Schuman, Ravel."

"Two country girls make it big on the world stage?" I say.

"That's one way to say it. But this war ruins it all."

"The war will end," I say. "Germany can't hold out much longer."

She frowns. "I wouldn't be so confident. I think it will take at least another year or two. And then, when it ends, will we even be able to go back to the way it was before? If we survive, that is."

I kiss her on the forehead. "We'll survive," I say bravely. Later, we finish the wine Georges Bosquet gave us. In the distance, the last of the light lingers on the peak of a mountain. Élodie tells me it is the Pic de Saint-Barthélemy. I take her into my arms. "How about a little snogging?"

We fall back and make love and sleep lightly until we hear the morning twitter of swallows, the plaintive call of a dove, the low of a cow, the crow of a cock. I yawn and stretch, and look up at the sky.

"The war could be on another planet."

"We should go quickly," Élodie says. "Perhaps we can get to the home of the Duponts before anyone sees us. It's on the edge of the woods. We'll cut through the trees."

"You said you know these people?"

"Very well. They are lovely people. You'll see."

Outside the barn, a low fog creeps over the farm fields at knee level. In the distance, the summit of Pic de Saint-Barthélemy is bathed in a golden light. We move stealthily through the trees. Only the snaps of twigs under our feet threaten to reveal our presence, but the sound is drowned out by the twitter of song birds and the squawk of crows. In the distance, a dog barks. The rising sun creates a blinding aureole of brightness at the perimeter of the woods. We emerge a hundred feet from the Dupont house, our long shadows stretching before us. We are startled when a door flies open.

"*Qui est là?*"[41] The questioner is a stocky woman in her 50s with a yeasty countenance and kind eyes.

"It's me, Odette. Élodie Bedier."

"*Élodie! Mon dieu! Est-ce que vraiment tu?*"[42]

"Yes. It's truly me."

"But why do you speak English?"

"I have an American with me," Élodie replies. She turns to me and says, "Before the war Odette taught beginning English."

Odette Dupont rushes to greet us. "Élodie! Élodie! It is so good to see you after so long a time." She kisses Élodie first on one cheek, then the other.

Élodie introduces me to Odette and says, "We have a message for Ruth and Elsie Benjamin. Isaac wants them to know he's alive and well."

"You saw him?"

"Along with Auguste Pauly and several others. They are all well."

"I am relieved to hear it." She pauses, then asks, in a low voice, "Did they tell you about my house?"

"Obviously, we know you are sheltering Ruth and Elsie Benjamin and we know they are Jewish. It's very dangerous."

"War is dangerous," Odette says. "Isaac wanted them to escape and go to England, but they refuse to leave him."

"They are brave."

"Perhaps too brave. It has become much more dangerous in recent weeks. It's as if the allies have poked a ... *comment on dit, nid de frelons?*"[43]

"A hornet's nest," Élodie says.

---

41   Who is there?

42   Élodie! My god! Is it truly you?

43   How does one say, hornets' nest?

"Yes, it's as if they have poked a hornets' nest. The Boche have increased their efforts to send as many Jews to the camps in the east as possible. They are crazed. You've come at just the right time. I don't know what to do."

"What do you mean, the right time?"

"Auguste and Isaac didn't tell you about the children?"

"No. What children?"

"Children sent to us by their parents, some who were bound for the concentration camps. In some cases, the parents were sent to Drancy."

"Drancy?" I ask.

Élodie turns to me. "It's an internment camp near Paris. Jews are kept there before being deported to concentration camps in the east. The rumors say they are extermination camps. We know of Auschwitz and Dacau. There are others."

"I fear they are not rumors," says Odette. "I think many are killed as soon as they arrive at those death camps. Most of the children hiding here have no idea where their parents are. I, for one, think the worst. And now the Nazis will want to finish the job by sending the children to their deaths. That's why we need your help."

"What can we do?" asks Élodie.

"You must escort them over the Pyrénées. Like you've done with the airmen."

"The children?"

"*Oui. Les enfants.*"

"How many are there?"

"Eleven."

"Eleven! We can't take eleven children. They'll never fit in the car."

"What car?"

"We have an old, wood-burning Citroën."

"Impossible! The Boche are all over the main roads up the Ariège valley."

"False papers? A train?" Élodie asks.

Odette shakes her head. "Several of them have already experienced the trains, and being caught, and having to escape again. They are far, far too fearful. *Ce n'est pas possible!*[44] They would panic if they saw guards, or the Gestapo. Also, the Boche are watching the trains much more closely now, since the invasion. And, besides, some of the children began their journeys in horrible ways that have left them so very vulnerable. For example, the three Godowsky children were smuggled out of a ghetto in coffins. Can you imagine how frightening that would be for such young children, to be placed in a coffin and having the lid closed? And there is Kamilá Brodny and her brother Józef: They escaped under piles of potatoes in carts. Some of the other carts were stopped and men poked through the potatoes with bayonets. They heard the screams of other children as they died but, somehow, they were spared. There are other stories. No, no, no. For all these reasons, you must walk. The children are too vulnerable. It will be very difficult. Some of the children might die."

"But my American friend was wounded in the leg. It hasn't completely healed."

"That can't be helped." Odette looks me up and down as if examining my worth. "You mentioned a car. Where is it?"

"Behind your barn."

"We must hide it," Odette says. She hurries to the door of her house and calls inside, *"Gaston! Viens ici, s'il te plaît."*[45]

Moments later, a stout man appears. He carries a wood gouge and wears an apron on which curls of wood shavings cling. He brushes his hair and one or two shavings fall to the floor like oversized dandruff. He nods and greets Élodie with a broad smile. *"Bonjour, Élodie."* He turns to me. *"Bonjour, Monsieur."*

Élodie explains that I am American and that I don't speak French. Gaston shrugs. Odette speaks to Gaston, and Élodie turns to me. "Gaston is going to hide the car in the barn."

After Gaston leaves, Élodie asks, "The children, how old are they?"

"The youngest is three, the oldest is twelve."

"May we see them?"

---

44   It's not possible!
45   Gaston! Come here please.

"Not yet," Odette replies. "If you see their sad, anxious faces it would put too much pressure on you to say yes. Besides, it might also raise their hopes needlessly."

I ask, "Are there others who can take the children?"

"Everyone who is fit enough is with the *maquis* fighting the Boche or has betrayed us by joining the Milice. And, in any case, the journey over the Pyrénées must be done two or three more times."

I don't understand and ask, "Why two or three more times?"

"I hear, through my network, others are on the way to me. That's another reason you must take the children who are here now. We need to create more room."

I look at Élodie, then back at Odette. "Then the decision is made. Isn't it?" I say. "Bring us to the children."

Odette hesitates. I feel her studying me, considering her options. Finally, she says, "They are in the hidden cave. We must climb the hill."

I turn to Élodie. "The hidden cave?"

"It cannot be seen from the village," she says. "It's where young lovers have always gone to be alone together."

"Were you one of these young lovers?" I ask with a smile.

She pokes me in the ribs. "You ask too many questions."

We climb through stands of chestnut trees along a path dappled with sunlight. Élodie puts out a hand and urges me to walk more slowly so we are beyond whispering distance from Odette. When she is satisfied Odette cannot hear us, she asks, "Do you fully understand what this means for you?"

"I'm not sure what you're getting at," I say.

"My mission was to escort you out of France so you could rejoin your American comrades."

"Yes. But taking the children will only delay it."

"You don't understand."

"I do understand. What you don't understand is I'm not in as much of a hurry as I was before."

"Why?"

"I don't know. Oradour. These children who have no one else to take them. You. Especially you...."

Élodie shakes her head, brushes a lock of hair from her forehead. I see her hand is trembling. "What if after these eleven, there are another eleven? And then after them, yet another eleven?"

"What about it?" I say, taking hold of her hand. "If you need the help, I'll be there for you."

"No, you still don't understand. A few weeks for the first group. A few more weeks after that for the next group. A few more weeks after that. At what point do you turn from being missing-in-action, to becoming a deserter?"

"A deserter?" A squirrel scampers across our path and into the underbrush.

"It could be said you are fighting with a foreign force. The Resistance is not considered regular French Army. We may be allies, but you will still be fighting for a foreign force without permission from your superiors. If the American army is like most armies, that will count as desertion, and we both know what the penalty for that is in a time of war. A firing squad! You must give this serious thought. They will *shoot* you!"

I smile and shrug. "Nobody's perfect."

"I hate you! How can you be so—I don't even know what the fucking, goddamned English word is—*blasé?*"

"I think it's 'blasé'."

"It's the same word?"

"Yeah, I think so," I say. "I think we borrowed it from you French."

"Seriously, Henry. They could execute you."

"Of course, they could."

"And that doesn't worry you?"

"Sure, it does. But there's nothing I can do about it now. We can't leave the children to the Nazis. That's simply out of the question. I'd have to turn in my membership card to the human race. So, I'll just have to deal with it when the time comes. I'll make up some story. Hell, it's only a problem if I survive, anyway!"

Élodie stares at me but says nothing, and then we continue up the hill without a word. When we catch up to Odette, who has paused to recover her breath, I look behind me. In the distance, I see Saint-Barthélemy, and, beyond, the snow-draped Pyrénées. "Do the mountains ever lose their snow?" I ask.

"Not usually above three thousand meters," says Élodie. "Even in July there's snow."

"And we'll be crossing them?"

"Yes. But the passes should be clear unless there was more snow than usual."

"How far are they from here?"

"To the other side? Spain? About a hundred kilometers."

"Hmm."

"Yes," Élodie says with a grim sigh. "It's a dreadful undertaking. Especially with your leg."

"As the lady said, that can't be helped."

"Then you will do it?" Odette asks, looking back and forth at the two of us. "You have made your decision?"

"We have made our decision," I say. "We'll take the children."

Élodie narrows her eyes at me, and I reach for her hand and give it a squeeze.

Odette nods, turns, and heads into the cave as she calls out. "It's all right. You can all come and meet some very nice people."

In small groups of two or three—and singly—eleven children move toward the mouth of the cave, squinting and shading their eyes from the harsh sunlight. They stare silently, suspiciously, at Élodie and me.

Odette says, "We have several nationalities here. Most of them speak no French and, of course, no English, except for Max Jäger, here, and another boy I'll introduce you to." She places a hand on the shoulder of a thin, blond boy. "He's the oldest, at twelve. He's German."

Max looks at me and asks, "Are you taking us away?"

I nod. "Yes. Out of France. To safety."

"Well, I shall help you with the other children and I shan't permit myself to cry because my mum told me to be strong."

"Your mum?" I ask.

Max squares his shoulders. "My mum was British. But she was put on the train to Drancy all the same." His voice quavers but he does not cry.

I turn to Élodie. "The internment camp near Paris?"

"Yes. Really, a transit camp where they stay whilst waiting for a train to take them east to the other ... camps."

Odette steps forward. "I'll introduce you to the rest of the children. "This is Jerzy Godowsky and his sisters Elżbietá and Klará. He's ten and they are eight and seven. They fled Poland after their parents were arrested. They have no idea what happened to them after that. They speak only Polish." The three children stand close together. The boy, in the middle, has his arms around his sisters. All three children have blond hair.

Odette stands behind two smaller children, a hand gently on each head. "This is Kamilá Brodny and her brother Józef. They, also, are Polish. She's seven and he's six. They, too, speak only Polish."

The boy, Józef, approaches and wraps his arms around my right leg and says, "*Tata?*"

His sister reaches for her brother and pulls him back, shakes her head, and says, "*Nie!*"

Odette says to me, "He wanted to call you Papa, or Daddy. His sister said, 'No.'"

I tousle the boy's hair and let my hand rest on his head.

Odette places her hands on the shoulders of a boy and girl who are standing together. "This is Rebekka and Stephan Weiß. She is eight and he's seven. They come from Vienna and have been on the run since their parents were arrested shortly after the *Anschluss.*[46] Apparently, no one knows what happened to their parents."

Élodie smiles, says, "*Grüß Gött.*"[47]

Apparently surprised she greeted them in their southern German dialect, they reply, "*Grüß Gött.*"

---

46   The "joining." Refers to the forcible annexation of Austria by Nazi Germany.

47   The common greeting in southern Germany and Austria. You can tell where a person comes from according to whether the greeting is *Guten Tag (Northern Germany/Prussia), Grüß Gott* (Southern Germany/Austria) *or Grüezi (Switzerland)*

In a low voice, Odette says, "Rebekka went to a local, private school in Vienna where the headmaster arranged for a bonfire into which he threw all texts written by Jews. The man then tied Rebekka to a tree and ordered the other girls in the class to file past her and spit in her face. She won't talk about it. Stephan told me."

Élodie frowns, and I can see the muscles working in her cheeks as she tries not to cry—or scream.

"Son of a bitch!" I say under my breath.

Odette next introduces us to two sisters, Leni and Renata Gottfried from Dusseldorf who are five and six years old. She eases forward an older boy, Aron Klotz from Zitau in Saxony, who is ten. "Zitau is on the border with Poland, so Aron speaks Polish and English as well as his native German. That will help with the five Polish children."

Suddenly, there comes a loud, metallic crash. Leni and Renata Gottfried, backing away from Élodie and me, have knocked two milk cans from a shelf. As the cans roll across the floor with repeated clangs, the smallest child runs away from them in circles, flailing her arms, her mouth open in a silent scream, her eyes wide with fear. Odette reaches down and takes the little girl's hand. "No, no. It's all right, Mitzi. Don't be afraid," she says soothingly. "Do not be afraid. *N'ais pas peur.*" She looks up at Élodie and me, and says, "Of course, she probably does not understand English, or French. We think she's German."

Élodie crouches before the girl and says, "*Fürchte dich nicht.*"[48]

The girl brings a finger to her mouth and stares at Élodie.

"Her name is Mitzi," Odette says. "That's why we think she is German, but that's only a guess. We know nothing of her parents or where she comes from. She appears to have been adopted by other children as they traveled. It was Aron and Max who brought her to us. We are guessing she is about three. As you can see, she is afraid of loud sounds. I think she must have witnessed bombing. And she doesn't talk, poor girl."

Élodie bends down and lifts the girl in her arms, but the girl struggles and reaches out to me. Élodie smiles and passes the child to me. "I guess she wants a man. She must have loved her papa."

---

48   Do not be afraid.

Odette points to a small pile of backpacks and canteens. "You'll need these. There are just enough for you two, and the older children. They would be too heavy for the younger children in any case."

"How did you collect all this?" Élodie asks.

"From dead maquisards. If they can no longer fight, their kit will. But for the littlest one, we must improvise."

"Yes," Élodie says. "It's unimaginable she could walk all that way."

"That will be no problem," I say. "We'll just take the largest rucksack and cut holes in the bottom for Mitzi's legs."

An hour later, we are gathered with the children in the Dupont's roomy kitchen. Gaston has spread a large map out on the table and he, Élodie, and I study it while Odette cuts leg holes in one of the rucksacks and sews extra layers of cotton to the edges of the holes to guard against chaffing.

"Now for their protection against the weather," says Odette. She shows us a scrap of material and says, "Pascal Bibaud, a house painter who lives in the next village, gave me *des bâches*. I don't know what it is in English."

"I think 'tarpaulin'?" Élodie says, looking at me for confirmation.

I feel the material between thumb and forefinger and nod. "Tarpaulins, or painter's drop cloths."

"They will protect the children from the rain," Odette says. "Ruth and Elsie Benjamin helped me make ponchos with … *des capuches?*"

"Rain hoods," says Élodie. "Brilliant. Well done, you!"

"Pascal said nobody can afford to paint these days anyway," Odette says. "It's best the children stay warm and dry. But what about you two?"

"We have American army-issue ponchos," Élodie replies. "Henry has his own and I have one I took from a dead paratrooper."

"Good," Odette says with a business-like nod. "You'll probably need them because the escape route was designed mainly for British and American airmen. With the children, you won't be able to move nearly as quickly. It's likely the distance between the safe houses Gaston will be telling you about will be too great some of the time. You'll be forced to make *les bivouacs*. Do you understand my meaning?"

"It's the same word in English." Élodie says.

"Good." Odette hands me a dozen lengths of chord. "Gaston tells me soldiers can make small tents using this chord, the ponchos, and sticks planted in the ground."

"Yes, we've all done it."

"*Bon!*" Odette reaches on top of a cupboard and produces a large square of cotton. "For you, Monsieur Henry, since you will be carrying little Mitzi."

"What is it?" I ask, bemused.

Odette smiles. "*Une couche de bébé.*"

I shrug, look at Élodie who has a broad grin on her face. "What's goin' on?" I ask. "You look like Odette's put a bee in your bonnet."

Still smiling, Élodie says, "That's American slang. I don't know what it means, but I can tell you that *Une couche de bébé* is a nappy."

I shake my head. I'm still confused. Élodie continues. "In America, you call it a diaper. Since you will be carrying Mitzi, her needs become your responsibility."

My eyes widen. "Well, that's a lame-brained idea! What do I know about those things?"

Élodie laughs. "It will be alright. I'll help."

"You're serious!"

"Of course."

"Well doesn't that beat all?" I shake my head, amazed at the idea of me changing diapers along an escape route across the Pyrénées.

Odette, who looks like she's trying to suppress a fit of giggles, says, "Now you have all you need, Gaston will go over the route with you."

We sit at the table and Gaston begins tracing a path with a pencil as Élodie translates for me. "He says if we follow this route, it will give us the best chance of getting past the Germans. It offers at least three caves where we could possibly hide overnight plus find protection from the weather. They are la Grotte du Mas d'Azil and maybe La Grotte de la Vache or La Grotte de Niaux. 'Grotte' is 'cave' in English."

Gaston explains something to Élodie at length, after which she turns to me. "The first safe house is in a small commune called Lagrâce-Dieu, or Grace-of-God. It is the third house after the church, and a woman named Lombarda will be expecting us." She places a finger on the map.

"Gaston says it's important to stay west of Foix, here, because he thinks there are German units stationed there. And, also, west of Ax-les-Thermes where he knows, for certain, German officers go to use the baths. But that should be no problem. Our route is never closer than thirty kilometers to those places."

"And they are the only places he knows for certain where there are Germans?" I ask.

"As far as he knows. But he can't be sure."

"He doesn't sound all that confident."

"He's just being realistic. In case you haven't already realized it, this is a very dangerous proposition."

"So, after this Grace of God, what is the rest of the route?"

"We'll only know it a stage at a time. Lombarda, which by the way is a code name, will tell us about the next safe house when we see her. That way, if anyone is caught by the Nazis, they could only expose one link in the chain.

We decide to wait until evening before slipping out of Aquilac under cover of darkness. Our plan is to spend the first night in an abandoned barn two kilometers west of Aquilac from where we will start our journey early the following morning on paths well out of sight of the main roads. While we wait, Odette, defying all prohibitions and food rations, prepares a large pot of the cassoulet for which she and the area are, I'm told, famous. Normally it will contain white beans, duck confit, garlic, onions, carrots, ham hocks, white wine, and pork sausages, but she adds more duck and leaves out the ham hocks and pork sausages. When Gaston complains, she says, *"Mais, les enfants sont juifs!"*

I look to Élodie when everyone laughs. She says, "Gaston complained because she left out the ham and pork and she reminded him that the children are all Jewish."

Finally, when everybody is fed, and daylight is seeping from the sky, we prepare to leave for the abandoned barn. Odette lifts Mitzi and places the toddler on my back with her legs through the holes of the rucksack. Mitzi wraps her arms around my neck and puts her cheek against mine. I reach back and pat her on the head. After a few rounds of cheek kisses, Élodie and I slip out of the house, edge round to the back, and set out along an ancient, barely perceptible track toward the abandoned barn. We are surrounded by the younger children, some of whom want their hands held, while Max, Jerzy and Aron—the ten- and twelve-year-olds—lead the way.

Though the sun has disappeared, it has left footprints in the sky, splotches of pink-rimmed clouds, and, in the distance, sunlight still sits on the snowfields of the Pyrénées. Once we arrive at the barn, we find the excitement has left many of the children sleepless and cranky, and it is several hours before Élodie and I can sleep. Also, the presence of several bats keeps everyone on edge. But finally, everyone is asleep. And Élodie and I soon follow.

After a fitful night, we rise long before light, step outside and study the night sky. To the west, Jupiter and Mars are low on the horizon. The "W" of Cassiopeia is in the north, and in the northeast the arms of the Northern Cross hover over us.

Élodie folds her arms across her chest, shivering, and I put my arms around her and pull her close. "I've been watching Mars the last few nights," I say. "I think it's in retrograde."

"What makes you say that?"

"It seems to be closer to Cassiopeia than it was. Like it's moved eastward."

"Perhaps," she says. "All I know is it's a good thing there's moonlight. We can be on the trail south before dawn, and well out of sight of the roads."

I kiss the top of her head. "I'll wake the children."

In the first, fragile moments of morning, with moonlight still pawing the ground and before the day has gathered strength, we begin our journey southward toward the Pyrénées.

❦

New York City sits beneath a bright and sunny afternoon when the doorman at the Waldorf-Astoria waves down a taxi for me. "Brooklyn Cruise Terminal," I tell the driver. The people at Cunard suggested I arrive at the terminal by two in the afternoon for the five o'clock sailing.

A half hour later we pull up to the cruise terminal. I pay the driver, step from the cab, look up at the bow of *Queen Mary 2* towering above me, and smile. It takes me over an hour to go through the check-in process. Finally, I cross the gangplank, find my cabin, and unpack. I sit for a while in a lounge chair on the balcony of my cabin to catch my breath. It's been a little more strenuous than I'd anticipated.

There is an emergency drill at 4 o'clock during which I find my way to my assigned muster station. But after that, I am free to stroll the observation deck and watch the departure.

A deep-throated rumble from the ship's horn—a characteristic bass A as if tuning an orchestra of giants—signals our departure. With the band playing, Glenn Miller's "Moonlight Serenade," we pass the Statue of Liberty, and soon travel under the Verrazano Narrows Bridge and into the open Atlantic. My back aches and my legs are beyond tired, but I don't want to miss the departure.

At last, an hour later, in the Todd English restaurant, aft on Deck 7, I settle into a comfortable chair. I choose the "Crispy Duck with a ginger sesame glaze served over root vegetables & sweet and sour cabbage" plus a half bottle of Beaujolais—far better than the hospital food that was part of my life the last several weeks. The duck makes me think of Odette Dupont and her cassoulet. Perhaps that's why I ordered it. No doubt she and Gaston are long dead. They had to be at least twenty years older than I. So many of the people I knew then are dead, I'm sure. I wonder about the children and I draw a sharp breath when I realize the youngest among them, Mitzi, would now be about 75. I shiver at the thought.

After dinner, and taking many breaks along the way, I stroll the deck further aft toward the stern where the red British ensign whips smartly in the breeze. On a deck below, I'm delighted to find a children's pool, and I lean on a railing and watch the children play. Their joyful shouts and laughter make me smile. I tilt my head back and look up into the night sky to find Mars. I don't know if it's in retrograde or not, but it makes me think of Élodie and those children and our long-ago southward journey, and I am filled both with anticipation and trepidation for what I might find in France. In my mind, I reach up with both hands, like a curator in a museum straightening a picture, and make sure the face of the moon is turned squarely toward me.

I'm still lost in these thoughts, when I'm startled by a voice over my shoulder. "I'm not at all surprised to find you here. You always loved the sound of children's laughter."

My heart jumps into my throat as I whirl around and fall back against the railing. "Callie!"

PART 2
MARS IN RETROGRADE

The ultimate test of a moral society is the
kind of world that it leaves to its children.
—Dietrich Bonhoeffer

She said, I'm tired of the war,
I want the kind of work I had before,
A wedding dress or something white
To wear upon my swollen appetite.
—Leonard Cohen

Chapter 10
The Carrots Are Cooked

I regain my balance and push myself off the railing. "What are you doing here?"

"I thought I'd keep you company." Her smile is devilishly self-satisfied. "But shouldn't the real question be: What are *you* doing here?"

I have no idea what to say. I stand dumbly, mouth agape.

"Never mind," she continues. "I know exactly what you're doing. At least you took our advice not to fly. Good move."

"But how the hell did you find me?"

Callie removes a slip of paper from her pocket and hands it to me. "You left this on the desk in your condo. I don't know, it almost seems like it was intentional." I look down at the paper, torn from the notepad I keep on my desk.

Cunard 800-728-6273
Brooklyn Cruise Terminal
72 Bowne Street, Brooklyn

Callie shakes her head. "One phone call was all it took to confirm what I suspected. And, yes, they did have some empty cabins."

"But what about Danny and Ashley?"

"Tom has them while I'm on vacation. I told you that before, but you were probably too busy planning your jailbreak to hear me. So, Papa, was it intentional?"

"What?"

"Leaving this slip of paper out where I was certain to see it."

"I forgot to take it with me. I'm an old man. I forget things."

"I'll bet you have another copy in your pocket right now."

I turn my pockets out to show they're empty. "Like I said, it was a mistake."

"Sure." She says slowly, appraising me with a skeptical eye. "Anyway, if you don't mind my company, I have three weeks."

"Goodness! Of course, I'd love your company."

"Good. I want to see what this D-Day ceremony is all about. I took the brochure from your desk where, as it happens, you had conveniently left it. And, by the way, I turned off your computer and unplugged it from the internet. You shouldn't leave it hooked up like that in case of lightning."

"I guess I just forgot. I was in a hurry."

"People pulling off a jail break usually are. You know, you're gonna have a fight on your hands with your insurance company when you get back. They don't take kindly to patients leaving against medical advice."

"I'll fight that battle when I come to it," I say. "Where is your cabin? Have you already paid for it? Can I help you with that?"

"An inside cabin on deck five. And no, thanks, Papa. I'm good."

"At least let me buy you a drink."

"Now *that*, I'll accept."

"Good. Let's take a walk. There's the Commodore Club near the bow, one deck up. And on this deck, just below it, is the library. I'd like to visit it first."

Callie smiles. "To see if they have any of your books?" She knows me well.

"Now, I didn't say that."

"You don't have to. I've seen you check out every library and bookstore you come across." She slips her arm in mine and we start walking along the teak deck.

"Guilty as charged," I say with a laugh. We walk to about midships when I say, "Let's take a break." I stop and lean against the rail.

"Tired?" she asks.

I nod.

"You only have yourself to blame. You busted out before they were finished buffing you up. I think we should spend some time together in the gym during the crossing."

I nod again and wait until I feel ready to continue our stroll.

When we arrive, I'm delighted to find that the library is surprisingly large and richly appointed. The bookcases are made of darkly polished wood and are divided into glass-door-fronted cubbies, presumably so the books won't fall out if the ship lists in heavy seas. Sofas and reading chairs are distributed throughout, some facing the windows over-looking the bow. Callie helps me search the bookcases, and we quickly find a copy of my *Reluctant Salvation: WWII Refugee Children and the Roosevelt Administration*.

"You should offer to sign it," Callie says.

"You don't imagine I ever miss a chance, do you?"

When I show the young librarian the book, and the embarkation card containing my picture, she says, "Yes, of course, Mister Budge. We'd be delighted if you would sign it. And I'll be sure to message the captain you're aboard. He always enjoys meeting famous guests."

Famous. I couldn't help a laugh at that.

The Commodore Club is lit in soft blue. A group of people are gathered around a piano, laughing and talking. A pianist plays show tunes. When Callie and I walk in, we hear the last notes of "Somewhere Over the Rainbow," before the pianist segues smoothly into "Memory" from *Cats*.

We take a table near a window overlooking the bow and page through a menu of drinks. "What the hell kind of drinks are these?" I ask. "Rhubarb mule, Secret Garden, Japanese Dynasty, Passion 'n' Orange smash? Can't I get a simple martini?"

Callie laughs. "Here you go," she says with affected snobbishness. "A Beluga vintage vodka martini with a dash of Noilly Prat to your taste." She turns the page. "Oh, my god! There are two pages of martinis!"

A waiter arrives and stands poised with order slip and pencil while Callie flips quickly through the menu and finally says, "I'll have a 'Crazy in Love.'"

"What in hell is that?" I ask.

Callie reads from the menu. "Stolichnaya Raspberry Vodka, Watermelon Syrup and Strawberry Purée, topped with Champagne. You should have one, too. Isn't that what this trip is all about? Crazy in love?"

I give her a sideways glance and look up at the waiter. "Can I get a simple martini?"

"Certainly, sir. What would you call a simple martini?"

"Bombay Sapphire, two olives?"

"Of course."

"There, see?" I say to Callie. While we wait for the drinks to arrive, we remain silent, listening to the music as the pianist transitions to "Life is a Cabaret."

At last, the drinks arrive. I take a sip and ask, "Did your mother know you were going to do this?"

"No. She didn't know. I called her after we left the pier. She was frothing at the mouth when she learned you skipped out of rehab. I think she was ready to sic the freaking Interpol on you. I expected she'd react like that, so when I deduced where you had gone—because you had so brilliantly left that piece of paper on your desk—I kept it to myself."

"Good girl! But, why did you call her after we left?"

"I figured if she knew I was with you, at least she wouldn't panic and call the police."

"What did she say when you told her?"

"She was apoplectic." Callie shakes her head. "Honestly, I've never heard her swear like that. Then she insisted I turn you right around when we got to England."

But I'm not listening to Callie. The pianist has taken a break, and one of the passengers from the group standing around the piano is now sitting at the keyboard playing "We'll Meet Again" as his friends sing along. I stare across the room with a tightness in my throat. Callie places her hand over mine. "Papa, where have you gone? What's wrong? You just went far, far away."

"She sang that," I say. "She taught the children to sing that."

"Who?"

For a brief instant, I see Élodie. She has the children gathered around her, enthralled. They are singing with her. I can almost hear them. "It was the last night," I say.

"The last night of what?"

"It was after Andorra."

"Do you mean Élodie?"

"Yes. Élodie. She taught the children to sing that song."

"What children?"

I shake my head. "Maybe later," I say. I'm not sure I want to get into all of that now. I pause, take a sip of my martini, and ask, "So, when your mother told you to turn us around as soon as we got to England, what did you say?"

"Not a chance, I told her." Callie replies. "I said I planned to stay with you through the Normandy ceremonies."

"... keep smiling through,
just like you always do
till the blue skies drive
the dark clouds far away ... "

I tear myself away from the song. "How did she react to that?"

"How do you think she reacted," Callie says with a snort. "She was royally pissed."

But I am still thinking about France, about the children, about Élodie. "What? I'm sorry. I wasn't listening," I say.

"I said she was royally pissed." Callie gives me a questioning look.

"Good!" I say, trying to sound bright. I glance up at the group around the piano. There are six middle-aged men, bleary eyed, top shirt buttons undone, bowties untied.

"When we get to England, I'll call to assure her you're okay," Callie says. "That should keep her at bay for a while."

"... so, will you please say "hello"
to the folks that I know..."

"Good plan," I reply. I glance up at the group again. "I saw her in person," I say.

*"... they'll be happy to know
that as you saw me go
I was singing this song."*

"Who? Élodie?"

"No. The song they're singing was sung by Vera Lynn. I saw her perform it."

"Who was she?"

"They called her 'the Forces Sweetheart.' She was a British singer who went around to bases to entertain the troops."

"Like Bob Hope?"

"Yes, like Bob Hope. I saw her in England twice before D-Day."

An elderly couple has joined the group and are dancing in the background. The man is still thin enough to wear his World War II uniform. Ivy leaves on his shoulder patch, the 4th Infantry Division, slogan: "Steadfast and Loyal." The guys who attacked Utah Beach. The guys for whom I was supposed to help take out the German 88s aimed at the beach. One of the men in the singing group raises a boisterous toast. "To the men of Normandy!" They clink glasses and say, "Here, here!"

"They're talking about you, Papa!" Callie exclaims.

I shrug. I don't know what to say. I don't want to say anything.

"I'm gonna tell them you're here." She starts to get up, but I grab her wrist.

"No, don't. I don't want to grandstand." *And they might ask too many questions.*

"Don't be silly. They'll love meeting you." She lifts her drink and walks over to the group at the piano. She speaks with them for several minutes, then returns, a satisfied smile on her face.

"Papa, they're members of a D-Day club."

"What the hell?" I say. "There's a D-Day club? What is it, some kind of fan club?"

"They're all history buffs. Two of them have read your books. Come say hello to them."

"I don't know," I say. I see the 4th infantry guy mingling with them.

"Oh, come on. They'll enjoy it. And it'll do you good."

Sometimes, Callie doesn't know when to give up, when to stop doctoring. With a sigh, I rise and shuffle to the piano group. They greet me with handshakes. A tall man—the one who had proposed the toast—says, "It's an honor to meet you, sir. All you guys of that generation are heroes."

Another man asks, "What unit were you with?"

Damn, I can't lie! "Eighty-Second Airborne," I say.

"Really? Wow! You guys really saw some action."

"I guess."

"Were you with the five-oh-fifth regiment? The one that captured Sainte-Mère-Église?"

"Sainte-Mère-Église?"

When I regain consciousness on the edge of the flooded field I reach down and feel the wound in my thigh and examine my hand in the spill of moonlight and it glistens with blood and I hear the dull blasts of 88 mm flak guns and the sporadic sharp mutter of machine-guns that seem to come from a great distance and it's as though when I jumped from the C-47, across the face of the full moon, I somehow jumped clear out of the war.

"Papa," Callie says, "the man was asking you about your unit."

"Yuh, the five-oh-fifth," says the man.

"Uh, no. I was with the five-oh-eighth." I pause, take a breath. "You guys seem to know your history."

"It's our hobby."

"Hobby?"

"Yuh. Didn't you guys in the five-oh-eighth miss your drop zone by quite a lot? Some of you up to ten miles away?"

"I guess."

"In fact, some of your guys even went missing. It must have been tough."

"I guess," I say. I reach behind me, find the arm of a chair, and lower myself into it. I take several deep breaths.

"Papa, are you okay?" Callie asks.

"Why aren't you wearing your uniform?" one of the men asks. "Lots of the vets wear their uniforms at the D-Day commemorations. Like John here."

"I'll be fine," I say to Callie. I look at the man standing above me. "I guess I don't like to draw attention to myself."

"That's understandable," the man says. He looks at Callie. "A lot of the veterans don't like to talk about their war experiences. It's not that they're hiding something. Isn't that true, Mister Budge?"

"I suppose."

"What was it like?"

"What was what like?"

"Missing the drop zone. How long did it take you to hook up with your buddies again?"

"I don't know. It was quite a while." I turn to Callie. "I'm very tired. I think I'll go to my cabin."

Callie nods. "I'll walk with you." She looks up at the men. "It was nice to meet you, but if you'll excuse us."

"Of course," the tall man says. "Maybe we can talk more tomorrow. Always love to talk with vets." Again, he raises a glass. "Here's to you, sir."

The others raise their glasses, clink them together. "Here, here!"

Callie and I start to leave, but the man from the 4th Infantry Division blocks our path. He extends his hand. "Private First Class John True, Fourth Infantry, Second Battalion, Eighth Infantry, Charlie Company" he says. "I went ashore at Utah on the first wave."

"You fellers did well," I manage to say.

"Despite incoming artillery. Freakin' eighty-eights. Way more than we expected."

"Yeah," I say, sliding past him. "Excuse me, but I really am very tired."

But Pfc. True again blocks my way. "That guy asked about Sainte-Mère-Église. I was there. After that, we took Cherbourg."

"Well done," I say, again making a motion to pass him.

But he continues. "We went on to help liberate Paris. Ernest Hemingway was with us. Imagine that! Then the Siegfried Line,

Hürtgen Forest in Belgium, the Battle of the Bulge, and we crossed the Rhine at Worms."

What can I say? "Sounds like you had one hell of a war. Now, if you'll excuse me, I really am very tired." Finally, I manage to slip past him and, moments later, Callie and I emerge onto the promenade deck and start to walk aft. I hold onto the rail as I walk, and after a few moments, we come to a wider area where deck chairs face the sea under lifeboats hanging from their davits. "Do you mind if I sit for a few minutes?"

"Of course not! I could see you were really getting tired in there."

"Yes."

"You seemed to be under some stress with those people."

"I guess it's like one of them said. Some of us vets don't like to talk about the war."

"Well, I'm gonna be watching you closely. I don't like that you were having trouble catching your breath. You may have done some damage by skipping out on your rehab."

"I'll be okay."

"Still, if you're having trouble tomorrow, I'm gonna ask for a tour of the medical facilities on this ship, and I'm gonna take you with me."

"I wonder about that man," I say.

"What man?"

"Private first class John True."

"Why? He seemed like a nice man to me."

"The guy managed to get promoted just once, from buck private to private first-class, while fighting all the way across Europe," I say with, I admit, a bit of a growl in my voice. "Christ, with so many combat casualties, guys were getting promoted left and right!"

"Papa, you sound positively angry and that's not like you."

"I'm sorry. Let's drop it."

"No. I'm not gonna drop it until you come clean. It's more than those D-Day groupies or Private True. You've gone somewhere profoundly sad."

As always, Callie is on to me. I stare out at the ocean for a long moment, glance up at the life boats suspended above us, and finally say, "You and I talked before about closure and grief."

"I remember."

"And I said there is no such thing as closure. There's only dealing with it better."

"But with Élodie, it isn't about closure. You said it's about a final chapter to your story."

I sigh and turn to look at her. "And learning to handle the grief better. But sometimes it's more difficult than at other times and those people brought me back to that time when I first lost her. The way it works is at first the grief makes you feel your life boat is swamped and you think you will surely sink. You bail like a body possessed, but it feels like you'll never catch up. Then slowly, over time, you're able to bail just enough to keep the boat afloat and eventually the waves of grief get smaller, but they are always there, and you're always bailing. And every so often there comes a giant wave and you're in danger of sinking again. That's when some people give up."

"And you've felt like that sometimes," Callie says. "That's what we talked about that day of the family gathering in Gloucester."

"Yes. But you need to have faith that the giant grief-wave is like the real ocean ones called freak waves. Like in that movie, *The Perfect Storm*. They pile up when several wave trains from different storms converge in the same place at the same time. It's like that with grief. Several things come together—a song, a sad movie, a memory, people unwittingly dragging you back to a painful time—all of it converging at once."

"The D-Day fans?"

"Yes, because that's when it all began with Élodie."

"Will you tell me the whole story? When it's not too painful, I mean."

"You'll be the only person I'll tell the story to in person ... without a bound memoir between us, that is."

❦

Moonlight silvers the tree trunks as Élodie and I lead the children down a meandering path to the riverbank. We wear our ponchos against the morning chill. Silently, we cross the ancient Roman bridge at the edge of the village which Élodie said has been long thought by the locals to be the gateway to the Pyrénées. But for this strange procession— white caped, tiny monks led by two taller monks in kaki—I hope the bridge is the gateway to life.

Once across the river, we turn south and follow the west bank of the Ariège along a path lined with smooth, gray beeches, gnarled oaks, and arched canopies of chestnuts. Cascading down from the melting snow fields of the Pyrénées, the river here is a little over fifty meters wide, and as it cataracts over rocks with a spumy roar, the moonlight transforms the roiling water into sprays of sparkling diamonds.

Now and then, we come to places where farm fields reach down to the river. In these places, Élodie and I gather the children into a tight group and lead them across the exposed field at a run. The first time we do this, I feel Mitzi bouncing on my back and laughing and squealing, *"Lauf, Papa! Lauf!"* It is the first time any of us has heard Mitzi speak.

"*Lauf* means run?" I ask Élodie.

"Yes," she replies. "Now at least we know, for sure, she is German."

With a lump in my throat, I reach behind me and pat Mitzi on the head. Élodie gives me a tender smile and I think this must be the way parents look at each other. Mitzi rests her head on my shoulder and murmurs, "Papa."

"Well, doesn't that beat all," I say to Élodie.

"It's brilliant!" Élodie says.

Max, the twelve-year-old British-German who has been lagging a little behind, says, "Some of the children are tired. Can we rest here for a little while? Just a little while?"

"Of course, Max," says Élodie. "Thank you for looking after the other children. Well done, you. And you should rest, too."

Max flashes her a smile of delight. "Isn't it cracking that Mitzi spoke?"

"Yes, it is, Max. It's brilliant."

Sitting in a circle under a broad-domed chestnut tree, we tear off pieces of the baguettes and cheese Odette has given us.

After a short break, we resume our journey. When we spot, in the distance, the church and castle of Vernet-les-Bains against the backdrop of the Pyrénées, we turn slightly to the west to avoid the cluster of buildings and follow narrow dirt roads limning the edges of farm fields. Thus, zigzagging from field to field, we finally arrive at the outskirts of Lagrâce-Dieu, a tiny commune where the first safe house is located.

"It's the third house after the church," Élodie says. "Stay with the children whilst I make sure everything is good."

I shake my head. "No. I should go in case there's trouble."

"Don't be daft! If there's trouble, I can deflect suspicion in three languages. You would be revealed instantly. Stop trying to be the protective male. Just make sure the children are hidden and they remain quiet."

She's right, of course. Reluctantly, I reach out and squeeze her hand. "Go, then."

A half hour later, Élodie returns with good news. "It's all clear. Follow me."

Lagrâce-Dieu is a tiny hamlet of no more than 100 or 200 people. The few people we see pay us no attention as we hurry past the house into an adjoining lambing shed where the woman, code name Lombarda, awaits us. *"Vite! Vite!"* she says with waves of her hand, ushering us through the door. She is a young, attractive woman. A boy and a girl stand at her hips and gaze at the children passing into the shed, some older, some younger, than they. The interior of the shed is a grid of drop pens, lambing jugs and creep feeders, all bedded with a thick floor of straw. In one corner is a large, rusted scale for weighing new-born lambs. Several water troughs sit on the floor.

Lombarda says, *"Je vais apporter un peu de soupe. Il est tout ce que je peux offrir."*[49] She pushes her children before her and they head toward the farmhouse.

Élodie translates for me. I nod and sweep the shed with my arm. "Where are the sheep?"

"Probably in the high pastures with her husband." Élodie explains to me the practice called transhumance by which livestock are moved from one grazing ground to another. "June is the right time for it."

---

49   "I will bring a little soup. It is all that I can offer."

Suddenly, there are squeals of delight from the two Polish girls, Elżbietá and Klará. Elżbietá cradles a long-haired, bushy-tailed, black-and-white cat, and Klará is stroking its head.

Élodie smiles and says, "All sheep farmers keep cats to protect the cheese from mice."

Lombarda and her daughter return with a large, ceramic soup tureen, a ladle and a dozen bowls and coffee cups of various sizes and shapes. The boy carries a huge wedge of cheese on a cutting board.

Lombarda ladles the soup into the bowls and cups and hands them out to the children. *"L'azinat,"* she says to Élodie who turns to me and says, "It's a specialty of the Ariège. Cabbage soup with carrots and potatoes. Usually it has pork and duck, but I doubt she is able to get meat of any kind these days."

The soup is, indeed, meatless. And thin. And not for the first time, I wonder how the people of France survive with such shortages. And I remember Odette Dupont's cassoulet and marvel again at her resourcefulness.

Élodie asks Lombarda a simple question: *"Où sont les moutons?"*[50] which launches the woman into a long, rambling narrative that brings tears to her eyes and ends with Élodie placing an arm around the woman's shoulders and holding her close while she sobs.

Élodie turns to me and says, "Her real name is Rachelle Monsigny. Her children are Adrien and Yvette. The sheep are not in the high pastures with her husband, as I had thought, because they were all confiscated by the Germans. Her husband, Yves, is at a work camp in Germany. He left last year as part of the so-called STO, the *Service du Travail Obligatoire.*[51] It's a Vichy program to recover prisoners-of-war. For every three men who go to Germany to do forced labor in factories and mines and so forth, the Nazis promise to release one prisoner. Lombarda's husband volunteered, hoping he could help get his brother released. But they're both still in Germany. She's invited you and me to join her in her house once the children are asleep. She has a little wine."

---

50 "Where are the sheep?"
51 Obligatory work service.

While the children are settling down to sleep, exhausted after the first day of the escape march, Élodie and I decide to bathe Mitzi and change her diaper. Neither of us having done it before, we struggle together, trying to improvise getting a fresh diaper on the little girl. But it keeps slipping down her legs. Finally, Rebekka Weiß, the eight-year-old Austrian girl, tells Élodie her mother used to take in children for care during the day and she taught Rebekka how to do it. The girl folds the flat diaper into a triangle, tucks one corner between Mitzi's legs and brings the other two together over her belly where she attaches them with a large safety pin. When she is finished, Mitzi smiles, reaches up to her and touches her lips. Rebekka looks at Élodie and asks, *"Was will sie?"*[52]

Élodie shrugs. *"Ein Kuss?"*[53]

Rebekka leans forward and plants a soft kiss on Mitzi's forehead, then abruptly turns and throws her arms around Élodie and bursts into tears and her shoulders shake and Élodie comforts her with caresses on her cheek and Rebekka's brother Stephan joins them and he, also, is crying and all the other children stare at them with sad expressions, some weeping in empathy.

"What is this all about?" I ask.

Élodie, a tear sliding from the corner of her eye, says, "Mitzi's mother must have kissed her every time she changed her nappy, so she asked Rebekka to do the same. Undoubtedly, that made Rebekka think of *her* mother, which made her cry. And Stephan, too. And the others. These children are so very, very fragile. It breaks my heart! Most of them don't know what happened to their parents and fear the worst. We must be extremely gentle with them."

I suddenly find it difficult to see as a bit of moistness tingles in my hardened, American, gun-carrying, paratrooper eyes.

An hour later, the children are asleep in the lambing shed, and Élodie and I slip out quietly. We cross the barnyard, which is puddled with moonlight. We hear the staccato, machine-gun cackle of the boreal owl

---

52   "What does she want?"

53   "A kiss?"

followed immediately by the scamper of a critter through the under-brush. A cool breeze, carrying a rumor of snow, streams down from the distant Pyrénées. We arrive at the farmhouse and knock quietly. The door opens almost instantly. Rachelle greets us with an anxious look. She motions us to the table where she has placed a bottle of wine and three glasses. She pours the wine. She hesitates, stares at Élodie and says, "*Je vous prie de m'aider.*"

Élodie translates. "She's begging our help."

"With what?" I ask.

Élodie turns to Rachelle and asks a question in French. Rachelle's reply takes a long time. When she finishes, she rises from the table and goes into the next room.

"She seems troubled."

"She is. She lied to us about why her husband volunteered to go to a German labor camp. It seems the local Vichy police were eager to show the Germans how good they could be at rounding up men for the forced labor camps. They were going from house to house and bullying men to volunteer. But the real problem came when they started sending women east. So, Rachelle's husband decided to volunteer to take the pressure off. He guessed they wouldn't visit if they knew he was already in Germany."

"That seems a drastic thing to do."

"He felt he had no choice. Rachelle, as it happens, is Jewish. They were desperately afraid she would be found out and sent not to a labor camp but to a death camp. And the strategy worked. Once they knew he was in Germany, they left her alone. But now, she feels time has run out on them."

"Why?"

"She asks a good question. With the allies continuing to break out from Normandy, what happens if Hitler feels he is losing? What if he becomes a cornered rat? They've already accelerated sending Jews eastward. She feels it will just get worse. The more Hitler loses, the more insane he'll become, and the more the killing of Jews will go on. And they'll start killing everybody, including the French workers in the labor camps. He'll see it as some sort of crazy Wagnerian *Götterdämmerung* in which everybody and everything dies. His own version of Armageddon. That last part, by the way, is *me* talking; I doubt Rachelle has ever heard of Wagner."

"I've heard of Wagner," I say. "But I don't know about that other thing."

"*Götterdämmerung?* It's the fall of the gods."

"Hitler thinks he's a god?"

"I don't know. Something like that, I suppose. In any event, Rachelle said we have no idea how impossible it is for her to sit at home and wonder if Yves will ever return. She said she will go crazy." Élodie pauses, places a hand on my cheek, takes a deep breath, and says, "Henry, she wants us to take her children with us." Her voice catches in her throat.

"What? Seriously? But, why?"

"Because she wants to go to Germany to find her husband."

"Is she crazy? Christ Almighty, how the hell would she do that?"

"Being part of the underground network, she knew where to get papers forged. She has false birth and baptism certificates, I.D. cards, even food stamps, for both her and her husband. She plans to travel backwards along the chain of safe houses until she reaches Essen in Germany."

"That's nuts! She'll never make it!" I can't believe the woman could even conceive of such a hairbrained plan."

"Please don't raise your voice."

"I know, sorry, but—"

"She's desperate."

"And her kids?"

"She knows how dangerous it is. She doesn't want to expose them to that."

"So, they come with us?"

"What choice do we have?"

I say nothing. Again, she's right.

Élodie takes a long drink of her wine. "I tried to talk her out of it, but all she said was, *Les carottes sont cuites.*"

"Meaning?" I ask.

"Literally, the carrots are cooked. It means it's too late to change things."

"The die is cast."

"Yes. That's what you say in America. In short, she's made up her mind."

Moments later, Rachelle reappears and shows us the documents she's had forged. She insists we examine each one as if to prove to us her plan is feasible. And, once more, she begs us, in a whispered voice, to take Yvette and Adrien with us. She promises they are good children, full of love and compassion, who will get along well with the others. Adrien, especially, she says, is a sweet boy who loves all animals, especially dogs. She tells us he may well adopt one of the many stray dogs that wander the war zones and that the companionship would be good for him. When Élodie says, yes, Yvette and Adrien can join our company, she hugs Élodie, then me. And, after another glass of wine, Élodie and I return to the lambing shed and the children.

⚗

We are woken in the morning by the loud wailing of two children who, apparently, have just discovered a new darkness in the world, and a mother's voice coming across the barnyard, tearfully imploring, full of grief. I need no translation. I feel the agony like a weight on my shoulders, or like a small bird trapped in my breast. And when Rachelle appears with Yvette and Adrien, the eyes of all three are red and moist. Élodie and I embrace Rachelle and gently usher all the children, now thirteen in number, out of the lambing shed and into the harsh moon-light. Yvette and Adrien move slowly, gazing over their shoulders at their mother until we turn a corner and they can no longer see her.

A short time later, at the far end of a neighboring field, in the soft early morning light, we see a farmer herding some of the sheep he's managed to save from confiscation into an enclosure. Only the heads of his sheep are visible above a ground fog. He, himself, seems to float with no lower body. He gives no sign he notices us. I realize we, ourselves, must be a strange sight with most of our charges hidden by the same ground fog as we set out for the next safe house in a tiny village called Sainte-Aimée on the Lèze River where we are to seek out a local priest named Peire Basc.

Chapter 11
The Sheep and the Rose

As we had arranged the night before, I sit at a table in the King's Court Restaurant on deck 7 awaiting Callie. The plan is to have breakfast and then to go to the gym, which is all the way forward on the same deck. There, Callie will test my breathing with some light exercise.

When she appears, we take trays and go to the breakfast buffet where I lift two waffles onto my plate and Callie orders a vegetable omelet. Callie watches me as we eat, until finally she says, "Do you feel better this morning, Papa?"

"Lots better."

She gives me a skeptical smile. "We'll just have to test that."

"Christ, I feel like I'm back in the military again."

"Speaking of which, I think we should try to avoid those D-Day enthusiasts. You were getting a little stressed."

"You mean the *hobbyists*?" I ask. "Can you imagine? They make a hobby of it."

Callie points her fork at me. "Now, that's what I mean, Papa. Already, there's smoke coming out of your ears. Eat your waffles and don't get so worked up about it. After all, you were there, in France. You're way ahead of them on that score."

I don't answer. She neglected to mention Pfc. John True. I drag a forkful of waffle through a puddle of maple syrup and stuff it in my mouth. After a few moments, I look up at her. "Do you remember that time we had planned to meet for dinner and I called you from the Boston Common?"

"The night of the vigil?" she asks.

"Yes."

It was a Saturday night two and a half years ago—mid December of 2012—when we'd planned to meet at "No. 9 Park," a restaurant near the State House and Boston Common. The previous day, there had been a mass shooting at the Sandy Hook Elementary School in Newtown, Connecticut. I had been sitting alone, transfixed, in front of the television, cursing at the horror of it, crying openly, wishing Anna was still alive so she could sit with me and we could console each other just as we had on that terrible Tuesday in September of 2001 when planes hit the twin towers and the Pentagon and crashed in a field in Pennsylvania, or in the days after the assassination of JFK, and again the dark days in April and June of '68 with the assassinations of MLK and RFK. At such times, nobody wants to be alone, so I called Callie who said she would come over and cook dinner and sit with me. And I said, "No, I don't want to have you cook. Let me buy you and the kids dinner."

"David has the kids for the weekend," she said.

"Oh. I was hoping to see them. Well, okay, then, just you and me. I want to get out. I want to be with people."

"I understand," Callie replied. "I'll be happy to have dinner with you."

"Good. Speaking of the kids, have you talked with David since the shooting?"

"Yes, Papa. And I told him not to let the kids watch the news."

"Good for you."

Later, when my taxi arrived at the intersection of Tremont and Park, less than 200 yards from the restaurant, I saw a mass of flickering lights. "What's going on here?" I asked the driver.

"It's a candlelight vigil for those kids killed in Connecticut. God, can you imagine? Those poor little kids! Their parents! I have two kids about the same age. Goddamn!"

Immediately, I thought of Élodie and Rachelle Monsigny ... and Adrien. *The carrots are cooked!* The thought of Élodie made me realize how much it would have meant to me if I could talk with her about the

Newtown children. "Let me out here, please," I said. "I'll walk the rest of the way."

I remember standing in the lee of the concrete blockhouse that was the Park Street subway station, and saying, under my breath, "I have no words, my lovely Élodie."

"Who can say anything, my love?" she replies. "This should never happen to children."

"We saw too much suffering, you and I."

"And experienced it, too."

"Yes. Of course."

"At least we helped the children. We can be glad of that."

"But now, in the face of this, I feel so helpless. I wish, so goddamn much, you could be here with me." I press my hand hard against the rough wall of the blockhouse and instantly a fleeting image appears of me leaning, with Élodie, against the parapet of the stone bridge over Noguera Pallaresa River in Spain.

"Don't speak, *mon chou.*[54] We did all we could."

"But it wasn't enough."

"It was all we could do."

"We were so much in love."

"We were young."

"We were old, as old as the war made us."

"Think of the children we helped."

"Adrien."

She touches her lips lightly with her fingers. Oh, that familiar gesture! "Yes, there was Adrien, too."

"And you still think we did all we could?"

"What more could we have done?"

And as quickly as she appeared, Élodie vanished.

I called Callie. She answered on the second ring. "Hi, Papa. Are you there already?"

"No. I'm at the Common. Meet me here. There's a vigil for the children."

---

54   Sweetheart.

"God, Papa, every time I think about it—"

"Yes, I know. Come to the Common. I'm standing in front of the T station."

"I'll be there shortly."

While waiting for Callie, I gazed at the sea of lights, candles held by hundreds of people, one hand holding the candle, the other cupped around the flame to shield it from the wind; the tall, conical Christmas tree with thousands of lights and topped by a blinking star, the necklaces of lights hanging in loops from the elms and the maples, the oaks and the lindens. And I saw a brief image of Élodie cupping her hand around a match as she lit a lantern in one of the caves where we were forced to bivouac. The dancing reflection of the flame in her eyes. The hopeful gazes of the children. It's all burned into my memory.

A soft singing rose up from the crowd. I made out the words to "Amazing Grace."

"I once was lost, but now I'm found ..."

Clouds of condensation from the mouths of the singers filled the chill December air. In a quiet voice, I sang along with them. A frigid blast of wind funneled down Tremont Street and struck me in the face. My eyes watered. I knew the appalling damage automatic weapons could do to a body, especially a child's body. I had seen it in the war. I remembered. Oradour. A child's pram. I shivered at the memory. With my forefinger, I wiped away a tear. A cloud drifted and graceless moonlight shrouded the Common.

❦

"What in the world made you think of that now?" Callie asks as she finishes her vegetable omelet in the King's Court Restaurant aboard the luxurious Queen Mary.

"Hmm?"

"Newtown was more than two years ago. What made you think of it now?"

I shrug. "I don't know. Maybe seeing those kids in the pool on Deck 6." But I know that's a lie. The truth is I had been thinking a lot, lately, about Élodie and the children in the Pyrénées, some of whom had been about the ages of the Sandy Hook children. And I had been watching a young boy at the buffet filling his plate with French toast, sausages, cinnamon buns, sweet rolls and topping off with a cataract of maple syrup over everything.

Later, in the fitness center, I mount a stationary bike. As I pedal, I say, "Do you know when you were a baby, Nana and I used to babysit you?"

"Sure, I remember."

"But did you know it was always I who changed your diaper?"

"Of course, I knew. Then you would kiss me on the forehead. It's one of my fondest memories." Callie gives a small, incredulous laugh. "What made you think of that?"

"I don't know," I say. "Trying not to think of my legs, I guess."

"Are they hurting?"

"Burning a little."

"Lactic acid," says Callie.

Less than two minutes later, I am gasping for air.

"You better stop, Papa." Callie frowns. "I should have seen the signs first thing yesterday. That's one of the problems of being a doctor where family are concerned. There's a tendency to entirely miss the signs or, conversely, over-read them."

"What signs?"

"You're not nearly complete with your rehab. Will you come to see the ship's doctor with me?"

"You really think it's necessary?"

"Yes. You clearly are experiencing dyspnea. I want the doctor to check it out."

"Dyspnea? You've gone all doctor talk on me."

"Labored breathing," she says. "But you know that."

"Just giving you a hard time."

"Don't I know it!"

We get directions to the medical office: midships, deck 1, port side. "I'm not surprised," she says. "Midships on the lowest deck will be the most stable place for medical procedures."

"What medical procedures?" I ask. "I've had enough of that!"

"Don't worry. I meant for other patients. If my diagnosis is right, there's no real procedure involved. Just some antibiotics and some breathing exercises."

In the medical unit, I sit on the edge of an exam table while Callie briefs the doctor, a young man named Clarkson, on my recent medical history. As she speaks, he furrows his brow and finally interrupts to ask, "Are you a doctor?"

Callie nods. "Yes. Doctor Calliope Roza. Emergency medicine. Massachusetts General Hospital in Boston."

"Brilliant! It's good to have you aboard. How about we see what his OSAT is?" He asks the nurse for an oximeter and places it on my forefinger.

"What is OSAT?" I ask.

"Stop playing dumb, Papa. You know it means oxygen saturation. Why do you play these games?"

"Have you experienced rapid, shallow breathing," Dr. Clarkson asks, "or just difficulty catching your breath?"

"Rapid, shallow."

"Coughing?"

I nod.

Dr. Clarkson reads the oximeter. "Your oxygen saturation is ninety." He looks at Callie. "Atelectasis?"

"That's my thinking," she says.

"We can confirm it with an x-ray. If we were at a shoreside hospital I might order a CT-scan, maybe a bronchoscopy, but we're not equipped for that and, besides, I don't think it's necessary."

"I concur," Callie says with a thoughtful nod. "Antibiotics and incentive spirometry?"

"Exactly."

I hold up my hands in protest. "Okay, now I'm truly in the dark. Enough doctor talk. What does it all mean?"

"It means I become a rehab therapist and we resume your rehab," Callie says. "Do you remember putting a tube in your mouth and breathing in hard?"

"Yes."

"That's incentive spirometry. That's what you would have been doing at the rehab center if you hadn't sprung a jail break."

"So, does this mean I have that condition you said prevented me from flying?"

"Pneumothorax?"

"Yes."

"No. This is different. What we were worried about then was air collecting in the pleural space outside your lungs. But with atelectasis, air doesn't escape into the surrounding cavity but the alveoli inside the lungs deflate and lose air. It's like a collapsed lung from the inside. Except in your case, I think it's only partial."

"So, what does this all mean?"

"It means, if you don't improve, we'll have to get you to a shoreside facility with a pulmonologist," says Dr. Clarkson. "But we can afford to wait and besides, we've no choice. It's not even an option for a little while yet because we must be within about two hundred miles, maximum, of a helicopter base capable of carrying out a medical evacuation. We're already out of range of the American and Canadian Coast Guards. Ahead of us is Iceland, the Faroe Islands and Ireland, all of which can airlift a patient, but we won't be within range for a little while yet."

"Meaning?"

"Meaning we have a lot of work to do to get you through this."

"And if we can't?"

"I'm afraid if you can't get through this, we'll have to put you into a London hospital until I can take you home. And that would mean no Normandy."

"That's out of the question," I say, my voice a bit more adamant that I would have liked.

Callie glances at Dr. Clarkson and then shrugs. "Okay, then. Time to get to work."

The morning ground fog gives way to a brief period of sun. In the distance, deckled clouds scrape and shred over the mountains, followed by thicker, impasto clouds layered with a golden glow that fades as the clouds roll over the Pyrénées and smother the light. The mountains themselves disappear behind clouds that drag over the tops of the nearby foothills which are like curry combs, shrouding the conical pines in mist. Élodie looks up and points. "I wonder if there is snow in those clouds."

"In June?"

"At the highest levels, there's often snow year around. I'm worried there will be snow in the passes. It would make it much more difficult for us." She puts a hand on my elbow and whispers, "We could lose some of them." She stops. The procession of children comes to a halt. "It's time to put on your ponchos," she says to the children, first in English, then in French and lastly in German. "Rain is on the way." Looking back along the path we have been following, she says with a frown, Yvette and Adrien have fallen behind again. We must wait."

"I'm afraid it's hard on them," I say, as I shrug off the rucksack and lower Mitzi to the ground. The child immediately embraces my leg in a hug and murmurs, "Papa."

At last, Yvette and Adrien rejoin us. Élodie leans toward them and whispers something. I can't hear what she says, but I instinctively know she is comforting them while also telling them they must try not to lag behind. Finally, she rises, nods to me, and sings the first line of *La Marseillaise*.

"Allons enfants de la Patrie …"[55]

As she sings, she sets out with an exaggerated marching stride, arms swinging stiffly like a drum majorette, eyes glancing to the sky. Looking for storm clouds? German planes? Allied planes? Giggles and laughter float up from the children. Even Yvette is laughing. She elbows Adrien, trying to get him to participate, but he remains silent.

---

55   "Let's go children of the Motherland."

Raindrops arrive less than half an hour later. At first, the leaves, hanging by the side of the path, bead with raindrops, bend under the weight, then snap back as they shed the water. But soon the rain is too hard, and the leaves stay bowed toward the ground. Our refugee column, with the paint-splotched ponchos, trudges through a field of borage where the white, star-shaped flowers are pressed to the earth.

The rain is too intense for the ponchos, and by the time we reach Sainte-Aimée, everyone is soaked through to the skin. When Abbé Peire Basc greets us at the door of the rectory, which is attached to the small stone church, he surveys us head-to-foot and clasps his hands together. "*Mon dieu!* What has God delivered to my door? A colony of drowned rats!" His English is heavily accented.

Élodie pulls off her poncho and says, "I am Azalais."

"No need for your *nom de guerre* here, Élodie Bédier. I know who you are. I saw you play a concert in Carcassonne. Quite beautiful. You introduced a new piece of music."

A smile flits across her face. "Ah yes. The first movement of the Barber Violin Concerto."

"From the stage, you said it wasn't finished."

"It wasn't. Mr. Barber worked on the concerto in Switzerland, but then Americans were warned to leave Europe because of the coming war, which he did, but not before stopping in Paris where I met him. He showed me the score and gave me permission to perform the first movement. I performed it in Carcassonne as a kind of protest against the war." Élodie pauses. "But tell me something. You greeted us in English. Why?"

Abbé Basc gestures toward my boots. "American boots. Americans don't speak French."

Élodie and I exchange glances and she says, "Our plan was to say he took them from a dead American."

The priest shakes his head. "One should never think the Boche are stupid. But enough of that. We must get these poor children dry and warm. Wait here for me." He hurries into the next room and returns, moments later, his arms cradling quantities of cloth. "*Bien,* now follow me." He leads us out of the rectory and into the street. Abruptly, the rain stops and a swath of sunlight spreads over the hills and over the village. Three men with expressionless faces rise from where they are sitting at a table—on which rest a bottle and three glasses—under the covered arcade of a medieval half-timbered house and cross the street toward us. I protectively step in front of the children and face the advancing men. One lumbers toward us on a pair of wooden legs; the other 2 limp on one good leg and one wooden. As they near, I see their faces are not frozen at all. Instead, they are wearing masks.

Élodie says, "It's okay, Henry. They mean no harm."

"How do you—" I start to say, when one of the men, the one with two wooden legs, reaches out and grasps my hand. *"Vous êtes Américain?"*

I don't need it translated. "Yes, I'm American." I see, through the holes in his mask, he has doleful eyes.

The man embraces me. I feel the hardness of his copper mask against my cheek. The other two men also shake my hand and offer embraces and, as quickly as they appeared, they return to the table under the arcade. There, they lift up their half-filled glasses and sip from straws.

"What the hell was that about? Gratitude for the invasion?"

"No. I don't think so. They are the men we call *'gueules cassées,'* or 'broken faces.' We also say, *'mutilés.'* They are veterans of the last war who suffered horribly disfigured faces in combat, as well as other wounds like missing limbs. I saw many when I was in England. They had masks made at a hospital in London that had a department the Tommies called the 'The Tin Noses Shop.'"

"So, these men went to England for their masks?"

"No, no. Paris. But that's why they wanted to shake your hand."

"I don't get it."

"The person who made their masks was an American woman who studied the process in London, then moved to France. Her name was Madame Ladd."[56]

---

56   Years later, I learned this was a sculptor named Anna Coleman Ladd who—coincidentally—came from Manchester-by-the-Sea, less than 10 miles from my Gloucester home! The masks were made from gutta percha, a type of latex, overlaid with a thin film of copper, then painted to approximate the man's

"So, it wasn't because of the Normandy landings?"

"Maybe some of that, but mostly gratitude for their other American, their mask-maker."

"What are they drinking?"

"Pastis,"[57] replies Abbé Basc. "And those are bamboo straws which they must always use because of the masks. But now, please follow me." He leads us through a side alley into a field behind the rectory. In the sky, the sunlight appears as crepuscular rays fanning out from the cloud bottoms. It is the kind of light often called God rays. And on the land, long shadows stretch from right to left across the field, ten times longer than the pines casting them are tall. The sun, peeking through a break in the clouds, appears about to be impaled by the serrated tops of the trees at the western edge of the field.

After a brief intermission, the rain begins again. On the other end of the field is a stone barn with a red tile roof. The stones appear pink in the slanting sunlight. As he strides ahead of us, wheezing with the exertion, bent over to avoid dropping the cottons and linens held tightly to his chest, Abbé Basc says, "That barn belongs to Madame Esclarmonde Cazenave. As you can perhaps tell from her name, she and her husband come from ancient Occitan stock. She speaks French, Occitan and English. It was she who, in former times, taught me English at the local school. Her husband and two young sons were killed by the Boche last year when they tried to stop the devils from taking their sheep. Now she lives alone."

Élodie turns to me. "Esclarmonde means 'light of the world.'"

"And she truly is," says the priest. "When I told her you were coming with some children, she used up much of her month's allowance of butter and sugar and eggs to bake something special for the them."

The barn door squeals as he slides it along its track. An odor of old hay mixed with sheep dung wafts to our nostrils, though there are no signs of sheep. On the far wall, barely visible in the gloaming, written

---

original appearance. Ladd also created a bronze sculpture, called "Triton Babies" in Boston's Public Garden which I have visited.

57   An anise-flavored apéritif popular in France, especially in the south.

in red paint that has dripped like a blood spatter, is a cross of Lorraine with its one vertical and two crossbars, the symbol of the Free French. Under it is the dot-dot-dot-dash for "V," representing victory.

"Did Madame Cazenave do that?" Élodie asks, gesturing to the wall.

Abbé Basc nods. "Only yesterday. It was a foolish thing to do. What if the Boche see it? They have an encampment only a few kilometers from here. I suppose anger overcame her. But, *pas de problème*, she has agreed to paint over it and to do penance for allowing her anger to take hold of her senses. In the meantime, old Monsieur Clérisse has been creating a diversion to keep the Boche away."

"What sort of diversion?"

Abbé Basc flashes a perky smile. "One that pulls everybody away from the barn and to the other end of the village. You will see tomorrow when the rain stops. It will be a wonderful surprise for the children."

Élodie gives him an inquisitive look but pursues it no further. Instead, she asks, "What caused Madame Cazenave's anger?"

"We received news two days ago of a massacre in the Haute-Vienne."

Élodie looks at me and inhales deeply. "We passed through there two days after it occurred. It was in a commune called Oradour-sur-Glane."

"*Mon dieu!* Is it true they killed many women and children? Gathered them in a church and set it afire?"

"It's true. The animals!"

Abbé Basc makes the sign of the cross, shakes his head, and says, "No, no. No animal loved by Saint Francis would do such a thing. They are human savages, capable of far worse than the most monstrous brute." He presses the cloths to his chest with one hand and, with the other, pats Mitzi, whom I am carrying on my hip. "To kill innocent children like this! No hell is deep enough!" The priest looks down at the cloths as if he has forgotten what they are for, breathes deeply, and lets a tiny, shuddering cry escape from his lips. Finally, he spreads the cloths on an old wooden table, taking care to keep them far from the can of red paint that sits on one end, and says to Élodie, "For you and the American: altar cloths you can wear like *une toge*."

"Yes, a toga," she replies with a smile.

"They should be quite big enough. And for the older children, some priestly garments: three soutanes, a surplice, two cassocks, a chasuble, plus some of my secular clothes, including two coats. I suggest you separate the boys and the girls—one group can go into the milking room—and tell everybody to strip off their wet clothes and put these on. Madame Cazenave will bring more clothes for the smaller children."

A flash of lightning is followed, seconds later, by a crack of thunder. Abbé Basc flinches. Rain starts drumming on the roof tiles. From outside the door, I hear rainwater gushing into a metal cistern. In the diminishing light, Élodie ushers the girls into the milking room where she will help them out of their wet clothes and devise ways in which they can wear the new garments. Meanwhile, I do the same with the boys. Giggles and nervous laughter fill the barn. When we are finished with the children, Élodie and I help each other fashion togas from the altar cloths by tying two corners together over one shoulder. With a smile, Élodie asks, "Do you want to wear the embroidered crucifix on the back or the front?"

I laugh. "I think it would be disrespectful to wear it on the back and end up sitting on it."

Moments later, Abbé Basc returns with Madame Cazenave. She is a tall, slender woman with a kind face and a warm smile. There is no trace of the bitterness that caused her to risk painting anti-German graffiti. She and the priest carry clothes which they distribute to the smaller children. "They are clothes that belonged to my two sons," Madame Cazenave says. "Now help me carry the wet clothes into the house where we can set them out to dry."

Along with Abbé Basc and Madame Cazenave, we gather up all the wet clothes and carry them from the barn to the house. The moment we enter the kitchen, we are assaulted by heat emanating from a cast iron stove which is surrounded by four high-backed chairs. "I know it's June, but I started the stove to dry the clothes." Madame Cazenave loosens a thin rope from a wall hook and lowers, through pulleys, a rack from the ceiling above the stove. The rack has eight long wooden slats. "Spread the clothes on the rack. What doesn't fit, drape over the chairs."

When we finish hanging the clothes, a large puddle sits on the kitchen floor. It grows larger as beads of water slide down the clothes and drop to the floor with little plops. Madame Cazenave steps into an adjoining room and returns with a book tucked under her arm and a basket whose contents are covered by a cloth. Sitting atop the cloth is a stuffed toy. She hands it to Élodie. "Here is *un ours en peluche* for the little one. How do you call it in English?"

"A teddy bear. But for Mitzi, it's German name might be better: *ein Teddybär.*"

"That is appropriate because it's from the German company Steiff. But we won't hold that against it."

She lifts the cloth and shows us two dozen madeleines and says, "For the little one and the other children."

"Oh, thank you! They'll be very happy," says Élodie. "What book do you have there?"

"One the children may enjoy. My sons certainly did. It's called *Le Petit Prince* and it's by Antoine de Saint-Exupéry."

Élodie turns to me. "Saint-Exupéry is a famous writer and aviator here in France. Rumor is, at present, he flies with General Valin's Free French Air Force."

"A very courageous man," says Abbé Basc.

"When I was in England," Élodie says, "I read his book *Terre des hommes* which in English is called *Wind, Sand and Stars.*"

Madame Cazenave frowns, "I don't know this book of which you speak, but now we should read his *Little Prince* to the children while they eat their madeleines."

"Of course. You read in French and I'll translate into German and English."

"*D'accord.*[58] But first, in the next room I have set out four kerosene lamps. Help me carry them to the barn. Children often have a fear of the dark."

When we return to the barn, we distribute the lanterns among the children. Madame Cazenave presents the madeleines and there are

---

58   Agreed.

muffled cries of joy, but mostly there are tears of gratitude for the unexpected, and unaccustomed, kindness and I am forced to wonder when was the last time they experienced goodness in the world.

Élodie and I sit beside each other on a bench. Madame Cazenave sits in an old, metal chair with red paint stains, while Abbé Basc leans against a creep. Most of the children sit on the barn floor with legs crossed in the manner of children everywhere anticipating a story. A few lay prone on the floor propped on their elbows, hands cupping their chins. I watch the children relish the little cakes, which are shaped like scallop shells, and it makes me smile. Little Mitzi bounces to her feet and offers me a bite of her madeleine. I take the smallest possible nibble and she gives a delighted giggle.

The light from the lanterns illumines the faces of the children, causing their eyes to shine like cats in the night. Not since Élodie and I first met them, have they looked this free of fear, even if, as it turns out, only for a fleeting time.

Élodie announces, first in French then in German, that Madame Cazenave will read them a story about a little prince. She has already asked Aron Klotz to translate for the five Polish children.

In a voice tight with tension (she no doubt is thinking of her sons) Esclarmonde Cazenave begins to read the story in the original French. Almost simultaneously, Élodie translates the story into German and, while Aron further translates it into Polish, Élodie turns to me and repeats the narration in English.

Within moments, the children are transported from the rain-soaked foothills of the Pyrénées, and the grown-up desolation of war, to the clean Saharan desert where a pilot, whose plane has crashed in the sands, encounters a boy with blond hair who says he is a little prince from Asteroid B-612. The children hear how the little prince has traveled a very long way to come to this place and how he asks the narrator about his airplane and what it does and how the narrator says the plane allows him to fly great distances through the air.

"Like an eagle?" asks twelve-year-old Max Jäger.

"Yes, like an eagle, an eagle who can fly over fields and fences," replies Madame Cazenave. "And over German guard posts, too."

Élodie adds, "And even fly so high as to soar over the mountains of the Pyrénées with ease." Her words are translated until every child has uttered a gasp of wonderment and, with rapt attention, has turned back to Madame Cazenave for more. She reads on about how the pilot sketches a sheep, because the boy wants the sheep so it can eat the seedlings of the gigantic baobab trees that threaten to split the boy's tiny planet to pieces.

"Baobab trees are like the Wehrmacht," says Max.

Madame Cazenave pauses, looks up at Abbé Basc. Élodie and I exchange knowing glances. "Yes," says Élodie. "They can be like the Wehrmacht."

Madame Cazenave continues. She reads to the children how the little prince says sunsets can bring cheer and comfort to a person who is sad, and how the boy's planet is so small, he can see forty-four sunsets by simply moving a few steps and how the little prince worries the sheep will eat, in addition to the baobab seedlings, his special, unique rose, and how nothing is more important to him than protecting that rose, and how the prince loves the rose, and waters it, and covers her with a glass globe at night, and how on the day the prince leaves his tiny planet, the rose, who loves him, assures him she no longer needs him to water and protect her, but then turns her face away so he will not see her crying.

The barn is pin-drop quiet except for the voices of Madame Cazenave, whose once tense voice has softened, and the even more hushed voices of Élodie and Aron. The lamps cast dancing reflections on the walls which are, in turn, reflected in the children's eyes. And in those eyes, I see, if only for a short time, yearning memories of rainbows, and big-eyed teddy bears, and princesses with tiaras, and sweet lollipops, and gay balloons, and purring kittens, and long-maned ponies and chin-licking puppies ... and mothers' aprons and fathers' pipes.

Madame Cazenave reads on about how, in the course of his travels, the little prince visits many planets and many characters: the king who claims to rule over all the stars in the universe but who, in reality, has no subjects including the vain man who wants only to be admired as the finest man on his planet when, in truth, he is the *only* inhabitant of the planet; the drunkard who drinks to forget the shame of his drinking;

the businessman who has no time to answer the little prince's questions because he is busy counting the stars which he claims to own; and the lamplighter who lives on a planet so tiny there is room for only one lamp which the lamplighter must light every dusk and extinguish every dawn for a total of 1,440 sunsets every twenty-four hours because the planet spins so rapidly.

A twitter of laughter rises from the French children, followed quickly by the children listening in German and even more quickly—because laughter is infectious—by the five children listening in Polish. A rolling laughter that, in itself, draws laughter.

Madame Cazenave lowers her voice to an audible whisper and narrates how, on the 6th planet, the little prince meets a geographer who records information about places. But when the boy tells the scholar about his own planet and his rose, the man says he doesn't record roses because they are too ephemeral, which deeply saddens the boy.

Again, Élodie and I exchange glances. I feel a vague unease, the grief of love.

Madame Cazenave turns the pages to the final chapters and reads how the little prince finds a huge rose garden and is saddened to find so many flowers that look just like his rose, whom he thought was unique in the world, and how he lies down in the grass and cries and how, as he's crying, a fox appears, and how the prince asks the fox to play with him but the fox replies that the prince must first tame him.

After translating this passage into German and English, Élodie says to Madame Cazenave, "I'm afraid that doesn't translate well into English. Please allow me to explain to the American." She turns to me. "Madame Cazenave used the word *apprivoiser* which does, indeed, translate to 'tame.' But it is not 'tame' in the sense meant by the English word. For that, the French word would be *domestiquer*, meaning to make a wild animal domesticated. But to 'tame' in the *apprivoiser* sense means to make a loving connection."

"In that case, you may 'tame' me whenever you like. I won't resist."

Élodie flashes me a warm smile, then, becoming serious, says, "I hope we come across a stray dog that Adrien can 'tame.' It would help pull him out of his gloom."

I am aware of Madame Cazenave watching us. Her eyes are glistening, as if she is about to cry. She turns back to the book and reads how the fox assures the little prince that, by this act of taming, they will need each other, and each will become special to the other; and how the fox tells the prince to re-visit the rose garden to see why his rose, though not unique, is special; and how the prince comes to realize his rose *is* special because of the love they have for one another; and how, because of that, he asks the pilot to draw the picture of a muzzle for the sheep to prevent it from eating the rose.

As we sit beside each other on the bench, Élodie presses her thigh against mine.

Many of the children, though captivated by the reading, yawn. No doubt, it's the exhaustion of walking for several days. Madame Cazenave quickly finishes the story by skipping past a few pages to read the ending about how the marooned pilot and the prince discover a well of sweet water in the desert which revives the body and the heart of the pilot; and how, the following day, the pilot returns to the well to find the prince sitting on a wall and how the prince informs the pilot that he will, by the bite of a snake, be returning to his home planet among the stars and how the prince points to the stars above and assures the pilot they will always have a special meaning for him now that a loving friend, namely the little prince, is living among them, and how the pilot will always look up at the stars and hear the sound of many tiny bells and wonder about his friend, and worry if the sheep has eaten the rose.

Several of the children are already asleep. Madame Cazenave and Abbé Basc bid goodnight to those still awake and leave. Élodie and I move about the barn and extinguish the kerosene lamps. We step outside and look up at the sky and see an exuberance of stars splayed across the heavens. The moon is a waning crescent, a mere sliver of a fingernail. A cradle.

Élodie slips her arm around my waist and leans into me. "You seem glum."

"Just thinking about the ephemeral rose … and all those sunsets."

"The sunsets?"

"Fourteen hundred and forty in twenty-four hours?"

"Yes. On the lamplighter's planet."

"I'm guessing many more than fourteen hundred and forty people saw their last sunset today in this goddamn war."

Élodie says nothing.

The field is loud with the staccato squeaks and chatter of tree frogs and cicadae mimicking the clamor of the tracks and sprockets of Panzer tanks on cobblestone village streets.

Chapter 12
Roasted Chestnuts

The morning after seeing the ship's doctor, Callie and I have breakfast again in the King's Court restaurant on Deck 7, then trudge to the gym in the forward part of the ship, stopping several times so I can sit in a deck chair and recover my breath. A light-infused fog hangs over the ocean. The surface respires in long, slow swells. Several decks below, the frothy bow wave fans away from the ship, leaving a long wake. Old tars would have said she has a bone in her teeth. Not far to starboard we see flashes of light flying near the ocean's surface.

"Seagulls?" Callie asks.

I shake my head. "Not this far out. Probably flying fish trying to escape bluefin tuna. They are natural prey and predator." We continue along the promenade deck until we reach the outside door leading to the gym. "Before we go in, let's take a look near the bow," I say. "Have you ever seen porpoises frolicking?"

"No," she says. "Is this a delay tactic?"

"Not at all. Let's go forward and lean over the rail. We'll probably see some."

But we quickly learn we can go no further than the observation deck which ends with a V-shaped breakwater many feet aft of the prow. To starboard and port on the observation deck, gigantic spare propeller blades, each much taller than a person, stand upright, gleaming dully in the refracted light like pieces in a Henry Moore sculpture garden.

"Can't see the bow wave from here," I say. "Let's see if we can find somebody who can tell us how to get further forward."

"Papa, all you're doing is procrastinating."

"I'm not procrastinating. I want you to see the porpoises."

"You *are* procrastinating, and you know it. Now let's get to the gym. Doctor's orders."

Christ, she can sound like her mother sometimes! "Lead the way. I wouldn't want to deprive you of your sadistic fun."

In the gym, we sit in a corner doing breathing exercises with an incentive spirometer for ten or fifteen minutes. Then, at Callie's insistence, I mount a recumbent bike and pedal slowly for another fifteen minutes. When I finish, we go back out onto the promenade deck.

The fog has thickened, and beads of moisture cover the rails and the seat cushions of the deck chairs. The droplets shiver with the tiny vibrations from the ship's engines. Nobody is on this part of the ship which is exposed to the wind coming over the bow.

"It's too early for lunch," Callie says. "What do you want to do?"

"Let's go sit by the pool. It's a little cold here with the fog, and the pool is sheltered by the upper decks."

With me walking more slowly than usual, and stopping several times for a breather, it takes us almost ten minutes to reach the stern on Deck 7.

"Up one deck to the adult pool, or down one to the children's pool?" Callie asks.

"The children's pool is more sheltered, and it's down a flight of stairs rather than up. And I'd much rather watch children than overweight adults."

"Down to Deck 6, then," she says, offering her arm, which I happily accept.

The pool at the very stern of the ship on Deck 6, reserved for children, is called the Minnows Pool. Callie guides me to a chaise lounge close under the overhang of Deck 7 where I will be completely sheltered from the wind, then says she is going to the bookstore to get something to read. "Shall I pick up something for you while I'm there?" she asks.

"No. I'm just gonna enjoy watching the children."

"First, let me get you a blanket. It's chilly despite being in the lee."
She disappears inside and returns moments later with a woolen blanket
which she spreads across my lap. I immediately slip my cold hands
under the blanket and clasp them together.

Callie says, "Okay, I'm off. Would you like me to bring you something when I return? A coffee, maybe?"

"No, I'm fine."

"I'll be back in half an hour," she says. She kisses me on the forehead
and mounts the stairs up to Deck 7.

I look out over the stern, past the flapping union jack, at the roiling
wake—twin whirlpools of frothy turbulence gradually subsiding into
a long, straight scar on the ocean's surface, until it disappears at the
horizon. Laughter draws my attention to the children frolicking in the
pool, their whirling bodies splashing the water. I'm filled with admiration for how they move with suppleness and grace, their little muscles
rinsed with blood, their free-moving joints awash in fluid. The children
are beautiful, their arms, their legs, their torsos willowy and lithesome,
an opulence of grace moving with the effortless, flowing confidence of
dancers, a suppleness which, for my own ancient body, is just a memory.
The sun burnishes the gold of their bodies, and just as their bodies are
so wonderfully pliable, so are their spirits limber with laughter, a sound
like many tiny bells among the stars.

I remember a photo taken of me at Revere Beach when my father,
experimenting with color photography, used the autochrome camera he
inherited from *his* father. There I am, in a red bathing suit, five or six years
old, standing in water that sluices and foams around my knees as a wave
surges onto the sand. In the background stretches the long crescent of
the beach with its roller coasters, Ferris wheels, and other amusements.
I remember how the waves threw up spray and cold-licked my ribs and
how they caused me to stagger with their weight. The muscles of my
legs twitch as I recall the cold of the water, the sandy tug of my wet
bathing suit, the smells of coconut oil, and mustard, and seaweed from
the crowded beach with scores of blankets and umbrellas sprouting
from the sand like colorful mushrooms. And these memories bring to
the surface another memory, the night when Élodie and I talked of the

movie *It Happened One Night* and how we dreamed one day of finding a little island in the Pacific where we would jump in the surf together, and the moon and the water would become one with the stars, and the stars would be so close we could reach up and touch them. I remember how, despite the knowledge I could have been shot for desertion at the time, I had never felt so alive, so vital.

As I stare at the children in the pool, no longer really seeing them, I see those other children whose names are as fresh to me as they were seventy years ago: Max Jäger of the blond hair who spoke fluent German and English and whose British mother was sent to the internment camp at Drancy and then on to the east never to be heard from again; the Godowsky children from Poland, Jerzy and his sisters Elżbietá and Klará; two others from Poland, Kamilá Brodny and her brother Józef who wanted to call me "Tata;" and Rebekka Weiß—whose headmaster at her school in Vienna instructed her classmates to spit in her face— and her brother Stephan, who, even though a year younger, tried to protect her; and the sweet sisters from Dusseldorf, Leni and Renata Gottfried, who couldn't bear to be apart from one another; and Aron Klotz from Saxony who spoke Polish as well as English and his native German, and who was more than helpful as a translator for the five Polish children; and, of course, little, sweet Mitzi, who was as close as I ever got to having a child until, years later, I married and started a family of my own.

And then there was Yvette and Adrien, whose mother begged Élodie and me to take them under our protection while she went off to find their father. Christ, I remember how stupid I felt when I was nervous the addition of Adrien and Yvette brought the number of children to thirteen—*unlucky thirteen*—and then how I rationalized the thought away when I realized, counting Élodie and me, the number in our party had already been thirteen, and nothing bad had befallen us.

I remember them all. After seventy years, I remember them all and I wonder how many of them have survived through all that time.

The morning sky over Sainte-Aimée is clear as Élodie and I assemble the children in advance of setting out for the 3rd safe house, a dairy farm north of the commune of Le Fossat on the Salat River, a tributary of the Garonne.

Abbé Basc accompanies us out of the barn and escorts us to the far end of the village with a broad smile on his face. He says, "My nose tells me Monsieur Clérisse has begun his diversion. We will treat the children. The Boche never come until the afternoon."

Élodie makes a theatrical show of sniffing the air. I, too, sample the air. It's a familiar, but almost forgotten, aroma that makes me think of snowy fields in Maine on my grandfather's farm. "Roasting chestnuts!" I blurt, and just as I say it, we turn a corner and come face-to-face with an old, portly man wearing a checkered beret and a coat with sleeves so long only his stubby fingers emerge from the cuffs. A large, dented, long-handled roasting pan sits over a vigorous fire. As we approach him, Monsieur Clérisse gives a laugh, shakes the pan with a clatter, and says, *"Châtaignes grillées pour tous."*[59] To the side is a bowl where already-roasted chestnuts sit cooling.

Élodie echoes his laughter and turns to the children, and says, "Roasted chestnuts for everybody! *Geröstete Kastanien für alle!*" and Aron Klotz says, *"Pieczone kasztany dla wszystkich!"* A murmur rises among the children, and with shy, hesitant smiles, they come forward one by one and hold out their hands, like prayerful congregants at Holy Communion, and receive a half dozen roasted chestnuts each with a roll of laughter from Monsieur Clérisse, and a guttural but musical *"Châtaignes grillées pour tous,"* and only Adrien holds back until his sister returns to him with a handful of chestnuts and offers one to him, and he accepts it. She is followed by Max Jäger, who also offers a chestnut to Adrien with a smile, then Jerzy Godowsky repeats the gesture and is quickly followed by his sisters Elżbietá and Klará, so, in the end, Adrien has nearly a full share of chestnuts and the children look around and smile at one another with wide-eyed wonder, and I see the chestnuts must feel good in their hands—the

---

59   Roasted chestnuts for everyone.

heat of the chestnuts in their tiny, nervous hands—and it seems to momentarily wish away the war, and the ripples of laughter rising from the children (except for Adrien) make me smile until my cheeks ache.

After all the children have received their chestnuts, Madame Cazenave approaches Monsieur Clérisse who nods, smiles at her, and places a single chestnut in the palm of each of her hands and with his stubby fingers tenderly folds her fingers over them and leans over and kisses the knuckles of each of her closed hands.

Abbé Basc quietly says to Élodie and me, "One each for her two lost sons. It's a tradition between them whenever Monsieur Clérisse finds enough chestnuts to roast."

"Are they related?" asks Élodie.

Abbé Basc shakes his head and says, "Only in a shared human kindness."

As Madame Cazenave whispers *"Merci,"* and takes a step back from Monsieur Clérisse, Adrien bursts into the space between them and throws his arms around Monsieur Clérisse and presses his cheek against the old man's chest and Monsieur Clérisse lets out a surprised and happy laugh and tousles the boy's hair.

"What's Adrien doing?" I ask Élodie.

"I think it's been a very long time since a stranger showed him some kindness."

After bidding farewell to Abbé Basc and Monsieur Clérisse, Élodie and I lead the children away from Sainte-Aimée. Under a hot sun, we pass several farm fields, stands of chestnut trees, and meadows crowded with shrubs of white, clustering viburnum.

Élodie turns to me. "The flowers look like new-fallen snow,"

"Are you still worried about snow in the mountains?" I ask, gazing at the foothills that stand in a blue haze before us.

"We'll be there in two days," she says. "If so, it will be difficult for us." She lowers her voice to a whisper. "I am afraid we will—" her voice cuts off, choked by emotion

"No! Not on my watch, damn it! We're all going to make it through."

Élodie gives me a half-hearted smile. "Well said, you," she whispers.

Suddenly, a dozen or more distorted shadows sweep around the meadow in every direction like chaotic facets in a broken kaleidoscope. Élodie glances at the sky and frowns.

I follow her gaze and see a large, scramble of birds wheeling and circling, swerving and dipping, in confused patterns. "Hawks?" I ask. All at once I'm aware the songbirds in the meadow have gone silent.

She shakes her head slowly. "Lammergeiers. I think you call them 'bearded vultures' in English. They have ten-foot wing spans."

"What makes them congregate like that?"

Again, she shakes her head. "It's unnatural. I've seen them kettling before, but not so many of them."

"Perhaps there are a lot of prey in the fields around here."

"No. They're scavengers. They feed mostly on dead animals."

And, just as quickly as the lammergeiers appeared, they disappear beyond the tree-topped ridge to our south and a barely discernable thrumming appears, a drone we wouldn't have noticed except that the songbirds are still silent.

"Merde!" Élodie whispers. She continues to stare at the sky. The children must hear it, too, because they also have stopped in their tracks and are staring at the sky. Then I see it—a tight formation of a dozen planes appearing over the ridge, out of the scumbled, bright-edged clouds, sunlight flashing from their fuselages, and the drone of their engines gradually increasing and turning to a rumble that we feel in our feet as they pass overhead.

"Stukas?" I ask.

Élodie shakes her head. "The horizontal stabilizers are lozenge-shaped. On the Stuka, they're a hard rectangle."

"Meaning?"

"Meaning they're Tiffies."

"Tiffies?"

"Hawker Typhoons."

"British?"

"Yes."

"Then it's no problem," I say. "They're probably cleaning up pockets of Germans."

"Except, the fuckers don't know where the Germans are in this part of France. Only the Resistance knows that."

"So, what's the problem?"

"The allies refuse to listen to the Resistance."

"Why?"

"They don't trust them because there are Communists among the resistance fighters. Allied bombers have already killed many innocent people by not knowing where to drop their bombs."

"Shit!"

As the planes pass overhead, we see their shadows undulate away from us over the uneven ground and across the river and then we hear the first explosions from the direction of Sainte-Aimée.

Élodie grabs my hand. "What do we do?"

My heart pounds as I fight the desire to turn around, go back, do something. I feel the weight of Mitzi's make-shift carry pack on my back and see the fear on the children's faces. "I don't know."

"We can't go back," Élodie says firmly.

"Everything inside of me says we must return and see if we can help, except—"

"Except our first responsibility is here," Élodie says, gazing at the Pyrénées in the distance, beyond which lay a promise of safety for the children.

I drag in a deep breath. "Yes."

"We must go on."

"We have to."

But we remain frozen to the spot. More detonations. Less than two kilometers away. We feel the ground shake. The roofs of some buildings are still visible. Flames geyser toward the sky from one of them. Probably dry hay igniting in a flashover. Then another building is engulfed. The ground shakes. The hills echo the detonations. The urge to race back and help the people who so recently helped us is almost irresistible. Élodie and I exchange worried glances. We are holding each other's hand so tight it hurts. A chorus of crying and sobbing rises up from the children. All except for Mitzi who stands rigid, staring up at me, eyes round, mouth open, making no sound. She had been walking hand-in-hand with one of the other girls, but now she looks at me with such an expression of betrayal that I feel like I've been pierced through with flaming shrapnel. I reach out to take her into my arms, but she backs away and starts to run in silent circles, waving her arms frantically. I chase after her. At last, I'm able to gather her into my arms and hold her tight and kiss her on the forehead.[60]

Élodie goes around to the other children, trying to comfort them. She stops abruptly and says, "Where is Adrien?" I scan the area. No sign of the boy. Carrying Mitzi, I go to where Yvette is sitting on the ground, weeping. I start to ask, "Yvette, where is ..." before I remember she doesn't speak English. I look helplessly to Élodie, who turns to the girl and asks, *"Yvette, où est Adrien?"* Yvette says nothing. She only looks back toward where we came from. I follow her gaze and see Adrien at the far side of the meadow running back toward Sainte-Aimée. I'm hamstrung. I can't put Mitzi down. Not now. She'd think I was abandoning her. But I can't carry her and run fast enough to catch Adrien, especially with my wounded leg. Again, Élodie and I exchange desperate glances. She, too, is incapacitated. She can't leave the children to go after Adrien. It's unthinkable; they would panic if either of us left them now. Yet, we can't abandon Adrien. We are left with no choice. We must head back to Sainte-Aimée. And we must somehow find a way to lessen the shock of the bombing, do what we can to shield these innocents from the world that has so monstrously forsaken them.

We arrive back in the village to a cacophony of crying and shouting. A mini whirlwind of ashes and hot embers writhes along the street. A dozen people have formed a bucket brigade, shuttling water from the town fountain to the rectory. Already, they seem to have the fire

---

60   Only one other time in my life have I seen that look of betrayal in the eyes of a child. When she was four years old, Natalie's bicycle was stolen the day after we'd removed the training wheels. She looked at me as if I had somehow opened a gate and carelessly let evil into her world. After she went to sleep from the sheer exhaustion of crying, I scoured the neighborhood until midnight, hoping to redeem myself ... to redeem her world. The bike was red. We never found it.

controlled, though the building is gutted. The barn, however, is a fully engulfed inferno. The heat of the fire is so intense, it has created a small firestorm, drawing heated air into itself. A thick roof beam crashes to the floor in a cascade of sparks and instantly there comes the shriek of a panicked horse. I look to where the sound comes from and I see one of the face masks worn by the mutilated veterans, its fleshy enamel flensed and blistered, its copper blackened. Next to it, curlicues of smoke rise from a scorched wooden leg. There is no sign of the three veterans.

"Mon Dieu!" says Élodie. "Copper conducts heat. The mask must have become unbearably hot."

"So, he threw it away?"

"What choice did he have?"

"What about the others?"

"The barn took a direct hit."

She's right, of course. I look around to see if there are more people to form a second bucket brigade. That's when I see Monsieur Clérisse and Adrien. They are curled up on the cobblestones together and Monsieur Clérisse is stroking the boy's forehead with stubby fingers that barely emerge from his coat sleeve. The long-handled roasting pan is upended in the middle of the street next to a dead donkey, and chestnuts are scattered everywhere. Several fires roar in the background. My heart sinks when I see, on the opposite side of the street, the prostrate figure of Madame Cazenave who lies on her back, arms outspread, palms open to the sky. Next to each hand is a lone chestnut. Nearby, her copy of *Le Petit Prince* lies open, spine broken, its singed pages flipping with the fire-summoned breeze.

At the head of the bucket brigade, Abbé Basc grunts as he hurls water at the remaining flames licking at the rectory's door. I approach him. "Here, let me relieve you," I say.

He eagerly hands me the bucket. "I thought you left," he says.

"We're back."

"It's dangerous. The Boche will want to inspect the bombing. They'll come early."

"Don't you have a fire truck?" I ask. "It would go faster."

He gives a bitter laugh. "It's a nineteen-twenty-four Delahaye. It stopped working at the beginning of the war and there are no parts to fix it. *C'est un objecteur de conscience!*"

"Conscientious objector?"

"*Oui.*"

Suddenly, I hear Élodie give a cry of alarm. "Henry!"

I turn. "What?"

"Look!" She points to the road which runs straight into the village from the north. I look and see a small convoy of vehicles about a mile away. Even from this distance I can tell one of them is a light Panzer tank from its squared body and its upthrust gun. Several of the others are motorcycles.

"As I predicted," says Abbé Basc. "But even sooner than I thought."

"Hurry! We must hide the children," Élodie says.

"Yes," I reply. "But where?"

"In the rectory," says Abbé Basc as he helps us gather the children. "The fire is mostly out, but we'll keep the water coming. The Boche will never think to go inside."

"This is going to be hellish for the children," says Élodie.

"We have no choice."

Within minutes, Élodie and I are huddled with the children— all, except Adrien, who is still with Monsieur Clérisse—inside the rectory's pantry which is just off the alcove. The floor is littered with glass from canning jars shattered by thermal shock. Tomatoes, pickled cucumbers, applesauce and several other fruits and vegetables drip from shelves and puddle on the floor. "Be careful of the glass," Élodie says quickly in three languages. "And please, please be as quiet as possible." She nods to Aron who translates for the Polish children. She encourages the children to reach out and touch each other, and to stay touching, and she spreads her arms and touches as many as she can.

I feel the fear in Mitzi's rigid body. I kiss her forehead. I hold her tightly wrapped in my arms but lean to the side so Jerzy Godowsky can feel my body pressed against his and he, in turn, clings to Elżbietá who has an arm around Klará. We are in hiding, but we are connected.

I hear the rumble and clatter of the motorcycles and the tank. Through a small crack in the outside wall, I see there are also two light armored cars. I flinch when a splash of water hits my ankle. Apparently, Abbé Basc is trying to persuade the Germans the fire in the rectory is still alive and dangerous. I look around at Élodie and the children. Everybody must have grabbed onto the charred pantry door frame as we scampered to our hiding place, for, in wiping at their tears, the children have smeared soot all over their faces through which tears have etched channels. Élodie's face also is blackened and I assume I am the same way. We look like coal miners coming to the surface at the end of our shift.

Several of the children are weeping. I grind my teeth because it sounds so loud to me, but I think the rumble and clatter of the idling German vehicles will keep the children's whimpering from the ears of the soldiers. Also, there is much crying and sobbing from the villagers. Indeed, I hear a German officer, who is standing just on the other side of the wall, say, *"So schade! So viel Weinen und Jammern! Aber denken Sie daran: Es waren die britischen Schweine, die Ihnen das angetan haben."*[61]

· The German starts to pace up and down the street, examining the effects of the bombing. From my low angle, I see his boots stop beside the body of Madame Cazenave, pause for a moment, then stomp on one of the chestnuts that fell from her hands. It shatters, and he kicks the fragments away. Finally, he strides back to his armored car, gives an order, and they leave. As soon as I can no longer hear the clanking and grinding of the Panzer's sprockets and tracks, I lead Élodie and the children out of the pantry, out of the rectory, and into the street. Upon seeing us, Abbé Basc says, "And fire came down from heaven and consumed them, and the devil who had deceived them was thrown into the lake of fire ... but the *innocent* angels escaped."

"Thanks to your ruse," I say.

"It's a good thing we have buckets."

Élodie and I spend the next hour cleansing the children with buckets of water in the open. Since the barn is destroyed, we are forced

---

61   I later learn what he said was, "Such a pity! So much weeping and wailing! But remember, it was the British pigs who did this to you."

to sacrifice all modesty. No longer whimpering, they stand silent and shivering as the water cascades over their bodies. When, one-by-one, the children emerge clean, Abbé Basc dries them off with sacerdotal robes. Finally, with Abbé Basc improvising a modesty screen by holding a sacerdotal robe between outstretched arms, like Moses parting the sea, Élodie and I strip out of our clothes, dump buckets of water over ourselves, then dry each other off with an alb discretly passed over the screen to us.

All through that night, the children are inconsolable. Adrien, in particular, has withdrawn even deeper into himself. Élodie and I huddle with Abbé Basc and quietly discuss the situation, at last deciding to give the children time to recover as much as possible before continuing on.

☙

After two days rest, we leave Sainte-Aimée for the second time. Soon, we pass a dairy farm where the gate of the sheepfold has been left open. There is only one un-shorn Lacaune sheep in sight.

"I'd expect to see a flock," I say. "Where are the rest of the sheep?"

"Probably confiscated by the Boche and slaughtered for mutton," Élodie says. "I fear this one is next. They'll no doubt be back. I wonder where the farmer is. He wouldn't leave the gate open like that."

A bad feeling sweeps over me. "Maybe he resisted when the Krauts came. Perhaps we should check it out."

"No," says Élodie, shaking her head vigorously. "There's probably nothing we can do. It's likely he and his family are dead. It would be putting the children at too great a risk if there are Boche close by. Besides, if the family is dead, we don't want the children seeing that. They are far too vulnerable, too nervous, and they are always our first responsibility. Always!"

Suddenly, we hear a cry of *"Nein!"*[62] and we turn to see Aron Klotz running across the field toward the lone sheep. Several of the Polish children are running after him.

---

62   No!

"What the hell is he doing?" I ask.

"I don't know, but we must stop him before somebody sees or hears him."

We set out at a run after Aron and the Polish children. When we catch up to him, he has already reached the sheep and is pushing it toward the open sheepfold gate.

"Aron, what are you doing?" asks Élodie.

But I already know the answer. "Look," I say, and point to the ground where there is a single, wild, red rose. "He was stopping the sheep from eating the rose."

Élodie takes a deep breath. Smiles.

I look past the sheepfold to the stone farmhouse. "Since we're here—" I still have that bad feeling.

Élodie nods. "Yes, I agree. But let's be quick about it. I'll tell the children to stay back. They'll watch Mitzi for a few moments."

We advance toward the house. There is no sign of life. We go around to the back where we find an open door and we enter the house. The first room is a kitchen. We enter the kitchen and find two bodies, a man and a woman, lying on a blood-soaked floor, and we see that both have been shot in the back of the head, execution style, and that the blood has oozed into the cracks of broken floor tiles and dried, and we see a trail of blood leading from the kitchen to an adjoining room, and we follow the trail, and we find two children also murdered with bullets to the back of their heads.

I feel the sorrow and the hate and the bile rise up in my throat and manage to croak out a rough, "Shit!"

And then comes a child's scream.

Élodie and I whirl around to see the children standing in the doorway to the house. Probably too afraid to stay alone even for a few minutes, they are now staring at the blood-soaked scene in the kitchen.

"*Merde!* We must get the children away from here!" She moves to herd the children together and roughly pushes them out the door. Several are sobbing. "Now!" Élodie shouts. "Outside!"

Whimpering, Elżbietá whispers, "*Mamusiu! Tatusiu!*" Her sister, Klará, hugs her.

Élodie looks to Aron Klotz. "She said, Mommy, Daddy." His voice cracks as he says it.

Élodie turns to me. "I guess we now know what happened to their mother and father. Quickly, let's go away from this place."

"But, should we leave the bodies like that?" I ask.

"We'll tell people in Le Fossat as soon as we arrive. We must get the children away from here this instant. *This instant!* I saw ... during the exodus from Paris ... children ... after the bombing ... their innocence, their happiness, gone, probably forever. We can't allow that to happen to these children." She chokes back a sob. "Though I fear it already has."

I sweep Mitzi up in my arms and we stride so quickly away from the gruesome scene that some of the children must jog to keep up. We don't stop until we are well out of sight of the farmhouse. Here, we rest at the edge of the forest. Most of the children have stopped crying, but I still hear a few sniffles. Aron comes and stands before Élodie and me. He wipes a sleeve across his face and says, "The sheep didn't eat the rose."

Élodie gives a feeble smile. "No, Aron, you stopped the sheep from eating the rose, and we are proud of you for that. Well done, you."

After a half hour rest, we set out again for the next safe house in Saint-Lizier. By now, we are in the foothills of the Pyrénées and walking is becoming more difficult. We pass areas where limestone has erupted from the earth like broken bones through flesh and the stone seems to have a memory of the castles that used to mottle this land with some vertical outcroppings giving the illusion of turrets. For long stretches, the limestone cliffs hide the sky in all directions except immediately overhead where clouds sit heavy over the hills like clotted cream. But then we come to a break in the escarpment where we can see the sky to the west and what we see is voiced by Max Jäger in both German and French. *"Ein Gewitter! Un orage!"*[63]

"What is it?" I ask.

Élodie nods toward the west where a heavy wall of clouds with a ragged base, the kind, sailors and meteorologists call 'shelf clouds,' is advancing on us. "It looks bad," says Élodie.

---

63   "A thunderstorm!"

"More than an ordinary thunderstorm," I say. "That's a giant. We need to find shelter right away."

"There's a cave not far from here," says Élodie. "To the east, less than a kilometer. Let's hurry." As she rushes, violin case strapped to her shoulder like a rifle, Sten gun cradled in the opposite arm, and hustles the children before her, she shouts to me breathlessly, "There's another large cave nearby called Béideilhac that the Boche use as an airplane hangar. That might be what the Brit planes were targeting."

What the hell? "An airplane hangar?"

"Yes. It's very large. But the cave we're going to is much smaller. There shouldn't be Boche there."

"Shouldn't be?"

"Won't be. I'm sure of it."

"I hope you're right."

The air becomes noticeably cooler. As I jog, my thigh screaming in agony, Mitzi bouncing on my back, I feel the chill on my arms. Mitzi must feel it, too. She snuggles closer to me. The cold slash of air is followed instantly by the ozone smell of rain, an aerated odor peculiar to thunderstorms that I remember from days of sailing during Maine summers. I look behind me, past Mitzi's frightened face. She has just started saying 'Papa' again, and I hope this doesn't set her back. The wall of cloud stretches across the sky until it disappears in mist at both ends. The jagged bottom of the leading edge goes from gunmetal gray to black. Behind it, a bloom of lightening creates a ghostly cast on the atmosphere. Suddenly, the west wind backs violently to the south and hits us with a ferocious gust. The wind increases in strength. Limbs fall from trees. A savage ripping sound rends the air, and a white pine topples over as its roots erupt through earth like an extracted tooth through flesh. Day becomes dusk as the cloud wall passes over us and unleashes crackling hail. A flash of lightening casts everything in a surreal glow and is instantly followed by the crash of thunder. Mitzi buries her face in my shoulder and several of the other children cry out.

"There it is!" Élodie shouts.

I look to where she points and see a huge, crescent opening, almost hidden by bushes and trees, and bigger than the arched spans of the

Longfellow Bridge in Boston. Élodie and the children make a final sprint and are swallowed into the maw of the cave. Mitzi and I reach the opening just as a second bolt of lightning strikes only a hundred yards away. The crack of thunder is deafening and is still ringing in my ears as I drop to my knees and lower Mitzi to the cave's floor. She still has her hands pressed to her ears. Her eyes are wide with fright, and she is panting. She uncovers her ears, and waves her arms frantically, and starts running in tight circles. I gather her up into my arms and hug her close. "It's alright, Mitzi. It's alright."

Élodie says, "I must calm the other children." Starting with the youngest after Mitzi, she goes to each child in turn and speaks soft words. When she comes to twelve-year-old Max Jäger, he says, though with a tight throat, "I'm not frightened."

"Yes, you're very, very brave," Élodie replies, resting a hand on his shoulder. "Perhaps you will help me pass around food to the children. We have lots of bread that Abbé Basc gave us. And some chestnuts."

As Élodie and Max distribute bread, I hold Mitzi tight, and scan the inside of the cave. It runs deep and is filled with stalactites and stalagmites. Unlike many of the caves in this region of France, there is no sign of primitive art on the walls. I turn to Élodie. "How far is it to the next safe house? Le Fossat is it?"

"Only a few kilometers," she replies. "But the children have been through too much. We should stay here the night."

"Yes. That's wise. We can build a fire."

Élodie nods. "It should be hidden by the bushes and trees. It will be safe."

Ten minutes later, a consoling fire is snapping and throwing flickering shadows on the walls of the cave. The reflected red glow in the faces of the children mimics the blood red atmosphere of the storm outside. I see the flames twitching in Élodie's eyes and I place a hand on her cheek and I brush aside the hair the rain has plastered to her forehead and I say, "It will be alright. We'll take shelter here for as long as necessary."

She kisses me on the cheek. "Agreed," she says. Then, after a pause, she adds, "You know, we join a long list of people seeking shelter in these caves. It's like joining a guild of the oppressed."

"What do you mean?"

"All the caves around here have been used forever as shelter from enemies. Just a few kilometers away is the Grotte du Mas d'Azil, a giant cave used by the Cathars to hide from the Christian Crusaders, and again later by Huguenots hiding from Catholics, and recently by Spanish Republicans escaping Franco. No doubt others. Perhaps local citizens hiding from the Romans and later the Visigoths. Who knows?"

A bloom of lightning lacerates the air. More thunder reverberates in the cave. The children's eyes are wide with fright.

"I think we should have a song," Élodie says. She gathers the children round and teaches them the words to "*Frère Jacques.*"

"Frère Jacques, frère Jacques,
Dormez-vous? Dormez-vous?
Sonnez les matines! Sonnez les matines!
Ding, dang, dong. Ding, dang, dong."[64]

After she repeats this a few times, the children join in, one after the other. All except Adrien, who sits by himself in a far corner of the cave. Seeing this, I get a sudden inspiration. I go to Élodie and say, "Tell me how to say, 'I want to be your friend' in French."

"Adrien?" she asks.

I nod. "We need to try something."

"You say, *Je veux être ton ami.*'"

I repeat it several times until I think I have it, then ask, "Now, how would I say, 'Will you teach me French?'"

"You say, *Apprends-moi à parler français.*'" She shakes her head. "It won't work."

"I've got to try. Will you watch Mitzi?"

---

64   "Brother John, Brother John, are you sleeping? Are you sleeping? Ring the bell for matins! Ring the bell for matins! Ding, dang, dong. Ding, dang, dong."

"Of course." She extends her arms to Mitzi, but the child only clings tighter to me.

I smile at Élodie, shrug, and carry Mitzi over to Adrien, and I sit beside the boy, and I place a hand on his shoulder, and I say, "I wish I could speak French, Adrien. I wish I could make you believe everything will be alright." And then I try my French. *"Je veux être ton ami."*

No reaction.

"Apprends-moi à parler français?"

Again, no reaction. Adrien only squirms his shoulder away from my touch. I try for another five minutes until Mitzi insistently tugs at my arm to signal she wants my undivided attention, and I'm finally forced to give up.

⁂

This is where the *Queen Mary 2* is. She is at latitude 43 degrees, 2 minutes, and 32.04 seconds, north, and longitude 50 degrees, 1 minute, and 14.38 seconds west, steaming on a great circle course of 78 degrees magnetic at 26 knots. She is 1,092 nautical miles out from New York. Southampton, England is another 2,027 nautical miles off her bow. This position places her 76 nautical miles northeast of, and 12,500 feet above, the carcass of *RMS Titanic* and about a thousand miles southwest of Nanortalik at the southern tip of Greenland. Vega, the brightest star in the constellation Lyra, is 25.05 light years above, shining in a field of an infinity of stars, some living, some dead but with their light lingering. Also, in the northeast sky flies a British Airways Boeing 747-400 heading east and cruising at 37,000 feet, its wingtip lights blinking green and red.

As I sit at the captain's table, I see the young son of one of the other guests and think again, as I often do, about Adrien. If only things could have turned out differently those seventy years ago. If only I could have elicited a reaction to my clumsy French.

"Papa, did you hear the captain's question?"

It's Callie's voice. I turn to look at her. "Huh?"

"The captain asked you a question."

I look at the captain. "I'm sorry. I was distracted. What was your question?"

"My navigator tells me you were eager to know our precise position. I was just wondering where your interest in navigation comes from."

"I suppose it's always been a compulsion of mine to know exactly where I am," I say. "I guess it comes from being a sailor all my adult life. My father had a boat I sailed before the war, then my wife and I owned a sailboat in which we cruised New England waters."

The captain smiles. "Well, that certainly explains it. Did the navigator give you a satisfactory answer?"

"Yes. He explained about the GPS instrumentation you use. We didn't have any of that when I sailed before the war. We didn't even have Loran-C yet."

One of the members of the "D-Day Club," a man whose bowtie is skewed, raises his glass of wine and says, "Here's to you sir, and all the men of your generation. Like Private True over there at the next table." He rises, proffers the toast, puts his glass down on the table, and applauds. Everybody else at the table stands and joins in the applause. I glance at the next table. Pfc. John True remains in his seat, staring at me. I feel a flush of heat in my cheeks.

"You parachuted into France on D-Day?" asks another guest at the table, a young man whom I had heard was an internet entrepreneur.

I nod.

Another guest asks, "What was it like?"

I remain silent.

Callie puts a hand on my arm and says, "My grandfather doesn't like to talk about it."

The internet entrepreneur nods and goes on. "I read this book by Stephen Ambrose. He said most of you guys were dropped in the wrong positions, like, all over the place. And parachutes were caught up in trees so men were basically hanging there like, well, sitting ducks. Is that true?"

"I suppose," I say. I don't look, but I can feel Pfc. True's gaze on me.

"Were you, like, personally, dropped in the wrong place?" the entrepreneur asks.

"You might say that."

"Well, either you were, or you weren't."

"Then I was dropped in the wrong place, if it pleases you. Many kilometers from my drop zone."

"Well then, see? Perhaps that's why you always want to know precisely where you are."

I stare at the man. I don't know what to say. I crumple the napkin in my lap. I slide a knife from one side of my martini glass to the other. I twirl the olive spear through the liquid and then lift the glass to my lips and take a sip. I avoid looking at Pfc. True.

No one speaks. The only sound is a nervous cough from one of the other guests.

Finally, I look at the captain and ask, "What happens if the electronics fail? Or the GPS satellite falls out of the sky?"

The captain laughs. "We have a great deal of redundancy. All the same, every one of our navigators at Cunard is thoroughly trained in celestial navigation, so unless the stars fall out of the sky, or we misplace our sextant, we'll be fine."

"That's good to know."

The internet entrepreneur turns to me again. "Isn't it nice to know, with modern technology, there's almost no chance of getting lost again?"

I turn toward him, but Callie, her hand still on my arm, squeezes hard. She fixes the man with her gaze. "Earlier, I told you my grandfather doesn't like to talk about it. So, with all due respect, please stop with the questions." Under her breath, softly, barely above a whisper, she adds, "And shut the fuck up!" But there was mostly silence in the room at that instant and she is heard.

The man glares at her, says he is finished anyway, gets up, and leaves the table with half a drink left in his glass.

For a few moments, nobody speaks.

Finally, the captain looks from Callie to me. "I have a granddaughter, myself, sir. You are a lucky man." He raises his glass and says, "Here's to loving granddaughters!"

Chapter 13
Adrien

By the time we reach Saint-Lizier two days later, the children are exhausted. Some have bleeding blisters on their feet requiring immediate attention, but Élodie and I are out of supplies for bandages. We hope our contacts, Ian and Annabel Beckham—a British couple who have lived in France for twenty years—can find bandages and ointment. Élodie goes to the Beckham's house about a hundred meters from the octagonal tower of the small cathedral, while I wait with the children. The evening light is fading and only the nearby peaks of the Pyrénées are in sunshine. The blanched moon has made a shy appearance.

Ten minutes later, Élodie returns with a tall, middle-aged man who has a mustache and wears wire-framed eyeglasses. "This is Ian Beckham," she says.

I shake Beckham's hand. "Happy to meet you."

"Quickly, let's get the children to the house. My wife has laid out some food." Minutes later, we hustle the children through the back door of the small stone house. We are met with a yeasty wave of heat.

Annabel Beckham, who is rail-thin and almost as tall as her husband, wears a blue-and-white print dress that ends below the knees. A white apron is cinched at her waist. She smiles at Élodie and me and says, "The bread will be out of the oven in a few minutes. I'm Annabel."

After we exchange greetings, Élodie says, "Several of the children have blisters. Is it possible we can get ointment and bandages?"

"Indeed, you can," says Annabel. "We collect them because we get many people who have marched a long way. We have both P. K. Burn ointment and Wehrmacht *Mückensalbe* and a good quantity of clean cotton cloth."

Élodie places a hand over her heart and exhales a breathy "Brilliant!"

Annabel reaches for a pair of scissors and hands them to Élodie. "I'll spread the bed sheets on the table and we can cut bandages from them." Annabel leaves the room and returns moments later carrying several white bed sheets which she spreads out on the kitchen table.

Meanwhile, Ian says, "I'm afraid I have some unwelcome news. The route from Saint-Girons to Seix is compromised."

"What do you mean?"

"Jerry executed a couple of passeurs, day before yesterday. No way of telling if they tortured the men first and what information they might have gained."

"Passeurs are guides?" I ask.

"Yes."

"So, you're saying—"

"I'm saying you have to pick a different route, probably further to the east."

Élodie looks up from her task. "What about going through Andorra?"

Ian nods. "That's what I was thinking. We know somebody in Siguer who can help. From that point, there is a safe house in Merens. It's a little over twenty kilometers of difficult terrain, so you'll likely have to bivouac one or two nights. But that very fact means it will probably be free of Jerry. And then, Merens is about ten kilometers from the pass over the mountains into Andorra called El Pas de la Casa. Downhill the rest of the way."

"We just came from the area near Siguer," says Élodie.

"Yes, I know. It will involve some bloody backtracking, but it can't be helped."

Élodie turns to me. "Do you agree?"

"You know the area."

"Then it's settled," Élodie says. Turning to Ian she asks, "May we rest the children here for a couple of days?"

"By all means. We have an old barn out back where they can stay during daylight hours. And, of course, they can sleep there, so long as it doesn't rain. I'm afraid the roof is in bad shape."

The following morning, I step out of the barn at daybreak and walk around back through hip-high grass for a pee. The grass is bent with the weight of dew and I feel the cold wetness penetrate my pant legs. To the west, the sky is filled with an immoderation of stars. The moon is gibbous in the south. In the east, Venus is low on the horizon, its brightness soon to be swallowed by the sun. Only the very tips of the mountains are lit, like pilot lights, ready to ignite the day. Somewhere in the distance, a cock crows, a dog barks. Closer at hand, comes a dawn chorus of birdsong—first the twitter and whistle of the blackbird, followed soon by trills and peeps of the robin, then the louder warble of the wren. I take a deep breath of cool, clean air and, for the briefest of instants, I can imagine a world waking to the absence of war.

I hear Élodie call to me. "Henry, where are you?"

I adjust my pants and walk toward her voice. "Back here."

"Is Adrien with you?" she calls.

"No."

She appears around the corner of the barn, her brow furrowed. "I can't find him anywhere."

I grasp her hand. "C'mon. Let's check it out."

As we rush back toward the barn, I peer into the surrounding gloom for any signs of Adrien. There are none. We enter the barn. Some of the children are just now stirring. From the corner, we hear sobbing.

"It's Yvette," says Élodie. We rush to the child and Élodie drops to her knees. "What is it, Yvette? Where's Adrien?"

"Il est allé trouver notre mère. J'avais trop peur."[65]

Élodie rolls her eyes, translates. "He's gone to find their mother."

"Goddamnit!" I say. "He has no idea what he's doing! The danger!"

Élodie wipes the tears from under Yvette's eyes, the slobber from her nose. "He's only a child, Henry. He doesn't understand. All he knows is something hurts very, very badly, and he wants to make it stop."

---

65   "He went to find our mother. I was too scared."

"Ask her how long ago he left."

Élodie asks the girl, hears the answer, and turns to me. "He left just a little while ago. He gave Yvette his portion of bread and cheese."

"Christ! He's taken off without food! He'll be too weak to go very far. Maybe we can catch up with him."

Élodie approaches twelve-year-old Max and asks, "You heard what is happening?"

"Yes."

"We need to go after him and we need you to stay with the children. Are you brave enough to do that?"

"I will be exceptionally brave. You can rely on me."

Élodie squeezes his shoulder. "Well done, you!"

Élodie and I take up our weapons and rush out of the barn. "Which way?" asks Élodie.

"He'll try to go back the way we came, all the way to his house in Lagrâce-Dieu."

"*Mon dieu!* That was days ago!"

"Can you think of anything else?"

"No, of course not."

"Then let's go."

"Maybe at this hour the *Grenzschutz* won't be at their posts."

"The what?" I ask.

"The German border guards. You heard Ian Beckham. He said they're crawling all over this area. We've got to get to him before they do."

A half hour later, the gloom is starting to lift when we come to a fallow farm field bordered on all sides by trees. We are just starting across the field when we hear something scurrying through the underbrush on the far side of the field.

"A wild boar? A deer?" I ask.

"Or Adrien," Élodie whispers.

Suddenly we hear a cry of "Halt!"

"Shit!" I say. "It *is* Adrien and they've seen him!"

At that moment, Adrien bursts into the open at the far end of the field. He sees us and runs toward us, his arms flailing.

"Halt!" Two German soldiers crash through the line of trees at the far end, and into the open. They level their guns at the boy.

"I've got the one on the left," I cry. At the same instant, I fire, and hear Élodie's Sten gun stuttering. Almost as if choreographed in a macabre dance, the two Germans sink to the ground ... at the same time as Adrien.

"You go to Adrien," I say, "I'll make sure about the Krauts."

Moments later, I finish the two Krauts off with a single shot each and return to Élodie and Adrien. The boy is lying in the dirt. He is bleeding from two gaping bullet holes in the back, and his right hand which also took a bullet. While Élodie bends over to examine the back wounds more closely, I say, "Fuck them! Shooting a child! Shooting a fucking child! Fuck the animals!"

Élodie gives me a wounded look.

My big, fucking mouth! I know she's remembering the young German soldier she killed after Oradour-sur-Glane.

"He's badly hurt," she says. "We need to carry him back and see if Ian and Annabel know a doctor who won't be too afraid to treat him."

"Yes," I say. "But first let me drag those bastards into the bushes and hide them."

By the time I return, Élodie is naked from the waist up. She has removed her shirt, ripped it in half, and stuffed Adrien's wounds with the cloth. "This won't stop the bleeding," she says.

"Let's go, then," I say. I lift Adrien into my arms, cradling him. His breathing is erratic, and his eyelids keep closing. His complexion is blanched. "Stay with us, Adrien," I whisper.

Élodie kisses Adrien's forehead and says, *"Ne nous quittes pas, Adrien. Ne nous quittes pas."*[66]

We start back toward the old barn, and I feel the warmth of Adrien's blood as it soaks through the remnants of Élodie's shirt and drips onto my arms. A trail of blood drops stretches out behind us. I go as fast as I can, while trying not to jounce the boy too much. Several times, my heart skips a beat when I stumble and nearly fall. By the time we return

---

66   "Do not leave us, Adrien. Do not leave us."

to the barn, Adrien's lips are blue. All the children bolt to their feet and stare in horror as Élodie and I burst through the door with Adrien. Mitzi cries, "Papa!" and rushes to me. Several of the older boys glance shyly at Élodie's shirtless body and quickly avert their eyes. She plops down on a stool and says, "Give him to me, then go and fetch Ian and Annabel."

Gently, I lay Adrien across Élodie's lap so his body is resting across Élodie's right thigh and his legs dangle to the side and she supports his upper body with a hand under his armpit and his face is pressed against her shoulder. His blood drips onto her thighs. Blood glistens on the shattered knuckles of his right hand.

Moments later, carrying Mitzi, I return with Annabel. In her hands is a blouse. She says, "Henry told us what happened. He also said you needed something to wear. It's here when you're ready." She drapes the blouse over the rail of a stall.

"A doctor?" Élodie asks.

"Ian is fetching Doctor Delage. He's excellent. He speaks English and he's not afraid to treat Jerry's enemies. We've taken many British aviators to him."

Yvette is standing in the corner sobbing, and I go to her and lift her onto my hip, the one opposite to where Mitzi is already balanced.

The rain starts. We hear it gush from a spout and splash into the large, patinated cistern that sits just outside the barn door.

"Henry, Adrien's lips are dry," Élodie says. "Will you get some water from the cistern?"

"He's tending to some of the children," Annabel says. "I'll go." She returns moments later with a cup of water and holds it to Adrien's lips but it only dribbles down his cheeks and onto Élodie's breast where it dilutes the blood from his wounds. Élodie shivers. "Here, let me," says Annabel as she takes a dry cloth and wipes the blood and water from Élodie's breast.

And at that moment Élodie gasps, *"Oh, mon Dieu, non! Non!"*[67].

Adrien's breathing has suddenly become labored, loud and rasping, with a faint gurgling. Élodie puts her hand on his forehead. "His skin

---

67   *"Oh, my God, no! No!"*

has gone cold!" His mouth opens as in a yawn, he sucks in two breaths, and stops breathing. The barn is silent as everyone waits for the next breath that never comes. The only sound is that of songbirds outside the barn door.

❧

Later, when Doctor Delage arrives, he examines Adrien's wounds and says, "I would not have been able to do a thing. These are fatal wounds. Dear god, I hate what those weapons do!"

An hour later, while Annabel stays with the other children, Élodie, Delage, Ian and I bury Adrien behind the barn and disguise the grave with brush.

And again, it starts to rain. I look up at the scudding clouds and mumble, "Stop your fucking joke with the rain. This is not a fucking movie!"

Delage and Ian head for the barn. Élodie grasps my hand and starts to pull me toward the door, but I stay put, staring at Adrien's grave. "Not yet."

"I need to be with the children," she says.

"Yes. Go back in."

"Won't you come inside?"

"In a little while."

She stares into my eyes for several moments, nods, and goes back into the barn.

I can't stop wondering what I could have done differently. Back then, when Adrien bolted from us to run back to Sainte-Aimée, I should have left Mitzi with Élodie and run after the poor kid and hoisted him over my shoulder and carried him back. Why didn't I do that? Long moments pass, and I am scarcely aware the rain has stopped, when Élodie appears with Mitzi. "I'm afraid she's been impossible," Élodie says. "She keeps saying 'Papa' and trying to get out the door. I finally had to bring her to you."

I nod and hold out my arms and Mitzi runs into them and I fold them around her and I lift her up onto my hip. The rain clouds have passed, and the Janus-faced moon has invaded the barnyard with light. Rain drops gather at the axils of oak leaves, slide down the veins, hang off the tips then drop to the ground and the unweighted leaves spring back up. The moonlight forms dozens of miniature moons in the water beads that adorn the bushes covering Adrien's grave.

"There was nothing you could do," Élodie says.

I shake my head. "I failed him."

"No."

"Yes. When he ran to be with Monsieur Clérisse, we assumed it was because the man had shown kindness and given the children chestnuts. But that wasn't the point, was it? He ran back to Monsieur Clérisse because he needed a man and I wasn't available because Mitzi had already claimed me. He needed a substitute father and I wasn't there for him."

"His father had been gone a long time. He knew Monsieur Clérisse. He was familiar. You mustn't beat yourself over the head about it."

"How could I have been so fucking blind? He went looking for his mother, so she could bring him to his father! That's what it was all about, and I was too stupid to see it."

Élodie puts her hand on my cheek. "After the cave and that soldier I gave a haircut to, you said I shouldn't let it torment me. You said the same thing about the boy-soldiers after Oradour. It's the same thing. Don't let what happened to Adrien torment you. It's the war. It's the fucking, goddamned war."

I place my hand over hers and draw in a deep breath.

"We do the best we can," she says.

I let the breath out in a long, slow exhale. Fuck this fucking goddamned war.

⁂

Ian says, "You must leave straight away with the children before those two guards are missed and Jerry goes looking for them."

"Is there a danger of reprisals?" asks Élodie. "Will you be safe?"

"Don't worry about us. You have the children to care for."

A half hour later, Élodie and I and the twelve remaining children set off for the arduous trek to the east.

Three days after leaving Ian and Annabel Beckham's barn in Saint Lizier, we stop in an open field a few kilometers south of Merens-les-Val. We have had to bivouac each night and it's been hard on the children who have been having nightmares and seem in constant need of loving touches. As the sun disappears behind the ridges to the west, and shadows creep across the field, Élodie and I organize the children the same way we have the two previous nights. After they have eaten their portions of bread, and swallowed their allotment of water, I arrange them into a huddle with Mitzi sitting in the center surrounded in concentric circles first of the younger children, then of the older children, and finally an outer ring comprising me, Élodie and the oldest children. We press the circles tightly together to create a collective warmth. "It's the way penguins do it," I explained the first night, swaying back and forth, imitating a tuxedoed bird and hoping for at least a smile. Periodically, the outer two rings exchange places briefly, so the outermost ring has an opportunity to collect a reserve of warmth before returning to the outside.

In this way, we pass a long, cold, night in thin moonlight, and with wind snaking down off the surrounding slopes, and tongue-flicking every inch of exposed skin. And through the persistence of each night, Élodie and I can feel, as corporeal manifestations, the nightmares playing in the silence of the children's minds, for they reveal themselves in the agitated spasms brushed from limb to limb in the huddled circle at the center of which, like the one ember in a dying fire, is Mitzi, the only partially warm body. And that is how we stay until the blood-red light of the sun first paints the bellies of clouds over Pic Carlit, the mountain looming only a few kilometers to our east.

With stiff limbs, we break the circles apart, pass bread and water from hand to hand and, after a while, set off up the spongy, treeless slopes for the pass through the mountains a mere two kilometers away. When at last we reach the top of the pass, we see no signs of German guards. Instead, we see the green valleys of Andorra spread out below us, and begin along a path that descends, for a change. And the more we descend, the more our spirits are lifted.

Andorra la Vella, the capital, is twenty kilometers away and we make it by early evening. As we appear on the outskirts of the village, a cluster of mostly two- and three-story stone buildings, we are met by a portly, middle-aged woman who greets us first in Catalan then, after eyeing me up and down, switches to rudimentary English. She introduces herself as Vera-Lucia Ribó and nodding to the children, asks, *"Jueus?"*

"Yes," replies Élodie. "They are Jews."

"S'escapen? They escape Hitler?"

"Yes."

Vera-Lucia Ribó smiles broadly. "Is good. I will feed. Okay?"

Élodie's eyes water. "Oh yes, thank you! Thank you! They haven't eaten properly in many days."

The woman places a hand on Élodie's belly. "And you, too. Eh? I will make trinxat. You will enjoy. Follow." She turns and marches toward the center of the village. Élodie, the children, and I follow.

"Trinxat?" I ask.

"It's a mash of potatoes and cabbage, fried with bacon," says Élodie. "It's traditional Catalonian. When you were in England, did you ever try bubble and squeak?"

"Yeah. At a pub we frequented."

"It's similar."

The trinxat is a great hit. Most of the children have two servings and, while we are eating, Vera-Lucia Ribó goes around to several neighboring houses and returns with the news that she has found warm beds for everyone. "I do my part," she says. "We have been at war with Germany since thirty years."

"Thirty years?" I ask. "How can that be? The war is only five or six years old."

Vera-Lucia Ribó turns to Élodie. "You explain. My English is not good."

Élodie laughs. I realize it is the first time in many days I have heard her laugh. She says, "In the First World War, Andorra declared war on Germany. And then, when the war was ended by the Treaty of Versailles, the diplomats forgot to list little Andorra in the official papers. Therefore, she was, and still is, technically, at war with Germany."

Vera-Lucia Ribó purses her lips in a show of disapproval. "No, no. *No tècnicament en guerra, veritablement en guerra!*[68] For the children!" She takes Élodie's hands in both hers. "But what will you do now?"

"We were to meet some men in Esterri d'Àneu," Élodie replies. "But we are many days late because the route we were to take became unsafe and we had to go further east."

"I know the men of which you speak. They have escorted many people to Lisbon for the ships. I will send my nephew to Esterri d'Àneu. He will tell them you are coming. But you rest here for a day and I will find donkeys for you."

"Donkeys?"

"*Sí.* So you don't walk all the way."

"But—"

The woman holds up a hand. "The children must not walk one step more. I will not permit it!"

And, so it is that, two days after arriving in Andorra la Vella, Élodie, I, and the twelve children set out in a caravan of seven donkeys, most of them carrying two children each, and each led by a farmer holding the reins, bound for Esterri d'Àneu. Using paths only the farmers know, we stop often because the children want to pick flowers by the side of the road. Finally, we arrive in Esterri d'Àneu in the early evening. Élodie smiles at me as I sit astride my donkey with Mitzi braced in front of me and says, "You look like Don Quixote."

"And you look like Christ entering Jerusalem. Except he had palm fronds and I don't think he had so many flowers in his hair." The children have insisted Élodie wear flowers they have picked along the way.

Soon, we are welcomed by Àngel Barbera and Miquel Garriga, the two men who will shepherd the children to Lisbon, a journey of more than 1,200 kilometers, mostly by train. Barbera speaks English but Garriga speaks only Catalan.

The sun is beginning to set as we are brought to a large inn near an ancient stone, single-arch bridge over the Noguera Pallaresa River. The undersides of the clouds, fleeced into long strips as they drag across the

---

68   "Not technically at war, truly at war."

surrounding peaks, are gilded butter-yellow. The slow-moving current causes the golden reflections in the river to ripple. We are led through the front door of the inn, and into a large, wood-paneled public room. Four small tables sit in the center of the room adorned with, I later learn, popular card games from the Basque region, and *damas*, a version of checkers. At one end of the room is a huge stone fireplace that occupies the entire wall, and rises to the dark, coffered, wood ceiling. Against the other three walls sit several pieces of furniture including a sideboard, a cabinet of Spanish-Moorish design, two chairs with leather seats and backs, and two Moroccan sofas with seat and back cushions, also with Moorish designs. The floor is made of large, red tiles.

"We have arranged two rooms with beds and cots for you," Àngel Barbera says to Élodie. "One for the boys and the American, and one for you and the girls."

"I see." Élodie says. She turns to the children and explains the arrangements in French and German. She pauses while Aron Klotz translates her comments into Polish.

Instantly, there are tears and sobs of "*Nie! Nie!* from the Polish children which are quickly echoed by cries of, "*Non!*" and "*Nein!*" Even Max Jäger shakes his head slowly and mutters, "I'd rather not" in his best, polite British accent.

Élodie's mouth falls open. "Why not, Max? What's going on? Why is everyone so upset?"

"They don't want to be separated. I don't either. We all want to stay with you and Herr Henry."

Élodie and I gaze at the other children. The three Godowsky children are gathered close together as are Kamilá and Józef Brodny. Rebekka and Stephan Weiß hold hands and gaze back at Élodie and me. Leni and Renata Gottfried hug each other. Even Mitzi seems to understand what is happening, for she has her arms wrapped tightly around my leg.

Élodie turns to Àngel Barbera. "I'm afraid we can't separate the children. I'm sorry."

Àngel gives a broad smile. "I understand. No problem. You have great *duende* with them."

"*Duende?*" Élodie asks.

"How you say? Charm? Enchantment?" He gestures to Miquel Garriga, "*Segueix-me,*"[69] and the man follows him down a corridor that leads from the large room.

"What do you think they're doing?" I ask.

"I don't know," Élodie replies with a smile. She looks down at the toddler clinging to my leg. "But this I do know—that little girl is quite attached to you."

I tousle Mitzi's hair and whisper, "What are we gonna do tomorrow when we have to leave them?"

"I have no idea," Élodie says in a very low voice. "It will be difficult, but it may be only me who will be leaving them. We still have your situation to discuss. On the morrow are you going back to France with me, or are you returning to your outfit?"

Before I have a chance to answer, Àngel Barbera and Miquel Garriga return with arms full of cushions and pillows which they drop on the floor before sliding all the furniture together against one wall to leave a large open space in the center of the room. "This way the children can enjoy the fireplace through the night," he says to Élodie. "We will leave extra wood. But you and the American can have real beds."

"Thank you," Élodie replies. "But please don't be offended if I say I wish to stay with the children."

"As you wish." The man grins, turns to me, and raises his eyebrows inquisitively.

"I'll also stay with the children," I say.

Barbera nods. "I will instruct Miquel to light the fire now, so the children will sleep comfortably. You have had to bivouac, yes?"

"Several times," replies Élodie.

Barbera shakes his head in sympathy. "The mountains can be harsh."

Once Barbera and Garriga leave, the children gather around Élodie and me. Several move in for hugs, and Mitzi continues to hang onto me.

"What are we gonna do?" I ask.

Élodie shakes her head. For a long time, she remains silent.

So long, that I ask again, "What should we do?"

---

69   "Follow me."

"Let's teach them a song," she finally replies. "Let's get them to sing."

"Okay. What song?"

"Vera Lynn's 'We'll Meet Again'."

"Swell. I know it," I say. "Lew Stone played it often at the Dorchester on some type of strange organ."

"You went to dances at the Dorchester Hotel?"

"A few. When I could get leave."

"Well, it wasn't an organ. It was something called a novachord. He led his band from it." Élodie turns to Max Jäger. "Do you know this song?"

Max shakes his head. Instead, he asks, "Might we close the curtains?"

"Yes, of course," replies Élodie.

Max lets out a huge sigh, and smiles. "But I'm so sorry I don't know the song."

"It's alright," Élodie says. "I'll teach you all the words. Tell the others what we're doing and tell Aron to translate for the Polish children." Max does as she asks then turns expectantly. Élodie says, "Yes, then, gather around children. I'll play the melody on my violin then Monsieur Henry and I will sing the lines, and you all repeat after us. Here we go." She opens her case, takes a moment to tune, then notches the chin rest of the instrument against her neck and plays the melody. She then cradles the violin in her lap and nods to me, and together we sing the first line as she waves the bow to the beat:

We'll meet again …

Hesitantly, the children sing the line. Max and Aron translate the meaning. Élodie and I repeat the line and the children mimic us. We do this several times until the children can reasonably approximate the unfamiliar words. Then we move onto the second line and repeat the process, then the third, and so on until everyone has memorized the first verse. Finally, Élodie picks up her violin, and counts out a beat, and plays the melody one time through, and nods, and the children start to sing, and at first their voices are tentative and shy and then, gradually, the room swells with song and the children begin to smile and laugh.

We'll meet again
Don't know where
Don't know when
But I know we'll meet again
some sunny day.

The children insist on singing the song repeatedly and they revel in the fullness of their voices until, finally, one after the other, they are yawning and lying down on the cushions and falling asleep.

After the last child is asleep, we slip out the inn, and walk to the center of the arched, stone bridge. We brace our elbows on the chest-high parapet of the bridge and listen to the water flowing underneath. Above, silvered clouds drift under the moon, blocking its light, then revealing it again. Each time a cloud passes, the river beneath us responds with wavelets of reflected light. Élodie wears a scarf that is wafted by the breeze, floats out for a moment, and snags on the stone of the bridge. Gently, she lifts it away from the stone. "Are you going on to Portugal with the children?" she asks. "Or are you returning to France with me?"

I answer immediately. "I've been thinking about it," I say. "I might as well be hanged for a sheep as a lamb."

"If you mean what I think you mean," she says, "do you understand the implications?"

"I guess they call it desertion."

"You could be shot."

"Or hanged."

"Yes. Or hanged."

"It's worth the risk."

"Why?"

"Because I love you."

She lays her head on my shoulder. "Yes. And I love you."

"And I love the children," I add. "We have nothing to be sorry for. Those children have a chance to survive the war now, and I feel good about that. And, as you said, there will be others."

"I don't know what's going to happen now," she murmurs. "The consequences!"

"Nobody does," I say. "But whatever happens, we must bring more children over the mountains. I don't care about the consequences. I would rather die with you, doing our best, than live without you."

"Yes."

"It's a consequential life."

Élodie gazes into my eyes for several long moments. She places her hand on my cheek and kisses me. "Then we will go to Prades."

"Prades? Why there?" I ask.

"That's where Maestro Casals lives, and he has contacts. He will help us gather more children."

"But why not return to Saint-Lizier and Ian and Annabel Beckham?"

"Saint Lizier was good for when we were planning to cross the mountains further to the west. But now that we're using La Pas de la Casa, Prades is about half the distance."

Several hours later, the early morning light, liquid and golden, inundates the land like spilled egg yolk. It warms the faces of the children, glistens in the tear trails on their cheeks, and glints dully off the muddied metal surfaces of a waiting truck. Àngel Barbera and Miquel Garriga will take the children west to the train station in Huesca in Aragon from where they will travel by rail to Lisbon, and then by ship under neutral-flag, through U-Boat infested waters, to Britain.

The truck idles with a quiet rumble.

As Élodie and I approach the children, Élodie says, "I've been living in fear of this moment. I've grown so fond of them."

"Me too, frankly," I say. "But it must be done. We've brought them this far, you and I together. Now, we need to let them go."

"I'm just so afraid of putting a foot wrong, of saying the wrong thing."

As Élodie and I come alongside the truck, several of the children throw out their arms, and lean over the rail, and cling to us. Mitzi, who is not yet in the truck, has an especially fierce grip on my leg. I am forced to gently pry her hands away as Àngel Barbera bends down to lift her into the bed of the truck. She wails and reaches out for me. I stand at the side of the truck, and she leans out to hug me, and I pat her forehead, and I wipe away the tears on her cheeks with a finger. Several of the other children are crying. Even Max seems about to lose his composure. Surprising myself, and in what must look almost like a priestly gesture, I place my right hand on the boy's cheek and say, "You must be brave for your new journey, for at the end, you will be free," and I approach Jerzy Godowsky and his sisters Elżbietá and Klará and I place a hand on each of their cheeks and say, "Be brave for your new journey. At the end, you will be free," and I do likewise, one by one, with Kamilá and Józef Brodny, and with Rebekka and Stephan Weiß, and with the sisters Leni and Renata Gottfried, and with Aron Klotz, and with Yvette Monsigny, and, finally, with Mitzi.

"Time to leave," Àngel Barbera says.

"No," says Élodie. "First we must have a photograph." She reaches into her knapsack and pulls out the Voigtländer we took from one of the Germans she shot after Oradour. and hands it to Àngel Barbera. She assembles the children at the rail of the truck, stands against the side of the truck, calls for me to join her, and nods to Barbera.

Barbera takes several snapshots before handing the camera back to Élodie and, at last, he and Garriga clamber aboard the truck, grind it into gear, and start off with a lurch. The truck lumbers off slowly, raising clouds of dust that follow after it like swirling dust devils, partly obscuring the children who are staring back at Élodie and me as it grumbles down the road toward the mountains that are soft with a buttery light. One short-circuited taillight winks on and off and Élodie and I watch, unable to tear our gaze away from the receding truck until it turns a bend and is out of sight. And then in silence, feeling useless without the children, we head back toward Andorra from where we will go on to France and whatever awaits us.

⚜

In my cabin aboard the QM2, I stand under the driving shower thinking of that time in Sainte-Aimée when we poured buckets of cold water over ourselves and the children to rinse the soot away, or, another time in the foothills of the Pyrénées when Élodie and I stood naked and shivering under a waterfall. On an impulse, I turn the water to cold, and gasp. I close my eyes and catch a fleeting picture of her standing naked in front of me before the image fades and turns to a green-grey mackle behind my eyelids. After the shower, I shave and splash on some Old Spice and make my way out to the starboard side, forward, on the promenade deck, where Callie and I have agreed to meet to watch the ship steam down the Solent toward our arrival in Southampton.

Callie is already at the starboard rail, which is the windward side of the ship and her hair lifts from her temples just as I remember it doing when she was a child and running on the beach in Gloucester. She comes forward and hugs me. "You smell good, Papa," she says.

"It's for my return to Europe."

Callie gives me a devilish smile. "Where your great love affair blossomed."

"Now, don't tease an old man."

"I promise. No teasing if you live up to your bargain."

"What bargain?"

"Don't give me 'what bargain!' You know damn well what I mean. We made a deal you would tell me the whole story about you and Élodie when we got to London and I don't intend to let you off the hook."

I smile. Perhaps it is time.

In silence, we watch the ship maneuver in the tight channel, complete a full 360° turn so that her port side is parallel to the dock, and then slowly move up against the dock under the power of her bow thrusters and the azipod propellers mounted at her stern.

Passengers have lined the rails to watch as she arrives in Southampton. Among the people, is a boy about the age Adrien was when he died. I can't help but stare him.

"Do you know him?" Callie asks.

"Who?"

"That boy. You've been staring at him."

I shake my head.

"Something is eating at you," says Callie. "You have been distracted the last few days. The closer we've come to Southampton, the quieter you've become."

"It's nothing," I say.

"I don't believe that for a moment. Something's going on, and I wish you would share it with me."

I stare into her eyes for a long moment. It is tempting. I have never, in seventy years, shared my story fully with anyone, not even Anna. And if I were ever to do it, Callie would certainly be the right person. I had suspected returning to France would not only help me remember Élodie but would also dredge up certain misgivings about my time in France immediately after the invasion. It all became fresh when I ran into Pfc. John True. Is this something I want to talk with Callie about?

Callie turns to face me. "When we get to London, we'll see the pulmonologist Doctor Clarkson recommended. Then, if your condition allows us to continue to France, we'll rest up a day, go to a nice restaurant, get a good bottle of wine, and maybe you'll loosen up and tell me what I know damn well you want to tell me about the war years. Sound like a deal?"

I hesitate for a long moment before finally saying, "Deal."

Chapter 14
You Must Make It Sing!

Vera-Lucia Ribó is there to greet us as we pass through the main street of Andorra la Vela on our return journey to France. Wrinkling her nose, she invites us to her home. "You must each enjoy a warm bath," she says. No doubt, she could tell we'd been many days without bathing.

"Thank you for the kind offer," replies Élodie, "but we must try to get to El Pas de la Casa and to the French border just as the sun is setting."

"But why?"

"We will be approaching the pass from the west. If there are German border guards, they will be blinded by the sun, but they will also be lit up by the sun, so we should be able to see them and know what to do. We may have to abandon the trails and climb over open country."

"Well, I will fetch a bar of soap for you to take with you."

Élodie and I both laugh. "We'll be quite grateful," she says.

The woman goes across the road into her house and returns moments later and hands Élodie the bar of soap, and we bid her farewell, and set out for El Pas de la Casa. We arrive in the early evening and, by the time we approach the border, the sun is setting just as Élodie had anticipated. We see no activity, no French citizens, no German guards, but we decide to abandon the trail anyway, and trek through open country, until it is too dark to walk. And then we bivouac for the night.

In the morning, we begin the fifty-kilometer trek east to Prades and our route takes us through valleys with rocky escarpments on both sides.

This had once been a land of medieval castles and even the stones seem to carry memories of them where shadows play tricks and give the illusions of fortresses recessed into the hillside and vertical columns of rock that look like turrets or giant trilobites impressed into the rock face. Erupting from the land are limestone outcroppings, knobby as rheumatoid knuckles, where the earth wears its skin thinly on the bone like a half-eaten, partially flensed, carcass, and every so often the shadow of a griffon vulture rolls and swells across the undulant, fractured stone. The valleys through which we trudge, between the escarpments and the outcroppings, burgeon with purple and white saxifrage which flower from cracks and crevices of rock, blue trumpet gentians, white alpine butterwort, and blue and yellow monkshood. Butterflies flit before us and birdsong sweetens the air—rock thrush, red-backed shrike, woodpecker, finch.

"The war couldn't be further away," I say.

Élodie shakes her head. "No, my love. On the contrary, the war is inside us."

I stare at her for a long moment. There is a sadness in her eyes, a sadness so deep, tears will not come.

Soon, we arrive at a small commune called Vilanova in the late afternoon and go straight to the little stone church to ask sanctuary from the priest. I watch as the priest and Élodie engage in a long, heated conversation. Finally, the priest stomps off, and Élodie turns to me and says, "He's not very happy."

"I can see that," I say. "What's his beef?"

"He's afraid of reprisals, He says we put the whole village at risk. We can stay in the church, but he wants us out of here first thing in the morning. At least, he'll bring us some food."

We pass a fitful night, and the following morning we leave early after finishing the last of the baguette and cheese that the priest brought us.

"I stink," says Élodie. "And by the way, so do you. We can't appear on Maestro Casals' doorstep like this."

"What do you plan to do about it?" I ask.

"I know a place where we can wash ourselves and our clothes. It's a waterfall only a few kilometers north of Prades. And we have the soap Senora Ribó gave us."

"Lead on, Macduff," I say.

"It will take us a good six hours to get there, but it will only be another one or two hours to Prades. We'll be able to rest while our clothes dry because we don't want to enter Prades during daylight."

We move much faster without the children and arrive at the waterfall before noon. It is in a small, rocky ravine that has the internal volume of the nave of a country church. At the head of the nave, where the apse would be, is the waterfall, scintillating behind a standing rainbow and spilling its water into a clear stream. We climb down into the ravine and scramble over boulders until we come to a slab by the edge of the stream, flat as an altar, and there we strip off our clothes and we grasp each other's hand and we step into the stream and wade to the waterfall and step under it with gasps and shivers.

"My god, it's cold!" Élodie cries.

"You bet your sweet ass it is!" I say. "Jesus!"

"Speaking of my ass," Élodie says, "Here. Get to work." She hands me the bar of soap.

Quickly, we pass the soap back and forth and lather each other up, lingering in the intimate places with groans of pleasure, as the sun ignites diamonds in the cascading water. Soon, we are finished, and we emerge from the waterfall and wade back to where we left our clothes. The sun is now at its zenith, and its light penetrates the ravine fully, heating the rocks which, in turn, trap the heat in their embrace. We wash out our clothes like village washer women and then lay naked under the sun on a flat rock slab hidden from the world.

Élodie asks, "Do you want some of my perfume?"

"You mean that horse stuff?"

"*Mon dieu!* Horse stuff! You mean *Nuit de Longchamp?*"

"Longchamp is a horse race track, isn't it?"

"That doesn't make the perfume 'horse stuff,' as you call it."

"Now if you had some Old Spice," I say. "I'd take that."

"Is that an American men's cologne?"

"Yup. New. It came out a few years ago."

"Well, I don't have any. You'll just have to make do with your natural scent."

She gives me a teasing smile, but it quickly fades and her lips part and she holds my eyes in a fierce gaze and strokes my arm and says, "I want to have a baby with you."

I am stunned. For a moment, I am speechless. Finally, I take her in my arms and murmur, "Yes," and we make love, and in the unfolding of the afternoon we lie together, bodies golden under the warming sun and we make love again and I whisper, "As soon as the war is over, we'll get married."

"Yes." She trails her fingers up and down my chest. "And I'll wear something white."

Several hours later, as we stand on a hill on the outskirts of Prades, Élodie and I have a clear view of the peak of Canigou with the light of the setting sun refracting from the sharp ridges of its summit. Below us, Prades lies in the murk of twilight. We see no activity in the streets. Nevertheless, Élodie says, "We should wait until it is fully dark. The last time I was here, there were Vichy police, but they were not much of a threat. However, if the Gestapo has taken over, that's a different story."

"Then, let's wait," I say. "I have no desire to run into those bastards."

"I've never approached his house in the dark, but I think I can find it. It's called Villa Colette and there's a woman who lives with the maestro named Señora Capdevila. I believe she's a kind of administrative assistant. At least that's the post she held with The *Orquestra Pau Casals* in Barcelona. It was an orchestra he founded some years ago. I played with them once."

A half hour later, the light has completely disappeared. The moon is yet to rise, and we have difficulty stumbling down the hill and into the town and finding Casal's house. Once or twice we sense movement in the distance, and pause, and hold our breaths until it seems clear again. At last, Élodie says, "There it is! Quickly!" She grabs my hand and we take off at a run.

The house is a modest two-story affair. We must have been seen from the inside, for as soon as we approach the door, it opens and a handsome woman hurriedly ushers us inside and looks left and right before she closes the door, turns, and nods to Élodie. *"Mademoiselle Bedier, Maestro Casals sera heureux de vous voir."* [70]

"This is Henry Budge," Élodie says once we're inside. "He's American."

"Ah, then I will speak English," the woman says. She admits us to a small front room with two 19th century French tapestry armchairs and a Moorish rug in muted reds and blues. Against the wall, in the far corner, is an upright piano.

Footfalls sound on the stairs and Pablo Casals rushes to greet Élodie. "I heard," he says. "We must speak English. How are you my sweet? As Señora Capdevila said, I am so happy to see you. Were you seen by others?"

"I don't think so," replies Élodie.

Casals walks to the window, draws the curtain an inch or so and peers outside. Apparently reassured, he returns and says, "The Gestapo have been troublesome. Sometimes, they watch the house. We've been visited several times by them. I must ask you to hide your weapons out back in the trees. If we are visited by the Gestapo, it would go badly for all of us if your weapons were discovered."

"Yes, of course," Élodie says and leads me out the back of the house.

When we return, Élodie says, "Perhaps we should not have come. We don't want to cause you trouble. We should leave."

Casals nods. "It is best. I have found a safe house where you can wait for the children. The word has been sent back along the line."

"You are wonderful! Where is this safe house?"

"Mosset."

"Perfect!" Élodie turns to me and says, "The waterfall is halfway between here and there in the same direction. We'll pass it on the way."

"But not until we play some music together," says Casals. "Then, at the right time, we will drive you there."

"You can get petrol?"

"Not much, but, yes. On rare occasions, the Germans allow me to take food to the prisoners at Rivesaltes."

"Rivesaltes?" I ask.

---

70   "Miss Bedier, Maestro Casals will be happy to see you."

"It's a concentration camp just north of Perpignan," Élodie says.

"So many prisoners," says Casals. "And they send many from there to the death camps. When will it all end? When?"

Suddenly there comes a pounding on the door.

"The Gestapo!" whispers Casals. "Quickly, the two of you out the back door! Hide in the trees."

Élodie and I hesitate for a moment. "But what about you?" Élodie asks.

"Go! Go!" Casals says, urging her with a gentle push in the back. "We've handled this before. We know what to do."

"No, wait," Élodie says. "They must have seen us. How will you explain that nobody is here?"

Casals gapes at her but has no answer.

Élodie says, "Henry, you go out back and hide. We'll say there was only one of us and I … and I came with my violin for a lesson with the maestro. Go! Now!"

More pounding on the door.

"Go, Henry!"

I hesitate for only a moment, then bolt out the door. I crouch in the bushes next to where we hid our guns. If it becomes necessary, I will make sure the Gestapo man "discovers" them in the most unpleasant way possible.

Élodie later tells me, in detail, what happened while I hid outside.

As soon as she was certain I was well hidden, Élodie told Señora Capdevila to open the door. A man in plain clothes—which included the clichéd leather coat and Trilby hat of a Gestapo agent—entered. He was accompanied by a soldier wearing a grey SS uniform consistent with the practice of the Gestapo in occupied territories. The Gestapo agent marched up to Casals and asked, "And who is this *junge Dame?*"

"She is Élodie Bedier. She is a student of mine."

The man asked Élodie, "And who was with you when you came here?"

"Nobody. I was alone," she said. And when the German expressed disbelief and insisted he and his man saw two people, Élodie angered the man by saying, "It is dark. Perhaps you are mistaken." She then thought quickly and said, "Perhaps you saw my violin. I'll show you how I carry it." She described to me how she slipped the strap of the violin case over her shoulder and turned her back to the man and asked, "Do you see how it could look like a second person? In the darkness, I mean."

The man said nothing for long moments. Finally, he ordered the soldier to search the other rooms in the house. They waited in silence while the man searched. Finally, he returned and said he found nothing. But they weren't out of the woods yet, because the Gestapo agent said, "Show me. Teach Fräulein Bedier a violin lesson."

Élodie told me it was through an almost miraculous bit of silent communication that she and Casals conceived of a subterfuge. "Pablo looked me in the eyes," she said. "He asked if we should play *'Song of the Birds'* again together. But he said I should play with more vibrato than the other day." Élodie said she had all she could do not to smile, and opened the violin case, and lifted up the violin and tucked it under her chin, and purposefully neglected to check its tuning. And as she was making a show of doing all this, Casals took his position in a chair and propped his cello between his legs and they began to play. Élodie tried quite hard to play without enough vibrato, to play emotionless and, after several bars, Casals said, "No, no, no! More life! More vibrato," and he played several bars to demonstrate. Élodie played the same measures, this time with more vibrato, but still she deliberately held back, until Casals said, "More! You must make it sing!"

And after several more minutes of that back and forth, the Germans left.

⁂

Later that night, feeling our way without headlights in the glow of a waxing gibbous moon, a friend of Casals drives Élodie and me to Mosset in a Citroën. The trip goes without incident. He says his name is Nigel and offers no more, and we don't ask. We only know from his name and his speech that he is English. Turning off the main road onto a two-track dirt road, with tall grass between the tracks, we drive on for another ten minutes until we finally arrive at a small house nestled in a stand of conifers. Our driver says, "The house belonged to my sister and her husband. They were executed by the Boche. No one has lived here in months."

"Do the Germans know of this place?" I ask.

"No. My sister and her husband were executed some distance away in Rivesaltes. They were trying to help some Brits escape the prison there. You may have noticed how carefully I kept the tires in the tracks, so we wouldn't bend any grass. No one will know you are here." He leads us into the small two-room house. "We have put in supplies. There's a Sterno stove and plenty of fuel. Lots of canned goods. And there's a pond out back for fresh water."

"I'm sorry about your sister and your brother-in-law," Élodie says.

"Yes," he says. "I'd best be going. Someone will contact you when the next group of children is ready."

"Of course."

We watch him drive off. As soon as the sound of the engine fades, we become aware of night sounds—frogs in the unseen pond, crickets, cicadae. At the periphery of our vision are the flickers of fireflies. A slight wind soughs through the trees. I put my arm around Élodie's waist. "Peaceful," I say.

"Yes." She reaches up and kisses me on the cheek.

I turn to face her and kiss her full on the lips. When I pull back and look into her eyes, I ask, "Were you serious about wanting to make a baby?"

"Yes. Of course," she says. She returns the kiss and grasps my hand and leads me inside and turns down the covers of the bed and we undress and we embrace and we sink to the bed and we make love passionately and I am flooded with happiness unlike any I've felt before, happiness enough to bring tears, and when we are finished, we lay back, side-by-side, holding hands, as a density of moonlight, pouring through the window, washes our naked and sweat-sheened bodies. But it's a two-faced moon and I am convinced it is bone-white moonlight from its other face that now shimmers upon a world at war. It is the moon-light a prisoner in Auschwitz, 1,500 kilometers to the northeast, sees sizzling on the barbed wire at the edge of the camp as he thinks of his wife and the same cruel moonlight the man's wife gazes at through the tiny crack in the barracks wall of the women's camp at Bergen-Belsen as she thinks of her husband. It is the same unnatural moonlight that weighs heavily on all the broken and burnt-out buildings of London and Hamburg, of Coventry and Cologne, of Darmstadt, Cardiff and Düsseldorf, and it is the same light from the same obese, gibbous moon that hauls an ocean onto the beaches of Normandy, and that flashes in the whirling propellers of American B-17s and B-29s about to bomb a plant in Ruhland, Germany where the moonlight also glistens on the waters of the Schwarze Elster River, beside which a group of children play—*a group of children!*—and it is the moonlight that sparks off the buckled rail of a sabotaged train track north of Toulouse, and that sheens the decks of ships unloading materiel at a temporary harbor, called Mulberry "B," off Gold Beach in Normandy, and that glints off the nose detonator of a V-1 rocket aiming for London, and that refracts in the binoculars of a civilian volunteer in the Royal Observer Corps, standing spread-legged, and proud, on the roof of Selfridges in London's Oxford Street as he watches, with his pig-tailed, freckle-faced daughter by his side, for more V-1 flying bombs, and it is the very same perverse moonlight that gleams on the barrels of 75 mm guns on Sherman tanks waiting for dawn to attack their Panzer enemies in the hedgerows of Normandy, and the same oh-so-very-indelicate moonlight that glitters in the gold tooth of an open-mouthed corpse in a shattered street in Minsk, 2,200 kilometers away, and the same shimmering moonlight that soon, after a slight rotation of the earth, will glance off the rifle of a soldier of the 77th U.S. Infantry Division pulling guard duty on the Orote Peninsula of Guam, and that will flash on the periscope, as it breaks the ocean's surface, of the *USS Sailfish* on patrol off Formosa, and that will gleam off the decks of the Japanese cargo ship *Toan Maru*, so soon to fall victim to *Sailfish's* torpedoes, and it is the same unholy light from a pregnant moon, on that night of lovemaking, that also floods through the open, burnt-out roof of a church in Oradour-sur-Glane to lay a ghostly radiance on a mangled and charred baby pram, forsaken on the shattered altar.

We wake the next day at first light, having slept soundly and without fear for the first time in weeks. The moonlight that blanketed the house in the night is now replaced by the glow of new sunlight. I go outside in time to see the moon slide behind a mountain to the west just as the sun rises blood-red in the east, as if seesawed up by the dense, sinking moon.

Élodie joins me and puts her arm around my waist and we stand gazing at the mountains and she says, "No clouds. It promises to be a beautiful day."

"It almost feels like the war could be on another planet."

"Let's enjoy it while we have it. What do you want to do?"

"Nothing. Absolutely nothing." I push a tendril of hair behind her ear and plant a kiss on her temple. "Except make love to you and listen to you play the violin."

She sighs and leans against me. "That, my good sir, sounds like an excellent plan."

For breakfast, we eat some of the bread lest it go stale because we have no idea when Casal's friend might deliver more. "We can break into the baked beans and whatever else we have later," Élodie says.

Looking through a cabinet, I make a discovery. "Would you believe they somehow found a half dozen cans of Spam, a few cans of sardines, some other stuff with labels I can't read."

Élodie examines the labels which read *Les Anis de Flavigny* and *Bloc de Foi Gras de Canard.* She says, "This first one is a candy, the second one is duck liver."

"Do all French hideaways eat like this?"

"Maestro Casals is well loved. No doubt he asked for help."

"Yes. And didn't he also say the Krauts let him take food to the prisoners in … where was it?"

"Rivesaltes."

"Yeah, that's it. Obviously, he has sources."

After eating some bread, we return to bed and make love again, and sleep, and make love again, and sleep more, and it is afternoon by the time we rise and go out into the meadow that fronts the house. The field is alive with the twitter of songbirds, the buzzing of bees, the chirping of crickets. From the far end comes the nickerings and snorts of two Mérens ponies grazing side by side. Butterflies flit about the field which is a varicolored profusion of flowers—the blue carpet of gentians with their mossy fragrance, the rich aromas of orchids, purple, yellow and white, golden lilies, and the lavender of the bearded iris. And in the luxuriance of these scents, and these colors, we make love in the grass under the sun which heats our bodies and we feel the grass tickle our flesh and we listen to the sounds of the field and we taste the sweet salt of sweat on our bodies. And in the evening, we tune the wireless Casals has loaned us to *Radio-Londres*, the voice of the Free French Forces broadcast from London for news of the war and especially for music, like the many songs composed by Frenchmen and sent secretly to London so they could be played as acts of resistance.

For eight days, it goes like this. Days spent lying in the meadow, swimming in the pond, evenings listening to the radio and making love. Then, on the ninth day, we are jolted out of our reverie by the sudden appearance of the Citroën and Casal's friend, Nigel.

"It's time?" Élodie asks.

"It's time," the man replies.

When we arrive in Prades, Casals says only, "There are seven children waiting for you at Merens. There is an ancient stone bridge. They are in the house opposite. It has a blue door, the only one in the village. Nigel can get you to a tiny hamlet called Orlu about six kilometers from Merens, then you'll have to walk the rest of the way on mountain paths. Fortunately, there is enough moonlight."

Using only single-lane back roads, it takes us almost three hours to travel the forty kilometers to Orlu in the Citroën. After Nigel drops us off, we watch him disappear into the moonlit night. We climb until we summit a ridge and follow the ridge line westwards. Eventually, by the reflection of the moon in the water, we locate the Ariège River and follow with our eyes its silvery length to the village, a cluster of buildings that we assume is Merens. We hunt for a gentle slope that will take us from the ridge to the valley, and eventually find one. Carefully, we descend, feeling for the ground with our feet. At the base of the ridge we come to a small brook only a hundred yards from the bridge over the Ariège. First, Élodie crosses, stepping from stone to stone. "Be careful," she says with a whisper, since we are so close to the village. "It's slippery."

I begin to cross. I'm nearing the far end when I slip, and my heart sinks, and I make a desperate leap for the opposite shore. I land awkwardly, and pain shoots through me. I lay on the ground grabbing my ankle and cursing softly.

"You're hurt," Élodie whispers. "Where? Your ankle?"

I nod. "I think I broke it."

"Let's get you to the house so we can have light to look at it," she says. "Can you walk?"

With Élodie's assistance, I stand and instantly find I can put no weight on my left foot. I shake my head. "It's no good. I can't walk."

"Well, you can't stay here. I'll help you. Put your arm around my shoulder." She supports me as I hop, one-footed, and we make our way to the stone bridge. On the opposite side, as promised, is the house with the blue door. Élodie taps lightly. Moments later, the door opens, and we are greeted by a middle-aged woman. "You're late," she says.

Élodie replies, "I'm Azalais."

"I'm Céleste. No need for your *nom de guerre*. I know who you are. I adore your music. And this is the American Nigel told me about?"

"Yes. You know a lot. Where can he sit to take weight off his ankle?"

"I like to know what I'm getting into," the woman replies, as she guides us into the next room and points out a sofa.

As Élodie assists me to the sofa, she says, "You're French by your accent, but you speak excellent English."

"I went to school in England," the woman replies.

"Me, too. When the war is over, we must talk. In the meantime, is there a doctor we can trust?"

"Yes, of course."

"Can you send for him?"

"*Her*," the woman replies. "And no need, for I am the doctor. Let me look at this ankle." I start to untie my boot laces. "You've broken the little finger on your right hand some time ago," she says, pointing at my finger. "Why did you never get it reset?"

"I keep it as a reminder not to jump out of airplanes," I say.

Céleste smiles, takes hold of the boot with both hands. "This will hurt," she says. She gives a hard tug and pulls the boot off and I stifle a cry of pain. "It's best to do it quickly," she says with an apologetic tone. She removes the sock and takes my foot in her hand. "It's already swollen big as a grapefruit. You broke it, for sure. It's probably an avulsion fracture. In any case, it needs a cast and you won't be walking freely on it for several weeks. I have crutches you can have."

My heart sinks. "But, the children?"

"You'd be next to useless. *They* would have to help *you*."

"Where are the children?" Élodie asks.

"There are seven of them. It would be too dangerous for that many to remain here. We're accustomed to one, maybe two, aviators. The children are in a summer sheep barn in the high pasture about two kilometers from here."

"What should we do?" Élodie asks of both me and Céleste.

"You have no choice," Céleste says quickly. "The children can't stay where they are. You must take them, and you must do it without the American." She raises her eyebrows inquisitively.

"His name is Henry," Élodie says.

"Yes, you must go without your Henry. I will send word to Maestro Casals and he will send Nigel to collect Henry. But you must leave with the children tomorrow."

Élodie peers into my eyes for several long moments, her eyebrows knitted. At last, she says, "Then I will leave with the children tomorrow."

I sleep fitfully that night because of the lingering pain. And the prospect of parting with Élodie. When I finally slide out of bed, I see, outside the window, Élodie's silhouette against the sky. I hop outside on one leg and a crutch and turn my collar to the chill wind coming off the mountains and hug Élodie from behind and she looks over her shoulder at me. Her face is blanched by light from the moon that is still visible in the dawn sky. "You slept badly," she says.

"It was painful. You slept poorly, too."

"Yes."

"I hope the children slept peacefully."

"They are probably too frightened," Élodie replies. She reaches back and caresses my cheek. "What was it you called that kind of moon?"

"Gibbous," I say, looking up. Sheets of mist roll down the slope from the high pasture where the children wait.

"It's the same as it was that wonderful night in Mosset."

"Except, then it was waxing gibbous. Now, it's waning gibbous."

"It looks like a pregnant belly," she says with a hesitant laugh.

I echo her laugh. "You have a wonderful imagination."

"You could ask me not to go."

"I won't lie," I say. "I was thinking about it in the night. But, no, I can't. You wouldn't forgive yourself. You wouldn't forgive me."

"It will be much more difficult without you."

"I'm betting you'll handle the children fine."

"That's not what I meant." She turns in my arms, faces me, reaches up and kisses me. "I love you too much."

"Too much?" I ask, bemused.

"It makes this too difficult. I don't want to go without you."

"You must promise me to be safe. No unnecessary risks."

"I'll return as soon as humanly possible."

"Do you hear me? No unnecessary risks."

"Yes. I promise." She pauses, then says, "Maybe the war will end, and this will be the last time. No more children to rescue after this."

I force a smile. "Yes. Then we can go to our little island in the Pacific."

"My God," she says. "I wish you could ask me not to go and I could say, right then, I won't go. What if we don't make it through the war? We'll never have that island."

"We made our choices. We knew what we were doing. Just be safe. Please, by all that is holy, be safe." I pause and run a finger along her cheek. "And return to me."

From the corner of my eye, I see Céleste standing at a distance. I don't know how long she has been there, but now that I look her way, she approaches and says to Élodie, "You should start out now before the sun is too high."

Élodie nods. She lifts her rucksack and slips her arms through the straps and shrugs it onto her back. Then, abruptly, she puts the rucksack down again, fishes through it, and pulls out the Voigtländer camera we took from the dead German and holds it out to me. "Here. You should take this."

"Why?"

"It's … it's too much weight."

Of course, it weighs very little, and I am forced to wonder what she is doing. I reach out and take the camera. But I can't escape a sense of foreboding. Is she giving me a parting gift?

She gazes into my eyes and leans into me. We embrace for a long time until, finally, I take her by the shoulders and gently turn her so she's facing the path to the summer barn. "Go," I say. "The children are waiting. They need you."

She holds onto my hand for a long time before finally starting up the path.

And as she passes out of hearing distance, I whisper to myself "And *I* need you."

I lean against the rough stone of the side of the house and watch Élodie climb toward the leaden, grey-bottomed clouds that roll past the top of the ridge. Crepuscular rays pour down through the morning clouds, and Élodie passes in an out of the light and, halfway to the crest, she stops and turns and gazes back at me for a long time and, finally, she turns again and, within moments, passes into the shredded filaments of a low-reaching cloud, and out of sight.

PART 3
A MOMENT IN PARADISE

Ein Augenblick, gelebt im Paradiese
Wird nicht zu teuer mit dem Tod gebüsst.
(One moment spent in Paradise
is not too dearly paid for with one's life.)
—Friedrich von Schiller

Chapter 15
If Prayer Were Made of Sound

When Élodie ascended the path that day, seventy years ago, the sky was curdled with heavy, big-bellied clouds that the morning sunlight penetrated in bands. It is the same sky I see now as Callie and I disembark *Queen Mary 2* a little before noon. We catch the train for London and an hour and, a half later, arrive at Waterloo Station from where we take a taxi to the Dorchester Hotel on Park Lane, where I had booked connecting rooms, and where we take brief naps before going down to the Promenade Room for the 3:15 afternoon tea sitting. The maître d' leads us past coral-colored marble columns with white veins and gold leaf capitals to a divan which is trimmed in green to echo the many palm plants scattered throughout the room. The windows are adorned with heavy drapes, also coral colored.

After we are seated, Callie says, "I called Mom."

"How did she react?"

"She was beside herself."

"I'm not surprised," I say. "She'll get over it."

Callie waits for the waiter to take our order, then says, "I can't believe how luxurious this hotel is. What made you choose it?"

"I've been here before."

"With Élodie?"

"No. We were ships passing in the night in those days. She had been here before me, but by the time I got here, she was in France. I came to a few dances they held here for service men."

"Tell me about the dances. Did you meet British women?"

I chuckle and say, "Oversexed, overpaid, and over here."

Callie laughs. "What? What's that supposed to mean?"

"That's what the Brits said about American soldiers who went after their women. But we had an answer. We said they were underpaid, undersexed, and under Eisenhower."

"You were like high school boys insulting each other."

"We were young."

"Did you ... did you hook up with any of the British women?" A mischievous smile comes to her lips.

"I came mostly for the music. There was a band leader named Lew Stone. He played a strange instrument called a novachord. It had a keyboard and all sorts of electronic stuff like vacuum tubes and capacitors and such. And they played—"

"It sounds like what we call today a synthesizer," Callie says. "And it sounds like you're regurgitating a bunch of irrelevant details to avoid answering my question."

"I'm not saying anything about British women. That wasn't part of the deal."

The waiter appears with the raisin scones and Keemun Mao Feng black tea we ordered. When he leaves, Callie asks, "When was the last time you saw her?"

I nibble on my scone, take a sip of the tea, and finally say, "The last time I saw her, she was climbing a mountain path to meet up with another group of children. I had broken my ankle and was in no shape to go with her." It's strange how memory works! Just then, when I nibbled on my scone, I flashed on a memory of Mitzi—how, that one time, I took the smallest possible bite when she offered to share her madeleine with me.

"A group of children? You've alluded to children before. Please, Papa, tell me about the children."

I take a deep breath and say, "Yes. The children. But first I must tell you how I ... Élodie and I ... came to meet the children. I suppose to go back to the beginning, it really started when I climbed aboard a plane in England ready to jump into France on D-Day ...."

I told her how I was wounded on the way down and how I missed the drop zone and how I was cared for by Élodie and how we traveled south and how we came upon the aftermath of what happened at Oradour-sur-Glane."

"Oh, my god!" Callie puts down her teacup with a rattle.

"And I suppose that changed everything," I say. "Élodie damn near lost it. For a little while she was so deranged with anger, she could have shot her way through to Berlin and personally lined up Hitler, Goering, Himmler, Goebbels, and Keitel and mowed them all down. I think the only thing that saved her was the children."

"And you?"

"Perhaps." I go on to tell her how Élodie and I met the children in Aquilac. How Odette Dupont introduced us to Mitzi and the others. And I name them all.

Callie looks at me in amazement. She puts a hand over mine. "After seventy years, you remember all their names?"

"Uhm hmm. Yes." I look down at my folded hands. I can almost see them. I can almost see them as they are standing in the bed of the truck in Esterri d'Àneu.

"Do you ever wonder what happened to them?"

"All the time. I even tried to track them down after the war, but everything was so confused. There were displaced persons all over the continent."

"But I thought you said they ended up in England."

"Probably only for a short time. The idea of the U.N. group responsible for post-war displaced persons was to repatriate them to their countries of origin as quickly as possible." All at once I'm hit with exhaustion, telling the story. I rub my eyes.

"Are you tired?"

I nod. "Yes. But there's more."

She squeezes my hand. "I know," she says. "But let's get some drinks before you continue."

We pay the bill and go into the bar at the Dorchester, order martinis, and when they are delivered, I continue my story. I tell Callie about the trip south, about Rachelle Monsigny, who went by the *nom de guerre*

260 NORMAN G. GAUTREAU

Lombarda, and her children, Adrien and Yvette, and how she gave her children over to our care.

"That poor woman!" Callie says. "So brave."

"We couldn't save Adrien," I whisper. It surprises me that, after seventy years, it still hurts so much to say that.

"What do you mean?"

Through tears, I tell her how Adrien ran off in search of his mother, the German guards and about how he died in Élodie's arms.[71]

"Oh, god, Papa!" she says again and squeezes my hand.

After a long pause and a few sips of the martini, I tell Callie about the rest of the journey to Esterri d'Àneu, about the pain of turning the children over to the Catalan men, and about retracing our steps and going to Prades and visiting Pablo Casals.

"The cellist?" Callie asks.

"Yes. A beautiful man. He found us a place to hide out while we waited for another group of children." I tell her about the idyllic eight days and nights Élodie and I spent in Mosset and about the trek to Merens, and about breaking my ankle, and about watching Élodie disappear into the clouds. But now, how can I tell Callie what it was truly like waiting for Élodie? The hope. The pain. The thousand imagined greetings in those weeks. How I thought I would go crazy with worry and longing.

"And that was the last time I saw her," I say. "When I made it back to Mosset, I waited and waited, but she never returned."

Callie slides her chair back, rises, steps behind my chair and puts her arms around me. "Papa," she whispers. She kisses me on the cheek. "Did you ever try to find out what happened to her?"

I reach back and cover Callie's hands with mine. "Yes, of course," I say. "But it wasn't until a few months later. First, I had to avoid the firing squad if I could. Once my ankle healed, and she still hadn't returned, I decided to follow the same route through Esterri d'Àneu and make my way back to England. I learned, from the two Catalan men we

---

71   In my advancing years, I've become increasingly lachrymose—as given to tears as a child who's lost a pet—making it necessary to keep a hand-kerchief at hand at all times; a far cry from the hardened paratrooper I once was. (Pun intended.)

had dealt with before, that she had delivered the children to them and headed back to France. They had no idea what happened to her after that. Eventually, I made it back to England and, as it happened, my unit, the five-oh-eighth, was on R-and-R preparing for what would become known as Operation Market Garden, a jump into the Netherlands. But before I could rejoin them, I had to report to the Provost Marshall General's office to explain my absence."

"How did you manage that?" Callie asks.

"It was easier than I expected. I had the scars to prove my story of being hit on the way down, plus this broken finger, and there were lots of guys who ended up spread all over the place, many of them lost, missing in action."

"So, did you parachute into the Netherlands?"

"Yes. It was a mess. We lost that battle. But then there was the Ardennes, which you probably know as the Battle of the Bulge, then a few more actions in Belgium and Germany. At last, the war ended, and soon we were moved off the line and stationed in Chartres. I managed to get leave and immediately headed south."

✿

It is the 3rd week of May 1945, when I finally get leave. Hitchhiking in U.S. army jeeps and several farmers' carts all the way from Chartres, I finally arrive in Aquilac. I am pleased to see, in every town and village I pass through, people walking about freely. I go immediately to see Odette Dupont who greets me by saying, "You have come looking for Élodie?"

"Do you have any information about her?"

Odette shakes her head sadly. "No. I only know the last group of children made it to England, so we know she made it as far as the drop-off point in Esterri d'Àneu. But that was many months ago."

"And there's been no word at all? Not even a rumor?"

"None."

"The contacts we worked with? Abbé Basc? Pablo Casals?"

"They have heard nothing."

"The doctor, Céleste? Ian and Annabel Beckham?"

"I, personally, have sent people up the line to inquire. Nothing."

I don't know if I've ever had a sinking feeling like that in my entire life. Odette takes both my hands in hers and says, "You are very much in love with her, *n'est-ce pas?* And now you are, how you say, *dévasté.*"

I nod. Devastated is the right word. "What about the other fighters she was with," I ask. "Marcel, Claude, Jean-Baptiste? Perhaps they know something."

"They were never part of the rescue operation for children, so I don't know them. I've been told they live in Mirepoix. If you wish, Gaston will drive you there."

Of course, I accept. I'm desperate to learn what I can about Élodie.

Mirepoix is a well-preserved, fortified town, dating from the 13ᵗʰ century, where arcaded, timber-framed houses surround the central market square. It is here Gaston drops me off and heads back to Aquilac. A half dozen old men, drinking pastis, sit on rough benches under one of the arcades which is supported by massive posts and beams. I approach the men and in a mixture of English and rudimentary French ask if anyone knows three men—resistance fighters named Marcel, Claude and Jean-Baptiste. Fortunately, one of the men speaks a little English. He tells me that Marcel and Claude are dead, killed near Avignon where they were helping to support the allied invasion of the South of France that came a couple of months after D-Day.

"And Jean-Baptiste?" I ask.

The man spits onto the ground and says. "*Il est toujours avec la bouteille ou les boules de pétanque.*"[72]

When I frown and indicate I don't understand, the man mimes his answer. He tilts his head back and holds his open fist in front of his mouth. A man drinking from a bottle. "*Vin,*" the man says.

I nod. "Wine."

The man makes a bowling motion which I recognize immediately as the roll of a ball in a game I've seen several times.

I say, "Wine and pétanque balls?"

---

72   "He's always with the bottle or the balls of pétanque." Pétanque is the Southern French version of boules or bocce.

The man nods. "*Toujours.* Always." He takes hold of my sleeve and says, "*Viens avec moi.*"[73] He leads me across the street to the cathedral and circles around to the other side. I hear the click of pétanque balls. Four men stand on an improvised court which looks like it's normally used to park cars. On a bench to the side sits Jean-Baptiste. As if to confirm what my informant has said, Jean-Baptiste holds a bottle of wine in his hand. As soon as he sees me, he rises from the bench and starts to walk fast away from me. Within seconds, I catch up to him and grab him by the shoulder and spin him around and say, "You don't seem happy to see me, Jean-Baptiste."

"*Je ne sais rien. Laisse-moi.*"[74]

"Don't pull that shit with me. I know you speak perfectly good English."

Jean-Baptiste pulls away from my grasp. "What do you want?"

"I want to know about Élodie."

"She's dead."

I feel my knees go wobbly. I want to scream. I ask, in a voice that trembles, "How do you know? Did you see her? Did somebody tell you?"

"A *passeur* told me. A guide. He saw it happen. It was border guards."

"What's the man's name?"

"Why should I tell you?"

I grab Jean-Baptiste's shoulders and shake him. "What's his fucking name?"

"Luc Vidocq."

"Where can I find him?"

"He lives in Tarbes."

❦

"So, I went to Tarbes to find this Luc Vidocq," I say to Callie, "only to learn he was dead, killed by border guards. Probably at the same time

---

73   "Come with me."

74   "I know nothing. Leave me (alone)."

as Élodie. I knew that occasionally, she would work with *passeurs* for mutual protection."

"I'm so sorry," Callie says. "I can see from your eyes that it still hurts, even seventy years later."

"There was … *is* … this terrible sense of non-completion. As if we left something unfinished." I look up at my granddaughter. "That's why I need to go to Normandy. I need to see it again. I need to feel her, to finish it. Before I am finished."

"I think the doctor will give you a clean bill of health, Papa. We'll get you to France."

And, indeed, my appointment the next day with Doctor Nigel Hunt, a respiratory medicine specialist at University College Hospital, goes well, and I am given the clearance to travel to France. We waste no time booking on the Eurostar and heading for St. Pancras International station and, within five hours, we step off the train at Gare du Nord in Paris. While we were speeding through the Channel tunnel, Callie had called ahead to reserve a rental car in Paris and reconfirm my hotel reservation in Caen. From Gare du Nord, it is a three-hour drive to Caen in Normandy. We check into the Hotel Ibis Caen Centre, have dinner *al fresco* at the sidewalk café in front of the hotel, and go to bed early because we plan a full schedule for the following day: Omaha Beach, the 70th D-Day commemoration ceremony at the American cemetery overlooking Omaha Beach, and the Mémorial de Caen, the museum honoring the Normandy landings. When Callie mentions Utah Beach, I say that Omaha Beach is much more convenient to the American Cemetery and the ceremony.

The following day dawns clear. After a quick breakfast of croissants and coffee, we set out for Omaha Beach. Little more than an hour later, we pull into a parking spot and follow a sandy path, over and down a slight rise, to the beach. I pause at the top of the rise to gather my breath.

Callie reaches out a hand to steady me. "Are you, okay, Papa?"

"I'll be fine."

She slips her arm through mine. "It's a sad place."

"Yes," I say. My cane clicks on the cement walk, and on the cement stairs, as I approach the sand. I pause to steady myself and slowly stride toward the ocean. The sand is furrowed and ridged and moist. Like brain folds. And with every step, I pierce the sand with my cane. The wind assaults my ears like the roar of shells overhead. And, overhead, dozens of seagulls spool out bands of flight, skirling, swooping, skimming, a strangle of screeching motion, and in the sand a lone crab leaves a thin trail as it scurries for the safety of the ocean as in the distance more gulls soar and dip and I look down and see a seagull feather and I wonder what it had been like for the ancestors of these seagulls on that day seventy years ago, what the navy's guns and the German 88s had done to the birds, because nobody ever thinks of the other living creatures caught up in human-made hells. How many seagulls were blasted out of the sky by the shockwaves, vaporized? How many crabs were crushed under the boots of frantic men splashing ashore? On that day, along with a heavy, constant rain of hot metal and earth and sand and bloodied body parts, there must have also come a softer, gentler drizzle of white and gray feathers. Was the beach covered in seagull feathers everybody was too busy trying to survive to notice? Or, was the last thing some dying men saw the soft, bloodied down of a feather floating down to rest on the scalloped sand? Did some men stir the feather's downy barbs with their final gasps for breath, the seagull and the man united in death?

I'm overcome with sadness. Maintaining my balance in the uneven sand is difficult. I sink to my knees in the corrugated sand where retreating waves have scoured out ridges and valleys. A single, violent shudder convulses through my body.

"Papa! Are you okay?" Callie bends and offers her hand to help me to my feet.

"I'm fine. I'm fine. The sand is difficult to walk on." With her help, I rise and brush at the wet sand that sticks to the knees of my pants.

"Let me help you back to the car," Callie says. "We need to get to the ceremony."

I nod. "Yes. The ceremony."

It is a short drive to the American cemetery. In the parking lot, we are greeted by a young woman wearing the double gold chevron of a corporal on her American army dress blues. She pushes a wheelchair up to the car and opens the passenger-side door and offers her hand to me. She says, "Welcome to the Normandy American Cemetery and Memorial, sir." She checks the large accreditation badge hanging from my neck. "Mister Budge, my name is Corporal Maria Meléndez. I'll be escorting you to your seat behind the speaker's podium. And Ma'am," she adds, turning to Callie, "if you wait here for me, I'll show you how to find the family section."

"I don't need that," I say, gesturing toward the wheelchair.

"Very well, sir. If you'll just follow me."

"Wait," says Callie. She reaches into her tote bag and pulls out an olive drab baseball cap with a double "A" emblem standing for "All American" and the words "82nd AIRBORNE" on the front edge of the visor. "Wear this," she says.

"Why?"

"You refused to wear your medals, so I thought this would be okay."

"Where did you get it?"

"You don't think I know how to shop online? I ordered it while we were on board the ship and had it sent to the hotel in Caen."

"You must have been pretty confident we'd make it here."

"I know you. Now off you go to your ceremony. I'm so proud of you."

Corporal Meléndez guides me to my seat on a raised platform in a semicircular colonnade, facing west. I am appalled to find I'm in the front row to the right of the podium. No chance to hide. I pull my sunglasses out of my pocket and fit them over my eyes. I brush at the moist sand still stuck to the knees of my pants and look up to see an immense crowd sitting in chairs arranged in a kind of wide boulevard on either side of which are thousands of meticulously ordered white crosses and Stars-of-David. Immediately in front of me is the speaker's podium. I chance a quick look to my right and my left and see no sign of Pfc. John True. I don't dare turn around to look behind me.

A slow-moving cloud shadow drawls across the crowd gathered before me and, as quickly, moves away and is followed by a much smaller shadow. I look up to see a raptor—a hawk perhaps (or a lammergeier?)—peel off a thin layer of air and hover on it for a moment before gliding low over the rows of crosses and Stars-of-David, its shadow leaping over one gravestone after another, and then banking and floating over the crowd. I watch the shadow slide slowly across the rows of people, and then up to the entablature that wraps the memorial colonnade. I read the inscription:

This Embattled Shore, Portal of Freedom, Is Forever Hallowed
By the Ideals, the Valor, and the Sacrifices of our Fellow Countrymen

I look to my right where there is a loggia containing a giant mural map of the allied operations from June 6, 1944 to May 5, 1945. And across to my left is another loggia with a mural of the Normandy invasions—maps announcing the exploits that my brothers-in-arms had been achieving while I was traveling through the south of France with the woman I loved.

Just before 11:00 am, another shadow moves across the cemetery, this one is accompanied by the whop whop-whop of helicopter blades whipping the air. I look up to see the green of the president's helicopter with "United States of America" clearly visible in white letters. Some minutes later, I see, to my left, presidents Hollande and Obama walking between rows of topiary toward the speaker's platform.

A woman's voice welcomes the guests and announces the French and the American national anthems.

Soon, President Hollande is speaking, but I barely listen. Instead, I watch a flock of seagulls eddying and pinwheeling and pirouetting above the crowd until they disappear back to Omaha Beach as the raptor makes its appearance again. And suddenly my attention is snapped back to the podium by the sound of President Obama speaking. As I glance to my left to see the president, my attention is drawn to a flurry of motion behind him. I look over my shoulder and see several veterans standing and snapping photos of Obama. One of them is Pfc. True, who lowers his camera and smiles at me. I quickly return my gaze to the president who is saying:

"Friends, families, our veterans. If prayer were made of sound, the skies over England that night would have deafened the world. Captains paced their decks, pilots tapped their gauges, commanders pored over maps ..."

✾

Yes! If prayer were made of sound, the foothills of the Pyrénées would have rung the return of Élodie and I would have bolted out the door of the house in Mosset one glorious day and scanned the hills, as I did every day in that time, and she would have appeared, and her lilting gait would have told me it was her, and I would have run and hopped on my bad ankle to meet her, and I would have held her closer than ever before!

And if prayer were made of sound, the songbirds in the meadows around Oradour-sur-Glane, that place of prayer, would not have been obliterated by the jackhammering of boots in the streets.

And if prayer were made of sound, Élodie and I would have heard Adrien reply to our desperate calls and he would have returned to us before the border guards gunned him down.

And if prayer were made of sound, the stutter of Élodie's Sten gun would never have silenced the meadow where the boy soldiers died.

And if prayer were made of sound, the song "We'll Meet Again" would be a prayer.

✾

My mind is racing. Phrases from Obama's speech are like trip wires on my memory.

"And in the pre-dawn hours, planes rumbled down runways and gliders and paratroopers slipped through the sky ...."

✾

Yes, if prayer were made of sound, the world would have been deafened by the collective silence from the men when we heard the chaplain say, "Tonight is the night of nights" as we lined up to climb aboard our planes.

And if prayer were made of sound, the prayer would have been the hard click of the static line clip onto the anchor line cable I heard even over the rumble of the plane's engines, and the rattle of its rivets, as we lined up in sticks and watched for signals from the jumpmaster and tried to ignore the odor of sweat from the man in front or the odor of shit from another man further up the stick who'd messed his pants in fear.

And if prayer were made of sound, the jumpmaster's cry of "Go!" would have been a prayer.

※

Obama continues. "By daybreak, blood soaked the water, bombs broke the sky. Thousands of paratroopers had dropped into the wrong landing sites, thousands of rounds bit into flesh and sand ...."

※

And there was the terrible pain of the shrapnel slicing into my thigh, descending with others as if in a bloom of moon jellies ... my buddy hanging lifeless in a low tree amidst white blossoms, his blood staining red the parachute draped over him like a collapsed halo.

※

"By 8:30 a.m.," the president says, "General Omar Bradley expected our troops to be a mile inland. Six hours after the landings, he wrote, 'we held only ten yards of beach.' In this age of instant commentary, the invasion would have swiftly and roundly been declared, as it was by one officer, 'a debacle.' But such a race to judgment would not have taken into account the courage of free men. 'Success may not come with rushing speed,' President Roosevelt would say that night, 'but we shall return again and again.' And paratroopers fought through the countryside to find one another."

※

But not me. At the very instant men were dying and others were desperately trying to find each other among the fields, I was in a barn I mistook for heaven because an angel was playing the violin.

※

After Obama's speech, there is a moment of silence before he and President Hollande place a wreath to honor the dead, and that is followed by a 21-gun-salute. And through it all, I wait impatiently and, as soon as it is over, I stand and shuffle around the right wall of the colonnade and, when I reach the path, I am met by Corporal Meléndez who stands with an empty wheelchair.

"I thought you'd be tired, so I brought this."

"Excellent!" I reply. "I can walk, but I can't run and, frankly, I need the men's room. How fast can you make this thing move?"

She smiles. "Have a seat and try me."

I plop into the wheelchair and Corporal Meléndez takes off at a fast jog. People coming in the opposite direction smile at me as I speed past them. We quickly arrive at the visitor's center and the corporal waits outside while I shuffle into the men's room. And when I emerge, Callie is waiting for me.

"What was that all about?" she asks. "Are you and Corporal Meléndez taking up a new sport?"

"I had to go to the men's room."

"Well if you're finished, we need to be off," Callie says. "I arranged for a personal guide to take us through the D-Day museum and she'll be waiting for us."

※

Less than an hour later, we are at the Mémorial de Caen Museum.

"Can you manage the stairs, Papa?" Callie asks.

"I think so. If we take them slowly."

We climb two short flights of stairs separated by a broad landing, my cane clicking on the stone with every step, and we enter a vestibule where guards inspect the things we carry, and finally, upon nods from the guards, we enter a spacious lobby where a WWII British fighter-bomber hangs, suspended from the ceiling by cables.

"That's a Tiffy," I say.

"A Tiffy?" Callie frowns at me. No doubt she sees a darkness that must have come to my countenance.

"A Hawker Typhoon."

"Okay." She pauses, wrinkles her brow for a moment and says, "She said she'd be standing under the plane. That must be her."

Directly under the Tiffy stands an older woman who advances toward Callie with a broad, welcoming smile. "I am Elizabet Billings," she says in the Queen's English. "You must be Callie."

"I am." Callie takes the woman's hand. "And this is my grandfather."

"Very pleased to meet you, indeed." Welcome to the Mémorial de Caen, Mr. Budge. And on behalf of my country may I express my gratitude for what you and your American colleagues did those many years ago to help us help France gain her liberation."

I smile, nod, but say nothing.

"Right, then," the woman says, "If you'll follow me, we'll begin."

She leads us into a corridor that slopes downward and curves to the left. On the wall to our right is a chronological series of photographs and maps tracing the origins of World War II. I move slowly, keeping a grip on the red, metal rail to my left. It has been a long day and my legs ache from all the walking, especially the walking in the sands of Omaha Beach. Soon, I spy a bench in a dark corner and tell Callie I need to sit for a few moments. They sit with me and, as soon as they sit, we learn why the benches are in such a dark space. In front of us, a film starts showing. It is about the Warsaw Ghetto and shows the suffering of the Jews, including scenes of children clearly malnourished.

Elizabet Billings says, "It's so sad when these things happen to children. My mother was caught up in Operation Pied Piper. She was evacuated to the Cotswolds."

"Pied Piper?" asks Callie.

I lean forward. "It was the evacuation of British children from the cities to the countryside to protect them from the blitz. Some one and a half million women and children were evacuated from London alone."

Elizabet smiles. "Yes, that's right. You seem to know a lot about it."

Callie reaches for my hand and squeezes it. She says to the woman, "My grandfather here, helped save children like that during the war and he's devoted his life to writing about refugee children. You may have read his book *Reluctant Salvation*, by G. H. Budge."

I lean forward with my elbows on my knees. "But call me Henry. It's what I go by."

She gives me a pleasant smile, but I notice another woman, a guide with another group, turn and look at me with a strange expression.

"Well, I will certainly look for your book. Mr. Budge," Elizabet says.

"Henry, please."

"Yes, of course. Henry."

During the rest of the film, I feel the younger guide's gaze on me. Finally, I turn to look at her, but she's whispering intently with Elizabet. Billings. And then the film is over, and we rise and start down the corridor to my left. That's when I see it! "My God!" I whisper. I hobble down the corridor like a hooked fish being reeled in.

From behind me I hear Callie calling, "Papa, what are you doing?"

But I don't answer. I rush along the hallway and immediately bump into a man who is gazing at a display on the side wall, and the man turns and glares at me, and I mumble an apology but continue on and brush by a second person and accidently hit a third on the ankle with my cane, muttering apologies all along the way, and I stop only when Callie catches up to me and grabs my arm.

"Papa, what are you doing? Have you gone crazy? I've never seen you be so rude!"

I'm breathing hard. "That photo!" is all I can say. I wave my cane toward the wall facing us at the end of the hallway where an enlargement of a black-and-white photograph covers the entire wall, floor to ceiling. It is of a woman walking alongside a horse she is leading by the reins she grasps in her right hand as it pulls a cart down a road past a car piled high with boxes and household belongings. A small, large-eared dog walks at her heels. A Papillion, like Arlequin.

"What about it?"

But I can't speak. I can't catch my breath. I'm afraid I might hyperventilate.

"Papa, you must relax," Callie says. "What's got into you?"

"Are you okay, sir?" The guide who'd given me the sidelong glance is suddenly beside us.

I say nothing. I can't drag my eyes away from the photo.

"The title," the guide says, "is 'Mai-Juin, Mille Neuf Quarante, L'effondrement' which translates to 'May-June, Nineteen Forty, The Collapse.'"

Callie turns to me. "What's so interesting about this photo, Papa?"

"Please, Madam, pardon my interruption." The woman is speaking again, but I barely hear her. "My name is Francesca Dulong. I am a guide here, and I overheard you tell my colleague your grandfather helped save children during the war and that his name is"—she stops as if she can't get the words out—"that his name is Henry Budge."

"What?" Callie asks, frowning at the guide.

"Well, I ... I ... is your grandfather American? Mister Henry Budge from America?"

"Yes, why?" Callie looks between me and the guide.

Francesca Dulong puts a hand over her mouth and sucks in her breath. "I ... I ... Oh, my God! Oh, my god! I think Mister Budge knows the woman in that picture!"

I haven't taken my eyes off the photo.

Callie turns to me. "Do you, Papa? Do you know her?"

All I can do is nod.

With my mouth open.

And try to breathe.

Chapter 16
And the Gold of their Bodies

Francesca stares at me, mouth agape. "The woman is ... *Mon dieu!* ... the woman is my grandmother. Élodie Bedier."

Callie gasps. "Élodie? *The* Élodie?"

Again, I nod. I whisper, "Élodie."

Callie gapes at Francesca. "She was your grandmother?"

"Yes." Francesca nods and reaches out to lay a hand on Callie's arm. "But, not *was*. *Is*. She *is* my grandmother."

I stare at Francesca, mouth open. I shake my head. "No. No, there must be some mistake." My voice comes out in a squeak. "I don't understand. She's dead. He said she was dead. I looked for her!"

Francesca reaches out to touch my arm. "Oh, but ... but she's very much alive. She lives in Paris." Francesca raises a hand to her mouth as if just now grasping the enormity of what she's said. "Oh, my God!"

"It's impossible!" Tears well up unbidden. "Not after seventy years." I shake my head and wonder if someone has given the moon a spin. "No. It can't be. That picture is not her. It's someone who looks like her."

"No, it's her." Francesca says. Her eyes are round. She seems almost frightened. She speaks rapidly. "It was taken by a photographer during the evacuation of Paris after the Germans came. She saw it at an exhibit years later, bought it, and donated it to the museum. I was with her when they unveiled it. Oh, my God!"

I simply can't believe it. "Perhaps she had a sister," I say, struggling to comprehend what's going on. "Did she have a sister?" But, I know she didn't have a sister and I know for certain it's her. And at her heels is her little Arlequin.

"No. I tell you, it's her! It's my grandmother, Élodie Bedier. I call her Mémère."

Callie's voice is high, a slack-jawed expression of incredulity painted on her face. "She's alive?" Her voice has joined Francesca's and mine in the upper registers. People are staring at us.

"Absolutely," Francesca says. "And living in Paris."

"Impossible!" It can't be true, can it? The enormity of the idea is ... too much.

"If she's your grandmother," Callie says, "she had a child. Your mother? Father?"

"Mother," says Francesca, a circumflex of a crease forming on her forehead. "Her name is Adrienne Savary. But ... but ... her maiden name is ... that is, Mémère gave her the surname Budge. That's why I was startled when you told me your grandfather's name."

I lean heavily on my cane, and my hand, gripping the curved handle, rocks to and fro, the rubber ferrule tip fixed on the floor and acting as an insecure pivot point. If it were possible, the force of my plant would have driven the cane straight through the floor to the level below. "My god!" I whisper over and over again.

"Oh, my god!" Callie's voice reaches into an even higher register.

Francesca's hands frame her face as if she's in shock. "*Mon dieu!* I think I am going to cry."

"Me, too!" Callie uses a knuckle to wipe a tear from under her eye. "When was your mother born?"

"April tenth, nineteen forty-five."

Callie closes her eyes and counts on her fingers. I can see her doctor's mind working it out. Finally, she says, "She was conceived in early July of nineteen forty-four." Callie shoots me an inquisitive look.

I'm still confused, not sure of what is happening, and it's a long moment before I can reply. "Mosset. That's when we were in Mosset. I don't understand. I just don't understand."

Francesca says, "Oh, my god, yes! I'm definitely going to cry." Her eyes are shining, glistening tears poised, ready to fall from her lashes.

I'm losing my balance. I stagger and almost fall against Callie, who says, "My grandfather needs to sit for a while. He was recently shot and is still recovering. Is there a place?"

"Shot? As in gunshot?" Francesca looks like she just got news of the coming apocalypse.

Callie puts her arm around my shoulder to support me. "He stopped an attempted rape by beating the bastard over the head with his cane and ended up getting shot in the chest."

Francesca's hand flies to her own chest. "Oh, my god! Oh, my god!" Vaguely, I think this seems to be the winning phrase of the day.

"We need to get him someplace he can rest." Callie's voice is a mixture of pride and protectiveness.

"Yes," Francesca looks around. "This way. Come. There is a restaurant in the museum. *La Terrasse.*"

I say nothing.

I only nod.

I shuffle so slowly, supported by Callie, it takes us almost five minutes to get to the restaurant.

After we take our seats and order salads and wine, I say to Francesca, "Your mother is named Adrienne?"

"Yes."

"Do you know where it comes from? The name?"

"Yes. There was a boy named Adrien …."

It hits me like a body blow. "Jesus!" I whisper. I can't believe this is happening.

Francesca looks at Callie and then turns back to me. "Please forgive me, but may I look at your right hand?"

"Yes, of course," I say. I offer her my hand. "You're looking for the broken finger, aren't you?"

Francesca doesn't answer immediately. She only shakes her head in amazement. I see a shiver pass through her upper body. She takes a deep breath and finally says, "We've heard so many stories about you. But they all ended with you being killed." She examines my broken finger again. "It's exactly as Mémère described. *Mon dieu!* She will be so shocked. Both of them! I don't know how to tell them."

"I think you just have to tell them," Callie says. "And trust they'll be strong enough."

It's her doctor's mind at work. I can imagine her saying the same thing in some hospital corridor. I'm still confused. I still can't really believe it. And all at once a heat comes to my cheeks and I clench my fists. I look at Francesca and ask, "Did your grandmother ever mention a man named Jean-Baptiste? I forget his last name."

"No. I don't recall her ever mentioning someone by that name."

I nod grimly. "It would be good for him if he's already dead. That's all I have to say."

Francesca checks her watch and glances at Callie. "I think we should leave immediately for Paris. I will telephone Maman and arrange to meet with her first. She'll have a better idea how to break the news to Mémère."

Thus, within an hour, we are boarding a train at Gare de Caen scheduled to arrive at Paris' Gare Montparnasse some two and a half hours later. My legs are tired from all the walking I've done, and no doubt from the shock of this revelation, so Callie and Francesca help me into the car, one on each side. They take the first empty seats, the women sitting side-by-side and facing forward and me opposite them, facing the rear of the train.

"You don't mind facing backwards?" asks Francesca.

I shake my head. "When you've sat in a C-47 with a parachute strapped to your back and only a vague idea of where you are going, no mode of transportation ever bothers you again."

The train departs the station and soon picks up speed. The rhythmic click-clack of the tracks quickly has my eyelids closing. I doze fitfully. I wake several times to see Francesca staring intently at me, but I quickly close my eyes again. I hear her and Callie whispering, but I tune them out. There are so many things to deal with. Too many! Briefly, I wish I could be alone with Arlequin, walking the streets of the Navy Yard in Charlestown. A simple life. Uncomplicated. But as soon as I think of Arlequin, I'm drawn back to the photograph at the museum with Élodie and the horse and the cart and the butterfly-eared dog, and everything is complicated again. In one of my periods of wakefulness

I think I hear Francesca softly say, "*Pépère*," as if rehearsing. I doze off again and wake only when I feel a hand pressing my shoulder and I open my eyes and Francesca smiles at me and says, "We are coming into Gare Montparnasse … *Pépère*." She looks at me with raised eyebrows as if to ask if it's okay to call me "*Pépère*."

I glance at Callie who is sniffling and wiping her nose, then smile at my newly discovered granddaughter. I place a hand on her cheek and nod. "We have much to get used to."

We stand in the aisle waiting for the train to come to a complete stop. Callie impulsively hugs Francesca and says, "I can't wait to meet your mother. And grandmother!" Then, shaking her head, eyes wide, and lowering her voice, she says, "Holy shit!"

Francesca laughs. "In French we might say, *C'est pas possible!* I can't believe this is happening!"

Once we disembark the train, we climb into a taxi and Francesca says to the driver, *"Place de la Sorbonne, s'il vous plaît."*[75] She turns to Callie and me and says, "There's a café near the Sorbonne. I've asked Maman to meet us there. She teaches art history at the university. I told her Mr. Budge—*Pépère*—is recovering from an injury and the café is a nice place to sit."

"Is it possible," I ask, "to stop at a florist shop? I want to buy a rose for Élodie. No, two roses! One for my … for my daughter as well." "Daughter" comes out as a two-syllable sob.

"Of course," replies Francesca. "There's a shop called Rosebud Fleuristes in the Place de l'Odéon which is only a few minutes from where we are going." She leans toward the driver and gives him the instructions.

The small florist shop is next to a large gallery called Avant-Scene which Francesca says specializes in fine decorative furnishings. But I only have thoughts for the two most perfect red roses I can find. Roses no sheep would dare to eat. With Francesca's help, it only takes a few moments to find the right flowers, and two Waterford crystal bud vases, and, ten minutes later, we pull onto the Place de la Sorbonne and step

---

75   "Place de la Sorbonne, please." A popular plaza near the Sorbonne University.

out of the taxi at the corner of a pedestrian-only street. At the end
of the short street sits the domed neoclassical bulk of the Panthéon-
Sorbonne like a stern Roman paterfamilias at the head of the table.

"There she is. Maman is already here." Francesca leads us to a table
under a large awning that bears the name of the café, "Tabac de la
Sorbonne." When we reach the table, she stops and looks from me to
her mother and back again. "Maman, this is Henry Budge." She follows
that with a young girl's giddy laugh as if she can't believe what she just
said.

Francesca's mother brings a hand to her chest and her body goes
rigid and she stares at me for a long moment before saying, *"Mon dieu!"*
She makes the sign of the cross as she says, *"Au nom du Père et du Fils et
du Saint-Esprit.*[76] Can it be true?"

"Apparently," I reply with a soft smile. I hand her one of the
roses, unable to say anything more. I am overwhelmed by a wave of
unspeakable joy.

She stares at the rose in her hand for a long while, shakes her head,
and gives a short, nervous laugh. "Prove it. How did you know my
mother?"

"It was during the war. She was posing as a German nurse and I
was injured when I parachuted behind Utah Beach in the early hours
of D-Day."

Adrienne reaches for my right hand. "May I?" she asks. She examines
the little finger. "Did you never have it re-broken and set?"

"I keep it as a reminder not to jump out of airplanes."

She draws in a sharp breath. "Oh, my dear god! It *is* you! That's what
she said you said."

"It's me. I ... uh ... I ..." I dig into my pocket and fish out a handkerchief to wipe my eyes and nose.

Adrienne gives that nervous laugh again and reaches out and pinches
the sleeve of my jacket. "I don't believe it."

"But apparently it's true ... dear Adrienne." I try to keep my voice
steady. "I couldn't believe it at first. It all seems so impossible."

---

76   "In the name of the Father and of the Son and of the Holy Spirit."

"Maman, you have his nose," Francesca says, again with a giddy laugh.

I look into Adrienne's eyes and study her face. My daughter! *Our daughter!* "Do you think this will be too much of a shock for her?"

Adrienne laughs, and I reach out to steady myself with a hand on the table. "As you know quite well, she fought the Germans behind enemy lines, she guided two groups of children over the Pyrénées. What you perhaps don't know, is she survived one Nazi death camp … and …"—her voice breaks—"gave birth to me in another. There was no help. She even had to bite through the umbilical cord herself. I was born five days before the death camp, Bergen-Belsen, was liberated. She's the strongest woman I know, and I am proud to call her my mother." Adrienne places a hand on mine and holds my gaze. "She will handle the shock."

"Bergen-Belsen? She was at Bergen-Belsen?" I can barely breathe. I feel like I've been kicked in the chest by a mule. Callie pulls out a chair and I sink in to it. "The Brits liberated Bergen-Belsen. My outfit, the eighty-second, liberated a camp called Wöbbelin. Christ! If only it had been the other way around!"

"There's a great deal about that time you don't know."

"Tell me."

"No. It's for her to tell you … Papa."

There's that unimaginable—but confusing—wave of joy again! But then, a hard thought. "Tell me this, then," I say. "Did she ever marry?"

"No." Adrienne wipes her eyes and shakes her head slowly. "She often told me my father was the only man she ever wanted to marry."

We catch a taxi. I'm scarcely aware of our progress, or how long it takes. All I can think about is what will I say? What will she say? Should we be doing this? After seventy years? We each have lived all these years with a certain reality. Is it possible to change that now? Could we shatter that reality and reassemble the pieces into a different reality? Yet, what choice do we have once we know the truth?

The taxi stops opposite a café called "La Tourelle" and we all climb out.

Adrienne says, "This is the Saint-Mandé commune. That's her building across the street. See the windows on the third floor with the open curtains? That's her flat. Wait in the café. Have some wine or coffee and a pastry. I'll go tell her the news, and when she's recovered from the shock, I'll come and get you and bring you to her."

I look up to the windows which are one level below the mansard roof with its elaborate, second empire dormers, and then I gaze further upward to see how the roof is framed by heavy, impasto clouds, like clotted cream, that have gaps through which crepuscular rays shine down on us.

Callie, Francesca, and I sit in bright persimmon-colored, sunlit chairs at one of the sidewalk tables with a view of Élodie's building. We order pastries and a bottle of red wine. The order takes ten minutes to arrive and we have scarcely begun when Adrienne emerges from the building, crosses the street, and joins us.

"How did it go, Maman?" Francesca asks, pulling a chair back for her mother.

"I'm not sure she believed me," Adrienne answers.

I start to stand. "Should we go up?" I ask, anxious and afraid at the same time. Actually, I have no idea how to describe how I feel—incomparable joy for what I've found, immeasurable sadness for lost years, incomprehension that any of this is possible. And love. A swelling up and a blossoming out of love that threatens to choke me.

"Not yet," Adrienne says. "Just in case you truly are *her* Henry, she wanted a few minutes to freshen up. Give her ten or fifteen minutes. What's that compared to seventy years?"

"Be patient, Papa," Callie says, reaching out and patting my arm. "We're here. You just met your daughter! And you're about to see *your* Élodie." Her voice lifts at the end to a giddy register.

Adrienne and Callie are right, of course, but to me the ten minutes almost seem equal to the seventy years that have already passed. I sip my wine slowly. My hand is shaking. The little finger of my right hand, curled against the stem of the glass, aches.

At last, Adrienne touches my hand and asks, "Are you ready for this, Papa?"

I look into my daughter's eyes, hold her gaze, and then pick up the second crystal vase. "I'm ready."

To my relief, the building has an elevator. Of course! Élodie will be about my age so a walk-up wouldn't do. It's a shocking thought. In my imagination, in all my memories, she is a young woman. I don't know what to expect. Will I recognize her?

The elevator is absurdly small. It is scarcely able to accommodate the four of us and I feel awkward brushing against the bodies of family members—especially family members who are also strangers. The elevator lurches to a stop and we spill out. Across from us is an open door.

"Maman has left the door open." Adrienne gestures me forward like a gracious hostess.

My heart beats rapidly as I step across the threshold. An old woman leans against the marble mantel of a small fireplace, watching me from across the room. We stare at each other warily. I have no idea what to say. Is this, indeed, Élodie? I venture a few steps.

"You have brought me a rose," she says.

"It's the special rose that loved the little prince, and he her. The one he would give his life to ensure she is not eaten by a sheep."

The woman sucks in her breath as she steps forward and takes the rose from me.

Because I'm feeling awkward and shy with Callie and the others present, I quickly glance around the room. There are several framed portraits on the mantel. I study them. Each is a portrait of a young, beautiful violinist with a conductor. In one picture, she stands with a white-haired conductor before a structure I recognize—it's the music shed at Tanglewood in western Massachusetts. The conductor is Serge Koussevitzky, elegant in a bowtie and a white double-breasted suit. The clothes and the building confirm the picture must have been taken during a summer in the late '30s, for that was when the music shed was built. That would have made Élodie barely out of her teens, at the beginning of what, I know, was a prodigy career.

"I must look in those pictures very much like the woman you knew seventy years ago," she says.

I turn to gaze into her eyes. It is the same melodic voice I remember, just a little more thready. "Yes," I whisper.

A bracelet jangles from her wrist as Élodie holds out her hand and says, "Please. Come to me."

My cane taps the floor lightly as I cross the space between us. When I'm close enough, Élodie reaches for my right hand. She examines the broken pinkie finger for a moment then lifts it to her lips and kisses it. She looks into my eyes. "Hello my love, *Mon cœur*. What does one say? I can scarcely …. I don't know … I just …." She sucks in a deep breath. "How has your day been so far?"

A dam bursts. I explode into laughter.

Behind me, Callie, Francesca, and Adrienne all bust out laughing. It's as if, together, we have pushed an elephant out the window and now there is space to breathe.

"It's just become a great deal better," I reply. "There are so many questions." My hand is still in hers. Something doesn't feel right. I look down and see her knuckles, gnarled and swollen. I frown.

"Seeing you now is like seeing a character from a much-loved book suddenly come alive," Élodie says. "I feel I've dreamed our story all these many years and now, suddenly, here you are, straight out of the pages of a fantasy."

I start to say, "We both thought the other—"

She puts her fingers on my lips. "Don't. Don't speak of it. It's too ghastly. Let us allow all this to sink in before we ask how this … this … stupid nightmare can have happened."

"Adrienne says you were at one of the Nazi extermination camps."

Élodie flinches. She drops my hand and turns and walks to a sofa and sits. She sits silently for long moments and I begin to fear I made a terrible mistake. Finally, she pats the sofa, motioning for me to join her. And, when I am beside her, she says, "I suppose it will explain some things, so it's only fair I should tell you my whole story." She turns to Adrienne and says, "Please, *mon ange*, make martinis for everybody."

"Of course, Maman," Adrienne says. "It will be a pleasure to make a martini for my papa."

Élodie smiles at that and turns to me. "I never, ever, wanted to talk about it. But you need to know, for it will explain why you never saw me again."

"I went looking for you after the war," I say. "I went to Mirepoix because I discovered that's where Claude, Marcel and Jean-Baptiste were from. I learned Claude and Marcel were dead."

"Yes, they were killed in Dijon during the allied invasion in the south."

"But, Jean-Baptiste, survived."

"Yes." She frowns. "How unfortunate."

"He was the one who told me you had been killed by German border guards in the Pyrénées."

"He made it up. Probably to get rid of you as a competitor."

"But he said there was a witness," I say. "Someone named Luc Vidocq. I could never locate him."

"Luc Vidocq was a famous *passeur*. He was killed a year or so before you even appeared in France. Jean-Baptiste knew that."

I frown. "It was a lie the whole time!"

"Yes," she says. "And it was Jean-Baptiste who told me he saw you dead in a field hospital near Marseille. I knew he had joined other resistance fighters in the Battle of the Vercors Plateau in July and was with the fighters who aided the allied landings near Saint-Raphaël and the liberation of Marseille. I believed him because I knew all these things happened in July and August of that year and he had a wound that would have been treated at a field hospital. I had no reason not to believe him. Especially since it was some time after the war before I saw him. It took me a long time to recover from the camps."

"In July, my unit was in England preparing to jump into Holland," I say. "That's when I rejoined them. After the war I was stationed in Chartres. I got leave and went to see if I could learn anything about you. I saw Odette Dupont." I pause, then say, "Wait! You, too, must have seen her sometime later. Why wouldn't she have told you I was alive?"

"*Oh, mon dieu!*" Élodie raises a hand to her mouth.

"What?"

"It took several months before I was fit enough to make it back to Aquilac. I was in hospital, recovering from … from the camps. By the time I made it back, Odette had died. Gaston, too. People said he died of heartbreak only a week after her. It must have been soon after you saw her."

"Jesus!"

"I heard Jean-Baptiste died some fifty years ago. We should go spit on his grave," Élodie says with steel in her voice.

"Or piss on it."

She exhales slowly. "But we shan't, shall we?" she says. "We saw too much hate back then to bring it back into our lives now."

I nod. "If France and America can forgive Germany, who are we to carry on a hatred for a man who is long dead anyway?"

Adrienne appears with the martinis and hands one each to Élodie and me. Élodie takes a long sip, places her hand over mine, and says, "Even so, I don't know why I believed him so easily. I shouldn't have. But after everything that had happened, it seemed to make sense. It seemed nothing good could ever happen again." She looks up at Adrienne and smiles. "I had our daughter, but it was difficult. I had seen too much. Gone through too much. I was on my back foot. Perhaps I was still traumatized by Ravensbrück and Bergen-Belsen." She takes another long sip and stares at the opposite wall for a long time with an expression that suggests she is seeing through the wall to some distant memory. "It was a long time before I was able to think clearly, and, by that time, I suppose, I had become reconciled to you being dead."

I run a thumb over her gnarled knuckles. "How did you end up—"

"On that last trip through the Pyrénées, I was captured by the Spanish at the border. They locked me up in Barcelona for a while, then turned me over to the Gestapo. That's how I ended up in Ravensbrück. It was a concentration camp for women." She pauses, then says, "Oh, *mon dieu!*"

"What?" I ask.

"I saw Rachelle Monsigny there. Do you remember her? The mother of Adrien and Yvette?"

"Yes, of course."

"She was close to dying. I let her think we got both Adrien and Yvette to safety. That's all she needed to hear. She died within the hour."

Élodie averts her eyes and gazes into the distance. She makes the sign of the cross. She is silent for a few moments before continuing. "All these years there is one image that never ever has left me: moonlight reflecting off barbed wire. I would stare at it from the tiny window of the barracks. Sometimes it looked like a string of Christmas lights, and I would think of you, and I would wonder if I could survive long enough for the war to end and I could find you and we could be a family. Moonlight played such a big part in our story, I thought we owned it … or it, us. There was always moonlight. Always. Those nights in Mosset. The light in the mountains."

"I remember."

"Seventy Christmases have come and gone," Élodie says, her voice barely audible.

"It's only six months to the next one," I say.

"Can we make it?"

"We can try."

Élodie makes another hurried sign of the cross, then says, "You frowned earlier when you saw my knuckles." She holds both hands out to show me.

"I'm sorry," I say.

"Don't be. These are not the hands of an old woman. *They* did this."

"The Nazis?"

"First, they destroyed my violin. And when I protested, they smashed the knuckles of both hands with rifle butts."

"Bastards!" I say. "They wanted to take away your music."

"But, that's one thing they never had the power to do. I taught others. I fancy my music lives through them."

"I kept looking for your name. Some concert appearance. Something. Hoping there had been some mistake Hoping you were out there somewhere."

"Unless you happened to come across the program notes of one of my students and that person mentioned me as his or her teacher …." She gives a bitter laugh. "When you think about it, they didn't destroy my music, but they did destroy us."

"What do you mean?"

"Think about it. If my hands were whole, I would have resumed my international career. As you just said, at some time, in some place, with some orchestra, perhaps the lovely Boston Symphony, I would have received a review in a newspaper or magazine that you read, and you would have come looking for me."

"I would have turned the world inside out to find you!"

She touches my cheek and nods. "After the war, when I was doing better but had to accept that I could not resume my music career, I joined the United Nations Relief and Rehabilitation Administration to work with displaced persons, especially children. After UNRRA, I went to medical school and became a doctor. A pediatrician. And in nine-teen-seventy-two, not long after *Médecins Sans Frontières* was founded, I joined them. Adrienne was already twenty-eight and married, so there was no reason to stay rooted in France. They sent me first to Managua in Nicaragua where an earthquake had killed tens of thousands of people. I, of course, focused on the surviving children. A few years later, I was in Thailand where we had set up a refugee camp for the millions of Cambodians trying to escape the Khmer Rouge. After that, it was Lebanon during their civil war. Finally, I spent several years on the European lecture circuit, and then I retired." She places the empty martini glass on the coffee table. "Now you know my history."

I shake my head in wonder at such a woman. "Of course, I knew you were devoted to children but to such an extent? It's extraordinary." And then I ask the question I have no right to ask, a question Adrienne already answered for me. "You never married?"

"I was too busy. I made myself too busy." Élodie pauses before adding, "And you wonder if it was because of you?"

"No, no," I say. "I was just curious. And the violin?"

"I could never play again the way I did before they broke my hands."

"Could you play at all?"

She shakes her head. "It was never satisfying. It only served to remind me …." She reaches over and squeezes my knee. "Yes, it was."

"It was what?"

"It was because of you I never married. I was like a turtle dove, smitten for life. I assumed it would be like the violin, never satisfying if I couldn't play the way I wanted." She looks over at Callie. "But you have a beautiful granddaughter. A doctor, I am told. So you did marry." She pauses and turns back to me. "Henry, I hope you have had a happy life. Full of children."

I loved Anna, and for a moment I feel I am betraying her—or betraying my first love. But I was honest with Anna and now I must be honest with Élodie.

"Yes. It was … different, a different life. But it was happy. We had three children, and with the grandchildren and great grandchildren, there are thirty-two of us. Anna died two years ago. Ovarian cancer."

Again, she squeezes my knee. "I'm so sorry."

I don't know what to say. I never have when people express sympathy to me. In the reception line at Anna's wake, I was lost. Callie made sure she stood beside me. Perhaps sensing my discomfort now, she steps forward with her cell phone and holds it out to Élodie.

"In addition to all the children and grandchildren, Papa adopted this wonderful little fellow. He named him Arlequin."

Élodie gazes at the phto and gasps. My Arlequin!"

Callie nods and touches Élodie's hand. "I thought so."

I wasn't going to mention Arlequin for fear of dredging up a deep hurt, but Callie can never let things be. But then Élodie turns to me.

"Henry! I'm delighted. Well done, you! You honor me. He looks just like my poor, little Arlequin."

"Papa, I'm confused about something," Callie says. "It's clear why you never saw Madame Bedier's name in a concert program, or a newspaper, but couldn't it have worked the other way around?"

"What do you mean?" I ask.

"Well, given what Madame Bedier just said—"

"Élodie. Please call me Élodie."

"Yes, of course," Callie says. "What I mean to say is, given what you said about UNRRA and Doctors Without Borders, you probably should have seen Papa's name in association with a popular book he published that directly related to your field. *Reluctant Salvation: WWII Refugee Children and the Roosevelt Administration.*"

Élodie looks to me. "When was this book published?"

"Nineteen ninety-five," I say.

"Ah, I was already retired," she says. "And, sadly, I could no longer hear about, or read about, suffering children. I avoided it because it hurt too very much. I'd had a lifetime of it, and when I heard about those children in America … in the Connecticut school shooting … I wanted to die." Her eyes shine with tears and she pauses for a moment, then says, "Oh dear! I'm sorry. This has been such a shock, and I'm afraid I've had too much to drink. I'm not used to it."

"We must let you rest," I say.

She bows her head and whispers, "I need some time. I need to think."

"Of course," I reply. "I think we both do."

"We have scarcely begun to say what we must. How long will you be in Paris?"

I look over at Callie. "I haven't planned that far ahead."

"Good. We need more time. In the meanwhile, we should have dinner together tomorrow evening after we've had a chance to rest and recover ourselves."

"That would be perfect," I say.

"I'll make the reservations." Élodie squeezes my hand. "And perhaps I can arrange a pleasant surprise for you."

"A pleasant surprise?"

"You'll see."

⁂

The instant Callie and I step off the elevator the following afternoon, we hear wistful violin music. It reminds me of the many times, seventy years earlier, when I delighted in listening to Élodie play. As was the case the previous day, Élodie's door is ajar. Francesca must have heard the metallic scrape of the folding elevator gate, for she appears at the door and opens it fully. She hugs me, and says, "Hello, Pépère," as she kisses me on each cheek, "She is waiting for you."

As I walk into the room, the music engulfs me. It's like falling into Élodie's embrace again. A fire is crackling and spitting in the fireplace. Francesca has guided Callie to a seat and has taken one herself. Adrienne sits in a sofa facing the fireplace. Élodie sits with a wool Afghan draped over her knees in a quilted Chesterfield beside a small table on which sits an old gramophone with a shiny horn in the shape of a trumpet flower. The ammonia smell of metal polish stings the air. Also present is the subtle citrus aroma of wood polish, and I notice how the wood base of the gramophone gleams. There is an empty chair beside Élodie, and she pats the arm. "Come, *mon chou*[77], sit beside me. We never sat together before a fire that wasn't inside a cave. I can't tell you how many Christmas eves I thought of that and pretended you were beside me. How many New Year's eves."

"The music is wonderful," I say.

Élodie's eyes brighten. "It's a string quartet by Pavel Haas. He was a wonderful Czech composer who later was imprisoned at Theresienstadt Concentration Camp. While he was there, the Nazis made a propaganda film showing him conducting an opera with a children's choir to 'prove' to the world the Jews were treated humanely. But after the film was made, he and the children were transferred to Auschwitz where they were all sent to the gas chambers. I recorded the quartet in Paris with a small chamber orchestra in nineteen thirty-nine. It was my last recording before the war, the last time I truly played the violin in public. I haven't listened to it for years."

"It must take courage to listen to it now."

"Not in the least. I wanted to listen to it to honor Haas and the children."

"No. I mean …."

She raises an eyebrow. "Because of my broken hands?"

I nod.

She says, "It's nothing compared to the courage it took to live with a broken heart all those years."

I say nothing. I just gaze at her in wonder.

She continues with a smile. "The timing may seem suspicious—we made the recording the day before Hitler invaded Czechoslovakia—but

---

77   Literally, "My cabbage," but in this usage, a term of endearment like sweetheart or honey.

I'm quite confident Haas' music, or my playing of it, wasn't the *casus belli*."

I laugh. I turn to look at the others because they, also, are laughing. It's then I notice a new photograph has appeared overnight on the mantel. It is the group picture of Élodie and me with the children taken in Esterri d'Àneu seventy years earlier. I point at the photo. "I remember when that picture was taken by one of the Catalan guys."

"It was Àngel Barbera," Élodie says.

"You can remember that far back?"

"But you know I have that kind of memory," she says with a laugh. "Don't you remember how I had to correct you and remind you Clark Gable said, 'I've even been *sucker* enough—not, as you said, *fool* enough—to make plans.'?"

"Yes. I remember something like that. It was about that movie—"

"The movie was *It Happened One Night*. Clark Gable and Claudette Colbert. And something about an island in the Pacific."

"Yes, I remember now," I say. Of course, I never did forget. I stand and lift the photograph from the mantel and hold it before Élodie. "Look how little Mitzi is clinging to me. I can't help but wonder if she's still alive and, if so, what she's doing."

Élodie gives an enigmatic smile but says nothing.

I reach into my jacket pocket and produce another photo, the one with the crease through Élodie's face I've carried with me all these years. "Do you remember this picture?" I ask.

"I remember the German whose camera took it," she says. "His name was Fritz Dürbach. He had a wife and two children, a boy and a girl, and I shot him dead." She reaches for her drink, takes a sip.

The room has gone silent.

After a long moment, I ask, "That has stayed with you all these years?"

"I suppose one never forgets the people one kills."

More silence until, at last, I say, "Or the people who are kind."

"True." Élodie says, looking into the distance. "That reminds me, I did look for Aristide Charnay after the war as I told you I would."

"Aristide Charnay?"

"The compassionate man who helped me bury my parents. I told you about him that night in the barn when we drank wine and I told you about the evacuation from Paris." She squeezes my hand twice and gives me a coy smile and I know it's her way of silently adding, "the barn where we first made love."

I squeeze back. "Of course."

"I found his son. Monsieur Charnay had been killed by the Nazis."

The room is still silent except for the music and the gentle hiss from the fireplace. There is a sudden eruption of sparks as a log collapses and breaks apart. Élodie closes her eyes tightly. "Fucking, goddamn Nazis!" she finally whispers.

Francesca's eyes widen and she looks to her mother. "Shall I make more martinis?"

"Not for me," Élodie says. "We'll be drinking at the restaurant."

"What restaurant?" I ask. "Is that the surprise you promised?"

"One of Hemingway's favorites. *La Closerie des Lilas.* I remember how much you admired Hemingway."

"That *is* a pleasant surprise!"

"Yes," says Élodie, again with that enigmatic smile. "But now, what of us?"

"What do we do, now that we've rediscovered each other?" I ask.

"We can hardly go back seventy years, you know." She places a hand under her left breast and hefts it. "This won't ever ride high and pert again, you understand. It will never again point toward the heavens. And I can guess you are different in that way, too."

Adrienne's hand flies to her mouth and she cries out, *"Maman!"*

She is echoed by Francesca, *"Mémé!"*

Callie stifles a guffaw and shakes her head at me.

"You're as beautiful as ever," I say. "To me, you are perfect."

"Bollocks! Look at those pictures," Élodie says with a dismissive wave. "We were truly beautiful, then, you and I. Nevertheless, what I described are but a few of the ways—unimportant ways in the end—people change over the years. But at their core, people like us remain constant. And in a time of war, people exist almost solely at their core."

So, you're saying, *essentially*, we haven't changed in seventy years."

"Except for my boobs and your blessings, we knew each other mostly in the areas that don't change. So ... so welcome back, *mon chou,*" she says with a sudden flood of tears. "Oh, dear! I was wondering when the tears would come. It was bound to happen. Please forgive me." Her hands are shaking as she reaches for a tissue.

I take both of her hands in mine and pull her close and embrace her and put a hand under her chin and lift it and kiss her on the lips. "Yes," I say. "We loved the parts that were true. And I think we still do."

"Yes, *mon chou*, the true parts are still true. I understand you have once again played the hero and rescued a young woman from attack. And that you paid the price with a gunshot wound, one that I was not there to help heal." She holds my gaze. "That part of you I will never stop loving." She leans back. "But now, I must rest before tonight's dinner at the restaurant. You should do the same." She chuckles. "We're not as young as we once were."

That evening, after several hours rest and a change of clothes, the taxi drops Callie and me off at the restaurant *La Closerie des Lilas* on Boulevard du Montparnasse. The evening sun flares in the windows of the restaurant. Callie and I walk past the tall, intensely green bushes framing the entrance, to be greeted by an impeccably dressed man I assume is the maître d'.

"I trust you are Monsieur Henry Budge," the man says. He turns to Callie and says, "And you must be his lovely granddaughter Callie."

I stare incredulously at the man. "Yes. But how did you know?"

"Doctor Bedier asked me to watch for you—an elderly American with a lovely granddaughter. It wasn't difficult. Come, I'll escort you to your table."

It is still early for dining in Paris, so the restaurant is not crowded. As we walk past the piano bar, I pause. The pianist has abruptly stopped midway through some show tune and has launched into "We'll Meet Again," played piano bar style. Callie gives me an inquisitive look. The pianist smiles at us, nods. Several people at tables in the bar turn to look at us. After a moment's pause, we continue to follow the maître d' and emerge into a large room with a glass ceiling of many panes, lined at each long end with dozens of lights that augment the last slants of evening sunlight. The room has many tables with spotless white table cloths and red chairs. One table is arranged for a party of ten, and it is to this table the maître d' guides us. It is set for formal dining. Each place setting comprises four glasses—a water goblet, a champagne flute (three quarters filled) and glasses for red and white wines— three gleaming fork and knife pairings, several spoons cupping the ambient light in their upturned silver hollows, a place plate, a salad plate, a bread plate and a folded napkin. Six floating candles in votive glasses run along the center line of the table. Together, reflections of the overhead lights, the candles and the last of the sunlight create miniature dancing moons in the dozens of glasses and cutlery, a river of light at the end of which sits Élodie, head tilted in self-satisfaction and a cocktail glass held chin high. Adrienne and Francesca sit to her right and her left. "Ah, you are just on time, *mon chou*," Élodie says. "Come, give me a kiss, then you must take your honorary place at the head of the table."

I walk to the end of the table and lean down and kiss Élodie elabo- rately on each cheek and straighten up and ask, "What's this all about? Why so many place settings?"

"It's the surprise I promised," she replies "Quickly, go to your seat. *Vite! Vite!*"

I walk to the other end of the table and sit. I look to Élodie expec- tantly. Through the windows behind her, I see the moon. It is a good moon, waxing gibbous.

Élodie says, "And now, here comes your surprise. Look behind you."

I turn to see two distinguished-looking men walking toward me from the bar with big smiles on their faces. They look to be at least in their sixties or seventies, perhaps eighties. I rise to meet them.

One of the men looks at Élodie and says, "It's true!"

"Yes, it's true. Would I lie? He's very much alive."

The man turns to me. "Of course, you don't recognize me after seventy years, but I am Max Jäger."

Eyes wide, I suck in my breath. "Max?"

"Yes."

I start to tremble. My knees become wobbly and I grab hold of the back of my chair. "My god!" I whisper.

The second man steps forward and cups my elbow to steady me. "And I am Étienne Leblanc."

I give him a confused look and shake my head.

"But before I changed my name," he says, "I was Stephan Weiß."

"Stephan! It's you?" I gasp. How can any of this be happening?

"It's very definitely me," he says with a broad smile.

From her end of the table, Élodie says. "Max and Étienne are members of Club Henry Budge."

"What?"

"We meet once a year here at *La Closerie des Lilas*, all the survivors from that time."

Étienne says, "My sister Rebekka is usually here, but she has business in the states. When I told her about you just an hour ago, she was both overjoyed for you and distressed she couldn't be here."

I am overwhelmed. Stunned. Dizzy with it all. I feel Callie beside me, supporting me, and then a short, white haired woman appears. She gazes at me, and I say, "I should recognize you. You're also one of the children."

The woman says nothing. Instead, she throws her arms around me and murmurs, "Papa!"

I make a strange sound between a sob, a gasp, and a laugh. "Mitzi?"

"Yes. It's me."

"Dear God! I cannot tell you how happy I am to see you."

"Not half as happy as we all were to hear the news. And now to see you in person—"

"Is truly a blessing!" says another woman who appears beside Mitzi. She double-kisses me on the cheeks and adds, "I am Renata Gottfried."

"Renata!" I say. "I remember you and your sister Leni well."

A flash of pain crosses Renata's face. "Sadly, Leni succumbed to breast cancer three years ago."

"Oh, I'm so sorry."

"We all miss her terribly," says Élodie. "She always attended our little soirees." Élodie looks past my shoulder and says, "Ah, here comes Aron. We are all here now."

"Aron Klotz?" I ask, turning to see a bald man smiling at me.

"The same," he says. "How thrilled I was when Doctor Bedier called to let me know about you. It was a great shock, but a pleasant one, indeed."

Now that everyone is present, we take our places at the table with a scraping of chair feet on the tiled floor. Élodie raises her champagne and offers a toast. "Here's to our very own Lazarus."

There comes a chorus of "Here, here."

I take a sip of the champagne, pause, and say, "Wait a minute! It just came to me. You are all speaking English!"

"Doctor Bedier encouraged us to learn in your honor," says Max.

Mitzi laughs. "More like insisted, I'd say. After the first year, she would allow nothing but English at the Henry Budge table."

All at once comes a gush of conversation with everyone recounting what has happened in their lives in the intervening seventy years.

Mitzi says, "I was adopted in England and, for the first time in my life, given a last name: Peters. They told me I never spoke in those days. But after I married, my husband said I would never shut up."

"You're married?" I picture her as the little girl clinging to my leg.

"I was. Unfortunately, I am a widow. I married an Englishman, Vaughn Woodford, and we had a son. I bet you can't guess what we named him."

I *can* guess, but I spread my hands wide, and say, "I have no idea."

"His name is Henry. Oh dear, I only wish Vaughn had lived to meet you. He heard so much from me."

"And your son?" I ask.

"He's in Canada on business. He has two children, my lovely granddaughters."

I raise my glass toward Callie and Francesca, who are sitting next to each other. "Granddaughters are truly wonderful. Without them and our happy coincidences, I wouldn't be here with you tonight."

"As for me," Étienne Leblanc says, "I changed my name from Stephan Weiß because I wanted nothing to do with Germany ever again. I have never returned there. I married a Frenchwoman, Hélène, and we have three children, two girls and a boy."

Mitzi says, "We took a survey. Among only this small sub-group, we have twelve children, sixteen grandchildren and nine great grand-children. That's thirty-seven souls, not counting the five of us, that wouldn't exist if not for you and Doctor Bedier!"

"And that's to say nothing of the descendants *they* will produce," says Max.

Renata adds, "Which will number in the hundreds, no doubt. Monsieur Henry Budge, you and Doctor Bedier have done good."

Everyone raises glasses in a toast as Élodie and I exchange happy smiles.

And it goes on like this throughout dinner. I learn that Kamilá Brodny and her brother Józef were both killed in a suicide attack on a bus in Tel Aviv in 1994, and Jerzy Godowsky along with his sisters Elżbietá and Klará disappeared in the confusion of the post war displaced-persons crisis when they tried to return to Poland, looking for their parents. And Yvette? She was never heard from again.

It is late in the evening and the table is littered with empty wine glasses and half-empty wine bottles when suddenly, Max Jäger pushes his chair back and stands and approaches me and places a hand gently on my cheek and asks, "Do you remember that last day when you touched all our cheeks to comfort us and told us we were about to set out on a journey that would free us?"

I place my hand over Max's. "I do."

"Please don't be offended if I tell you it was a mother's touch. And I have never forgotten it. None of us have."

He is echoed with a chorus of yeses and I once again reach for my handkerchief.

And later, as the party is breaking up and we are bidding farewell to one another, each of them, one by one, places a hand on my cheek and says, "Thank you."

Several of them add, "We'll be with you tomorrow," and when I ask Élodie about it, she only smiles and says, "You'll see."

"Another surprise?"

"Yes. Another surprise," says Élodie. "Tomorrow. Perhaps a journey."

The following day, when the taxi pulls to a stop on the Quai Anatole France, I look out the window at a great, stately Beaux-Arts building I later learn had originally been a train station. A banner on a corner of the building reads, "Musée d'Orsay."

"We're going to the museum?" I ask.

"Not just any museum," replies Élodie. "Inside this museum is our island in the Pacific."

I give her a bemused look. "What do you mean?"

But Élodie doesn't answer. Instead, she says, "Oh, there are the others."

I turn to see all the people who were with us at the restaurant the previous night—Max, Mitzi, Étienne, Renata, Aron—walking across the large plaza of the museum. When they reach the taxi, Max opens the door and helps Élodie exit the taxi. Étienne comes to the opposite door and offers me an arm. Callie, Francesca and Adrienne pull up in a second taxi and join the others on the plaza.

"Long ago, you and Doctor Bedier escorted all of us to freedom," Max says. "It's our pleasure to return the favor."

I am more confused than ever. I am about to ask what he means, when Élodie says, "I called ahead for tickets for all of us. We are officially a tour group led by Adrienne as part of her Sorbonne work that will allow us to hijack Salle Seventy, which is small, for ourselves."

"What's in Salle Seventy?" I ask.

"Your little island in the Pacific. But first, you and I need wheelchairs."

"Why? I don't need a wheelchair," I say. "And where would we get them anyway?"

"The museum provides them. All we need do is go to a cloakroom and show some form of identification. And don't argue. We'll be here a while. You'll be glad for the wheelchair."

Callie says, "She's right, you know. Your breathing is not even close to being back to normal."

"You have a good granddaughter," Élodie says. "Two good grand-daughters, for that matter."

An attendant brings out first one, then a second, wheelchair. When we are seated, Élodie says, "Salle Seventy is on the median level. We can take the lift."

"The rest of us will take the stairs," says Max Jäger. "We should meet at the statue of Hercules. I think monsieur Henry will enjoy seeing it."

"But we came to see the Gauguins," says Élodie.

"Please, Doctor Bedier. It's important."

"Very well," replies Élodie after a pause. Looking over her shoulder at Francesca, she says, "We'll meet the others at the Hercules sculpture, then we'll go to the Gauguins."

Francesca pushes Élodie's wheelchair toward the small elevators and Callie follows with me as the others head for the stairs. When the elevator lurches to a stop, we emerge into a huge, bright tubular space with a high, arched ceiling made mostly of glass. We follow a long, open corridor and, moments later, converge with the others at the sculpture by Emile-Antoine Bourdelle called *Hercules Killing the Birds of Lake Stymphalis*.

Max rushes forward to greet us, his eyes sparkling. He says, "Look! Isn't it magnificent?"

I study the sculpture. The greater than life-sized bronze figure is full of power and tension—bone, cartilage and muscle sharply rendered as the archer draws the bow with his left foot braced against a rock while he kneels on his right knee. The way the figure's legs are positioned—the left leg stretched in a taut line from foot to hip, the right leg bent hard at the knee and trailing the foot at hip level—is exactly like a photo taken of me hurdling the water barrier before the final turn in the 3,000-meter steeplechase at a track & field event in my senior year of college. A brief thrill runs through me as I recall how alive my legs had felt during that race, how electric with energy.

"It's impressive," I say, "but I'm not familiar with it. What does it represent?"

"It's the sixth labor of Hercules," Max says. "The Stymphalian Birds were man-eating birds. They had sharp beaks made of bronze and knife-edged, metallic feathers which they could hurl at their victims. They were created by Ares, the god of war. Hercules killed them with poison arrows. Don't you see? The birds are like the Nazis, and you are like Hercules. Ever since the Pyrénées, you have been my hero. All my adult life. When I first saw this sculpture, I thought of you. I come to see it often. I even tried to learn more about you in the last decade or so when the internet made it more doable."

Once again, in these magical few days, I am overwhelmed. "You wouldn't have found me. Any entry would be under my author name: G. H. Budge." I give a short laugh. "Sounds more academic."

Élodie leans forward and looks up at the younger man. "You never told me this, Max."

"But you must know you are my hero, too. You are Athena who helped give Hercules the power. The two of you. You saved my life."

"And mine," says Mitzi, wrapping an arm around my shoulders.

Max continues. "You are the reason my children are in the world. And my grandchildren. And when I heard the news you were alive I ... I ...." He lowers his head and wipes his eyes.

For a long moment, everyone is silent. Finally, Francesca breaks the spell by saying, "Salle Seventy is almost empty," pointing to a group that has just emerged. She quickly propels Élodie into the room and places her in front of the painting Élodie points to and is followed closely by Callie pushing me.

Élodie explains that the painting before us is *Arearea* by Paul Gauguin, also known as *Joyousness*. Composed in greens, yellows and reds, it depicts two Tahitian women who sit in the foreground with a red dog. One of the women is bare breasted. In the background, three other women are worshipping a larger-than-life statue of a god.

"I come here often to look at these paintings," Élodie says. "They allow me to imagine what it might have been like."

I look from the painting to her eyes to her face which I want to reach out to caress. "You and me on our island?"

"Yes. You and me," she says. After studying *Arearea* for a while, she points to another painting and Francesca wheels her in that direction. Callie follows with me. The painting, called *Le Repas*, shows three children, a girl with a boy on either side of her, sitting at a table on which rests a large bunch of bananas, a bowl of coconut milk, and several oranges. Élodie says, "Perhaps we would eat like this. I'm sure we could find wine if the coconut milk doesn't appeal." She reaches out and touches my arm.

Soon, we move on to a third painting called *Femmes de Tahiti* which shows two women sitting on the sand at the edge of a lagoon. The woman on the left wears a white blouse and a red pareau, or sarong, with large white flowers. The other woman sits cross-legged and wears a pink missionary dress. She gazes warily to her left as she plaits a basket.

At last, we come before a fourth painting. As I stare at the painting, I hear Élodie breathe a little faster and I take her hand and, with my broken finger, I caress her broken knuckles and she gives my hand a slight squeeze.

"It's as if they are waiting for us," I say.

"They are," says Élodie. "The painting is called *Et l'or de leur corps*. It means '*And the gold of their bodies.*'"

In the painting, two women sit naked and bronzed—except for the tiny loincloth one of them wears—on a blue mat in a lush grassy area with a banana tree heavy with fruit and giant red blossoms which are probably hibiscus.

Élodie turns to me, and smiles, and asks, "Have you ever been in love, Henry?"

"You asked me that once before," I answer with a smile.

"Yes, and I ask it again. Haven't you ever thought about it at all? It seems to me you could make some girl wonderfully happy."

"Sure, I've thought about it. If I would ever meet the right girl, somebody that's real alive. You know, I saw an island in the Pacific once. I've never been able to forget it. That's where I'd like to take this girl."

"What sort of girl would this be?"

"The kind of girl who would jump in the surf with me."

Élodie's smile broadens as she says, "Our bodies would become golden and we'd play in the surf."

"What are you two talking about?" Callie asks, with a wide grin and raised eyebrows.

"It's a game we played back during the war," I answer. "We promised each other if we survived, we would go to Tahiti and live there."

"And the moon and the water would become one," says Élodie.

Callie smiles. "It sounds beautiful"

"And all would be one with the stars," I say. "A moment in paradise."

"And the stars would be so close we could reach up and touch them." Élodie squeezes my hand more tightly.

"Go!" Callie says suddenly.

"We'd drink mysterious water and live forever," Élodie continues, "and our bodies would become golden."

Callie moves to stand in front of us. She crouches and places one hand on my right knee and the other on Élodie's left knee. "Go!" she says again.

"What do you mean?" I ask.

"Go to Tahiti, damn it! Go!" Her eyes are shining. She glances up at Francesca and Adrienne.

I shake my head as if I haven't heard her correctly. "What?"

"Take Élodie to Tahiti like you promised. You know you can do it. I'll make all the arrangements for you. All you need do is ... is pack up and go. Francesca will help me."

"Of course, I will," says Francesca. "You must do it!" She looks to her mother and Adrienne just smiles and wipes her eyes.

With even more force, Callie says, "Go, goddamnit! The kids can stay with their dad for a while, and I'll take a leave from the hospital so you have a doctor with you."

And suddenly I see how it might be. I continue to stroke Élodie's broken knuckles with my broken finger as we gaze at the painting with the banana tree and the giant red hibiscus flowers and the golden bodies and, at that very moment, the chatter of a tour group around the sculpture of Hercules and the Stymphalian Birds softens to nothing, as do the microsecond clicks of camera shutters and the echoing conversations in the great open spaces of the museum, and all that is left is the soft throb of the pulse in my ears and the promise of the paintings shimmering before us, and I know somehow, later, no sound will be left but the sound of prayer and the rush of wind as we fly westward to a little island in the Pacific where, if prayer is truly made of sound, the air will be filled with the splash of waterfalls and the joyful cries of free children gamboling in the surf and with the singing of the women gathering bananas and hibiscus flowers and we will strip off our clothes and walk, holding hands, broken finger, broken knuckles, naked into the water, and sunlight will be golden on our bodies and we, too, will play and jump in the surf on nights heavy with a merciful moonlight that cools our bodies, nights when the stars are so close we feel we can reach up and stir them around, and we will kiss with wet lips, and our days will be filled with sunrises, and there will be moonlit nights overfilled with stars, until, in the fullness of time, we at last must turn our gaze to the west and the fearsome wonder of the setting sun.

Discussion Questions

1. There are several lenses through which to examine the governing metaphor of "the light from the dark side of the moon," including theological, biological, psychological, and physical. Given the passage below, what do you think of each interpretation?

> *I have never been able to erase the image of that damnable giant mirror. I can picture it up there, beyond the moon's orbit, wrathful in its precise reflection of the dark side, and I am filled with dread. This sense has never left me. Almost anything can bring it on: a news bulletin about children being harmed in some way, the view of a swollen moon in a sullen sky, a neo-Nazi parade anywhere in the world, a dead moon jelly on the beach.*

2. Which phase of the moon is most often descibed? What is its significance? When is it waxing and when is it waning?

3. Read the paragraph on page 217 that begins after the break. Why is Henry so obsessed with knowing exactly where he is in the world? Is it the experience of missing the drop zone or is it more than that? How does this tie in with the story of *The Little Prince?*

4. Read the paragraph on page 189 that begins, "The man embraces me." What aspect of Henry's experience is mirrored by the disfigured men in the scene?

5. Read the passage beginning, "Yes. Of course," she says. She returns the kiss and grasps my hand..." What do you think the author is trying to convey with the litany of monscapes?

6. After Élodie kills one of the boy soldiers (see pages 59 and 60), Jean-Baptiste makes a joke. Why does it make Henry so angry?

7. What is the significance of the name Adrienne?

8. What is the significance of the chapter, "An Ancient Moonlight"?

9. There are two passages in which Henry imagines a conversation with someone who is dead—one with Anna and one with Élodie. What do these types of conversations tell us about ourselves?

10. What does the cave at Lascaux and the incident with the Nazi soldier signifiy?

11. What do you think about the description the "Greatest Generation." What behavior or actions does it refer to? What behaviors do you see in Henry, if any, that fit the description? Do other generations fit the description?

12. How do you think the story ends? Do Henry and Élodie travel to Tahiti together?

Acknowledgements

For inspiration, support and patience, I thank my wife of 36 years, Susan Reynolds, whose help with plot, character and dialogue as we walk along the beach is one of the joys of my life.

A story is nothing more than a hope unless there is someone who sees its potential. For my entire literary career that has been my agent, Kimberley Cameron of Kimberley Cameron & Associates.

But unless there is someone who has the courage to launch a book as risky as literary fiction, the book would exist only as inchoate manuscript. For its existence as a bound book *The Light From The Dark Side of the Moon* owes its gratitude to Lisa Miller of Amphorae Publishing Group. And a novel would limp into the world deficient and disfigured were it not for a wise and meticulous editor who has the patience, grit and endurance to stick with it despite difficulties. For this book, that heroine is Kristina Makansi of Blank Slate Press, an Amphorae imprint.

But, however limber an expertly edited novel might be as it steps into the world, it would have no place to go were it not for someone who understands the marketplace. I am deeply grateful to my publicist, David Ivester of Author Guide, who is just such a person.

And finally, a book can't get into the hands of you, the reader, without someone who is expert at selling the book in the right channels. The person managing this feat for the book you hold in your hands is Laura Robinson of Amphorae.

My sincerest thanks to all these people and to you, my reader, without whom not only would this book not exist, but I, the writer, would not exist outside my lonely garret.

About the Author

A native New Englander with a life-long love of the sea, Norman's first novel, *Sea Room*, won the prestigious Massachusetts Book Award for Fiction in 2003, was an "All-City-Reads" choice in several cities, and was a BookSense® selection. He has since written several more critically acclaimed, prize-winning novels.

An avid reader, poet, sailor, runner and cyclist, Norman lives outside Boston with his wife Susan and three cats.

For more discussion questions and images of the book's setting, please visit www.normangautreau.com.